Ascending

From

Madness

(A Winterland Tale #2)

Stacey Marie Brown

Copyright © 2019 by Stacey Marie Brown
All rights reserved.
Published by: Twisted Fairy Publishing Inc.
Layout by www.formatting4U.com
Cover by: Jay Aheer www.simplydefinedart.com
Edited by Hollie www.hollietheeditor.com

ALSO BY STACEY MARIE BROWN

<u>Contemporary Romance</u>

Buried Alive

Shattered Love **(Blinded Love #1)**

Broken Love **(Blinded Love #2)**

Twisted Love **(Blinded Love #3)**

The Unlucky Ones

<u>Paranormal Romance</u>

Darkness of Light
(Darkness Series #1)

Fire in the Darkness
(Darkness Series #2)

Beast in the Darkness
(An Elighan Dragen Novelette)

Dwellers of Darkness
(Darkness Series #3)

Blood Beyond Darkness
(Darkness Series #4)

West
(A Darkness Series Novel)

City in Embers
(Collector Series #1)

The Barrier Between
(Collector Series #2)

Across the Divide
(Collector Series #3)

From Burning Ashes
(Collector Series #4)

The Crown of Light
(Lightness Saga #1)

Lightness Falling
(Lightness Saga #2)

The Fall of the King
(Lightness Saga #3)

Rise from the Embers
(Lightness Saga #4)

Descending into Madness
(A Winterland Tale #1)

Dear Santa,

Don't bother. We've all been naughty here.

Ascending from Madness

CHAPTER 1

Bitter cold nipped at my nose and fingers, mushrooms of condensation billowing out with every breath. The stars twinkled far above the still night, and the sounds of holiday music seeped through the sliding door, floating out over the silvery backyard.

The tumbler bumped my lips as I poured the whiskey down my throat, the burn wrinkling my nose. Instantly the alcohol calmed and warmed me, though I was pretty sure my ass had frozen to the bench. My outfit wasn't made for anything hovering around freezing temperatures, and the heavy blanket I had wrapped around my shoulders didn't feel like it was doing much.

Snowy scenes at Christmastime were my favorite, but I longed for the snow not to be…well, so cold.

Freezing as I was, no way was I going back inside. Partly—okay, mainly—because I embarrassed myself beyond belief. My reaction had been humiliating. The crazed laugh that I couldn't stop until my sister escorted me away was just the topper.

And that was saying a lot coming from me.

Being around the people inside the house was worse than becoming an ice block out here. I could still see the look of horror on my mother, sister, and even our new neighbor. Their eyes had been wide, each pair saying something similar.

Crazy. Bonkers. Mad.

Even to myself, I couldn't explain my response to our new next-door neighbors: Jessica, Matt, and their adorable, tiny son, Tim. The contradictory effect the couple had on me was extreme and confusing. I had hoped the fresh air would help center me, but it did nothing more than force me to stir up the feelings that would not go away.

Taking another gulp of whiskey, I sighed deeply, my shoulders relaxing. The moon was almost full and reflected off the snow in my backyard, creating a ghostlike glow.

It made me feel lonely. Sad. But I had been feeling unsettled since I woke up, my memory still stopping at a certain point, giving me no recollection of leaving work last night, nor driving home. I barely recalled feeling sick or being at the cottage with Gabe. Everything in the last few days felt faraway and dreamlike. Weeks ago, not yesterday.

Sitting on the built-in bench on our deck facing away from the house, my scarcely covered legs swung back and forth, trying to stay warm. The whiskey was helping with that and was also bringing me to the point I didn't give a crap anymore. A place where I wanted to pitch a tent and camp out for a while.

"Alice. Alice. Alice," I muttered my name like a rebuke while downing the last bit of my drink.

"Forgive me. Am I interrupting a conversation with yourself?" A deep voice skulked up my back, my head whipping around. Oxygen caught in my throat from fright and the fact this man brutally stole the breath from my lungs.

Holy Santa's helper...

My gaze drifted over his frame. Nearing six-four, his broad shoulders cast shadows down on me. His blue eyes, which seemed to glow, pierced me in place. He was beautiful and sexy, but something suggested a beast hummed at the edges of his finely tailored suit. Someone who really knew what to do with a woman's body...

Alice! I berated myself. *He's married! With a kid!* This did little to take away the beating of my heart and flutter in my stomach.

Taking a step closer, he tilted his head, as if he were waiting for me to respond.

Did he ask me something? Was I supposed to talk? *Good job, Alice, in not confirming you are off your rocker.*

"I'm actually curious how your conversation was going to go." He shoved his hands in his pockets, air puffing from his mouth.

"Think I made myself look crazy enough in there." A frown pulled my lips down, my gaze going to my empty glass.

"Is that why you are hiding out here?" He took another step to me. If I wasn't mistaken, he had a slight British accent, which only made him hotter.

"Yes. No." My shoulders shrugged. "I don't know." My attention went to the festivities in full bloom inside the house. "Rocking around the Christmas Tree" got a few people wiggling their hips, with much help from my either my father's holiday punch or my mother's mulled wine. "Not really my scene tonight."

Normally, I enjoyed my mom's annual holiday party, but this year it was the last place I wanted to be.

"Yeah." Matt bobbed his head, following my focus. "I'm not feeling extremely festive either. Actually, I'd like the whole holiday season to be over with."

"Wow." I grinned. "And here I thought I was the lone curmudgeon. Aren't you just the modern-day Ebenezer Scrooge?" The moment the name plunged off my lips, a dizzying sense of déjà vu had me pressing my palm to my chest. *Christmas cookies! What was wrong with me? Why did saying that feel so familiar?*

He froze and a strange expression dashed over his features before it disappeared with a head shake. "Yeah…" Scrunching his eyebrows, he cleared his throat, moving to the bench where I sat. "Something like that."

"You look nothing like the character, but why do I feel Scrooge fits you perfectly?" I tipped my head to stare up at him, my heart thumping loudly in my chest.

He let out a laugh. "You're probably right. It does seem to fit me. Maybe I'll change my name?" He winked at me, playfully, compelling a huge smile to part my mouth.

The moment went from innocent to sensual in a blink, both our smiles falling away as we stared wordlessly at each other. His figure loomed over me;

every cell in my body screamed at me to reach out and touch him, to let his weight crush me.

Damn, Alice. Stop!

"So." My eyes dropped away from him, and I shifted on the bench. "What brought you out here? I wasn't supposed to be seen. I'm hiding in my top-secret fort."

"Am I not allowed in your secret fort, *Alice*?" His voice rumbled my name, the statement filled with connotation, drawing up my chin with a hitch, my heart leaping up my throat with a *yes, come in.*

Holy, Saint Nicholas. I needed to pack myself into the snowbank. The way he said my first name was erotic, like he whispered it in my ear, his body moving over mine.

ALICE! STOP!

"Wow…" His eyebrows darted up, his hand going up to his face to rub his mouth, the other still in his pocket. "That came out wrong. *Very* inappropriate."

I couldn't hide the disappointment I felt inside, the twist in my gut wishing he had meant it, sexual innuendo and all.

"Please." I waved it off. "This is where the inappropriate and wrong go. Did you miss my show earlier? Clearly I shouldn't be allowed around normal people."

"Then it seems I finally found where I belong."

Breathe, Alice. Breathe.

Trying to not read anything into it, I motioned to the spot next to me on the bench. "Please, have a seat; the outcast meeting is about to commence."

A hint of a smile pulled at the side of his mouth, fluttering my heart even more. He lowered himself, facing toward the house. "Aren't you freezing?" He rubbed his hands together. "Or are locals immune to this unbearable cold?"

"This—" I lifted my glass—"is our immunity." I leaned closer, feeling the effects of the whiskey, putting my finger up to my mouth. "Shhh. That is a well-guarded secret to us New Britain natives."

"Your secret is safe with me." He grinned at me, leaning his forearms on his legs. "I have to admit when my wife said we were moving to New Britain, I was thrilled to be going home. She left out *this* New Britain was in Connecticut."

"So, you are from England? I thought I detected an accent."

His mouth opened to respond, then closed it, his fingers going to his temples, scouring them, like he was trying to stir up a memory.

"Yes..." he finally said, but he didn't look completely sure. "So long ago now. I went to Oxford University, but I hardly remember it. The details are lost...it's more a feeling. An impression."

"Impression?" I scoffed. "What was it—ten, fifteen years ago? How much did you drink through school?"

His mouth pinched together, his gaze staring off at nothing. Several moments passed. Finally, he flicked his head as if he were waking up out of a trance, twisting to me.

"Well, I am grateful for you letting me in on the well-guarded local secrets."

"You belong in the inappropriate and wrong club now, remember? We stick together."

"Do we?" One eyebrow arched.

Shit… I stepped into that figgy pudding.

"Sure." I swung my legs, peering back at the sky. "But to be a full-fledged member you must bring alcohol to the meeting." I wiggled my empty glass. "Initiation."

His smile never fully bloomed, but his eyes glinted with mischief. "That *is* a coincidence." His hand went inside his jacket pocket, pulling out a flask. "I came prepared."

"Damn, you really are Santa sent…" I sighed happily, licking my lips, not realizing what I said until his silence drew my gaze up to his eyes. He stared at me, once again his gaze tunneling into my soul like a gravedigger. "I mean…wow…I am not getting any better tonight. All sorts of awkward."

"Actually, it was perfectly said for my first meeting." He twisted off the cap, pouring the brown liquid into my cup. The rich, smoky aroma had my toes curling. "Hence our club name, Ms. Liddell."

"What?" My head jerked up. It felt like a dart shot straight through my gut, heat snaking down to my thighs. "What did you call me?"

"I—" He stopped, his Adam's apple bobbing, looking as if he had been shot by the same dart. Except faster than a blink, his expression turned to stone, clearing his throat again. "I called you Ms. Liddell. That is your name, isn't it?"

"Yes." Why did him saying my name so formally feel so informal? As if he were stripping me bare. It felt far more intimate than if he had called me some sexy pet name.

"Well, what should we cheer to for our first meeting?" He lifted his flask up in the air.

"*Your* first meeting." I brought up my drink to his. "I've been a dedicated member since birth."

"Sounds like you would have been all sorts of fun to grow up with." His mischievous gaze met mine. His eyes were bottomless and crammed with naughty trouble.

"I was."

His mouth lifted cheekily. "A salutation to a *merry* holiday?"

"Bah, humbug." My lips twisted up, matching his impish expression.

A soft chuckle came from him, his gaze growing even more intense. "Bah, humbug." He tipped his head, tapping his flask against my glass, both of us about to take a drink.

"Matthew!" A woman's voice barked, jolting us to the figure standing at the unlit back kitchen door.

This woman froze me with just a look, like she was the Snow Miser. Her icy blue eyes latched on to us, her body stiff and regal as she stepped out farther onto the deck. A frown wobbled on her face before she corrected it, a small laugh puffing out.

"I have been looking for you everywhere, *dar-ling*." She strolled closer, everything about her screamed well-educated, well-bred, monied, pampered, and extremely controlling. She seemed cold and snobbish, not at all a good match for the man next to me.

She was a sexy woman, and it didn't matter if she was older or not. I hated the uptight bitch for reasons I couldn't comprehend. I didn't even know the woman except she had the man I felt unbearably drawn to. Craved. That needed to end now.

"You know I hate being away from you," she purred, reaching out her hand for him to take it. He tucked away his flask and promptly received her hand. Like a trained dog.

"I'm sorry, love." He kissed her knuckles, and I watched her shoulders ease down, a smile growing on her perfectly painted lips.

"It's past Timothy's bedtime." Her fingers coiled around his. She pretended I wasn't there, but I could feel the force of her possessiveness shoving me back away from him.

"It's only eight o'clock. Surely, my love, we can let him stay up tonight. He's was having so much fun dancing and eating all the gingerbread cookies."

"Exactly," she snapped loudly. "I mean…" A smile appeared back on her face. "He will have all that sugar in his system. You know how I feel about him eating sweets. Not healthy. We don't want him to get diabetes now, do we?"

Oh. She was one of those moms.

"I don't think he'll get diabetes from one night of eating a few cookies." I could hear the annoyance in Matt's tone.

"I have a terrible headache from the music." She pinched her nose. "And you have just gotten over being ill. Sitting outside in this bitter weather…I thought you smarter than that, my love."

He took a deep breath, standing up, rolling his shoulders back. Tension moved his muscles under his fitted jacket like snakes.

"You're right. We should get home. A good night's sleep is exactly what I need." He dropped her hand but put it on her back to steer her toward the sliding glass door.

"Have a good night, Ms. Liddell." He nodded at me. "It was a pleasure meeting you."

"Yes, Alice. It was lovely." Funny she said that, but it was not what her expression was saying. "Come, my darling." Jessica stepped in the house.

"Night, Mr. Hatter." I tried to say it as properly as I could, like everything out here had been formal and above censure.

He turned when he got inside, his hand on the door handle. His gaze latched on mine, his lips rolling together. He looked like he wanted to say something, but at the sound of his son's voice calling him, he turned away from me and shut the door.

I swallowed back the lump in my throat, swiveling back to face the yard. What the fuck was wrong with me? Guzzling down the rest of my whiskey, I tried to understand why his leaving made me feel so alone. I had just met him a few hours ago.

Leave it to you, Alice, to crush on a married man.

I felt gutted. Lost. As if whatever I had been searching for, I finally found, then lost it again.

Chapter 2

Milk rolled through the dark liquid, twisting and churning with murky swirls. Entranced by the courtship between coffee and milk before they gave in to the meeting and fused together, I stared at my cup like it would reveal the images and impressions my mind had been filled with all night.

Mentally and physically tired, I had hoped for a soundless sleep. That was not what I got. Every time I closed my eyes, it felt as if I were falling down a dark hole, paralyzed, and where figures danced just outside my view. All I felt was terror that I was too late. That I had to get somewhere. Save someone. Lives were in my hands, but I was stuck. The darkness itself was pinning me down, locking up my muscles.

Three times I bolted awake, fighting with my covers, my heart beating, fear lining my forehead with sweat. Finally, I gave up around dawn, stumbling downstairs for coffee before I went back to my sketches. The lure back to them, to keep inventing, was stronger than anything I had ever felt. The muse had surfaced and was singing like a siren, calling me back to my designs.

"Alice?" My mom's shocked voice popped my head up. She looked beautiful; her silky hair brushed her shoulders. She wore a knee-length plaid skirt, long-sleeve blue blouse, stockings, and ballet flats. At fifty-two, besides a few gray hairs and laugh lines, my mother really could be mistaken for my older sister. "What are you doing up so early? I usually have to drag you out of your bed at noon."

Complete exaggeration. Maybe ten years ago when I was in high school, but my job in the city had me at the office at eight a.m. She seemed to only recall me at fifteen, not twenty-five and forgot I lived on my own, took care of myself.

"Couldn't sleep." I shrugged, taking a sip of coffee, watching my mom retrieve her own mug of caffeine. "Why are you up? You don't work Sundays."

"No, I don't. But oddly, Rose called me this morning saying she was sick." Mom's eyebrows clicked up.

"You mean the Rose who was here last night, dancing on our sofa, a table decoration on her head, doing shots of Dad's holiday punch while singing a Run-DMC Christmas rap?"

"That would be the one," Mom smirked. "Somewhere from here to her apartment, she swears she got the flu."

"Too much of Dad's punch is now code for flu," I snorted.

Mom chuckled, swiping a banana out of the fruit bowl. "How are you feeling?"

"Fine," I lied. Nothing felt fine. My nightmares weren't the only thing keeping me up. Thoughts of Matt Hatter had me tossing and turning, reprimanding myself for every thought, clean or dirty, I had of him.

"You had us all worried last night. And then you disappeared."

Inhaling more caffeine stopped me from responding.

"Alice."

"Mom."

"Just know I am really concerned. You have not been yourself."

"I was off *a day*. Getting over some bug."

"No, it's been longer than a day. It's been going on for a while now."

A while? Really?

My head tried to file back to the last weeks when I had returned home after losing my job. It felt like running through mud, my mind struggling to remember the block of nothing before it skipped into the weeks prior. Hazy and distant, I did recall coming home. Granted I was a little depressed, but I had just lost my job and supposed boyfriend, having to move back home at twenty-five. That would demoralize anyone.

Mom poured coffee into a travel mug, adding a flavoring from a bottle I didn't recognize, observing me through her lashes. "So…what are your plans today? Did you see those catalogs I put in your bag?"

"You mean the *dozens* of college brochures? Yeah, kind of hard to miss." I went back to drinking my coffee.

"Sweetheart, you need a focus. You need a degree if you want to have a chance to advance. Do you think they would have chosen that guy over you if you had a degree?"

I had been let go from the job before my last assistant job with my ex. The boss's nephew was hired instead, who knew nothing about the company.

"Yes." I set the cup down with a clink. "And even without a degree, he had two things I didn't...a blood relation and a dick."

"Alice." Mom frowned.

"I was the best fit, knew everything about King of Hearts Cookies." I worked in customer service for three years, where I realized quickly I didn't really like people and was hoping to get the job in their marketing department. I actually hated it there and felt working in corporate sucked out my soul, but it would have been amazing money. The job went to Bill, the lizard. No joke. He looked like a lizard, constantly flicking his tongue.

"Well, please take a moment to look at them again. I'll be back around six." She kissed my forehead. "Oh, and you should try the homemade creamer Jessica brought over last night. I swear I could drink it in everything. It's so *divine*." She grabbed her purse and went out the garage door.

My eyebrows pinched at her choice of description, but I glared at the label-less bottle on the counter. I wouldn't be touching anything that woman made. Plus, Jessica didn't look like someone who did "homemade" anything, and I was sure she didn't bake, cook, or even know where the kitchen was. She probably bought generic syrup from the store down the street and put it in another bottle.

Pushing off the stool, I went to stand up and out of my peripheral saw a large, child-size, blurry white object hop across the lawn. My neck snapped to the glass, my gaze searching for what I saw.

Nothing. Our fenced backyard was empty of anything but a few trees and a lawn covered with snow. We got little critters, especially bunnies in the spring, but this seemed *far* larger than any bunny we had in these parts. We didn't grow toddler-sized rabbits here, and our cottontails were brownish, not pure white.

"I need to get some sleep." I shook my head, turned away from the slider, and headed back upstairs. I was tempted to go back to bed, but my ass plunked down at my desk chair, my fingers picking up my pencil, like I had no choice in the matter.

My hand flew over the page, tendrils of my dreams jumping up and down on the back of my neck, controlling my arm.

I started to draw.

And I didn't stop.

🎩 🎩 🎩 🎩

"Alice?" I heard my name, but it sounded more like a faint wind licking at tree leaves. "Oh my god!"

A figure crashed down next to me at my desk, grabbing my arm. "Alice. Stop!"

"Din-ah. Let go," I snarled as my sister's hand tugged at the charcoal stub in my hand.

"*You* let go," she snapped, ripping it from my hand, twisting my head to hers. Her brown eyes were wide and full of alarm. She was dressed in her elf costume. My attention went over her shoulder to the night filling my bay window instead of morning light. *What the hell? How was it night already?*

"What is wrong with you?" She waved at my hands.

My gaze slowly slid to my hands and the sketchpad on the desk. Covered in blood. Red liquid pooled and smudged across the sheets, coloring in the scarves around the countless top hats I continued to sketch over and over, like I was using my blood as a coloring crayon. Feeling like I just woke up from a deep sleep, I blinked at my raw and cut fingers smeared with charcoal and blood.

"Did you do this to yourself?" Her voice went up as she went back up onto her feet, snatching up my X-Acto knife I used to cut patterns, the blade caked with drying blood. "Holy shit, Alice. You sliced yourself?"

I blinked up at her. The alarm in her tone and the speed of her movements confounded my thoughts. I couldn't remember cutting myself, but the wounds over my hands, going down to my wrist, suggested otherwise.

"I don't know." I held up my hands, trying to recall any pain when I had done it. All I remembered was sitting down in the early morning. Now it was nighttime again.

"You. Don't. Know?" She emphasized each word, her hands on her hips. Puffed up in the skimpy green-and-red costume with red-and-white-striped legs and curved boots on her feet, her cheeks were scarlet.

"You are one very pissed-off elf." A bubblelike chuckle fizzled up my throat.

"This is *not* funny." She grasped my shoulders. "Have you even left this chair today? Do you remember me saying goodbye to you? Eight hours ago?"

No. I didn't recall.

Her head snapped back to the drawings, really taking them in. "God, Alice…you used your blood to color in the scarves?" She touched the top page, flipping through the hundreds of sheets I had already drawn on. Her attention fell to the floor. There were dozens of sheets ripped out, carpeting my rug in layers. "What the…" She pinched her lips together. "They are *all* the same. Every single one. And dozens on a single page."

She picked up another sketchpad that was pushed to the other side of the desk. This one was full as well. Mostly of top hats with a few penguin heads and rabbit ears.

She slammed the pad closed and stared at me like I was some extraterrestrial. Her mouth parted, her eyes darting over me.

"Dad! Mom!" she yelled.

"Dinah." I stood, reaching for her. "Don't."

Batting away my hands, she screamed louder for them.

"What, Dinah?" Dad pushed open my door wider, Mom following behind him. "What's wrong?"

"Look!" She motioned to me, then at the room, picking up the nearest notebook, flicking through the pages. "Thousands of them. The same damn thing." She tossed the book down, picking up the X-Acto knife.

"Dinah," I pleaded.

She glared at me, fixating on our parents.

"She used her own blood to color in the designs." She waved the blade around, pointing at me. "Look at her hands."

Mom pushed past Dad, her mouth dropping as her gaze zeroed in on the wounds.

23

"Fudge…" She swept up my hands in horror. Yes, my mother was one of those who said fudge instead of fuck. "Alice?" Her eyes met mine. "Did you really do this to yourself?"

Did I? I didn't remember. But I felt it would be worse to say that than admitting it.

"Yes," I whispered.

"But why? Tell me! Why would you do this?" Fear and confusion peaked her voice, making it identical to Dinah's.

My dad sensed Mom was a step away from losing her mind. Pushing in, he took my hands from her. "Alice. Talk to us. Why would you cut yourself?"

"I ran out of red?" I shrugged one shoulder.

There are many times I wish I could take back what my mouth slipped out. This would probably be one of those times. Even my dad closed his eyes, bowing his head, knowing what would come from my response.

"WHAT? WHAT?" My mother screeched, starting to circle like a frantic bird around a nest, pecking at my drawings, my blood stirring a frenzy in her. I never really noticed until now, but in a "crisis" she couldn't control, my mom totally lost it. Dad was the calm one.

"Is she serious, Lewis?" She talked to my father like I wasn't there. "I can't believe our baby is cutting herself."

"No, I'm not, Mom."

"Really?" She motioned to my injuries. "What are those then?"

"Creative liberty?" My dad glowered at my response. "Look at Van Gogh."

"Not helping," he muttered, shaking his head.

"Carroll, calm down."

"Calm down? You want me to relax?"

"Yes." He nodded. "You flying off the handle will not help the situation."

Mom shut her eyes, taking in a deep breath, blowing out, a few times. We all stayed silent as she reclaimed her self-control. When she opened her eyes, she was organized and in command.

"Sit down, Alice."

I bit back the groan in my chest. I was about to be lectured. At twenty-five you really hoped those would be over with.

"Alice…" Dad said softly, beseeching me to sit without a fight. "Dinah, please leave us alone with your sister."

"What? Why?"

"Because." He eyed her. "I said so."

She rolled her eyes, stomping from the room in a huff, her bell shoes tinkling, making it hard to take her anger seriously.

Flopping down on the bed, I waited for the censure to begin.

"Can you not see how upsetting this is?" Mom started, her voice controlled but not yet composed. "So please, tell us. Why did you decide to slice into your skin? Use your blood to color?"

My mouth pinched together. It was hard to defend something you couldn't recall. I should have been freaking out about that aspect, but strangely I felt relaxed, for the first time since I woke up the other morning.

"Mom, I wasn't trying to hurt myself or anything like that."

"That did not answer the question." Leave it to my dad to know when someone was trying to avoid answering directly.

"I don't know."

"I don't understand how you don't know." Mom licked her lips, taking even breaths. "At one point you picked up the blade and decided to cut into your skin. What made you decide that?"

"I don't know."

"We are going to need a better answer than that, young lady." Dad folded his arms.

"I can't give you one."

"Why?"

"Because I don't…I don't reme—" I snapped my mouth closed. My gut screeched at me to shut up, having no memory of the situation would only scare them more.

"Yes?" Dad lifted his eyebrow.

"Look. I'm sorry I scared you. I was just caught up with my designs. I wasn't trying to hurt myself. Really."

"That's another thing." Mom picked up one from the floor. "For two days now, you've been sketching the same thing for hours and hours, like you're possessed. You don't hear us when we come in. I called you three times for dinner tonight. You probably wouldn't have stopped until one of us made you."

"I'm really inspired right now."

"Inspired?" Mom scoffed. "I am not taking away

your talent, Alice. But they are just top hats, with a red scarf. To see you draw them over and over is really disturbing." She sighed, setting the paper on my desk. "I know what you went through with the breakup and losing your job. It must be difficult. But this level of depression is beyond the normal dejection."

"Normal?" I sputtered. "Normal could be abnormal, and abnormal could be quite ordinary to some."

Where the hell did that come from?

Both my parents blinked at me.

"I think it might be best if you speak to someone."

"What do you mean? A therapist?"

"Yes." Mom nodded. "Actually, I had been thinking it for some time now, but after last night and speaking with Jessica—"

"Jessica?" My spine bolted up in a rigid line. "What does she have to do with this?"

"We talked a lot last night. I can't tell you how wonderful it was to get to know her. She's *such* an amazing lady." There was no denying the reverence in my mother's voice. "She really made me see. We talked a lot about you. About your issues."

"About me?" Indignation hoisted me up to my feet. "What did she make you see? And why are you talking to a lady you *just met* a minute ago about me anyway?" My mom was someone who had people in awe of her, not the other way around. Nor did she ever talk to strangers about family problems. She barely talked to us about them. And now she was spewing them to the one person I *hated*.

I didn't understand my loathing any more than I understood my mom's esteem of her. Neither of us knew her well enough to feel either way, but thinking about the woman, I wanted to beat the crap out of her.

"She thinks you should talk to someone."

"I don't care what she thinks."

"Alice." Dad used his warning tone. "We only want what is best for you."

"I'm fine!" I tossed up my arms. "Today was a fluke. I promise I will be back to myself tomorrow. I'll even look at those college pamphlets." Sometimes you had to pull out the big guns. And college was one of those for my parents.

Several painful minutes passed before Mom nodded. "Fine. But you're coming to work with me. I know you don't have a shift at Santa's Cottage. The library is a good, quiet place you can read through the catalogs or use the computer."

"I could do it at home."

"No. You are coming with me. End of discussion." Mom shook her head.

She didn't want me left alone. She needed a place she could watch me and keep me away from sketching and X-Acto knives. I wouldn't be spending the day with my mother or even the librarian. I would be spending it with a warden.

Chapter 3

Streetlights illuminated the sidewalk, shadowing the row of darkened homes along the road. The late hour had everyone tucked in their beds fast asleep. An icy breeze coaxed me farther into my jacket, my nose sniffling every few seconds. Pulling down my beanie, I strolled forward with no destination. Again, I didn't care how cold it was, it was worth the numb skin to get out of my claustrophobic house. Away from vigilant eyes and judgment.

Even asleep, I swear I could feel my family's condemnation seeping under the door, pressing down on my body.

The more logical part of my brain suggested I should be terrified as well. I *couldn't* remember drawing all those sketches or cutting myself. *At all.* But in my gut I knew I wasn't trying to harm myself. I wasn't someone cutting herself to feel something or as a cry for help.

All my family's actions did was make me feel even more isolated and restless. They kept a close eye on me until they *thought* I was sleeping soundly. A trick I pulled so many times in high school before sneaking out. Finally, when the house was still, I slunk out. I needed fresh air to clear my head. Feel *free* for a moment. Nothing worse than having freedom, living on your own, and coming back to prying eyes, questions, and rules. I had to find a real job and move back to the city. Soon.

Shoving my hands in my pockets, I flinched as the tender wounds rubbed against the fabric, reminding me what happened earlier wasn't some bad dream.

I burrowed my head down, my breath ballooning out in front of me, my feet set forward with no real direction.

"Little late to be out." A deep husky accent came from the dark.

"Holy shit!" I yelped, spinning toward the direction of the voice. A huge outline of a man leaned against a tree; tendrils of smoke twisted and wrapped around the hibernating apple tree branches. Blue eyes shined through the darkness, emotionless while they sliced right through me.

"Are you out spying on me?" A pillow of smoke drifted to me, a skunky odor of pot wafting up my nose. "Tell me, are you a spy, Ms. Liddell?" Matt took another pull, the rings of smoke circling around him like a peel of an apple.

"A spy?" I pinched my lips together coyly. Why did this feel so familiar? "No...certainly not. But if I were, would I tell you?" The words flowed off my tongue easily, making me feel I had said the same thing before—to him.

"No," he replied, staring right into me, drawing me to him like a magnet. He was dressed in nice gray sweatpants, a beanie, boots, and a black puffer jacket, looking relaxed and so frickin' sexy, I had to reprimand myself again for my dirty thoughts.

It didn't stop me from walking to him instead of away like I should have. Stepping off the pavement, I treaded over his lawn, ceasing a few inches from him. He didn't move, but the way his nostrils flared, my sudden nearness put him on the defense.

"I think you would be a very cunning player," he rumbled. "Have a man so bamboozled he wouldn't care what secrets you robbed him of."

"Is this one of your secrets?" Smiling mischievously, I reached over and grabbed the joint from his fingers, a spark barbing my chest from the slight touch. I put it to my mouth, inhaling deeply. The smoke hit my lungs, and I tried not to choke and cough like a rookie.

Holly and mistletoe… He liked the strong, pure stuff. "Damn." I blew out the remnants, my eyes watering.

A smirk wiggled his mouth as he watched me pat my chest.

"To answer your question, yes." He adjusted his shoulder on the trunk of the tree, his gaze sliding back to the house for a moment. "Jessica hates it."

"Wow. That was easy," I teased. "Spilling your secrets. I didn't even have to pull out my torture equipment."

"Something to look forward to then," he replied evenly.

Holy fuck. He was much better at playing this game than me. I looked away, my chest and thighs constricting in response.

"Is that why you are out here, getting *high*, in the middle of the night?"

"*Relaxing*." He lifted an eyebrow, correcting me. His finger curling around mine as he took the smoke back. His eyes were on me as he lifted it to his lips, like he wanted me to see his mouth go where mine had just been. "Unwinding. There's a difference." He puffed out circular clouds to the side. "What is your excuse for being out at this time of night?"

"Not much different from yours. Going for a walk, but I think your plan is better." I nodded at his joint.

"No reason we can't do both." He pushed off the tree, holding the roll up for me to take as he brushed by me, heading for the sidewalk.

Shit, Alice, tell him no. This is a bad, bad, bad idea. My problem? I always seemed to jump straight into the hole of terrible ideas.

He waited for me to catch up before we strolled silently down the street. We both knew this was wrong, but pretended it was an innocent walk at three in the morning.

"How long?" I cleared my throat, taking another drag, tossing the huge elephant down on us. "How long have you and Jessica been married?"

His chin lifted, his stare drifting off far down the street, his teeth digging into his bottom lip. "Five or six years?"

"Is that a question?" I snorted, my head fuzzy enough to consider it funny. "Oh, wow. Do you know your anniversary?"

He blinked, his forehead scrunching.

A laugh burst from my chest, like champagne bubbles.

"Shut up." He tried to chide me, but a naughty boy smile stretched out over his face. "I do…I…I just can't think of it right now. Shit…" He rubbed his head. "Can't seem to remember a lot of things lately."

"Makes two of us." I handed him the last bit left of the bud. "You know, to most women anniversaries are a huge deal."

"To most women?" He took the last hit before flicking it onto the street. "Why does it sound like you exclude yourself from that?"

"I'm not like most women." *Stop flirting, Alice.*

"I believe that." His eyes slid to me, creating more bubbles in my stomach. "But why do you think that?"

"Don't plan to get married. Have no desire to." I shrugged. "So…no need to get fussy about anniversaries."

"What if you met someone?" He stared forward, shoving his hands in his pockets. "Knew he was the one. You wouldn't marry him?"

"Honestly, I don't see the point, but I'm also not against it either. Guess life will let me know in time."

He turned, gaping at me.

"What?"

"You certainly aren't like other girls I've ever met, Ms. Liddell," his voice low. "Different. You have more…" He paused. "Muchness."

Muchness.

My feet stopped, bile burning the back of my throat. My head spun with murky pictures I couldn't make out.

Pinching the bridge of my nose, I tried to ease the sudden dizziness.

"You all right?" He halted a few feet in front of me.

"Yeah." I nodded, keeping my focus on the line in the sludgy pavement. "Maybe it's the pot making my brain fumble, but I just had the most acute sense of déjà vu or something. Getting it a lot lately."

"Makes two of us," he muttered the phrase back to me, staring up at the sky. The moonlight trickled through the tree branches, shadowing half his face. "An electrical malfunction in the brain. One side gets the same information twice, so you think that event happened before." He shook his head. "Well, it's what Jessica tells me over and over anyway."

"You don't agree?" I moved to him, not realizing how close I got. My neck creaked back, my body feeling the desperate need to touch him. To slide my hands in his jacket, feeling the warmth of his body under my palms. Like it was mine. Mine to touch freely.

He peered down at me, not stepping away, his expression grave.

"I don't know what I agree with anymore." He spoke quietly, but the sentiment felt like a fissure, the meaning going far deeper than what it appeared from the outside. Something I completely understood.

"I know." My eyes searched his, feeling that strange bond tie tighter around my gut. His eyes went back and forth between mine before he inhaled sharply, yanking his head up, taking a step back.

"We should go back." He pivoted, not meeting my gaze. "Jessica might wake up and come looking for me.

And Timmy…he gets night terrors a lot. Wakes up crying for me."

"That's awful, I'm so sorry." I reached out to touch him, but stopped, clearing my throat. "My sister used to get them when she was young. Used to say the Miser brothers were kidnapping her."

"Miser brothers…Heat and Snow?" He tilted his head, his forehead wrinkling like he was trying to recall something. He shook his head, letting out an exhale.

"Yeah. We watch a lot of Christmas movies. She was probably a little too young when we saw it. Haunted her for years."

"I wish it was that. Tim's dreams are *much* darker." He stuffed his hands into his pockets, blinking. "Last one he woke up screaming saying he wasn't real, that he wasn't supposed to be here." Matt's throat bobbed. "That I had killed him."

"Wow." My head drew back in surprise, my heart aching for the father.

"Yeah, well." He shrugged. "Between my illness and this move—we are all out of sorts. Things will calm down soon." His sentiment was set with determination, but the words ricocheted like they were hollow inside.

"I better go." He gestured to his house.

"Yeah…yes, of course." I pinched my lids together for a second, shaking my head. "I should get home too."

We walked in silence. I was smart enough to know I was playing with fire. A blaze that would annihilate everything around me.

He had a wife. A son. No matter how much I felt this connection to him. For once I had to do the right thing, the responsible thing, and stay far away from him.

Matt Hatter was not a rabbit hole I could fall down.

CHAPTER 4

The squeak of wheels echoed down the row of books, the cart wobbling as I pushed it through the children's reading section. Mom put me on shelving duty when I frowned at reading college catalogs this early in the day. It was well past noon already, and I hadn't had enough coffee for my brain to be working at any capacity.

Between the pot, lack of sleep, my thoughts constantly leaping to Matt, and my general feeling of edginess, I was not a ray of sunshine this morning when Mom woke me up at seven. Okay, I was never a ray of sunshine. At least while restocking, I didn't have to speak to people and could get lost in the aisles of imagination.

Grabbing a stack of books, I slid them into their proper place on the shelf, some of the illustrations too tempting not to look through before putting them away. There was something about children's books and their detailed pictures that flickered at my imagination. Each page gave you a scene you wanted to jump into. Be part of. I would much rather be on the cushy bean bag they had in the corner, my nose in the book, instead of putting them away, but Mom was set on keeping me busy. Hence the never-ending books to be shelved or checked in.

The wheels on the old cart squeaked down the aisle as I moved across the sections. This one was children's crafts, baking, and things for them to do when stuck inside. Very popular in the winter.

Stuffing a book with bright colors and the title spelled out with different crafts, I reached for the next one, almost shoving it into place without looking, but my gaze snapped to the jacket. *Gingerbread Fun.* The cover was full of differently decorated gingerbread men and houses.

My fingers gripped both sides as I stared at it, a strange sensation forcing me to swallow. The déjà vu impression flooded back, my pulse in my neck thumping. The taste of gingerbread laid on my tongue, as if I had actually taken a bite of one, the sweet, spicy cookie melting on my tongue like a phantom.

"It's a party!" A light giggle whispered like a flower petal floating in the wind.

At the same moment I saw a flash of black and white from the corner of my eye, and an oval toddler-sized figure waddling across the walkway. I jerked my head to the end of the row. Nothing.

Caramel fudge.

What was that? Licking my lips nervously, I crept to the end, peering down where the kid might have run.

Nothing.

No kid, no sound of pounding feet, or even breathing.

Absolutely nothing.

Curious.

I couldn't deny this time a trickle of genuine fear scratched at the back of my throat. Yesterday's incident hadn't done that, though it really should have. I couldn't remember hours of my time, of cutting into my skin. But this sank into my belly like rocks.

Nothing's there, Alice. Shaking my head and trying to ignore the pang in my gut, I returned to the cart and rammed the gingerbread book in its place without looking at it again. Propelling the cart forward, I curved it toward the farthest section, the lights not as bright and never filled with people. When I was little, I used to think this part was creepy and not in the spooky fun way. The kind that felt as if a nail was being dragged down your spine. Eyes watching you.

The whine of the wheels as I drifted down the last row had my hair standing on the back of my neck.

"Don't let your imagination get the better of you," I muttered. "You're not a kid anymore."

I quickly grabbed at a book, finding its home, and reached up to put it away. A red glowing light flickered by before it slipped behind the shelves. I swiveled sharply, my heart jumping up in my throat, scrambling for the end of the row, peering around. The walkway was vacant. I shook my head, taking in a deep breath. I went to turn back for the cart, when I saw the blur of red light on the other side of the shelves from me and a dark shadow falling over the books as it headed down the aisle toward the end.

Fear slammed my pulse against my neck, but I propelled myself to move, scooting round the rack to the next row, ready to find something there.

It was empty.

Curiouser.

"What the...?" I gaped, staring at the blank wall where the row dead-ended a few yards away. There was nowhere to go. Nowhere to hide. Dread dribbled down my throat, forcing me to swallow.

"Switch! Switch!" Giggling voices jerked my head to the side. At the edge of my vision, two toddler-size figures darted into a row, a blur of green and red. Reacting instantly, I chased after them, determined to find the brats messing with me, ignoring the notion I needed to see they were real. I wasn't losing my mind.

Jogging after them, I shot down the aisle. The kids were nowhere to be found, and panic generated tears behind my lids. Distant giggles kept me moving, *needing* to find them. The desperation to prove they were there pounded adrenaline through my veins. Zigzagging through the shelves, I tried to catch them.

Darting out into the kids' reading area, I found it empty.

A giggle, sounding like a little girl, made me jump around. "Stop it!" I yelled, my gaze scanning every inch, trying to find movement.

"It's a party!" Another kidlike voice circled me around, ripping the air from my lungs.

"I said stop! You guys are going to get into trouble."

"It's a very Merry un-Christmas." A girl's voice sang behind me, whirling me back.

"To me?" A boy's voice crooned back.

"I said stop it!"

"No, to you!"

I didn't see anything, but their voices lobbed all around me. My teeth sank down into my lip, my chest heaving for air, true terror skulking down on my shoulders, dropping beads of doubt into my gut, whispering, *Alice, you are going mad.*

"Stop!" I screamed, my hands going to my ears. My back curled as their giggles echoed in my head, thumping at something so deep in the far reaches of my mind bile flushed up my throat. I dropped to my knees, nausea spinning my head.

"Alice?"

"Stop it!" I repeated over and over, pressing the heels of my palms into my ears, trying unsuccessfully to block the giggles and singing in my head.

"Alice!" Hands grabbed for me, tugging at my wrists, trying to yank my hands from my head. "Oh fudge…Alice! Stop hitting yourself." Fingers tore at mine. "ALICE. STOP!"

The pitch of my mother's demand halted the voices instantly. As if a switch was turned on, the pressure leaked out of my skull like evaporating fog, easing my lungs.

Slowly, I lifted my lashes, looking at the few people in the library standing around, staring at me with horror. Gulping, I licked my lips, my gaze darting to the woman crouching beside me. Her dark brown eyes held even more terror. Her hands still wrapped around my wrists like she was afraid I would hurt myself, her fingers pressing into the wounds still healing.

She stared at me for a few beats, searching my eyes for an answer, some logical reason for my actions. I had none.

"What. Just. Happened?" She kept her tone emotionless, but her nails digging into my tender injuries spoke the truth under her façade.

"Mom…" I croaked. "I—I…" I looked around at the few people still gawking. They were all older. A man with gray hair dressed similar to my father, a thirty-something woman, and a couple around their sixties.

No kids.

Their wide eyes pinned on me like I was part of a freak show. A thing in the cage that scared you, but you couldn't turn away from.

Alice. Let the madness in… I heard a whisper run through my mind.

Bolting up, I tore from my mom's hold and ran for the bathroom, needing to break from the scrutiny of their eyes, the truth and pity in their expression.

Freak. Mad. Crazy. Mentally unstable. I could feel their disapprovals.

Shoving through the door, I ran to the sink. Taking in slow breaths, I lifted my face to stare into the mirror.

My reflection stared back at me. My dark brown hair slid over my shoulders, falling around my flushed face. To anyone who hadn't seen my crazy episode, I looked like an attractive, *normal* girl. By people's comments, I knew I was considered striking. I had the uniqueness of my mother's Bulgarian heritage of olive skin, silky, long dark hair, dark eyes, and full lips.

The problem was men treated looks as if the prettier you were, the stupider you were. I might not have liked school, but I wasn't dumb. Nor did I deserve to be patted on the head while an inexperienced man took the job I earned because A) I was a woman; B) A pretty one. So I must not be smart or be taken seriously.

Something like this just added to the stereotype. Really pretty girls were also half crazy. I couldn't deny I felt like I was losing my grip on reality.

My fingers squeezed the edges of the sink, my gaze locked on my reflection as if it was calling me to step through the glass. I had a strange feeling my copy in the mirror was shedding me of myself. And the more I stared at it, the more I couldn't identify the girl in the mirror or which one was the real me.

Taking a deep breath, I turned on the water, splashing my face. My gaze drifted up to my likeness again when I saw a snowman with a top hat and pipe standing in the stall behind me.

"The madness is seeping in. You will be one of us in no time," it spoke.

A cry sprang up my throat as I spun, the noise sticking in my throat when I searched each empty cubicle.

No-no-no-no…this can't be happening to me. I fell back against the sink, my lids squeezing together.

"Alice?" The door squeaked open, my mom stepping in.

I didn't look up or move from my spot, not wanting to deal with answering her right now. There was nothing I could say.

"Alice." She said my name tentatively, moving in front of me. "What happened out there?"

My shaky inhale was my only reply.

"I am so scared right now," she whispered hoarsely. "I don't know what to do, and you are not talking to me."

"There's nothing I can say," I muttered.

"Really? That's your only response? After yesterday…then the episode earlier?" She grabbed my hands. "Alice, please. I don't know what's going on with you, but this is serious. You acted as if you saw and heard something. Telling someone to shut up. No one was there. Do you understand why you are terrifying me? Self-harm? Hallucinations?"

"Mom."

"No." She shook her head. "You are not going to brush this off like you did the other night or blame it on being sick. I will not ignore both incidences, nor my mother's intuition. You have been extremely depressed since you have come home." *Extremely?* That seemed highly exaggerated. "You need to recognize there is something going on with you right now."

I had no argument, nothing I could say would soothe her. It was like the saner I felt, the more I was really sliding away from reality.

"I am making an appointment for you to talk with someone." She nodded, reassuring herself of the plan more than me. "We'll nip this in the bud." She squeezed my hands before running one of her hands down my face. "Sweetheart, we'll do *whatever* we need to get you healthy again."

I watched her walk out, full of confidence, determination setting her shoulders back, her plan set in front of her. Her checklist to "curing" me mapped out in her head.

All I could hear was, "we'll do *whatever*" looping around my lungs, cinching in…

Like a noose.

Chapter 5

Skipping dinner, I went straight to bed when we got home. I yearned to sleep, but anxiety flipped me all over my bed like a dying fish, listening to my parents argue and talk about me downstairs. Being twenty-five and regarded as no more than a toddler who couldn't control their actions caused a need to run.

The impulse to slip out the window, get on a train, and head back to the city had me jumping up several times to pack. Then the seeds of doubt would drop in my stomach and clamp down on my lungs, telling me I really might be going crazy and accepting help was the most responsible thing to do.

The house grew quiet as the hours ticked by, while I watched the moon shift shadows across my bedroom floor. Though the necessity to escape itched at every muscle, for once I understood my impetuous need to flee would only make things worse for me, proving I had a reason to run.

Shoving off my blanket, I wandered over to my wall, now pinned with my hat drawings. Reaching up, my fingers slid over the sketches, the pads of my fingers feeling the texture of my dried blood coloring in the scarves.

An image of a man with glimmering blue eyes wearing the top hat, kept appearing in my head, like it had been made for him. Stepping right off the pages of a Dickens novel.

Matt!

My modern-day Scrooge.

The moment his name drifted across my mind, I jerked toward the window, feeling a pull as if strings yanked at my gut. Nothing moved outside. The streetlamps and darkened homes along the lane looked like every other night. No sign of movement or life out in the freezing night, but instinct moved me to my dresser.

Slipping on a pair of yoga pants, I tiptoed out my room and down the stairs, every creak making me pause, listening for any signs someone in the house was up and moving. Shoving my feet in boots, I pulled on my coat, scarf, hat, and gloves and slipped out the front door, doing the very thing I told myself not to do. But this desperate need to see him, to feel normal for a moment, was too powerful to fight.

The icy air slammed down my throat and smacked my face like a boxer, forcing a hitch in my lungs as I tucked in deeper into my scarf. I stepped off my porch, my destination set. Uncertainty settled down on me the closer I got. Dark emptiness surrounded the apple tree in my neighbor's yard, and my stomach sank.

Did you think he was out waiting for you or something? Such an idiot, Alice.

Trying to fight back the roaring wave of

disappointment, I didn't let my steps slow as I started to pass the house.

"We need to stop meeting like this, Ms. Liddell." His voice rumbled from the dark, concocting a strangled yip from my throat. "I might expose more of my secrets."

Moving from around the back of the tree, Matt leaned into the trunk, the swirl of smoke coiling around from the joint in his hand. Wearing something similar to what he did the night before, he looked even sexier than I remembered, not helping me regain my breath.

"But more of your secrets is exactly what I'm after, Mr. Hatter." The flirty tint coloring my words had my cheeks rushing with heat. "Otherwise my spy skills are for nothing."

"Well." A glimmer of a cheeky smile tugged at his mouth. "We are at quite the impasse then, as I really don't have many secrets to confess."

"Why do I think that's a complete lie?" My boot crunched under the snow coating the lawn. "I have this feeling you have nothing but secrets."

His blue eyes stared into me, not answering, but the twitch of his jaw told me what I said was true.

Identical to the night before, I reached out for the joint, our fingers rubbing against each other, sparking warmth in my veins. He didn't fight as I got it from him, inhaling deeply, the smoke curling around like the creamer in my coffee.

"I hope I'm not initiating a bad habit." He nodded at me.

"You are far too late to be a pioneer in my bad habits." I took another drag, feeling the tension ease from my muscles. "I had them all down by my teens. If anything, I would be the instigator."

"Doubtful." He smirked, taking it back. My gaze locked on his mouth as it curled around the roll. The desire to feel his lips on my body created a layer of sweat down my back. "Think I've been up to no good before you were even born."

"Please." I scoffed. "What are you, thirty-five or something?"

"Age is nothing but a number." He tugged at his beanie, staring up at the sky. "I feel as if I've been around for centuries."

"Today I feel like that too." I flicked my head to the footway. "Walk?"

He moved off the tree, following me down the sidewalk. We passed several houses before I spoke. "Do you sneak out every night?" I realized my gaffe immediately. "I mean… I didn't mean to insinuate you were sneaking…or you needed to."

"Why not? I am." He exhaled up into the air before handing me the smoke. "I don't remember if I always did…but since we've moved here…*every* night. The moment she's sleeping deeply."

"You don't remember? Maybe I should cut you off." I tried to joke.

He smiled, but it fell fast, never reaching his eyes. "I got very sick before we moved here. My fever reached such severe temperatures, it gave me a form of amnesia."

"Amnesia?" My attention snapped to him. He kept his head forward, frustration wrinkling his forehead. "Seriously?"

"My past before moving here is mostly blank. Images, impressions, but nothing concrete. Every once in a while, a smell or object will trigger something, like it's there waiting. But as soon as I try to grasp on to it..."

"It slips through your fingers," I finished, understanding so well what he was feeling.

"Yeah." He half turned to me, studying me in wonder as we continued to walk.

"Believe me. I get it." I took a puff, handing it back to him. "Nothing like you. I mean, I remember my past and even last week, but it's strange that ever since I woke up after being ill, I feel something is missing. Like a chunk of time is gone, even though it isn't." My lashes fluttered, the strain of the day finally hitting me. "I know it must sound crazy." I wagged my head.

"Not at all." Our pace remained slow but steady down the street. "Nothing sounds crazy to me right now."

I turned us down a path leading to the public park. A playground set spread over the lot, the swings creaking with the light breeze and freezing temperatures stiffening the chains. I sat down on the frozen plastic seat, cringing as the initial stab of cold seeped through my pants. Matt fitting himself on the seat next to me.

"Didn't even know this was here. I'll have to bring Tim here sometime."

The mention of his kid twisted guilt in my gut like a knife.

"Yeah. You should," I replied, swinging back and forth. We stayed quiet for a moment before the weight on my chest became unbearable.

"Something happened to me today." I gulped. "Not sure why I'm telling you... You are practically a stranger." *And married.* "You have your own issues."

"But?"

"Huh?" I peered up at him.

"There is a question mark at the end of your sentence." His voice was low, his breath billowing out of his mouth.

I glanced back at my feet, digging into the snow. "I don't know why, but I feel comfortable talking to you. Everyone else would think me absolutely mad."

"And I won't?"

"No." I turned back to him, our eyes locking for a few seconds before his head nodded in understanding.

"I feel the same." His gaze still latched on to me. "Jessica gets angry every time I bring up the past or ask questions, saying how much the experience upset her. Almost losing me. That I'll remember in time, when my mind is ready." He flicked up his eyes like he didn't believe it for a moment. "She won't even tell me how we met or about the moment when Timothy was born."

"Shit," I whispered. "I can't even imagine. Not to remember your son's birth or even your wedding."

He stayed silent for so long I was convinced he no longer wanted to talk about it, but then he sucked in a breath, staring off into the night.

"I look at Jessica." He swallowed, talking quietly. "And I can't for the life of me recall what made me fall in love with her."

Wow. How do I even respond to that? And I hated the part of me that wanted to scream, *because you aren't. You're not supposed to be with her.*

"I stare at our wedding photo, we look so happy, and…nothing. Not even a spark of familiarity." He licked his lips. "It's odd, right? You think of all things our wedding day should trigger something in my memory."

"Damn." I curled my gloved fingers around the chain, leaning my head against it. "You win."

"Didn't know we were in competition." He tipped his head to me with a grin. "I guess before we declare the winner, you have to tell your story."

"It's nothing." I stretched my legs, pushing out the swing. His was a genuine loss of memory, while mine was a case of truly losing my mind. "Thought I saw something today. Something that wasn't there."

"Like a hallucination?" He stopped moving, his interest sharp on me.

"I think I'm going crazy…and what's worse is I don't feel crazy." Fear croaked my voice as I faced him. "Isn't that the true sign someone is losing their mind? Only the insane are so sure of their sanity?"

He stopped moving, his brows furrowing. "Why do I feel I've heard that before?"

"I don't know." I paused, trying to think where it came from. "Might be from a book or something?"

His lips pinched together, adjusting on the seat, his spine rigid. "So…what did you see and hear?"

"That's the problem. I can't really say. I thought some kids were messing with me. But there were no kids there. Everyone stared at me like I was several cards short of a deck. But it felt so real to me." Emotion clotted my throat. "I'm scared. I feel like I am losing my sanity, and there is nothing I can do to stop it."

What was it about him that I couldn't seem to stay away from? Married men in the city—I mean drop-dead gorgeous men—constantly hit on me at work, at bars, on the subway, but I had never gone there. I drew a hard line and never had a problem walking away.

Matt Hatter changed that the moment he walked into my house. "Force beam" was the perfect phrase. Even when I tried to walk the opposite way, I seemed to find myself standing in front of him

"Probably the lack of sleep, being sick, and possibly the pot the night before." I tried to play it off with a wink. Though I knew in my gut he'd listen, the thought of him really thinking I was crazy would send me over the edge. He was this strange lifeline, and if I lost it, I would go down and drown underneath the paralyzing fear building inside me.

"Don't hide from me," he rumbled, inclining closer to me, his intense expression making my heart thump noisily in my ears. The sensation of being like this with him previously captured my breath. Everything about him felt familiar, even the underlying sense of fear that of all the things dangerous in this world, he was the most threatening. It only added to my draw to him and the overwhelming desire to lose myself in him.

As if he could read my every thought, my slight change in mood, his pupils expanded, darkening his eyes. His already intense focus zeroed in. Not thinking, I bit my bottom lip, causing his gaze to drop to my mouth. Lust infested my veins, turning my chilly body to boiling hot.

The atmosphere strained with anticipation as if it was holding its breath. The condensation between us built as our breaths came quicker. I didn't think I moved, but we still seemed to be getting closer. His warm breath stroking across my lips and cheeks.

Eight maids a-milking. I wanted him to kiss me so bad it ached in my bones.

"Alice," he rumbled, his lips almost brushing mine. "I can't…"

"I know."

But neither of us moved away, our mouths only a breath apart, like we got caught in that force beam and had no control over our actions.

A pained huff twisted from his chest and he sat back, closing his eyes. "I won't be one of those cliché tales." He crunched his teeth together. "My son is *my world.* My focus. He comes first."

"As he should." My lids batted quickly, and I swallowed down the jab of rejection because he was right. We were completely in the wrong.

"With my memory loss, I feel I've lost all this time with my son. I've been given this second chance, and I don't want to waste a moment. I want to be the best father to him. And if Jessica—"

"I get it." I cut him off, knowing where he was going. If Jessica found out about us, she'd probably take Tim away from him.

"You don't know how much I wish the situation were different." He exhaled, staring up at the stars.

"Yeah." I nodded, rising to my feet. "I do."

"We probably should stop this." He stood, not meeting my eyes. "It would be for the best."

"Definitely." I stared down at my snow-covered boots.

"Do not seek me out." His voice went firm, cold. An order. "Don't even look at me if our paths cross." Resentment twisted the muscles in his jaw as he stuffed his hands in his pockets. "Don't even think of me…"

"Excuse me?" I stepped back, defensive anger straightening my spine. "Someone's ego is a little inflated."

He stepped forward, looming over me. "Tell me I'm wrong."

"You're wrong." Insolence spat it out, flopping on the snow with little substance.

He smirked. "You are a terrible liar."

"But you're the one lying to yourself."

"I have to." His boots hit mine as he snarled. "Hating me is the only way, Alice, because I can't allow what I truly want."

He turned, stalking away from me, leaving me gasping for air. The whisper of the same words stabbed my mind, bending me over, grasping for reality. Suddenly I was laying on a soft white rug, the sound of a fire crackling blazing in the room. The smells of pine and cinnamon drifted into my nose, the taste of sugar cookies and mulled wine was on my tongue, and my lips still felt puffy from being kissed. Hard. The feel of him over me, touching me, uttering the identical sentiment flickered so forcefully in my brain, my knees dropped into the snow.

The vision was gone as fast as it came, but the aftereffect was a strike to my stomach and head. Grappling to take in oxygen, I stared at the dirty snow, not feeling the wetness seeping through my leggings.

Stunned by the onslaught to my senses, every detail of the vision felt so real. Even though I knew it couldn't be, I still felt as if I tasted sweetness on my lips.

Harsh snaps of air sucked in and out of my nose as I tried to get my feet back on solid ground. I sat back on my heels, letting my head drop back, a tear sliding down my cheek.

In that moment, dread sank to the bottom of my belly, a boulder of truth. Hallucinations, visions, voices that felt as real as the world around you all amounted to one thing.

I was falling.

Down. Down.

Into the darkness.

Chapter 6

Snowflakes fluttered across the windshield, pirouetting and skipping, acting out the Nutcracker ballet. Lost in the beauty of their delicate dance, I watched the drama play out.

"Alice?" Mom touched my arm, jolting me away from the theater taking place outside the car. I didn't even care that she looked at me with fear and pity. "You ready?"

Nodding my head, I rolled my lips together. Was I ready to go sit in a chair where someone would ask me, "How does that make you feel?" or "Why do you think that?" until I really would *actually* lose my mind. Sure. I was ready.

This morning, I didn't even fight when my mom told me she set up an appointment for that afternoon. My sister clearly was told even before me and had already set it up with our boss she'd be taking my shift at Santa's Cottage. I sooooo loved feeling like a two-year-old.

Once again my sleep had been restless, and I ended up sketching designs for the remainder of the night, which peeved Mom even more when she checked on me in the morning.

"Alice." She clutched her cup of coffee, the smell of peppermint coming from her cup, the scent of Jessica's homemade flavoring. "What are you doing?"

"Drawing," I quipped.

"I see that."

Then why did you ask?

"What are you drawing?" She took a gulp from her mug.

"Elves having sex."

"What?"

I rolled my eyes, tossing my pencil down, standing up. "Mom, I'm fine. I need to get ready for work."

"No, your sister is taking your shift. She already let your boss know."

"What?" I swiveled, my hands going to my hips. "Why is Dinah—"

"Because." She stopped me. "You have a therapist appointment this afternoon."

"Mom."

"Not one more word, Alice. I got today off to take you." Because I wasn't old enough to drive myself? Or she didn't trust me to get there? "You. Are. Going," she demanded. "Now, come downstairs and have some breakfast." She exited my room and headed to the kitchen.

Now as we walked up to the therapist's office, I contemplated running for the woods behind the strip mall. The office was in the same center as the library, and for the life of me, I couldn't recall it being here before. The grocery store, dry cleaners, drugstore, the three fast-food restaurants, and the nail place… Yep, those were always here, but the therapist? It was as if it magically slid in with the other stores like in some Harry Potter movie.

We stepped through the door, and a shiver ran up my spine. The space contrasted with the old warn strip-mall façade on the front. This place was sleek, modern with glass and metal all in black and gray, with a few touches of red. A black leather sofa was placed against one wall with deep red pillows, a glossy coffee table, and a few sleek side chairs. Black-and-white modern impressions hung on the walls. Something about them made me pause, tilt my head, and try to make out what the artist was attempting to express.

"Checking in for Alice Liddell," Mom said to the woman behind the desk. She had her blonde hair pulled back in a bun, her slim figure dressed in all black, as her red nails clicked the keyboard. She reminded me more of a robot than a real person. She had a sour face, but nothing about her stood out. Someone who easily blended into the crowd, but I couldn't deny there was something familiar about her. Was it because she looked similar to a million other people, a general face that represented so many? But I kept seeing her face screwed up in wild fury, her eyes burning into me, screaming for my head.

"Have a seat. She will be right out." The receptionist nodded to the seating area, her expression blank of a single emotion.

"Thank you." Mom smiled, walking over to the sofa. "This place is so modern. It's lovely, isn't it?"

"No," I blurted out, staring at my mom with confusion as we sat down. "You hate modern. Always saying it has no personality."

"This is different." She waved me off, removing her travel coffee thermos out of her huge purse and taking a sip. "I like it."

I hated it. Kept me on edge. Uncomfortable. Defensive. Seemed like the opposite effect you'd want a client to experience.

Heels clicked over the marble floors, a woman stepping out into the lobby. *Holy-fucking-silent-night.* My mouth dropped open, fear lobbying up my throat.

No. No frickin' way.

"Al-ice." A cool smile raised her red lips. "I'm so glad you decided to come."

Jessica Winters stood before me in all her ice-queen glory.

She's a therapist? *My* therapist?

"No." I bolted up, my head shaking violently.

"Alice!" Mom stood up next to me, glaring at me with astonishment.

"No. I'm not doing this. Not with her." I stared at the beautiful older woman, looking elegant and stylish in her black pencil skirt, gray cashmere sweater, red heels, jewelry that screamed wealth, including the blinding rock on her finger. The ring binding her to the only man I craved like a drug. Every night since we met, he had impassioned my dreams so intently I woke up touching myself to the feel of him, the taste of his kiss.

Mom's nails dug into my arm, irritation coloring her cheeks. "I did not raise you to be this rude to people. To strangers or friends."

"She is not my friend."

"*Alice.*" My mom's voice snapped at me, diving into her calm fury, which was far scarier than her outraged anger.

Jessica's smile curved up more. "Do not worry, *Carroll.*" She purred over my mother's name like she was stroking a cat's head. "This reaction is normal. People who really need help are the most resistant to it."

"Need the most help?" I blinked. She hadn't even talked to me, had no idea what was going on with me, besides the tidbits my mom might have shared, but it was as if she already diagnosed me.

Ignoring me, Jessica stepped up to Mom, air-kissing her on the cheek. "It is so good to see you. I was telling Matthew this morning how we need to have dinner together soon. I had such a wonderful time at your party."

"That would be fabulous," my mom gushed, forgetting the tense interaction just a moment ago. "I was saying the same to Lewis this morning. We both rave about your creamer. I think you have us all addicted. I literally can't stop drinking it."

"How lovely. I'll have to bring you more. We have so much of it we couldn't possibly use it all. It's my little hobby when I'm home. Matthew loves it." Jessica's mouth curved together. "How would tonight be for dinner? We are in much need of a night together without kids. Maybe one of your girls could babysit Timothy while we go out?"

"Absolutely." My mom nodded eagerly, motioning to me. "Dinah is working for Alice tonight, but Alice would be happy to do it."

Wait. What the fuck was happening? One sentence and I could feel my power sliding away, my actual age being dismissed as a child. A babysitter. Not someone who could sit at the adult table. Be their equal.

Especially Matt's.

Jessica's icy blue eyes slid to me. We both knew what she was doing. She wanted to put me in my place. Keep me far from her husband.

"I wouldn't think you'd want a *crazy* person looking after your son." I did not take my eyes off her.

"What is wrong with you?" Mom shook her head, disappointment bowing her features. "You are being unbelievably disrespectful. It's so not like you."

She was right. I could be blunt and awkward, but I was never out right rude. Jessica seemed to bring it out in me.

"Follow me back, Ms. Liddell." Jessica turned back to the hallway, not responding to me, which somehow made me even smaller.

My feet didn't budge.

"Alice…please. Do this for me." Mom clutched my hand, her gaze pleading. Refusing my mom was always difficult, but the pooling grief and hope in her eyes pushed back my stubbornness.

"Fine." I stepped past her, knowing this next hour was going to be hell.

🎩 🎩 🎩 🎩

Mrs. Winters lived up to her name. Her office was just as cold as the rest of the place: black leather chairs, a glass desk, some modern paintings, and floor-to-ceiling windows facing out on the woods behind.

"Have a seat." She motioned to a square black leather-and-metal chair that could probably fit two people in it. She grabbed a file off her desk, slipping on stylish black-rimmed glasses, sitting in an elegant curved swivel chair. She crossed her legs, her red heel tapping at the air like it was counting the seconds on a clock.

Settling in the chair, I tapped my fingers on the arm in rhythm to the invisible clock.

Tick. Tick. Tick. It clicked in my head, making me even more restless. I felt like I was running out of time, and I had to find something before it was too late, but I had no idea what or why.

Twisting my head, I glared out the window. A few fluffy squirrels hopped around branches, knocking the snow off the limbs.

They are adorable, but probably would chew your face off if given the chance. Wait. What? Where did that come from? *Yeah, Alice, don't be silly. That's chipmunks…not squirrels.*

"Your mother said you were having full-blown hallucinations yesterday?" Her voice veered my attention to her. She folded her hands on the file, staring at me, her eyebrow slightly curved.

Snubbing her question, I faced back out the window again. I came in here for Mom. I didn't say I would talk. It was like giving ammo to your enemy.

"I'm here to help you, Alice. The faster you realize it, the smoother this will go."

"Help me?" I snorted. "Why don't I believe that?"

"I don't know. Why don't you tell me?"

A bitter laugh cut through the air, dying away just as quickly. "Let's cut the bullshit, Jessica. I don't think you have my best interest at heart." My attention went to where I was expecting to see the rabbit foot hanging around her neck, like I knew she never removed it. The absence of it only triggered my anger, wondering where it was, what she did with it. It was another thing I wanted to take from her, and I had no idea why. All I kept thinking…it wasn't hers to have.

"I don't know where you got that from. I am only here to help you get better." She leaned over to the coffee table, pouring a glass of water from the jug sitting there. She set the glass on a coaster and pushed it closer to me. "Now, can you tell me what you think you saw?"

I stared at the glass, a single drop running down the side of the cup. "Don't you guys usually start with going into my past? Losing my job? My boyfriend-slash-boss dumping me so he could screw his new teenage assistant? A far less qualified one at that. You know…the reason I might be experiencing the things I am." I reached out, clutching the glass, taking a drink. It tasted strangely sweet on my tongue.

Curious.

"Sure." Her lips compressed with amusement, her scrutiny completely on me. "We could start there. Though it sounds pretty typical. A man putting a woman down in some way because her power upsets his fragile ego. The story is nothing new. Actually, it has been going on since the beginning of time…"

As she talked my focus snapped back to the window as a large white object darted just outside my peripheral across the snow.

Tinsel toast. Not now.

Muscles along my shoulders tightened, and I shifted in my seat. Forcing my head forward, I drew a veil at the window, not allowing myself to look again.

"Alice?" Jessica drew me back, my gaze going over her shoulder. "Can you tell me where you just went?"

A gasp caught in my throat, terror gripping my lungs, tugging at a scream.

On top of the desk behind her, a cartoon looking penguin waddled around, flapping his flippers and kicking at stuff on her desk, but nothing knocked to the floor, like he was only projected there.

I blinked.

Gone. The vacant spot on the desk jolted me; my head darted around. The animal hadn't even looked ghostlike. He had appeared as solid as anything else in this room.

Real.

"Alice?" Jessica turned peering behind her, her eyebrow curving. "Are you seeing something now?"

My nostrils flared, trying to keep calm. The thought of her seeing it happening felt dangerous. Instinct kept my jaw locked together, not admitting anything. Lowering my lashes, I tried to center myself.

High-pitched giggles tore my lids open, my head twisting to the windows.

"Oh blustery bells." I jerked back as two forms ran by the glass. I could see a small girl and boy with matching green and red outfits, leggings, and hats. Elf costumes. He grabbed for her hand, swinging it as her long braids flapped against her back. My attention went directly to her pointed ears before they vanished without a trace.

Holy Christmas cookies... My hallucinations were getting stronger.

"The madness is seeping in. You will be one of us in

no time," a voice said in my ear, matter-of-factly, jerking my head to the blank space next to me.

Bitter dread covered my skin in hot and cold flashes, causing me to leap out of the chair. Feeling the room was closing in on me, I ran for the door, hearing Jessica call after me. I needed to get out of here before my mind crumbled all over the marble floors. Darting past the receptionist and my mother, I shoved through the doors, running until my lungs gasped for oxygen. Bending over, I sucked in.

"Alice!" I heard my mother yell from far behind me, but it was the closer voices that dropped me to my knees.

"Ms. Alice, come play with us." Three high-pitched voices leaped around me, floating along with the flakes tumbling down from the sky. *"We miss you. Come play."*

"Shut up." I covered my ears. "Go away!"

"Alice?" A hand touched me.

"No! Go away!" I felt tears spill from my eyes, sobs hiccupping up my throat.

"Alice, it's me." Mom moved in closer, pulling me into her chest. "Shhh. It's okay." She wrapped her arms around me, rocking us slightly. "It's okay."

"No, Mom." I peered up at her, feeling utterly lost and broken, tears sliding down my face. "It's not okay. *I'm* not okay."

"You're right, sweetheart, but we'll make it better again. I promise. I'll do *whatever* it takes to make you well again."

There was that phrase again.

And it scared me even more than it did before.

65

Chapter 7

My duplicate blankly watched me, the glass reflecting the shell of a girl I had once known. The streetlamp outside sparked the encrusted frame like glittering snow in my dark room. My parents' voices still murmured downstairs, talking about me, while I numbly stared at the girl in the mirror, trying to find the cracks in her veneer.

I had always been sort of a loner but never really lonely. Now isolation crept around me, building a wall and separating me from my family, friends, sanity, and even myself. To no longer be able to trust yourself, your own mind, was debilitating. Every decision was in question, and every thought or sound you doubted. And the only person I wanted to run to was the one person completely forbidden to me.

The bizarre need to grab him and run away—fall through the glass and disappear from this world— thickened the band of fear wrapping around my chest.

A week ago, I was a normal girl with normal problems. A few minor setbacks, but nothing I couldn't handle with plans to get back on my feet again. How fast the ground slid away beneath me, like quicksand.

Like an LSS. Liquefied Snow Sink. The thought rushed in from nowhere, bubbling a groan from my throat as I rubbed my temples. It didn't even make sense. "There's no such thing," I mumbled, turning away from the glass. My gaze roamed over the fresh sketches.

All top hats.

Emotion drained in the back of my throat, making it hard to swallow. I could see why this made me look nuts. There was no longer even a variation, sprinkled with other hats here and there. It was all the same. All with a red scarf. But I couldn't explain the need to sit down even now and do more, like if I didn't, it would make me go crazy. I had never been OCD or anal about anything in my life. That was the problem. I jumped around, nothing holding my attention. Now I went to the extreme the other way. The bad version of Goldilocks.

And yet, I still didn't feel crazy. At all.

Only the insane are so sure of their sanity. The thought skated through my mind, dropping me onto the edge of my bed, feeling the weight of the truth hanging on each word. Exhausted, I wanted to crawl in bed, pull the covers over my head, and forget everything happening. Wake up to it all being a dream.

With a sigh, I turned to do just that when I heard our doorbell. As if it was a warning, a shiver ran up my spine, pausing me in place. I listened intently.

My father's mumbled voice moved toward the front door. The rise of his timbre sounded like a greeting in response to another voice.

I couldn't tell if it was a woman or man, but my gut twisted. I stood up and moved to my door, cracking it open.

"Thank you so much for coming over. We appreciate it so much. I felt Lewis needed to hear your professional thoughts on the matter." My mom's sentiment drifted up the stairs.

Oh, hell no. I stepped out into the hallway stopping at the top of the stairs, already feeling the temperature drop from her presence.

"You don't have to thank me. You did the right thing, Carroll." Her frosty voice slithered up to me, icing my lungs. "I am only here to help. I also want the best for Alice."

"I am so grateful for everything you've done. Honestly, if you hadn't moved next door...come into our lives when you did," my mother cooed. "I don't know what we would have done. Knowing you are there, trained in these matters, has been such a solace through this awful time." Mom sounded like they had been "dealing" with me for a long time. Not just a few days.

"I'm glad to be of help." Jessica paused. "And here, I brought these for you. You said you were running low."

"Oh my gosh. Thank you!" Mom seriously sounded like a fan girl. "Lewis just finished off the last of it in his cocoa."

"I did." My father chuckled. "I don't know what you put in it, but it is seriously addicting."

"An old secret family recipe," Jessica twittered.

"Well, it's delicious. Please come sit down." Dad's voice drifted as he led her into the living room. My toes brushed the carpet on the stairs but stopped a few steps down. My presence would curb what they said, color it. I wanted to hear what they thought when they didn't think I was listening. The unfiltered truth.

Sitting on the top step, I leaned against the wall, hidden by the ceiling of the second story. I tuned my ears in on the three in the room straight across from me. Noises drifted up of them settling on the sofa and chairs, and there was a small pause before my mom spoke.

"Lewis, not being there and not seeing it for himself as I have, of course feels a tad more reserved about the situation. But you have seen it firsthand as well. What do you think? I'd love to know your expertise on this."

"Well," Jessica let out a sigh, which locked every vertebra in my back in a straight line. "It's far more serious than I imagined from our conversations."

A chair creaked as if someone shifted in it.

"Her mind is declining at an alarming rate."

"It's only been a few days," Dad barked in defense.

"Lewis, it may feel that way to you, but Alice has been suffering a lot longer than that. It may have gone undetected, but she is already at the level of full hallucinations, hearing voices."

My stomach churned with acid at her statement, and I struggled not to stomp down there and tell the bitch to shut up.

"Lewis, your daughter has had a psychotic break. I know it is scary to hear, but I want to be straightforward, so we can face this head on. Deal with it instead of ignoring it. It helps no one to sugarcoat a situation as serious as Alice's."

"Yes. That's exactly what I want." I could almost see my mom's nodding like a bobblehead. What the Christmas dumplings was wrong with her? She never acted like this. She was the leader in a room, not a groupie. "Handle the problem directly."

"What do you suggest?" Dad spoke again, sounding far more skeptical than my mother.

"First I want to start with some antipsychotics. Get her on them right away and see if that helps with the visions and voices. I also want to see her again in a few days."

"And what if it doesn't work?" Mom asked. She always liked to be prepared for all situations. "What should we look for?"

"Extreme paranoia. She will act as though everyone is after her, most likely me. It's usual for them to think their therapist or doctor is trying to harm them instead of help. The visions, voices, and her mood swings will become more severe."

"Oh, God," Mom whimpered.

"It's okay, Honey, we'll handle this together," Dad reassured her. "Alice is strong. She will get through this."

"I agree, Lewis. Alice is *resilient*," Jessica replied. It sounded more like an insult than a compliment. "Let's try this first, then we can go from there, but I feel the medication will really *help* her." Her emphasis on that term coiled in my chest like a serpent. "Wanting nothing more than to get Alice healthy as fast as we can, I took the liberty of filling a prescription for her already." The rattle of pills in a bottle tinkled in the room.

Everything in my gut chimed with alarm at the notion she conveniently had these pills in her bag already.

"Thank you so much. I can't express how much we appreciate what you are doing. You have been so kind. So attentive," my mom babbled.

"Please, we're not just neighbors; I feel we are practically family now. I want to help in any way I can. Alice is important to me too." I was important to her? *Rash on my ass.* Her feelings for me were clear and mutual. "I should get home." I heard rustling and movement toward the door. Her figure came into view as she stepped into the foyer. The shadows sliced right at her neck, like her head had been chopped off, but I swear I could feel her focus somehow find me.

"Sorry we couldn't go out together tonight. Maybe some other time. Though it was for the best, Matthew made me this *romantic* dinner for just the two of us. He is the best husband. After all these years, we are still *so* in love."

My hand slapped over my mouth, holding back the snort shoving against my palm. *He doesn't remember marrying you, bitch. Or why he did.*

"Awww," my mom replied. "That is so lovely to hear. You two make such a beautiful couple."

"We make a great team. He's my general, operating the home and little army while I work."

Mom laughed. "That's such an adorable analogy. Well, your family is picture-perfect, and we love that you guys are next door to us."

"Us as well." Her heels clacked over the wood floor, sounding like a clock marking time. "Good night. I'll check in tomorrow."

"Have a good night as well. And thank you again, Jessica," Dad said. I heard the click as the door opened then shut.

"Lewis..." Mom croaked the moment the door shut. By their shadows on the floor, I could see him put his arms around her. "I'm scared."

"Me too." He hugged her closer to him. "But you and I have been a good team. We have faced a lot of things together. We'll face this."

"I'm so lucky to have you."

"I'm the lucky one." He kissed her head, dropping his arms away.

"Okay." Mom exhaled, stepping back. "Step one. Get Alice started on these pills right away. I believe it will help."

Hell no! I wasn't taking them. I didn't trust Jessica. At all. Every fiber of my being screamed she wanted to hurt me.

"Extreme paranoia. She will act as though everyone is after her, most likely me. It's usual for them to think their therapist or doctor is trying to harm them instead of help."

Fuuucck.

She just pulled another rung out from underneath me. Robbing me of any power I had. If I refused, I played right into her plan. If I took them, I declared I was mad.

But wasn't I? Was this the paranoia talking? Dragging my knees up to my chest, I bowed my head onto my knees. The sanity I felt so sure about the other day was slipping through my fingers, leaving only doubt in the spaces.

"Alice?" a deep voice whispered my name, jerking my head up. My spine slammed into the wall, knocking the back of my head.

"Oh, Christmas fudge…" I breathed out in a frightened whimper, staring at the form sitting on the same step, only inches away from me. Half man/half deer, he was the most uniquely beautiful creature I had ever seen. His antlers tipped back and forth as his soft brown eyes analyzed me.

"You look like Alice," he said frankly. A squeak chattered through my teeth as he leaned in, and my back painfully pressed against the wall, not allowing me to move any farther. My chest heaved with terror as his dewy nose snuffled my hair. Warm air brushed down my neck, the feel of it tugging at my skin as he continued to sniff me. "You smell like Alice."

"Go away." I tucked deeper into myself, too scared to reach out and touch him, knowing without a doubt, I would touch a solid being.

I was truly going insane.

He sat back, a sadness filling his eyes. "But you are not *my* Alice," he stated. "My Alice had much more *muchness*. She was a fighter."

"Go away. You're not real." I shut my eyes, covering my ears so I could no longer hear the velvety voice twisting at my gut. "You're not real. You're not real."

"Alice?" Fingers touched me and I batted them away, repeating my chant over and over.

"Alice!" Mom's terrified voice snapped me out of my safety bubble. Raising my head, my gaze went to the body which now sat across from me, meeting her pained expression. Tears threatened at the edges of her eyes, her forehead wrinkling as grief and fear swirled through her.

"Alice..." she cried my name softly, gutting me even more than I already was. The guilt and heartache I possessed brought this on them. I felt like I was letting her down, my whole family down, and causing them unbelievable pain, stress, and agony.

So when she held out her palm with two pills, handing me the small glass of water, I didn't hesitate, swallowing them back in a gulp. Fighting this would only cause them more grief.

My mom's arms wrapped around me, and I fell into her embrace, letting my tears flow out.

"I'm so sorry, Mom." I cried into her shoulder. "I'm so sorry."

"Shhh. It's okay, baby." She rocked me back and forth. "We're going to fix this. I promise. It's all going to be okay."

"Have I gone mad?" I asked, wanting to believe her so badly, but a voice stirred up in the back of my head, crackling with laughter.

"I'm afraid so. You're entirely bonkers."

Chapter 8

My eyes darted nervously to the corners of my room, my body not moving a hair. Watching. Waiting. Every light was on in my bedroom. The Christmas lights trimming our house shone through my window, painting my floor in dull blobs of color. The two days since Jessica had stopped by, since I saw the deer-man, seemed like years ago. Every minute I was slipping more from myself.

Tonight was a perfect example of that. *It was just a movie, Alice. Wasn't real.*

Sitting in the middle of my bed, keeping my hands and legs far from the edges, anxiety thumped my heart in my ears, waiting for giant, green lizard-bat things to crawl out from under my bed and sink their sharp teeth into my skin again.

Again?

My door opened, allowing darkness to seep in from the unlit hallway, my sister's silhouette stood in the doorway timidly. Afraid. *Of me.* "Alice?"

Not moving, my ears picked up on the TV still playing in her bedroom across the hall. We had been watching our annual Christmas movie together tonight, a normal night. My reaction had destroyed the chance at anything ordinary or lighthearted, which seemed to be my specialty lately.

Like an Advent calendar, Dinah and I counted down the final fifteen days to Christmas with our favorite holiday movies. It had been something we did since we were little. Scott had joined us for the last couple years, introducing him to some of our favorites.

Popcorn, drinks, candy…we were all set for a good night. Scott and Dinah stretched over her bed, I sat at the foot, leaning back into her mattress, feeling somewhat normal for once in a long time. Even though every day not seeing Matt was agony. The nightly and *detailed* erotic dreams were only heightening my craving for him. The sensations of his weight between my legs and the feel of his mouth tortured my mind until I let myself pretend he was there. I couldn't explain how I felt, except the time away was making things worse not better. I thought a movie night would take my mind off him, but it did the exact opposite. Worse than a ghost, he felt even more dominant in the room as we watched the cult Christmas movie.

Halfway through the film, one I had seen a dozen times, lizard-looking creatures with bat ears multiplied over the TV. Seeing the leader Spike and his white mohawk on the screen caused something to snap. A scream tore from my throat. Jumping up, I backed away from the screen.

"No. No. No." My head shook back and forth, the room slipping away from me. Gazing down, I saw my bare feet in snow. Red and bloody. Like a goopy cherry snow cone. No longer in my sister's bedroom, darkness and trees surrounded me along with gut-wrenching fear and panic. It felt as if someone I loved was dying, but I couldn't reach them.

"Alice... What's wrong?" A woman's voice morphed to a man's, pulling my head to the side. An obscure snowy landscape outlined a man's tall physique, blue eyes shining through the shadows. I couldn't make out his face but instantly felt a name slip into my head and heart.

Scrooge.

The leader of the gremlins yelled from his perch on a rock, tweaking my attention back to him. His beady eyes glared down at me, like he was telling me my end was next. I stumbled back, my head shaking. His group beat their sticks, howling into the air, calling for our death. Spike shrieked, lifting his spear, and the hundreds of scaly bodies descended on us like swarming ants.

Not able to move, I watched them coming for me, their teeth snapping, eager to taste my blood, their claws longing to tear into my flesh. The first one leaped in the air, coming down on me. I hit the ground, covering my head, screeching from the pain I was expecting to feel.

"Alice!" Hands grabbed my arms, shaking me. A familiar voice wrenched my head up. Scott's green eyes met mine. He tried to hide the panic in his expression, but he wasn't that good of an actor. "Alice, you're okay."

I was back in my sister's room. No creatures attacking me. No snow. No man. Nothing. My gaze went over his shoulder to my sister prancing by her open door. Mom and Dad rushed in, heading directly for me. Scott moved to the side as my parents crowded my space.

"What happened?" Mom asked me first, but when I didn't say anything, she flipped to my sister. "Someone talk to me! What happened?"

My sister opened her mouth, but nothing came out, her body trembling.

"She freaked out," Scott spoke for her, pointing to the TV. "The moment the gremlins came on the screen, she started screaming. I mean gut-wrenching..." He shook his head, appearing as startled as my sister.

"The gremlins?" My dad's brow furrowed. "She's seen that a million times. Loves it... Why would it suddenly upset her?"

"You know what Jessica said to us the other night on the phone. Ordinary things might trigger her now."

They spoke like I was no longer in the room. My opinion or thoughts didn't seem to matter anymore anyway.

It had only been a few days since I started taking the pills. Mom kept saying it took time for them to really get in my system and work, but all I felt was a decline.

Now, I sat on my bed with all the lights on, imagining green monsters blending in the dark shadows, ready to spring on me the moment the lights went off.

Seeking revenge.

Now Dinah treaded softly into my bedroom, sitting on the edge of the bed like I would shatter into pieces. "You really scared me."

"I know." I no longer knew how to console my family. The amount of times I uttered the sentiment, "I'm sorry," in the last few days meant nothing anymore.

She went to reach for my hand but stopped. "Help me understand what you're going through."

"I wish I could. It's not a math problem you can solve." I glanced up at my ceiling. "I don't even understand."

"But it's real to you." She licked her lips, tucking a short strand of hair behind her ear anxiously. "You really think it's happening?" Her question felt more like a statement, than an actual inquiry.

Curious.

"Yes," I replied numbly, the medication Mom had practically shoved down my throat after the incident was finally working through my system, the fight in me dying away, leaving me empty and pliable.

"So...did the gremlins jump out of the screen and come after you?"

"No." Exhaling, I searched for the right phrasing. "It's not like that. I wasn't in your room anymore...I was somewhere else." *With someone else.* "It's as real as this." I lifted my arms to my bedroom. "It was as if I had been there before. Reliving the experience again. This sick feeling that someone I loved was dying or hurt..." My fingers pinched at my forehead, like the answer was right there, needing to be plucked out.

Dinah's hand covered mine, her eyes swimming in emotion, a single tear slipping down her cheek. She seldom cried. She'd rather solve the problem than weep about it.

To see her crying over me broke me a little bit more. I gripped her hand in mine, pulling her into a hug. "It will be okay." I tried to comfort her, wanting to be the older sister who protected her for once. "I promise."

She nodded, wiping at her face. Standing up, she gave me another quick hug and smile before leaving.

She exited my room, neither of us believing me.

Hours later, the downstairs clock ticked, echoing through the silent house. I stared out into the cold night, searching for the one thing that made sense right now. For days I had been good, stayed away, and it had been like fighting against a vortex that wanted to pull me in. But tonight my defenses were nothing, and I didn't want to stay away anymore. Not when I knew I had seen him in my vision on that mountain. I had called him Scrooge, which was odd since we teased about that, but it felt *right*.

In the bizarro world of being attacked by gremlins, his presence next to me was the most real thing about it, as if we had lived many lives, slayed dozens of monsters together. It was silly, but it didn't take away from a core part of my gut that agreed we had been together before. Were previous lives possible? Had we known each other in some other life? It sounded more like one of my fantasy books, but the idea wouldn't go away.

Sleepless nights and stress added to my jumbled mind, but the drugs had only made everything worse. I should have fought, stood up for myself, knowing Jessica was trying to harm me. It was like she had this all planned out, which made no sense. She barely knew me and had just moved here a week ago. She definitely was insecure when it came to her husband, but was that enough to do this to me?

I needed to see him. To talk to him. Quickly dressing in warm clothes, I slipped out into the night, a fugitive heading straight for the tree.

"Matt?" I called softly, searching desperately for the puff of smoke curling around the branches, his gorgeous physique leaning against the tree, waiting for me.

A figure moved from around the tree, and a smile burst over my face, feeling lightness for the first time in days. "Matt."

The silhouette stepped out. My feet came to an abrupt stop, fear spread down my veins, my stomach dropping like a block.

Jessica stepped out from the tree into the light. *Coal in my stocking.* Dressed in a long black wool coat with fur trim, the rabbit's foot dangling from her neck, and even at this time of night, her lips were perfectly coated in deep red.

"I figured you'd eventually come again." She brushed her leather-covered hands together as she traveled closer to me. "Like an elf to sugar, you can't seem to stay away. It seems you have a weakness for *other* women's husbands."

"It's not like that," I croaked, trepidation heating my skin.

Jessica's mouth curved in a malicious smile.

"Don't treat me like a fool, girl. I've known about your little rendezvous from the *beginning*. You really think *a wife* wouldn't notice her husband slipping away in the middle of the night?" She eyed me as I swallowed nervously. "Don't fool yourself. He's a weak-willed man. Like all the rest. But in the end, he will always come back to me. You really think Matthew would choose you over his son? He will do whatever it takes to keep him this time. You are nothing but a shiny distraction."

"Guess you're the kind to take a child away from his loving father because of a hurt ego," I retorted brusquely.

"Me?" She motioned to herself, her eyebrows curving up. "*You* are the one who will end up taking Timothy away. And he will *hate* you for it. Either way, I win." She tipped her head. "He wants nothing to do with you, so stop making an embarrassment of yourself."

"Is that what he said? *He wants nothing to do with me?*" I couldn't explain the desperation to fight for him. Nothing had happened, nor did I have a clue how he actually felt about me. But something so profound was between us; I couldn't walk away. I knew that.

"See for yourself." She twirled her hand to the second-story window above us.

Matt stood in the window, staring down at me with a stony expression, his jaw locked firmly. His gaze met mine. Our eyes were locked for two full beats, expressing things I didn't understand before his lids closed and he abruptly turned...walking away. From me. From us.

Emotion thickened my throat, my lashes batting back the betrayal and unexplainable hurt.

Jessica's smile widened.

Stupid Alice, when will you ever learn people, especially men, only deceive and hurt you?

A strange sensation came over me that I had thought this before, said the same thing when he saved his own ass and threw me to the wolves, going back to her. But how could that be true?

"Still a shame. I liked you much better than his first. You have so much power, Alice. *Very unique.* And I thank you for getting us here. I was not expecting it from you." Her gaze roamed over me with disgust and curiosity. "But now you are simply a thorn in my side. Too much temptation for him."

"What are you talking about?" She was the one muttering nonsense now.

Her focus zeroed in on me, and I felt a pressure cram into my head, like shoving a sleeping bag back into the tiny bag. A cry came from my throat. I gripped my head, and my eyes slammed shut.

It dissolved as fast as it came, and I opened my eyes. I was all alone. Jessica was no longer in front of me. An alarm in the back of my mind was telling me I should wonder why, but it never made it to the surface. A spark out of the corner of my eye caught my attention. To the side of the house, a small red light flickered, being carried by the deer-man I had seen a few days ago. Only wearing a pair of brown cargo pants, his bare chest gleamed with the red light, his stomach rippled with muscle. His antlers swiveled to me; his large ears pointed in my direction. *Santa's sleigh*, he was more beautiful than I remembered.

A slow smile crept up his mouth. "You coming, Alice? We're going to be late."

"Late?" I asked.

"Hurry. We are very, very late," he said and twisted back, leaping down the street. Nothing around me was important anymore. Only the desire to follow him. A need I couldn't seem to control. I could hear the clock ticking in my head, flaming the demand that time was running out. I *had* to follow him.

"Wait!" I called after him, my boots crunching across the snow as I ran after him.

He twisted, regarding me again before darting deeper down a side trail leading to the woods, springing forward with determination.

"Deer-man, wait!" I didn't think and sprinted faster, frantic not to lose him. Curving and zigzagging, I tried to keep up with the red light darting along the dark trees. A strange fear that they would reach out for me or start talking picked at the muscles in my legs, pumping them faster. I weaved through the woods, glimpsing the red light before it disappeared again.

"Alice! Please…" a voice cried out for me, echoing off the trees. "We need you."

"Ms. Alice…*hurry*."

"Come back now!"

"Alice, hurry before it's too late."

"I'm trying. I'm trying." I fumbled in the slush but righted myself, trying to get to the voices, each one stabbing urgency and pain through my heart.

My boots caught on a log, and I face-planted into the snow with a thud. Exhaustion snapped my bones like I had been running for days, and I struggled to get up. The desperation in the voices grew more frantic, becoming so gut-wrenching and painful it stripped at my skin and mind. Shutting my eyes, my hands went to my ears, and I curved into a ball.

I started to scream.

And scream.

Chapter 9

"Alice? Oh my god…Alice!" Hands fell on me, and I swung and kicked at the touch, feeling so raw I thought I was going to crack. My wails still ringing sharply through the air, burning my throat.

"Alice. Stop." The recognizable voice splintered my lids, and I glanced up at my father's face. Swirling red and blue lights flickered off my parents' forms as they hunched over me, highlighting the terror etched on their features. Tears streamed down my mother's face as my dad pinned down my arms so I couldn't move.

What the hell?

Lifting my head off the pavement, I glanced around. EMTs were climbing out of the ambulance, a cop car was parked right behind as neighbors wearing bathrobes and slippers hovered on their lawns, watching the drama play out. I was right in front of my house…

My brain couldn't understand. No forest. No voices calling for me. I was in the middle of the street in front of my house. It had all been in my head. Blinking back my own tears, I lowered my head back down. Dark emotions filled my head. Humiliation. Shame. Fear. Anger.

"Let us through." A female EMT bumped past my mother. "What happened? Is this your daughter?"

"Yes," Dad answered, still holding my arms down. "She's not been well."

"She was getting better, Lewis."

"No, she wasn't, Carroll," he snapped, his temper on the fringe. "She was getting worse, and you know it."

Mom nodded, her hands covering her face.

"What's her name?" the woman asked, pointing a flashlight into my pupils.

"Alice," Dad replied.

"Alice? Can you hear me?"

I glared up at her. Seriously?

"Alice. I want to hear you answer."

"Yes," I snarled. "I can fuckin' hear you. I'm not deaf." I wiggled under my dad's hold. "Let go." He hesitated before easing back like if he did, I would burst into a rabid animal.

Commotion whirled around me, my head aching. It thumped with a shattering pain, as if someone had been inside drilling.

"Can someone tell me what happened?"

"She woke up the entire neighborhood screaming and chasing after something that wasn't there," the guy who lived across the street spat out. "I called the cops…I mean, she was acting completely insane…like she was on something."

"You on any drugs?" the EMT asked, shining the light into my eyes again as another one moved in where my father was. "Molly, special-k, coke—"

"She's on an antipsychotic," Mom answered. "That's it."

The woman turned to her partner, both giving each other a look of *oh, she's legitimately crazy.*

"Ms. Liddell is under my care. I'm her doctor." Jessica's voice came over me, her figure stepping up, slamming loathing through me that clogged my throat. *She. Did. This.* I felt it in every fiber of my being. Somehow, she had caused my hallucination. "However, her mind is deteriorating so quickly, the drugs I have her on aren't helping anymore."

Shoving everyone back, I got to my feet. "You fucking bitch!" I screamed, lunging for her. "You are doing this to me. I know you are."

Dad and the EMTs grabbed for me, holding me back.

"Let go! She's the one. I was fine until she started me on those pills. She is doing this to me."

"Ms. Liddell, you need to calm down." The male cop stepped in, holding up his palms. "Just take a breath."

"No!" I yelled, struggling against the hold on me, my arms pinned behind my back. Staring at Jessica smirking at me, I had another impression of being here with her before. Images of me being held captive while she stripped all power away from me. "I'm not crazy! But she's making people think I am."

"Alice…" Mom's expression splintered with agony. "Don't do this, sweetie. You know you're not healthy right now."

"Mom, please believe me," I pleaded. "You just met her. Don't take her word over mine. Please, listen to me. She somehow has you completely under her spell."

Yule log scones. The moment I uttered the phrase a connection snapped in my brain like a puzzle.

The syrupy creamer.

Was it possible?

My whole family was addicted to it. I wouldn't be surprised if all my neighbors were as well. I had no idea how she was doing it, how it was even feasible, but my gut just knew—she was controlling their minds with it.

"Isn't it strange since she showed up and started me on those drugs, I've gotten worse? She's hurting me, Mom. Please see this!"

Mom turned away, her shoulders shaking as she held her grief back.

"Alice." Dad shook his head, pity twisting his mouth.

"Jesus. She has you all in her trance." My head whipped around, catching my sister standing not too far off, exhibiting the identical expression as my parents. "It's the syrup. I don't know what she puts in it, but she is brainwashing you guys." The words shot from my mouth, and even I knew how crazy it sounded, but I couldn't stop.

Everyone stared at me silently, their stances stiffening. Dad started crying, which was like a thousand cuts slicing my heart. "Jessica told us this might happen." He croaked through a sob, wiping his eyes. "I can't believe this is materializing."

I knew what Jessica said. She set me up perfectly. Anything I said...*I* would sound like the crazy one. Nothing I said would be taken seriously. And maybe I was insane, but I wasn't wrong about her.

"Lewis, you know it's the last thing I want, but after this, I must insist you take the recommendation I made earlier on the phone seriously." *Recommendation?* What the hell had she talked to them about? "Look around." Jessica motioned to the disturbance around us. "Alice is no longer safe—from *herself*."

"Fuck. You." I tried to leap back to her, my teeth bared, but I was yanked back. "You are loving this, aren't you? Why? Because your husband would rather be around me? Smoke himself into an oblivion so he can forget he's married to *you*? A callous, ice-cold bitch?"

A gasp burst through the neighbors who were watching.

A nerve flinched in her cheek, acting for the audience like what I said hurt her, but I knew better. Her smugness multiplied. I had no idea how, but everything going on with me was because of her. She had orchestrated it all. And now I looked like the scorned fanatical lover going after another woman's husband, while she played the honorable victim.

I could see it in all their eyes: the ridicule, pity, and judgement.

"I've known you my whole life. But I'm the one you turn on immediately," I yelled out at the crowd. "Seriously?"

None of them moved, their eyes wide, hungry for the spectacle. My brain tickled with a vision, a group of people staring at me the same way, licking their lips for my head, zombies under her control.

"She has you all in her web. Don't you see it? Or all you see is the crazy one in her natural habitat? Well, I hope you enjoyed the show. The zoo's closed. You can go home now." I threw up my arms, hating how the neighbors ate this up without question. Tossing out years of knowing me and my character and standing behind her.

"Alice, please. You're only making this worse." My mom's touch flicked my eyes to her, allowing me to slowly gaze around at all the faces staring at me. From horror to pity, the neighbors stared at me like I was the freak in the circus. "We love you so much. We want you to get better." She gripped dad's arm as he gave her a little nod. "We will do *whatever* it takes to help you."

Damn…that word again.

"What are you talking about?" I could feel it, whatever decision they had been contemplating was firmed in their mind.

"You need to be somewhere safe. Somewhere with people who can truly help you heal and get healthy again."

My world tipped on its axis, acid scorching my stomach. "Noooo," I whispered.

"I'm sorry, Alice." A few more tears slid down Dad's face. "We don't want to do this. But it's for the best. For your safety."

"Y-you're sending me to an insane asylum?" I screeched, looking back at my sister for help. She only buried her face in her hands, crying.

Instinct had me search around for Matt. He understood me. Knew this was wrong. But his absence just solidified the feeling. I was utterly alone.

"I'll set everything up," Jessica said sweetly to my parents. "All you need to do is be there for your daughter. We can do the paperwork in the morning." She stood there, cool and collected, offering my parents hollow condolences, while her eyes glinted with triumph.

Seven maids a-milking! She had this all ready to go, as if she were expecting this outcome tonight.

"Officer, I don't think she will come willingly." Jessica batted her eyes at the officer, and he quickly nodded, reaching for me.

"Wait. I don't think that's necessary." My dad frowned, but the cop clutched my arm, pulling me away from them.

"You bitch," I seethed at Jessica as I fought against his grip.

She leaned into me like she was hugging me. "Don't challenge me, Alice," she muttered maliciously. "As I told you before, I am ruler here, and there is only room for one."

I stiffened at her familiar words. *Shit.* I knew she didn't like me, but it was more than that. She was pointedly after me.

The cop yanked me back, dragging me to the car, not caring if any of this was even legal. She had them all bamboozled. And the more I tried to suggest she was the evil one, the crazier I sounded.

Stuffed into the cop car, the lights flicking off the window, she smirked at me while Dad, Mom, and Dinah stood behind her, huddled together.

Checkmate. *Well played.* I stared at her. *But I'm coming for you, bitch. Count on that.*

She thought she took out a pawn, but I was going to remove the queen.

As an adult you have this delusion you are in control of your life. Decisions are yours to make.

How easily that can be stripped away.

Staring down at my hands, my torn nails dug into my palms, the scratchy material of the light-cornflower blue scrubs they put me in was a constant reminder I wasn't dreaming. My life had taken a sharp turn, swerving out of my control in the wrong direction.

"Alice, do you understand?" A small, plump doctor sat on the other side of his desk. His round, rosy cheeks and stubby nose flared anger through me. He looked like the poster boy for gluttony, shoving food down his gullet while his piggy eyes narrowed on me.

"Alice? Do you understand what the doctor has said?" Dad brushed my tangled hair away from my drooping head. My parents sat on either side of me and gripped my arms so I couldn't bolt and run.

Escaping was the last thing I was capable of doing. The drugs they had injected to "calm me down" left me nothing more than a sleepwalker, a shell in my own skin. I had been quite upset when dumped off here in the middle of the night, reasonably enough. They acted like I was at a level-ten freak-out because I kept asking questions, challenging their authority, asking to see the person in charge, wondering how any of this was even legal. It was as if we stepped back into the 1800s or 1900s when a husband would consider any outburst from his wife an insane act and toss them in the nuthouse without question or proof. She could have been upset he was cheating or being a dickhead, but the institution would take the man's word, and the wife's life was destroyed. Her word meaning nothing, no way to fight for herself.

We weren't much more advanced today.

One of the many faceless nurses stabbed a needle in my arm, my body instantly going lax. After that I was a robot, staring off into the world as if I were no longer part of it, though my mind still understood what was going on.

Mindlessly, I changed my dirty, wet clothes into a prison-looking outfit and sat on my single stiff bed as the sun came through the single window, listening to other patients waking up. Screams and mutters echoed down the corridor, a few curious wards hovered at my door, but I just stared at my hands, waiting for my parents to show up and realize this wasn't the place for me.

Two hours after the sun rose, they did show up, but it wasn't to take me home. It was to sign the paperwork, giving the institution full rights to treat me. My dad was the one who seemed a little unsure.

"Doctor Cane, I want to be clear how you will be treating my daughter. This seems a little excessive." Dad motioned to the bars on the outside of the windows. "I mean, this place feels like a jail. It's kind of extreme for Alice."

"Mr. Liddell, I understand your concern. The bars are merely an extra precaution." Dr. Cane shifted in his seat, his belly knocking into the desk. "But from what I've learned from Dr. Winters, Alice needs this place to handle *all* her needs."

"Lewis." My mom peered over my head at her husband. "If Jessica says this is the best place for her, then I fully support whatever they will do to help. You promised me."

My lips curled into a snarl at her name. Fucking Jessica Winters. Only a week of knowing this woman and she had more power over me, over my parents, than we did of ourselves.

"I remember, Carroll, but I don't know…" He shook his head, eyes filling with tears. "This seems so fast and severe; don't you think?"

"We said *whatever* it takes," she muttered to him like I couldn't hear her, even though I sat in the middle of them. "She could have gotten killed tonight or hurt someone. We are not capable of watching her twenty-four seven."

"I know. I know." He bobbed his head. "You're right."

No! She's not. Please, Dad, help me. I could hear my voice cry in my head, but nothing came to my lips. Terror burned at my stomach lining, but none of my thoughts or feelings bubbled to the surface, whatever they gave me keeping me silent. Obedient.

After another thirty minutes, my parents had signed and asked everything they needed to. Dr. Cane rattled off all the right-sounding answers to appease them, sounding more like a brochure than an actual doctor.

"Visiting days are Sundays, right? We can come then?" Mom and Dad stood up.

"Usually yes, but we think it's best the first couple of weeks she has no outside influence."

"What?" Dad burst, his head wagging violently. "No, no way. You didn't tell us that. Are you saying we can't visit our own daughter?"

"I'm sorry, Mr. Liddell, but those are the rules for any new patient. No phone calls or visits the first two weeks. They need to get used to the schedule and rules. Think of it as a reset for her mind."

"That's bullshit!" Dad exclaimed, throwing up his arms. "I can't be with my daughter on *Christmas*?"

"Those are the rules, Mr. Liddell."

"Lewis." Mom moved to him, clutching his arms, turning him to her. "This kills me too, but if this is the way we get *our* Alice back, to see our daughter get healthy again, then we must put away our heartache and think of her. Alice comes first."

Dad gripped my mom's face, a croaked sob escaping his throat before he nodded slowly. "You're right. Alice is the most important thing," he whispered, holding my mom, his lifeboat. His rock.

Gently they both kissed and hugged me as if I were so broken a squeeze would crumble me onto the floor like an egg.

"We only want the best for you." Mom kissed my head after Dad. "We love you so much."

She took my father's hand, and both left the office, my mother's sobs resounding down the hallway as they left me there screaming inside my head.

CHAPTER 10

Because I had been driven up to this facility in the dark, scared out of my mind, I couldn't recall what the outside of the building looked like. But from the inside, it was built like an old mansion turned hospital, having two wings off the main area in the middle. With only two accessible stories, it wasn't huge but held a vastness that was cold and creepy. There was no warmth to the tiled corridors or the limited design in the main room.

The "hangout" area consisted of a few sitting areas with tables. On one side were two newish dark gray sofas and chairs facing a giant TV. On the other side, games and a few books were on a single shelf against the wall. On another wall were three large barred windows facing out onto the gardens, but that was it. No art or decoration on the walls. No personality. No feeling of being "lived" in.

It was like it had been staged for a movie set.

"This is where you will spend your time outside of therapy and meals. The bedrooms are just for sleeping." The nurse motioned around the room, where twenty people mulled around, along with a handful of orderlies. Women, men, all odd-looking and peculiarly youthful, though I couldn't put an age on any of them. Short to tall, large to small, they varied in size and shape. They either stared off in space or played at the craft table or a card game. I saw one lady who would randomly scream out from her chair by the window but would then go quiet and space out, getting lost in the world inside her head.

All of them were sleepwalkers pretending to be alive.

"With points you can earn TV time." The nurse drew my attention back to her. Nurse Green was a *very* plump woman who reminded me a lot of Dr. Cane. So much, I was convinced he was her twin or sibling. Same rosy cheeks, stumpy nose, and brown hair. Her head only came to my shoulder, with a deep snarl marking her face. She didn't look like the cushy woman you wanted to hug, but more as if she'd beat me with a huge wooden spoon if I looked at her cross-eyed.

"Breakfast is precisely at seven a.m. Lunch at noon. Dinner at five p.m. In your rooms at nine. Lights out no later than ten. In between, you will have various therapy sessions. Once a day you have an hour to go outside. If you are a good girl, you can expand that by earning merits."

"Good girl? Merits?" I snapped, sensing the drugs they gave me were wearing off. What the hell? Was I two years old?

"This is not Mommy and Daddy's house. We have schedules and rules here. You will abide by them all." She swung to me, seeming to relish my position, glaring like I had wronged her in the past. "And any snotty remarks or resisting? You. Will. Be. Punished. Every ding will put you further down on the naughty list."

"Naughty list?" I laughed, my eyebrows curving up.

"For that you already have a ding on your record. The more you defy me, the worse it will be for you here. I promise you that." She shoved her fat sausage finger into my face, her voice going low for just me to hear. "You should have lost your head that night. You have only made things problematic for us all."

"What?" I stumbled back. *Off with her head!* A blur of a picture of a woman screaming this at me whipped through my mind faster than I could grasp it, but I could feel the fear now like it really happened. "What did you say?"

"Everly!" Another nurse stepped up, her unibrow curving down in censure. "Take a break."

"I'm sorry," Nurse Green muttered. "I just couldn't stop myself."

"Just go. I'll take it from here," the blonde nurse ordered, her name tag displaying the name Pepper. She was the exact opposite of Nurse Ratched. So skinny her cheeks were sunken in, with a long nose and pointy chin. She was my height, but so boney, all legs and arms.

Green glowered at me. Turning, she stomped away.

"She's pleasant," I quipped.

"Nurse Everly Green is to be respected here." She twisted to me. "You understand? We are all to be if you want to do well here."

I knew myself too well to think I was going to do well in this place. I didn't like authority, my mouth always blurting out my thoughts, and my stubbornness would fight just to spite them.

"Sure thing, Nurse Pepper," I smirked.

"Only those who have earned it can call me by my first name. You call me Nurse Mint."

My mouth dropped open. "Pepper. Mint. Are you kidding me?"

Her beaklike nose lifted in a huff, her arms folding. "For that. No lunch. You will sit in our quiet room and think about your attitude."

I blinked at her. This place felt unreal.

"I'm a twenty-five-year-old woman." I stepped into her space, my jaw locking. Her eyes widened as she swallowed. "Treat me as an adult and I might consider pretending I respect you. *You* understand?"

Her throat bobbed with fear before she locked down her expression. "Now you will go without dinner," she snarled. "Noel," she called over her shoulder.

A stocky man stepped out from behind the desk. He was only a few inches taller than me but was so wide his arms rippled with huge muscles. He was massive. His smooth, dark caramel skin and glowing, light amber eyes stilled the air in my lungs. He was beautiful, but the scowling expression and hunched shoulders headed toward me like a linebacker.

"Mashed potatoes and gravy," I muttered, stumbling back. He nabbed my arm, gripping me tightly.

"Take her to the quiet room. She will spend the day there." Pepper Mint smirked at me. "She will learn who is in charge here. No room for *rebels* here." She waved me off.

Noel grunted, yanking my arm and forcing my body to follow.

"Hey!" I thrashed against him. The flimsy indoor shoes they gave me squeaked across the smooth floor, giving me no grip. "Let go of me!"

He gripped tighter, his head forward.

Wiggling and kicking, he effortlessly dragged me into the elevator, the buttons on the panel showing there were more than two floors.

He hit the B.

Basement?

Fudge pudding. In my pants.

"Please. Let me go!" I elbowed him and jabbed my foot into his leg. With a swoop of his arm, he locked me against him, my back to him, my arms pinned to my sides, my legs too close to kick at him.

"Stop," he grumbled into my ear, his voice grave but strangely calming. And fuckin' sexy. "No use to fight." The doors dinged, opening up. He walked me out, and my heart dropped to my toes, terror scratching up my throat.

The basement was directly out of a horror movie: dark, dank, smelling of death and rot with rows of windowless cells down the spine-chilling corridor. Only one light hung in the passage, shadowing creepy shapes along the metal doors. Tapping from leaking water and groans from a furnace just iced the disturbing cake.

"Nooooo," I cried, battering against his stone body. "This can't be legal!" As if I was being forced back into unending darkness, the yearning to be in the sun, outside, stabbed fear behind my eyes.

"Girl," Noel hissed in my ear. "Do as you're told.

Keep your head down. *Be smart. Learn.*" It should have been a threat, a warning for me to behave, but the directness in his timbre felt more intentional. As if he were trying to help me instead.

Curious.

I stopped fighting and turned my head to him when he reached for a door, opening it to a tiny lightless room. He gave nothing away, but when he pushed me into the space, his eyes landed on mine, and he stared at me with intention and intensity.

Curiouser.

His face disappeared as he shut the door, the squeal of metal raking up my spine as the door slammed shut, a cry breaking from my lips in the pitch-dark room. With the crank of a lock, my fists banged on the door in panic.

"Let me out. I promise. I will do as I'm told," I screamed, but only darkness answered me back. Claustrophobia itched at my skin, pumping my lungs.

Sliding down the wall, I tucked my knees in and closed my eyes, pretending I had control over the suffocating blackness. The room was no more than three feet square.

Tears burned at my eyes, but I bit them back, my mind rolling over Nurse Noel's words.

Be smart. Learn.

I didn't trust a single asshole here, but his sentiment kept rolling around in my head, his tone stressing words like he was telling me to be smart with my actions. Learn your surroundings. Study every person here. Weakness. Strengths.

Fight the clever way.

"The more absurd you are, the more rational you become," I muttered to myself. Having no idea where the declaration came from, it felt bizarrely accurate. "And Alice, you are about to go utterly bonkers."

Chapter 11

The screech of the door popped my lids open, and I flinched against the dim light. My bones were locked into a ball in the corner.

"Are we going to be a good girl today?" Peppermint Patty put a hand on her hip, staring down at me over her long sharp nose.

I didn't answer as my vision tried to adjust to the assault of light.

"Answer me, Alice. Or no breakfast."

"It's morning?" I croaked, stretching my muscles from their frozen position. Twinging with pain, I pushed to my feet. Dirt coated my skin. The memory of bugs crawling over my skin made me shiver. Sleep had been a fleeting desire. Fear, strange shrill noises, bugs, the cold, not knowing the hour, and my stomach aching with hunger only let me surface sleep in tiny measurements.

"Yes." She nodded. "You will learn your actions have consequences here." She motioned for me to move. "Now, let's get going. You have a session right after breakfast."

"Figuring no time for a shower?" I took a step, my arms wrapped around my stomach.

"The hour between six and seven is for that. It is now breakfast time."

My teeth dug into my lip, trying to hold back a lippy comment. It wasn't my fault I missed "bathing hours", and the hole I had been locked in came without an ensuite.

Nurse Mint eyed me like she was waiting for me to spout off, a smirk growing on her face when I stayed silent. Fine. If she wanted to believe she was winning, I'd let her. But I would win the battle. I had no other choice. In my gut I knew they would never find me "cured."

Peppermint Stick led me back up to the first floor, where the middle area was both the dining area and check-in desk. The wings of the building were used for the kitchen, therapy sessions, and doctors' offices. The second floor consisted of more patient living areas on one side and the orderlies on the other side. I did find it strange that most workers seemed to live here and not have a home outside this hellhole.

"Get your breakfast. Someone will be back promptly at seven fifty-five to take you to your session."

"Oh goody," I mumbled.

"Excuse me?" she asked sharply.

"I said, *thank you*." Saccharine sweet, a smile curved my mouth. "I appreciate y*our* kindness to me." Okay, so I couldn't go cold turkey.

She stared at me, her nose wrinkled, but I knew she couldn't tell if I was being serious or not. She seemed to have no understanding of sarcasm.

Walking away before she could decide, I went straight for the cafeteria-style setup. A few people were in front of me, holding trays, waiting for what looked like slop to be dropped on their plate. Silently we all inched along, the kitchen staff behind the counter looking as happy to be here as I was.

Giving us runny eggs, toast, and one link of sausage, they moved us down the line, controlling our portions. Even starving, I grimaced at the meal, scooting over to the coffee. No sweeteners or milk were offered, only a single tagless bottle stood near the pot. Picking it up, I sniffed at the opening. The smell chilled my skin, icier than I had been all night while sleeping against weeping stone walls.

Peppermint.

"No." My stomach dropped as I peered around the room, anxious she would suddenly show up. The one who had my family hooked on this stuff.

"You using that?" A man came next to me, pointing at the bottle. He was extremely short, the top of his head coming below my chest.

"No." I dropped the bottle back on the table with a thud.

"You're missing out. It's the only good thing here. They don't let us have anything sweet. So this is my daily slice of heaven. It's so good." He licked his lips, pouring an obscene amount into his cup. "I'm Happy."

"Alice."

"Welcome to crazy town. The more you drink, the better it is." He smiled brightly, tipping his cup at me before strolling away to a table.

Staring at the bottle like it was poison, I backed

away, hiking to an empty table in the back.

I ate slowly, watching, analyzing, my eyes rolling over the patients and staff, taking everything in.

"Be careful. Sanity is like a flame. Poof! Out goes the light." A woman slid onto the bench next to me, causing my head to jerk to the side. A crazed laugh bubbled up her throat, her eyes glimmering with light. It was the same woman who had sat by the window, erratically shrieking out nonsense. Great. The truly insane were attracted to me.

Her shoulder bumped me, and she giggled, stuffing a spoonful of eggs into her mouth. Something about her felt familiar and reminded me of someone.

She appeared young but also felt older than me. Her black hair was split into two braids, plaited down to the middle of her back. She had a cute button nose and huge brown eyes with the rosiest cheeks I had ever seen without the help of makeup. That was another thing not allowed here. Not that it mattered to me; I never wore much. But it seemed a tad extreme.

Shifting a little away, I tried to swallow the watery eggs.

"Oh, Alice." She sang my name. "The girl who changed it all."

"How did you know my name?" I snapped to her.

"Oooohhhh," she cooed. "Everyone knows who you are, Alice. You..." She bonked my nose with a deadly seriousness. "Changed *every-thing*."

Her face went from blank to fully whooping with giddiness.

Shit! This girl is the nuttiest Yule log ever... I paused, my lashes fluttering with a twisted sensation, my head bizarrely picturing the penguin vision I saw at Jessica's office.

"I see it." The girl leaned right up to me, tapping my temple. "It's all in there. Spin it! And let it all fall out."

"Okay, Bea." The huge nurse tapped the girl's shoulder. "Remember what we said about personal space."

Bea grinned up at the beautiful Noel, her cheeks turning an even deeper pink.

"Alice is different." She spun on the bench, turning herself to him, opening her arms wide. "It's time! Switch! Switch!" She leaped up, darting off across the room.

"Wow." I shook my head, taking a sip of the bitter coffee.

Noel leaned over and set a plastic cup in front of me. My eyes went to the pills, feeling my shoulders droop. Medication to keep me nothing more than a functioning dead person. Someone who couldn't find the will or energy to fight back.

"Every morning you will be given your medication." His deep gravelly voice reminded me of a movie actor. "You can take it while I walk you to your session." He nodded for me to pick up the cup.

I did what he asked, rising with my coffee and cup of pills, and followed him out of the cafeteria. As we walked, his eyes slid up to the video camera on the far back wall before they went down, staying on something longer than natural before he faced forward again. My gaze traveled to the same spot.

A garbage can.

A tiny flutter of hope drew in and out of my lungs.

Instinct took over, whether he meant to lead me to this or not. I angled my body away from the camera, so they only saw my back, drawing the paper coffee cup up to my mouth, gulping the last bit before chucking it in the trash…along with the plastic cup of pills.

It was seamless.

No one would even blink at it, but anxiety still twisted my guts in knots. Nurse Noel did not even give me a second glance as he continued down the hall.

He stopped at the last door, lightly knocking.

A muffled "Come in" seeped from inside.

He twisted the handle, opening the door for me to step in.

My body came to a halt, disbelief and horror pounding in my ears. "Oh, hell no," I snarled, stepping back, ramming straight into Noel's physique.

"Alice." Her red lips arched up. "Right on time."

Jessica. Fucking. Winters. In all her sleek, icy glory.

Even in this madhouse, I wasn't safe from her.

Chapter 12

"Why are you here?" I contemplated the office, the modern style, similar to her office in town, already telling me what I knew but didn't want to accept.

Jessica swiveled in her chair to the side, crossing her legs, ignoring my question. She was dressed in an expensive gray blouse, black pencil skirt, and her trademark blood-red heels, which matched the color on her mouth.

"Come, have a seat." She motioned to the empty chair in front of her desk.

"No." I scowled, not moving from my spot. "Why. Are. You. Here?"

"I run this place. It's mine." She sighed like she was bored.

"So...what do you do? Seek out people through your other place to become patients here?" I spat. "Convince their families they're crazy, take their money, and trap them in here for your own entertainment?"

"I didn't need to convince anyone. You did it all by yourself."

"You are a sick, twisted bitch." I skewered each syllable at her.

"You are testing my patience. Now sit down."

"No."

"Noel?" She signaled to the huge mass behind me. Large beefy hands grabbed my biceps, shoving me forward. Noel relocated me from the door to the chair, forcing my ass to slam down on the seat, a grunt puffing from my lips.

I glared up at the beast, but his expression was locked down, his eyes empty of anything.

"Did she take her medications?" Jessica stared at me, directing her question to him.

"Yes, ma'am," he grumbled, his hand landing heavily on my shoulder. "I watched her. Should be kicking in any time now."

I didn't move or even twitch a finger, not wanting to react to the fact he lied to Jessica. Was he on my side? Or was he just another person with his own agenda? Though, with his comment, I felt him helping me again. I was supposed to be on something that would probably make me not so combative.

"Good." Jessica dipped her head. "But I would still want you to stay here."

"Yes, ma'am." He stepped back against the wall, with a nod, folding his arms in front of him.

"Have them all potty-trained?" I snorted, not able to help myself.

Her nose wrinkled, her blue eyes glistening with hate. "How I wish I could purge the world of you. Do everyone a favor…including the man you can't seem to stay away from." Her detestation oozed through her teeth. "But of course, I can't."

My eyebrows lowered. "Is your hate and insecurity

so deep you would go through all this to keep me away from Matt? Are you that sick and demented? I think it's you who needs to be locked up in a padded room, not me."

"You think this is about Matthew?" She cackled, twisting back her chair, to face me. "Please, Alice. Give me more credit than that. Do I look like a woman who depends on a man? I certainly don't need one to make me feel whole or worthy. He was only a bonus in *all* this."

"All what?"

"In torturing you." She lifted her brow and grinned, gazing around the room. "Though he also deserves recompense for his own disobedience. This," she gestured to the room, "is all for you."

"For me?" I sat back, my mouth dropping open. "I-I don't understand. Why me? What did I do to you? I barely even know you."

"Why you? Oh, how many times I've asked myself the same thing." Her gaze crucified me as it went down my figure. "Unfortunately, you are valuable to me, Alice, and I need to understand if you are *her.*"

"Her?" Trepidation prickled from my stomach down to my calves, making me want to bolt from the room. Noel, acting the guard dog, hovered close to my exit. My gaze drifted over her shoulder to the barred window. "I don't understand."

"You don't need to." Her sharp eyes followed my focus, a smirk forming on her lips. "Go ahead, Alice. Try to squeeze through the bars or dart for the door. You won't get far. This place is well guarded inside and out, far from anyone who will help you. It would be better if you cooperated and learned I am the *ruler* here."

"You are crazy." I stood up, backing away from her.

"No, dear, that is you. Everyone saw it... May I applaud you on your great performance? You made this so easy for me." Her smile turned wicked. "With just a little push, you stepped right into my plan."

Fuck-an-elf! She was crazier than I thought. Nothing she was talking about made sense. Why did she want me? She just met me a week ago.

"Your files tell me nothing. Average girl, average town. Blah, blah, boring..." She waved her hand at the folder in front of her. "But maybe a loose tongue and your blood will tell me."

"What?" Panic gulped me down, turning off my logic.

"Noel." Jessica nodded at the nurse.

Run! My gut told me to go; my life depended on it. Whipping around, I darted for the door. Noel leaped for me. His arms wrapped around me, pinning me in place as I continued to struggle and lash against him.

Jessica pushed out of her seat, her heels clicking as she walked around to me.

"Keep fighting, Alice; it will only wear you out." She tapped my cheek, walking into the hallway, ordering Noel. "Bring her to the room."

"Stop fighting," Noel huffed into my ear, easily moving me into the corridor. "Making it worse."

Jessica stepped across, opening the door to another room. A shriek caught in my throat.

Holy mistletoe.

The room looked like a lab and an operating room had a baby. A dentist-looking chair with straps sat in the middle of the room, along with a tray filled with needles and operating instruments. Jessica sauntered over, picking up a syringe off the tray.

Noel pushed me farther into the room, heading straight for the chair.

"Noooo!" I screamed, my feet kicking, my body thrashing against my captor. Terror punctured holes into my lungs like a drill corkscrewing into the earth's core, spurting up bile, burning the lining of my throat. "No. Don't do this!"

"Hold her down." Jessica tapped at the needle. Noel forced me into the chair, his huge hands holding me easily in place as he lashed my wrists into the straps, his eyes not meeting mine.

"Please..." I begged him, wiggling around like a toddler wanting desperately to be let down. "Please. Help me."

Noel's vivid amber eyes slid up, securing to mine, his fingers digging into my arms where he tightened the restraints. Once again, I felt he was trying to tell me something, but I had yet to figure out the code.

"Clearly we need to up her medication. It does not seem to be working. She might be more resilient than others." Jessica moved to my side, disregarding my pleas.

"Yes, ma'am." Noel strapped in my legs, then stepped back.

She wiped a pad across the inside of my elbow, the harsh odor of rubbing alcohol stung my nose.

"No. Shit. This isn't even legal. You have no right."

I hissed, yanking at the binds, trying to twist my arm to no avail.

"Don't I?" Her eyebrow curved. "Your parents were so desperate for my help, to *fix* you, they gave over all rights to me on how to cure you, my dear."

"What?" Dread sank like a cannonball in my gut. "No, they wouldn't…" My parents were the kind to read every warning label, wanting to know everything before they did something.

"Oh, they did." Jessica grinned. "For two people so logical, they crumbled when faced with something so illogical."

My nostrils flared. "And I'm sure that had nothing to do with you controlling their minds."

"Controlling their minds?" Her eyes widened in a false shock. "How could I possibly do that?"

"Don't even…" I growled. "I know you put something in your peppermint syrup, manipulating them somehow."

"Wow, I'm influencing them with some flavored creamer?" She let out a low chuckle. "You know how crazy that sounds, right?"

"Fuck. You," I seethed, jerking against the restraints. I did know how insane it sounded. No one would take me seriously if I spouted it, chalking me up to a mad conspiracy nut. "I don't know how you are doing it, but you are."

"What an overactive imagination you have." She leaned over, the needle pinching my skin. "But we encourage that here. The more truth you tell, the more they will think you belong here." She jabbed the needle into my arm, driving a whimper from my lungs. My eyes tracked the clear liquid leaving the syringe and going into my arm.

"Nononono!" I clenched my jaw. A rush of heat scorched up through my veins. "What is that?"

"That was a little something to help you *relax*." Jessica set the empty needle on the tray.

"What are you going to do to me?"

"If you're good? I'll take a little blood. Ask a few questions," she replied. "If you're bad? Well, let's say there are severe punishments for disobedient little girls."

My head began to spin, the drugs already working through my system, weighing down my lashes. Butting against the need to close my eyes, I crunched my teeth together, compelling my lids to stay open. The fluorescent lights above my head blurred and swirled with other colors, splaying across my vision. My eyes and mind sludged through at different speeds, distorting my understanding of things.

A hazy object darted behind Noel, my lids narrowing on what looked like a three-foot rabbit...and I swore it was wearing a holiday-themed apron. I knew from its more humanlike qualities it was a boy. I blinked, strangely feeling calmed by him instead of scared. Like he was a friend sent to comfort me.

My mouth slurred as I pointed, "Vhere."

Noel turned to where I was pointing, then looked back at me with confusion, not seeing what I was pointing at. Another entity suddenly appeared on top of the counter to my right.

A penguin?

It flapped and waddled around, but this time I could hear it singing a Christmas song, sounding warped in my ears.

"It's kicking in," I heard Jessica say, but my gaze caught on the movement behind her. Bumping into each other were two distorted figures, small children dressed in elf outfits with pointy ears and round rosy cheeks.

"Alice, come play with us." The girl flipped onto her head, clicking her heels, colors swirling around her like a stream of sunlight catching on a soap bubble. "It's not scary from here."

"Sometimes looking at something from a different perspective changes everything." A man's deep voice rumbled through the room. I jerked my head to Noel, but he stood there silently guarding.

Sprinkles and frosting! What was happening to me?

The whole room wobbled with colors and distorted figures, their voices chatting away, growing louder and more distorted in my head until it was bursting.

"Alice. Alice. Alice. Alice!"

"Stoooppp." I closed my eyes, but their voices still twittered. Familiar, but the more they pulled at the veil in the back of my head, the more the pressure built behind my eyes, stabbing them with pain. "Please stop!"

I had gone under general anesthesia a few times in my life; I knew what it felt like. This wasn't the same. Whatever she injected me with was causing my hallucinations to come fully alive, crashing into me all at once. It reminded me of the one time a boyfriend and I tried mushrooms together, but it was not as intense as this. Sight, taste, hearing, and sound swirled and twisted, heightening until you could experience the rainbows of color bursting around.

Jessica moved into my line of sight. Sweetness turned to ash on my tongue, the hues turning to black like she was a tempest, bringing evil down on the happy kingdom, obscuring the voices and visions around the room.

"Alice." My name clung to the air like smog, Jessica's face bending as if she were in a kaleidoscope. "Tell me how you were able to *travel* through the looking glass?"

"What?' my mouth said, but my brain had no connection. It felt like it was floating inside my head, and my thoughts drifted to a space where I was suddenly surrounded by diamond-crushed mirrors and continuous images of me spinning around in fog and snow.

"Only one has enough magic to do that. No one, especially a human, should be capable of traveling through a portal. There's *no way* you should be *her. You're human.*" Her nose wrinkled with repugnance. "How were you able to fight the Land of Lost and Broken and enter the Valley of Mirrors? How did you do it, Alice? How did you pass through the mirror?"

As if I was suddenly set in that snowy-white place, where I felt no cold or heat, mist laced around my ankles. I watched my feet stroll up to the mirrors, blue eyes reflecting in the glass, beckoning me to come through, his voice commanding and deep.

"Let go, Alice. Let the madness in..." His voice swathed my heart, wrapping it up with bliss. Something I couldn't get enough of. I didn't just want *more, I*

needed *it.* *"Once you let it in. Everything will be right again."*

"I-I…" I felt my arm rise, reaching out to touch him…the desperation to be near him, the desire to follow him anywhere. The man's blue eyes and deep voice were like a dream, one I wanted to wrap myself into.

"Yes?" She got closer to my face.

"I just stepped in," my mouth answered, but I had no connection to my responses, like someone else had taken over my body.

Her lids narrowed, her back going rigid as she straightened. "You. Simply. Stepped. Through? You didn't do anything else?" Jessica spat out with irritation. "And woke up in Earth's realm?"

"Yes." I nodded my head, and it felt as if the whole room bobbed along with me. "He asked me to…reached for me…and I followed."

"Who, Alice?" She folded her arms. "Say his name."

"Scrooge." The name slid across my tongue like a hot toddy—warm, strong, comforting, and it tingled through me. Though I had no idea why I said that name.

A strange grin twisted her mouth; black and grays spun and dipped around and over her. "I knew he'd be the perfect bait. As you are for him. I enchanted the mirrors to show you the person your heart craves the most. To entice you. While I piggybacked on you to come here."

"Let's see if you'll be more useful to me for this." She moved closer to me, her face a distorted Picasso painting. "Tell me where *he* is hiding. I know you have seen him. There is only one reason you'd be in the Land of the Lost and Forgotten. I know he's on Mount Crumpit, but he is veiling himself from me, constantly moving." She pinched her lips together. "Tell me where he is, Alice."

"Whhhooo?" I puffed into her face, drawling out the word.

"You know who," she clipped. "The man who destroyed my life. My husband." She gripped the arms of my chair, moving into my face. "Nicholas. Where is he hiding, Alice?"

The rabbit, penguin, and the two elves fluttered around the edges, shaking their heads like they were my conscience telling me not to speak.

"Don't tell her, Alice!" the girl elf pleaded, her eyes big and wide.

I nodded, knowing I wouldn't have anyway. It was an instinct I couldn't even describe; my mouth clamped shut.

"Tell. Me!" Jessica grabbed the hair at the back of my head, yanking it back painfully. "Or you will lose that pretty little head of yours."

The words came out of my mouth as if they were put there on my tongue. "You better watch out. Don't cry. He knows if you've been bad or good."

Hues of red burst from her like flames as her nails dug into my scalp. "You asked it for it, Alice," she seethed, grabbing for another needle on the tray. This one was attached to a tube and bag. "I told you there are consequences for being disobedient to me." She pierced my vein with the needle, my blood filling up the tube, darkness bleeding at the edges of my vision.

"I just need to keep you alive. Enough to keep the door open. Then I will destroy him once and for all and slam that door shut for good. Ending the legend of Santa and the silly girl who's supposed to save him. Though looking at you, I can't fathom how it could be you." Her voice sounded as if it were moving farther away, and maybe I was. Blackness and nausea pulled me down as my eyes closed. "When I'm done, take her to the dungeon. She needs to learn not to disobey me."

"Yes, Your Majesty."

Dungeon? Majesty? My confusion only skimmed through my thoughts before I seeped further into unconsciousness.

"Know this, Alice: You are never getting out of here," Jessica whispered against my ear. "Ever."

Then darkness crept in, nabbing me like a thief.

Chapter 13

Time was running out.

Running. Searching. Lost. Darkness.

Stuffed animals floated by me. A rabbit. Penguin. Reindeer. Snowman. Elves. Their huge stitched-on eyes staring at me with accusing expressions, as if I was failing them.

I felt a desperation to find something, but I had no idea what. Tears slipped down my cheeks. The pendulum swung back and forth, the hands of the clock speeding around like a car race, trying to win.

Panic pounded my heart, the need to call out for someone, but the name dissolved on my tongue, disappearing before I could capture it.

"Alice." My name drifted over the wind in a whisper, stopping my feet. Nothing but darkness and strange toys floated by me; their pain and agony radiated off them. The call of my name, the deep husky voice, was the only warmth in this place. It was my lifeline, the single link to my survival. My head swiveled, blood pounding in my ears.

A crackled laugh of a woman echoed in the air, chilling my spine. "Time's up, Alice. You lost...everything."

I was falling. Crashing through glass, the fragments spraying out. I couldn't see it, but I felt my end coming.

"Alice! Fight her!" His gravelly voice tried to reach for me, but nothing stopped my fall into the darkness.

My lids bolted open with a gasp from my lungs, my body jolting with the imaginary impact. My eyes only took in utter blackness. The kind so deep you lost yourself in the absence of light, your mind desperately trying to make shapes out of nothing.

Dread bubbled up a cry at the back of my throat. I clamped my jaw together, holding the frightened whimper back. Was I awake? Was this still my nightmare?

My fingers dug into my leg to feel pain, to know I still existed. The cold stone ground crept through the thin layer of fabric I wore, stealing heat away from my body. Huddled in a tight ball against the wall, my muscles ached from being cramped up. I wanted to move, to stretch out my legs, but I couldn't move, my body too weak to shift.

This wasn't like when my sister dragged me out for a long run, working me so hard I'd come home and pass out on my bed the rest of the day. My energy was beyond depleted; Jessica had drained me of my essence. Seized a piece of me. I recalled everything up to when she injected me, then it got muddled and really bizarre. Whatever she gave me totally messed with my head, creating dreams with talking creatures and odd questions about stepping through mirrors.

And him.

The man's voice still vibrated my body, the raw need and power in it, as if he were trying to push through my dreams into reality.

I hadn't seen him, but it was Matt's face and voice I felt in every nuance of the dream. Even here he haunted me. Not that I minded, though thinking of him and the idea I might never see him again was torture. He was the one slice of happiness in this place. The one thing they couldn't take from me.

Fight her.

Maybe I was insane in thinking he had reached through all logic and reality and tried to contact me in my dreams. To give me strength. Tell me not to give up.

Anyone would say I was speaking through my subconscious. It was probably why I was truly crazy because even now, I could feel him. Like a ghost hovering around me, he kept me company in the lightless pit deep in the basement. Did he see what happened to me? Did he care? Did he think about me and wonder how I was?

Every minute, Ms. Liddell. Every. Fucking. Second. I heard his voice in my head, knowing I was just trying to make myself feel better. For one moment I let myself believe he could hear and feel me too. We had this connection which transcended everything.

I must have drifted for a moment because the clunk of the door lurched me awake. Scrambling to sit up, which used all the energy I had, I pressed my back into the wall as the door opened, the shrill squeak of the hinges making me cringe. My lids narrowed, turning my head. The dull light from the hall pierced my eyes.

"Only two days here and already two days in the hole." Pepper Mint clicked her tongue, tsking me. Her thin shadowy outline stood in the door with her arms crossed. "I'm not surprised. You are wicked to the core. A rebel. You deserve to be punished for defying her Majes—Mrs. Winters." She cleared her throat.

I blinked, too tired to think about what she was going to say. Staring at Nurse Peppermint Stick, I watched her pointy face curl up with a snarl. She wore light gray scrubs, which only bleached out her pale face.

"Get up. It's breakfast."

"I need a shower." My shaky legs pushed me up the wall to stand. I knew Jessica had taken a lot of blood from me as I slept. It was violating, making me feel dirty.

"Well, once again, you are too late. We stick to a strict schedule here." She stepped back from the door. "Now move."

Weakly, I followed her upstairs, begging for at least a bathroom break.

"Fine." She huffed in front of a restroom near the cafeteria. "Hurry."

Slipping in, I took care of business, then went to the sink to wash my hands and face, my skin itching to be scrubbed.

A frown creased my brow as I stared at the wall.

Blank.

No mirrors.

For a flash, I was staring at another wall. Rustic wood paneling, a bronze sink. Warm and comfortable, but mirrorless. I blinked and it was gone. The cruel fluorescent light above my head buzzed and flickered with a cold detachment, the icy snow tile lay in front of me.

Squeezing my lids, I bent over, splashing cold water over my face, trying to rid myself of the strange vision. It felt so real. Like I had really been standing there. Somehow I knew a walk-in shower, a large tub, and a shelf filled with toiletries were behind me. It wasn't an assumption. I *knew* the fluffiness of the towels, the different-colored stone tiles in the shower.

"Fuck a toaster strudel." I leaned on the sink.

"Hurry up!" Nurse Mint pounded on the door.

Wiping my face with a paper towel and brushing back my loose tangled hair, I left the bathroom, the strange dreams hovering at the back of my head.

Mirrors. Why did I dream she asked me about walking through them? A sensation tugged at the back of my mind at the notion they didn't have any here. Now that I thought about it, there were not any.

"Why aren't there mirrors here?" I caught up with her.

"What?" She wrinkled her nose at me.

"Mirrors. Isn't it odd to not have one in a bathroom?"

"No. They only encourage vanity. You need to fix what's on the inside, not worry about the outside." Her glare rolled down me. "Like you need more reason to stare at yourself. Or figure them out."

"Excuse me?"

"Better hurry, you barely have ten minutes before breakfast is over." She tapped her watch.

Thinking it was safer to not engage with the Mint Stick, I shuffled into the cafeteria, getting what was left of the breakfast: glue-looking oatmeal, a banana, and coffee. I glared at the bottle of peppermint syrup. I hated everything peppermint now.

The same small man I saw the day before refilled his cup with just the sweet liquid, rolling his eyes in ecstasy when he sipped it.

"You really need to try some." He held the cup up to my face. "It's delicious. Try it."

"No," I growled, staring at the innocent-looking flavoring.

"A drug she's been pumping into their water for years, making them no better than zombies. You think all those people agree with her? She can only control one at a time. This is her way of keeping her minions in line." The thought came out of nowhere, but once again I knew someone had told me this, that it wasn't me making it up.

The wild dreams, the mirror...*this*. It poked into my skin like a splinter, irritating me and causing me to be even more restless.

"You should stop drinking it," I muttered to him before heading to a table. On my first bite, a figure dropped next to me, knocking into my hip.

"Hey, Not-Alice." Bea's shoulder hit mine, knocking the spoon from my mouth. "I see you are trying to climb out of the hole."

A snarl vibrated through my teeth, irritation spiking at her abrasive intrusion. "Not Alice?" I glanced over at her. What did she mean I was trying to climb out of the hole? I was out. Sitting next to her, *trying* to eat.

Bea's cute little heart-shaped face was abruptly in mine, her nose crunched up against my own, her eyes going back and forth between mine.

"What the hell?" I jerked back, her intense brown eyes still digging into me.

"Nope. She's still not there."

"Who?"

"You, silly." She giggled wildly.

Keebler elf... She was seriously crazy.

Without warning she lurched forward, her forehead bumping into mine, her demeanor going serious. "She's trying," she whispered. "Let go...she wants to come out, Not-Alice. She's the one with the story. This is just intermission. But the curtain's going up, the stage is set. And you are the understudy for the real Alice. A brilliant star in the battle for it all. Full of muchness."

Muchness.

"What did you say?" Cold sweat lined the back of my neck.

"Bea!" Nurse Green yelled across the room, jerking our attention to her. "What have we said?"

"That I'm a mindless puck." She covered her mouth, snickering with naughtiness.

Nurse Green turned a deep shade of purple. "We told you to leave her alone. Not to talk or go near her. You disobeyed." She pointed to the doorway. "Go to your time-out space."

Bea laughed, jumping up from the table, leaning into my ear, her little hands clutching my shoulder. "They think it's punishment. But it's my asylum in a madhouse. It's all about perspective," she sang in my ear as two guy nurses I didn't know rushed for Bea.

"Time to wake up, Not-Alice. Let sanity go, and everything will make so much more sense."

"Shut up. Now," one of the orderlies demanded, grabbing her. Both wrapped hands around her arms, dragging her out as her fevered laughter followed her down the hall.

Gaping at the empty doorway, my mind reeled with everything she said. Most of me wanted to think she was nuts and forget about it, but instead, it hung on me like heavy ornaments on a flimsy tree, drooping and weighing my shoulders down.

A plastic cup full of pills dropped down next to me. I peered up into Noel's amber eyes. Against his dark skin, they bloomed bright with a translucent yellow color. Emotionless, he nodded to the cup.

"You have a free hour before therapy. I got permission to take you outside for a walk."

I felt like a dog with a leash who was being let out to pee. He held up a winter coat he'd been holding, tossing it on the bench. It was mine, the one they peeled from my body when I first arrived here.

"Really?" I lifted my brow. "I thought that was only reserved for the good little girls and boys."

Noel grunted and swung around, striding for the exit.

Hopping off the bench, I grabbed the coat. Pills in one hand, coffee in the other, I jogged after him, not wanting to miss a chance to go out into the sun. I didn't care if snow covered the ground. The need to feel the rays hit my face and the cold temperature crash against my skin was too much.

"Take your pills," he shot over his shoulder.

My gaze slid to the garbage can we were passing,

and identical to yesterday, I twisted for the camera, giving my profile, while I pretended to down the medication, swigging it down with coffee. I dumped them in the trash with my cup and pulled on the one thing here that was mine. I stepped out into the cold winter sun, feeling a moment of peace for the first time since I got here.

If I'd realized what was ahead, I would have enjoyed it a bit more, knowing it would be my last.

The sun stroked my skin softly, the cold nipping at my nose and cheeks, clipping my lungs, but it felt magnificent. Alive. Free. Not a patient in an insane asylum, but a normal girl enjoying the minimal warmth of the winter sun.

It was the first time I really got to see the front of the building. Built with dark stone, the two wings stretched off the main building in the center, spires reaching for the sky. Beautiful, but something was haunting and scary about it. It reminded me of a 1900s sanitarium, which was used a lot back in the day. Hospitals for incurable diseases, disabilities, or for those with problems who didn't fit into society's norm and turned insane inside these walls.

Noel stayed close but let me wander, checking out the extensive grounds. They were gorgeous. Lightly sprinkled in snow, the landscape had me wondering if at one time it had to be some wealthy person's personal estate. The gardens held a large hedge maze, fountains, and perfectly manicured bushes and lawns. A huge rose garden was on one side, which in spring had to be lovely.

I was instantly drawn to the maze. Mazes held mystery and intrigue, like anything could happen within its walls. I did have the fantasy of being the girl wearing some gorgeous old-fashioned dress, running through the maze, laced with fog and darkness, brewing a slight eeriness to it. Playing a kinky game of hide-and-seek with my lover, who frightened me as much as attracted me.

Clearly, I watched and read too many romantic fantasies. Besides that, I wasn't normally all that girly. Not that there was anything wrong with it, but I had never been an overly hopeless romantic in real life. No, I was just hopeless.

"Are we being watched out here?" I muttered to Noel, my boots sinking in the snow as I trudged closer to the maze.

"We are always being watched," he replied, keeping his head straight. "Eyes are everywhere."

"Can they hear us?"

"No. Not here," he said, so low I barely heard him. "But never let your guard down."

I swallowed, my bluntness jumping off my tongue.

"Can I trust you?"

His silence danced in the freezing air, dangling in front of me like a carrot. One that was probably poisonous, but I took a bite anyway.

He rolled his jaw. "Don't trust anyone."

"You've helped me. Why?"

He stayed quiet so long I figured I wouldn't get a response.

"Because the tide is changing." His eyes darted back to the building. "And I recognize the part you will play

131

in this battle." He halted, his voice going even lower. "Until it is time, keep your head down. I can only do so much. Listen. Learn. She will not be easy to defeat." He turned around and started strolling back to the building.

My forehead wrinkled at his odd statement, though his choice of words was similar to Bea's.

About to follow him, a noise wrenched my neck back to the opening of the maze. The hedges were so tall they blocked out the low sun, shadowing the path.

"*Alice...*" My name hissed through the branches of the foliage. A red light glowed deep in the maze, outlining the large form of a man.

With antlers.

Fear gripped my lungs, but my feet inched forward, feeling this strange pull.

"Hurry. Time is ticking. Alice, you are *her*." The form disappeared down the path, slipping behind the bushes.

"W-wait," I croaked, darting into the maze, curving around the corner where I saw him.

Empty.

Whirling around, I searched the space for the humongous form. No crunching of snow under foot, not a wisp of movement or sound.

He simply vanished. As if I conjured him up.

You probably did.

My hand went through my hair, rubbing my head. It was the deer-man; I knew it. The one I had seen in a hallucination before. The one thing with my visions, I kept seeing the same creatures over and over.

A penguin.

Elves.

A reindeer.

A hare.

Even a snowman.

Like Christmas had decided to haunt me, bringing in ghosts, not from my past, but from my delusional mind, to torture me. *Like Ebenezer Scrooge.* I laughed to myself.

A tightness strangled my throat, the humor dying away instantly. The name sitting on my ribcage like a block. My hand went to my chest, lungs pumping up and down as I tried to swallow.

"He asked me to—reached for me—and I followed."

"Who, Alice? Say his name."

"Scrooge."

The blurry memory fluttered in my head from my session with Jessica, suddenly feeling it was not a dream at all. Every warped colorful fragment fit into my head like a puzzle.

Say it again. Say it out loud. My mind ordered me; it needed me to vocalize it. I swallowed nervously, feeling I was opening a gate that would let out a storm. Changing everything.

"Scrooge." It came out soft, timid.

Say it again.

"Scrooge." I let the name pass over my tongue with more strength, feeling a truth in it I didn't quite understand. The name felt more real to me than my own, not as an iconic name associated with the holiday season, but a real man.

Matt Hatter.

He was who I saw. Matt with a top hat…and a tattoo on his chest. My fingers had traced it. Knew the feel of the inked lines under my fingertips. A teapot scrolled with "It's always tea time" pouring into an upturned top hat, with a red scarf dangling off it, identical to the sketches I did with fervent repetition.

"Oh god." Frantic breaths puffed out of my mouth, my body bending over. Why was I so sure he had a tattoo and knew how his skin felt? I had never seen Matt's chest. Was I so far into my insanity I was making things up? Taking his image and inserting him into my wild illusions?

"Alice!" Noel's voice cut through the bushes. "Time's up. Let's go."

Gulping in more oxygen, I straightened up, my head feeling like a washing machine, thoughts, feelings, and images blending and bleeding together.

I had destroyed my family and ripped apart my life with my hallucinations—but this was the first time I felt truly crazy.

It's about time, Alice, a voice curled through my head. *Fall into madness…it's the only way to climb out.*

Chapter 14

Staring out the window of my room, the snow glittered under the moonlight. A weight rested in the air, a peculiar vibe which tingled against my skin. I could feel it. The calm before the storm, the earth holding its breath, waiting for the snow heading our way.

The full moon felt like an omen, creating a tension, pulling me out to the maze. Edgy and agitated, I wanted to leap out of my skin, slip through the bars and soar away.

Following Noel's advice, I kept my head down the rest of the day. It helped I hadn't had a "session" with Jessica. I kept to myself, pretending to read a book while I watched the orderlies. They still berated me when they could, but when bedtime came around, I found myself in a single bed instead of the hole for the first time. Yet I couldn't sleep any better here. I missed my family so much, but it was more than that. A gap existed in my heart, as if I missed people I didn't even know.

Lack of sleep and food was deteriorating my mind. And I no longer knew if I was truly mentally unstable or not, if I was so far gone visions and reality were one and the same.

"Only the insane are so sure of their sanity," I muttered to myself, pressing my hand against the glass.

Just let go, Alice. Let it in, a voice nibbled at me. Scared to truly let go, I grasped the things that made sense. Logical. Where there was still hope you could come back. If I let go...I would be lost.

Lost and broken.

"Not-Alice?" A knock tapped on the wall against my head. Bea's voice slipped easily through the thin walls between her room and mine.

Ignoring her, I hoped she'd think I was asleep. Lights out meant we were in our rooms, no talking or interaction with other patients. Sleep was the only thing allowed. And they checked on us hourly to make sure.

"Ms. Not-Alice," she sang with a giggle. "I know when you are sleeping and when you are awake."

"Bea, go to sleep," I hissed back. I had done so well to stay out of trouble today. Three nights in the hole with no hope of a shower after chipped at the walls I was trying to keep wrapped protectively around me.

"But don't you feel it? It's coming."

Don't take the bait. Don't take the bait.

"What's coming?" Crap on a nutcracker.

"The magic. The hope. The story is changing." She sounded like an awed child, still believing in Santa Claus.

Santa Claus? My forehead crinkled, a flash of a naked bearded man wearing a kimono and holding a gun flashed in my mind.

"Ahh," I croaked, wiggling my body in disgust. "That was stomach-churning." The fact I imagined Santa naked should tell me a lot about myself. I probably was better off staying here.

"You will find *him*," Bea emphasized the last word.

"Who?"

"The one who is lost and the one who is broken," she replied, her voice slightly muffled through the wall. "You are the key."

"Key?"

"Look, Not-Alice...the clues are all around you. You need to open your eyes and see them."

Rolling my eyes, I peered around the room void of anything but a bed, nightstand, and small armoire for our few clothes. Signs of what? What the hell was she talking about?

"Not only what is there, but what *isn't*." She giggled eccentrically.

Shaking my head, I gazed out the window again. The woman was certifiable, but there was a good chance I was too.

A cloud rolled across the moon, blocking the beams into my room. Deep blackness encased the space, obscuring the grounds below. A gasp hiccupped up my throat, my body jerking.

At the edge of the maze a single red light glowed, burning through the darkness. I could feel eyes searing into me, beckoning me to follow the light, like a ship caught in the storm. In a blink, the clouds slid past, the blue-white light spreading over my bed and hands, the red light vanishing.

"No. Wait."

I leaped up, and my eyes locked on where the light had been. I could still feel the intensity of someone's gaze, calling for me to come to them, the lure vibrating my muscles to move.

Not thinking, I shoved my feet into my boots and ran for my door. I yanked it open and stopped.

A nurse strolled the opposite way, her back to me, starting room checks. I knew more orderlies were on the nightshift milling around and stationed by the entrance downstairs, guarding this place. Not from what could get in, but from what could get out.

"Fuck," I mumbled to myself. The need to go outside flourished inside me instead of lessening at the thought I couldn't leave. It almost felt I had no choice. I had to get outdoors.

A soft click jerked my head to my right, Bea stepped into her doorway, grinning at me.

I wrinkled my nose, motioning with my head for her to get back in her room. She didn't need to get in trouble too.

Her smile grew, and mischievousness glinted in her eyes. She took a step farther out and winked at me.

Oh holy fuckin' night. Noooooo! I shook my head violently, glaring at her with warning. *Don't do this.* My eyes pleaded with her.

"Go, Not-Alice." She turned away, let out a spine-chilling scream, and started to run down the hall, her bare feet padding on the tile, her crazed cries following her to the opposite side of the building. Crashes and booms echoed off the blank walls like she was knocking and throwing things. I could hear nurses yell, their feet pounding toward her.

She was drawing them away so I could escape. I didn't know what they'd do to her, but I had no doubt being put in the hole was the best scenario here.

Go, Alice! Don't waste her sacrifice, I screamed at myself, and my legs darted to the staircase at the far end of the corridor, hearing people running up the main ones.

My boots slapped the linoleum flooring, gravity yanking my legs down the steps, almost making me stumble. I stopped at the bottom and peered out into the dimly lit passage. The front doors would be locked and probably set with alarms. But on my tour of the facility, I saw a side door, which led to the parking lot, where I saw nurses constantly slipping in and out. For a smoke break or what I didn't care; I only hoped it would still be open.

My heart thumped against my ribs, fear crawling up my throat as I inched for the door.

So close. So close.

Commotion rumbled around the front where the main station was, Bea's wails still filling the asylum along with loud bangs. But now I heard other patients screaming, joining in like a choir of crazies.

Watching over my shoulder, my hand clutched the handle and twisted.

Click.

Elation burst in my chest when the door swung open, icy air slapping at my face, goosebumping my flesh. If caught, a jacket would have been a red herring of my true plan, but now I wished I had one.

Stepping out, I shut the door behind me, rubbing my arms. True to me, I had no plan once I got out here, the need overtaking rational thought. But now that I was out, I knew I had to keep running. I darted toward the maze, the need forcing my legs to act out of my control. I had no idea what I was running to or why, but as usual, I jumped without thought.

Jessica would never let me go.

I would die here.

My breath clouded in front of me in large curls, my nose and arms stabbed with the frosty temperatures, my hair the only protection I had besides the blue short-sleeved scrubs they had made me wear, even to sleep in. Nurses Green and Mint seemed to enjoy all the layers they could use to break me, as if it was their personal mission to snap my sanity in half.

I glanced over my shoulder. The asylum glowed with light, nurses and patients running back and forth in the living areas, no one knowing one slipped out.

I slowed, creeping up to the entrance. The air skated down on me, heavier than normal.

Don't you feel it? The magic? I could hear Bea say.

Ridiculous. That stuff is in books. It's not real. I tried to lecture myself, but nothing stuck. Tip-toeing into the shadowy maze, my lungs tingled with energy.

"Hello?" My voice quaked, jarring the silent night, moving deeper into the maze. "Please. If anybody is here. Come out. Prove I've not gone utterly mad." I snorted, feeling even more crazy for saying it out loud, for believing something was there. I risked everything to come out here, but for what? On the encouragement of a woman whose insanity was beyond question?

Rubbing my face, I took a deep breath.

You're out, Alice. Run, the logical part demanded.

Save yourself.

"Alllicccceee…" My name rushed down the lane, filled with desperation.

My head wrenched up, oxygen halting in my lungs, my gaze flitting to every space and corner.

Terror clutched my chest, but slowly I moved down the path, the light from the moon casting an eerie blue glow on the surrounding snow. Shadows hung heavy, making me twitchy and jumpy. I curved down another path, my stance low and ready for an attack.

"Alice, hurry," the voice called out again.

"Show yourself," I growled. "Stop playing with me."

Silence followed my request, but down one of the lanes I saw a red light. Bolting forward, I sprinted toward it. Reaching the spot, the light had moved down another path.

Twisting and turning through the maze, I chased after the light, feeling oddly like I had done this before.

"Stop it!" I yelled, my lungs heaving to fill up. "Stop being a coward. Come out!"

Back down the lane I had come, a giggle of a little girl darted by, heading down another trail. A frustrated noise ebbed up my throat as I chased after her and came to a four-way split. No little girl.

The desperation to get to them, reach them, like they were bits of my soul I needed to capture and put myself back together with, rattled my bones. Tears stabbed behind my lids.

A boy's laugh bounded behind me, spinning me around, my legs leaping toward the aisle. Halfway down, a penguin slipped down another path, directing my feet toward him.

"Wait!"

The moment I'd think I had one, they would be gone, only their giggles echoing in the maze, as if this was some game to them. Phantoms inhabiting my head.

I burst out of a lane into an open area. Frustration and anxiety danced on the back of my neck, spinning me around. It felt like claws were tearing at my mind, the echoes of their happy laughter shredding me. My knees dropped into the snow, a cry strangling my throat. I was so tired. Fighting for sanity. For my life. To be normal.

Let go, Alice.

A sob wedged up through my teeth, a last hold to reason. It was in vain, and my will to hold on was collapsing on itself.

Let go...

The words were almost soothing, like everything would be okay.

I shut my lids, my shoulders drooping...

And I surrendered.

Chapter 15

"Alice!" A deep voice called to me through the darkness, but it sounded far away, like he was yelling through thick glass. Turning away, I tried to delve deeper into the blackness. Into the peace where I was light and unburdened. "No, Alice…wake up!"

Latching on to me, he pulled me from the darkness. "Shit. Don't do this to me. Wake up." A sting sliced across my face, causing an angry grunt to quake my chest, ripping my serenity away.

My heavy lashes beat against my cheek, struggling to rise. Blue eyes stared down at me with a mix of terror and relief. The moonlight streaked over his beautiful face.

"Scrooge." The name floated off my tongue before my eyes shut again. I let the hallucinations fully in, and they felt so damn real. I could even feel his warm breath on my face, the jacket he covered me in, his fingers touching my face. Why did I fight this? I didn't care if I was crazy. If being insane was wrong, I didn't give a crap. Not if I could live in a world where he was mine.

"Open your eyes, Alice."

Gravelly and deep, I wanted to stay wrapped up in just his voice. It felt like home. A blanket swathing me in warmth.

Gradually, my lids lifted. He was even more gorgeous than I remembered, with his black wavy hair, full lips, chiseled jaw covered with a heavy scruff, like he hadn't bothered shaving in days, and brilliant blue eyes that made me feel possessed with need. They tore down all my barriers, seeing everything in me, making me feel exposed. Naked.

"You scared the shit out of me." He pulled me higher in his lap, taking a deep breath. I did the same, inhaling his rich, sexy scent, which produced a whimper from me. Woods and cinnamon. "Don't ever fuckin' do that to me again. You got that?"

Jeez, my hallucination was kind of a bossy ass. But who was I kidding? I liked it.

He rubbed the puffy black jacket against my arms, sending tingles down my nerves, sensation coming back.

"What are you doing out here?" His hands moved all over my body, trying to warm me up, his touch feeling like electrical charges. "Why did I find you passed out in the snow, in the middle of this maze, almost frozen to death?"

"I should ask you the same thing, but since you are a figment of my imagination, I know why you are here." I tapped at my temple. "At least like this, we are together."

"Figment of your imagination?" His brows bunched together, his gaze scrutinizing me, bulldozing through my walls. "What the hell does she have you on? What have you taken, Alice?"

"Nothing."

"Don't lie to me. What drug does she have you on?" He growled, pulling me to sit up, his grip on the jacket tightening.

"Didn't take anything," I laughed dryly. "I'm naturally this crazy."

His brows still squeezed together, straining his forehead. Reaching up, my thumb brushed his cheek, rubbing over the frown. He jolted at my touch but didn't move as my fingers slid over his skin and down his face.

"I missed you so much," I whispered. "Isn't that silly? In real life I don't know you, but everything in me tells me I do." My hand cupped his jaw, feeling the bristles of his scruff tickle my palm. "The moment you walked into my parents' house, I felt like you were mine. That we belonged together. Damn, I wanted to fuck you. The dirty sex I've imagined us having? Wow," I blurted out, my hand sliding down his neck, feeling his Adam's apple bob at my declaration. "Damn, you feel *so* real."

"What do you mean?" His fingers wrapped around my wrist, squeezing. "Alice. Do you think I'm not actually here?"

"Shit, no. I'd never say these things to the real you. Hello. Embarrassing. And so wrong. Married man with a kid." I cringed.

"What if I told you neither are true?" His gaze dug into me.

"Huh?"

"I'm not a hallucination, Alice." His hands reached for my face, gripping my chin, forcing me to look in his eyes. "I'm *really* here."

I thought I was good at understanding what was real and what wasn't. I thought hallucinations were something you saw. A projection, but if you tried to touch them, you'd feel nothing. That was not how it worked with me. I could see, smell, hear, and touch them. No different from an actual person next to me. I no longer trusted my mind. My senses.

"You may be an undigested bit of beef, a blot of mustard, a crumb of cheese, a fragment of underdone potato." I pulled away from his hold. "There's more of gravy than of grave about you, whatever you are."

I winked at him, proud I could still quote *A Christmas Carol* on cue. My sister and I used to have contests, tossing holiday movie quotes back and forth until one of us had to bow out.

Matt tipped back, his eyebrow curving up. "Not sure if I should be insanely impressed or ridiculously terrified you knew that by heart."

"Probably both."

"I'm not a blot of mustard." He caught my hair between his fingers, trailing them slowly through, longing etched on his features. "I'm. Here. I've been looking for you since the moment she carted you away." He swallowed, looking down. "I am so sorry. She threatened to take Tim. I thought I was doing the only thing I could to protect my son."

I understood. I would choose the same, though it still hurt, watching him turn from me.

Looking away, I took in a breath. We were in the center of the maze, a snow-capped fountain in the middle, surrounded by benches. On the ground was a human-size game of chess, the black-and-white board peeking through the bits of snow.

Pushing up, I rose to my feet, my legs wobbling like Jell-O. He lurched up and grabbed me.

"You swear Jessica doesn't have you on anything?"

"She thinks she does." I stared up at him, his warm body looming over mine. My numb limbs gobbling up his heat. "I've been able to toss them out. This is all exhaustion and lack of food. But the other night I know she did something to me."

"What?"

"I can't remember. It's all jumbled up in a knot. She drugged me. Reminded me of being on mushrooms, but ten times more intense. I saw things. And I swear she asked me the most peculiar questions. It didn't make sense at all."

"What do you think she asked you?" He stepped back, his form going rigid.

"It's nuts."

"Doesn't matter." He shook his head. "Tell me anyway."

Pinching the bridge of my nose, I no longer questioned if he was real or in my head or if my story was completely bonkers. I had given in—let the madness in.

"She wanted to know…" I rubbed my temples. "How I traveled through the mirrors." The swirl of memories scattered around my head, each one making the picture seem more puzzling, not less. "And she kept asking where 'he' was...her husband...but I know she didn't mean you." I took a few steps, trying to dig in deeper. "I also remember she asked me who I followed here."

"Yes?" His throat bobbed, his built physique filling more than the space his body took up. Wearing nice boots, jeans, and a black sweater, all I saw was a fierce animal humming underneath his skin. Sexy. Beautiful. Brutal. And savage.

"I saw you. It was you..." I said, staring back at him, open and raw. No longer hiding anything. "I said a name. *Your* name."

He watched me, waiting for me to continue as if he knew what was coming.

"But I didn't say Matt."

"What name did you say?" His voice came out a hoarse whisper.

I licked my lips. "Scrooge."

Taut silence crammed the air, his eyes scorching me.

"Yeah." He dipped his head, his hands going to his hips. "That's me."

Chapter 16

"What?" Taking a step back, my spine stiffened. I stared at him, the cold night air ballooning out of my mouth. I tried to swallow over the dryness spreading over my tongue and down my throat.

He scoured his head, focused on the ground under his boots. "I don't know how I know…but it is." He growled, frustration rolling his jaw. "At least it's one of my names."

My toes curled trying to keep my footing, feeling I was about to plunge over a cliff.

"I've been having these dreams." He shook his head. "Vivid. More real than anything here." He motioned around. "I remember university, even playing in the street in London when I was a child. My name was Matt Hatter. But another thing I also recall?" He peered at me through his lashes, fear bobbing his throat. "I was a boy in the 1800s there."

My mouth parted, no response finding its way out.

"I know, it doesn't make sense, nor is it possible. Nevertheless…" He took a step closer to me. "There is no doubt in my gut it's true. I can still hear the clump of horse hooves and squeak of the carriages in the streets, the smell of grime and horse shit in the air, see the coal factories coating the city in fog. My friends and I played in the street rolling wagon wheels. I can feel the scratchy wool of my knickers." He shut his lids briefly, like he was reliving it.

"After Uni? My memory is gone, but I can feel something there, like it's being blocked. Flashes of things will come to me. Odd things. Things that should terrify me…have me committing myself to one of these places, except I feel with every fiber it's real. And whatever life I lived then I was Scrooge." He extended his arms, gripping my biceps. "And more than that, I know you were part of it."

A sharp inhale sucked through my nose.

"You feel it, too, don't you?" he asked.

My head bobbed, my eyes squeezing together. "Yes."

"You aren't the only one who felt the connection the moment we saw each other." He gripped my chin, lifting it up to his face. His irises darkened with intensity. "And the things I wanted to do to you too… Dirty. So fucking naughty. In front of the entire party."

Heat shivered through my body, my nipples hardening at his statement.

"I've been searching for you for days." He inched closer to me, our bodies flushing together. "The moment I turned away from you, I knew I did the wrong thing. You were everywhere. I could see you, smell you, taste you, hear your voice as if you were really there."

Every declaration he made was like he was peeling it

from my own mind. Another reason I didn't fully trust my senses. I could easily be projecting what I felt through this incredible illusion.

"You still don't think I'm real." He smirked, reading my thoughts. His hands seized the sides of my head. "Jessica has kept me very close, using Tim as a weapon. But tonight she got a call and ran out. I felt the pull to you. Knew I had to follow her. Things I can't explain brought me straight here."

"You asked why I'm out here?" I bit down on my lip, his gaze dropping to my mouth. "Because I also felt the draw. It was so strong. There was no question I'd risk everything. I didn't know why, but now I do." I tilted my head back, my full attention on him. "To get to you."

His nose flared, his fingers digging into my head as he pulled me closer, our lips only inches away.

"We need to go. Get far away from her and this place," he murmured, his breath stroking my lips, slipping down my neck. His forehead knocking against mine, desire heating every vein in my body.

"Yes." I agreed, my hands sliding around his solid torso, neither of us moving. The need for him to kiss me overpowered the instinct to run.

His fingers gripped my hair roughly, pressing against me. His mouth barely brushed mine, and electricity sparked my muscles, my back arching, a soft groan catching in my throat. The desperation for him exploded, engulfing me—drowning me.

As if it had been held back for a long time and he had torn the barrier away with a single touch, a deep growl originated from his chest. "Alice…" My name coarse and raw as his mouth descended down on mine. Hungry. Raw. Sparks flamed through my body.

"I'm sure I'm supposed to feel something, watching my husband cheat on me." A voice sliced through us like a guillotine, separating us with a violent cut.

Jerking away, our heads turned to the center's entrance. My blood iced with terror, my pulse hammering in my ears.

Jessica stood at the opening, bundled in a long white fur coat. Rabbit. Her blood-red lips bloomed against the white fur, her blue eyes flashing under the moonlight.

All the nurses and guards surrounded her. Nurses Green, Mint, and Noel were in front.

Matt turned fully to her, his lids lowering.

"I am *not* your husband."

A menacing smirk twisted her mouth; a shoulder lifted in a shrug.

"Maybe not technically, but are you going to deny the child we have together?" She journeyed forward, confidence oozing from her, regal and fully in charge. "Clearly you care little for him, since you are willing to risk everything for *her*."

"He's not *our* child," Matt replied low and quiet, like this was the first time he admitted it out loud.

Jessica's cheek twitched, but she started to circle us, a shark moving in on its prey. "A beautiful girl makes men go stupid. I knew you couldn't resist her and would eventually follow me here. You are pathetically predictable. As usual, a man only thinking with his dick." She rolled her eyes, going around Matt. "Though it's stronger with her. What is so special about her? From the moment you met her, she's completely ensnared you and every creature she has come across. She's been able to break through my powers on you. I don't get it. So far, I've come up with nothing unique. Nothing in her blood, nothing in her mind. Why her?"

She flipped her hand at me, though it sounded more rhetorical than a question. "Her tests showed me *nothing*." She stopped in front of us. "I guess I'll just have to go deeper." Cruelty laced her words. "Dig deeper into her brain."

"You aren't going to fucking touch her." Matt stepped closer to me. "You have a problem? Take it out on me."

"What?" I snapped to Matt, my head wagging, nixing that idea. "No elfin way!"

"Oh, don't fight." Jessica laughed. "I have plans for both of you." She clicked her tongue. "My notes have been expressing worry and fear about my husband's mental health for a long time now. The fear growing is that he might hurt our *dear child*."

"You. Bitch." Matt lunged for her. The four guards she had posted at the front gate and door jumped for him, grabbing his arms, trying to pull him back. Still, he dragged them across the ground, abhorrence vibrating off him like a wild animal.

He leaned into her face, his jaw locking with fury. "Leave Tim out of this. He's an innocent in this. A child!"

"Is he?" She curved her brow. "And who is watching our innocent child while you chase after Ms. Liddell here?"

Matt's chest fluttered, and I could feel more than see the defeat raining down on him.

"Exactly. What kind of parent leaves their child unattended in the middle of the night? Not a rational, stable one."

Matt dipped his head, mumbling so low, I couldn't hear him, but I swear he said, "He's not real."

"Noel?" Jessica clicked her fingers at him. "Escort Ms. Liddell back."

"Yes, ma'am." He stepped forward. "Back to her room?"

"No. Alice has been an exceptionally bad girl. She needs to be punished." Jessica's eyes lit up with excitement. "Take her to *the room*."

Noel's jaw tightened, causing my stomach to drop.

"The room? What the fuck is 'the room'?" Matt snarled, wiggling against the hands holding him.

Noel dipped his head, striding over to me. I shuffled back, but he nabbed my arm, yanking me forward.

"No! Let her go!" Matt pulled against the guards, trying to get to me. "Don't. Touch. Her."

"Don't be jealous, Matthew. Your turn will not be far behind." Jessica clutched her rabbit coat around her body, smirking at him. "You have actually done me a favor coming here tonight. No longer do I have to pretend I love you or that sickly excuse for a child."

A roar erupted from Matt, the guard's heels digging into the frozen ground, trying to keep him in place.

"I will *kill* you," Matt gritted through his teeth, his face an inch from hers. "Count on that."

"No, my love." She patted his cheek. "*I* will destroy *you*. Along with my actual husband and your precious Alice. For good. Everything you love, things you don't even remember you love, will all be gone soon." She twisted down her lips in sadness, reeking of mocking cruelty. "You *really* should have run when you had the chance."

She whipped around, strolling out of the maze, her procession scrambling to follow, like she was the queen.

The blood-red Queen of Winterland.

Noel hustled me forward, pitching the odd thought from my mind, his hold firm as he moved us quickly out of the labyrinth. Craning my head back, I tried to find Matt through the throng of people, but the narrow lanes and mass of people hid him from view.

"Matt?" I screamed back, my legs stumbling to keep up with Noel's pace.

Terror for him, for myself, hammered my heart viciously in my chest, trying to climb up my ribs into my throat. She had isolated me from my family, from my life. There would be no phone call to check on me tomorrow or even the next day. And if Matthew's theory about himself was right, he had only her and his son.

She had us exactly where she wanted.

"Alice!" His deep voice rumbled through the crowd, sounding far back, his voice the only truth and comfort I had. My anchor.

Our group stepped out of the maze, the lights from both inside and outside of the building tinting the snowy gardens a pallid yellow. My eyes went to the second floor, noticing Bea's room was dark.

"What did they do to her?" I flicked my chin up to the vacant room.

"Hole," Noel replied briskly. "But that is nothing compared to what she's going to do to you."

"What is she going to do?"

Noel gnashed his teeth. "Fight, Alice," he said into my ear. "I can't help you in there. You were made a lot stronger than you think. I know you are her." He yanked me up the stairs to the institution, marching in. The heat inside stung my face like a slap, my nose instantly running.

The few nurses on duty at the main desk watched our group parade through with wide eyes as Noel directed me down the right corridor, my wet boots squeaking over the linoleum. I knew exactly where Noel was taking me, my insides snaking into knots, panic hazing my mind.

"Take him to the Rose Room until I'm ready for him," Jessica ordered the men dragging Matt. I twisted to see him. Through the chaotic cluster hustling around us, my eyes found his. Our gazes locked. Not one word was said, but I could feel the connection, the words we both kept silent.

I will find you.

Chapter 17

Noel pulled me into the room, my breath coming out in puffs. It wasn't much different from when I was in here yesterday, but it frightened me far more. My eyes slid to the tray holding all the needles and instruments. In the middle of the tray was a hammer and an orbitoclast. A lobotomy ice pick...

"No." My feet ceased moving, terror so deep, bile burned my throat as I started to scream. "No, please!" My legs gave out, and my body plunged to the ground. Noel caught me and picked me up, dropping me in the chair.

"Please...Noel. You don't have to do this. *Please*," I pleaded. He worked at the straps to bind me down. The betrayal was a sword straight from the fire being rammed into my stomach. Even though he told me not to trust anyone here, I still hoped he would assist me when it came to something this horrendous. "*Help me.*"

He watched me intently, strapping me in. "You are tougher than you look, Alice. You have it. Extra muchness."

Muchness. I felt anything but strong at the moment.

This was the stuff of horror movies, the ones that really messed with your psyche because it could happen in real life. At one time they had.

The 1900s were brutal with narcissistic doctors who thought their "experimental practices" were better than love and kindness. The doctors who came up with these treatments to "cure" people were the ones who needed to be locked away and medicated, not the innocent patients who couldn't help their mental troubles, unlike the supposed "doctors."

Thrashing against my bonds, shrill cries bubbled from my lips. I looked exactly like the wild animal they were treating me as. Feral. Crazed. "No, *please*...you can't do this to me." I wiggled again and realized something.

Noel left my binds loose...

"Actually, I can." Jessica stepped into the room, sans her rabbit pelt, which made me want to skin her alive. Wear her as a coat. Today she had on black slacks and a gray cashmere sweater, black booties, her hair perfectly curved under her chin. Stylish and elegant even to perform a lobotomy. "The paper Dr. Cane had your parents sign gives me full right to do anything I deem fit to help you."

Whatever happened to the doctor? I hadn't seen him since Jessica had placed him there as a prop. Dread rained down on me with realization. "He's not even a doctor, is he?" I snarled at her while I twisted my wrists trying to inch them out without her notice.

A light smug smile bowed her mouth. "Your parents needed a second opinion. I offered them that."

"You. Demented. Bitch." I spat at her, saliva running

down my chin, my loose hair curtaining around my face, sticking to my cheeks.

"And yet it is you who sits in the chair, not me." She picked up a surgical gown, pulling it on. "Dr. Cane may not be a 'licensed' doctor, but he has done many procedures for me." A figure appeared in the doorway as if she summoned him from thin air. "Speak of the devil. We were just talking about you, Dr. Cane. All good things, of course."

The pudgy round man, who resembled the shape of an egg, waddled into the room, already dressed in a surgical gown.

"Serving you is my privilege, Majesty." He bowed his head, toddling up to the tray. His rosy cheeks and bright eyes glinted with excitement. His tongue slid over his bottom lip as he touched the instrument, like it turned him on.

"Noel, you can leave." Jessica nodded to the nurse. He dipped his head at her, peering through his lashes. His severe gaze fastened on mine, telling me to use the opportunity he presented, before turning for the door. "Wait!" Jessica screeched.

"Ma'am?" He faced her, his expression stone, but I saw his Adam's apple bob.

"Fasten her tight. I want to make sure she is secure. She already slipped away from you imbeciles earlier tonight."

"Yes, Majesty." He dropped his head, returning to my side.

"No," I whimpered. "Noel…"

He tightened my binds a little more.

"More." Jessica watched his every move.

He cinched all my restraints until they cut into my skin, carving out my last bit of hope.

"Go," she ordered.

He once again dipped his head in a bow, swiveled around and marched out of the room, shutting the door behind him.

The click boomed in my ears like a gunshot. The last string of any possibility to escape broke, hollowing out my chest. The absolute aloneness floated me out into nothing where hope and happiness would not touch me.

"Shall we get started?" Jessica picked up a syringe. Dr. Cane licked his lips again, nodding his fat head.

"Don't you want to do this with her fully aware?" He picked up the ice pick, ogling it like it was his favorite toy.

Fear comes in all different forms and intensities. The immobilizing terror which locked my entire body down went beyond every horror I knew could exist. I no longer felt attached to my body as shadows crept up around the edges of my vision, air not fully making it to my lungs, fright floating me away from any understanding except panic. Wild, guttural, raw panic. I understood how people lost bodily function or vomited, their system not knowing how else to deal with the crushing weight.

"Normally, yes. Especially for this one." She glared at me, tapping at the needle. "But I need her to relax, let the block on her mind unravel."

Panic scurried inside me like squirrels.

She stared down at me like a specimen, tapping my vein.

"What are you talking about?" A croaky voice came up from the pit of my stomach.

"The Land of the Lost and Broken took your memories and hid them, slithering through just enough you thought you were going mad. I used that. You got enough flashes, enough glimpses of truth, to step perfectly into my design. Feeling yourself going crazy, your family watched you lose your hold on reality. Slipping from yourself, when in truth, it was the exact opposite." She smiled at me cruelly, sliding the needle into my arm, pushing the drug into my vein. I stiffened, a cry breaking from my lips, still wanting to fight against her. There was nothing more helpless than when you had no control over your own body. Trapped in a prison of your shell. "Now, I *need* you to remember."

"Remember what?" I snarled as she pulled the needle out, the burn of the drug already zinging up my arm.

"Winterland."

"Winterland?" I furrowed my brow, the liquid she pumped into me crawling over my shoulders.

"I don't understand. You are human. Nothing special. You have no magic." Her lips rose up. "Not only did you get in, but you were able to travel through the mirrors. Only Nick can do that, but you opened the door, allowing us all to get through."

"Magic? You sure you're not the one who needs to be in this chair? You are nuts."

"Soon you will see I am not." She folded her arms. "But what does it matter, Alice? Your parents wouldn't even listen to you now. The more you refute me and spout about how crazy *I am*...the more *you are*...in their eyes. Humans are so easy to twist, making them believe something without question. Without facts. And toss all control away at the drop of a hat."

Elf on a shelf. She was right. Who would people believe? Her authority was indisputable to anyone not looking too deep. She acted the part of an acclaimed psychiatrist, and people easily gobbled it up because she said and did everything right. She had my whole neighborhood watch me melt down in front of them. I had no leg to stand on anymore. Even if I got out of here, they'd probably help her round me up again, thinking "poor Alice...she once seemed so normal."

"Can I start now?" Dr. Cane bobbed his weight from one foot to the other, holding the hammer. Bucking against the warmth trying to soothe my muscles, ice shot through my veins opening into my stomach. I had seen a movie where they did this to someone, and their screams had haunted my dreams for months.

"Patience, Dr. Cane. That's after her memories come back." Jessica waved the overeager oval ass back. He was even more cracked in the head than she was, getting off on the pain and torture of others. "I need her to give me the information first, then we will turn her into a vegetable."

Wrenching against the constraints, my muscles were growing weaker, not able to fight as before.

"I told you, Alice, you will never leave here." She leaned over me. "Did you know the lobotomy procedure can have severe negative effects on a patient's personality and ability to function independently? You will be merely a drooling decoration in the corner, a thing your parents only visit on holidays. I could kill you after I close the door on

Winterland for good, but that feels far too simple. Who knows, I might need you later for some reason. At least this way you will no longer be a thorn in my side."

Her lips were moving, but my mind couldn't really grasp on to anything beyond the superficial meaning of each word. Whatever she gave me to govern my functions, I still could hear the panicked screams in my gut.

The drug progressed through me, centering on my brain. A tingling pressure tapped over my head, as if fingers were in there, peeling back layers of my brain, trying to get deeper. It wasn't painful in the true sense, but it felt raw and exposed. I cried out, whipping my head back and forth, trying to dislodge the sensation. As if I could buck off the fingers digging into my head, I bowed forward with a wail.

"Don't fight it, Alice. The veil is coming down."

Flashes. Glimmers of images popped across my brain, coming in so fast and frenzied, like a montage but not a whole picture. Sitting at a table across from a large rabbit wearing an apron, I could see us laughing. A toddling penguin dancing and singing with such joy and innocence, it soothed my frantic heart. A little girl-elf swung our laced hands back and forth as we walked. A boy-elf running around a table, giggling wildly. A half man-half deer lay in a bed, his hands wrapped around mine, his brown eyes staring at me like the whole world revolved around me.

And then *he* flashed through, his body pressing into mine against a wall, his fingers sliding down my stomach.

Scrooge.

"No, Alice. You can't." A sweet little voice in the room dropped into my ear, curling my head up, just enough to peer over.

Hiding behind Dr. Cane, standing near the leg of the tray, was the little elf girl, her eyes wide, her head shaking. "Don't let them in," she pleaded with me. "Don't let her find him. Find us."

"Ms. Alice?" another voice to my other side whispered, jerking my eyes over. The penguin stood behind Jessica, the same beseeching expression on his face. "Please. You can't let her in."

"Hide your memories," the boy elf spoke, standing next to this twin. "If she finds us...all hope is lost."

"You let her in..." a voice hopped in next to the penguin. The rabbit folded his arms over his frilly apron. "And you'll never get to taste my mead, which in itself is a *fucking* tragedy."

A soft snort and smile wiggled my lips, and my heart bloomed. My eyes dropped down to his feet...one was missing. *Her necklace.*

"Alice," a deeper voice called from straight in front of me, my gaze darting to the deer-man through my lashes. His beauty and ripped torso had me blinking several times. "I knew it. You. Are. *Her.*"

Rudolph. I suddenly knew he was the famous reindeer I grew up with, but more...I *knew* him.

"What do you mean?" I asked him. Jessica had called me that too.

Jessica and Humpty twisted around, searching the room to see who I was talking to before looking back at me.

"It's working." She smiled smugly.

"You are the one with the power to defeat the queen," Rudolph responded. "The story of *her* has been a long almost forgotten tale, but I think it is true. There is a reason you were able to follow me, that you came to Winterland. *You* are the one who can fight the queen. Help save Winterland. But stories can always change, shift directions…you need to *live*. Don't let her strip away what makes you special. We need you, Alice. Fight for yourself. Fight for us." His words were unemotional, but powerful. "And Alice? *You* have the power. Don't forget who you are. Fight." He stared right into my eyes, and the sensation he had said this to me before whooshed through me. "*Wish*."

Wish. I blinked, the understanding right on the tip of my memory, the slight taste of it hinting on my tongue, teasing me.

"Stay with me?" I implored, needing all of them, even if they weren't actually there, because I knew they were my friends. People I loved. Not feeling alone eased my heart. *They* gave me strength.

"We're always with you," he answered impassively, but I felt the love in what he said. The belief and trust in me from him and the others in the room.

I dipped my head in a thank you, glancing at all of them. The instinct, the fierce need to protect them, had me slamming against the drug trying to rip through my head, crashing against barriers.

"So, Alice?" Jessica clutched my chin, yanking it up to look at her. "Tell me where Nick is. Where are your little friends hiding?"

Images of a huge hooked mountain top, a cabin set against a snowy backdrop. The cozy interior filled with scrumptious smells of vanilla, cinnamon, and a burning fire. A loft filled with books, and a rustic bathroom…with no mirrors.

I recognized it better than my own house.

Mount Crumpit. The name dropped on me like it had been waiting for me to pluck it out of obscurity. Most of my brain felt the urge to answer her question, my tongue ready to waggle, like it was being pulled between my teeth.

Forced.

Fudge balls. Did she give me a truth serum? Clenching down on my molars, I tried to strike against the drug attempting to steal my memories, spill them out on the floor.

"Can I tell you something?" My mouth spoke. *Fight. Alice.*

"Yes. Tell me *every* little detail."

I tipped my head in her palm. Huffing, my nose flared, my lids lowering in a glower.

"Go. Fuck. Yourself."

CHAPTER 18

The slap came swift, my head jerking to the side, but I didn't feel the sting, the drug numbing my skin. My lips curved in a taunting smile.

"You can't fight me. Do you even know who you are challenging right now? Bow down, Alice. I will crush you." Jessica leaned into my face, her eyes bursting with fury. "Now, tell me where Nick is."

Nick. Again, my mind went to the naked, white-bearded man, his snarling expression and sour attitude streaming into my head. Crunching down on my jaw like a steel trap was the only way to keep the drug from turning me into a gumball dispenser. Crank the knob, and I would pour out endless tidbits into her hands.

Most of the morsels melting on my tongue didn't make any sense to me, but they pushed forward with a righteous claim without caring what I thought. They believed in themselves, not needing me to, though deep down I did.

I fought against the need to tell her everything, my little friends still surrounding me, encouraging me to stay quiet. Their heads nodded, urging me to be stronger than her. To protect them at all costs.

"What did you give her, you idiot?" Jessica snapped up to Dr. Cane. "Sugar water? Why isn't she talking? This is your fault!"

"No, Y-Your Highness. It-it should have worked. I gave her a full dose of the serum. More, actually." Cane fumbled nervously, staring at the empty syringe like it would tell him something.

"Well, obviously, you did something wrong," Jessica seethed. "This is what I get for leaving it up to a man. You know what happens to people who disappoint me?" She swiped another off the tray.

"Maybe she has a higher tolerance than others, Majesty," he squeaked, his face flushing pure white. "I-I can give her more."

"Do. It." All niceties she showed him before were gone, her pretty face streaked with ugliness, my sluggish mind exaggerating her twisted features.

Dr. Cane bobbed his head, filling the needle with more fluid. My eyes slid to the clear liquid. I was barely holding on now. If I had more, would I be able to fight it? No matter how much I wanted to struggle, I was still human.

"Stop her, Alice," Rudolph spoke to me, his voice so steady. I clung to it like a rope. "You have the power within yourself if you ask for it."

"I ask for it," I blurted out, staring at the beautiful deer-man.

He chuckled dryly, his antlers wobbling. "I'm not the one you need to ask."

Help, I thought, having no real idea who I was talking to. Me or some fairy godmother. *Please help me. I need to fight.*

Nothing happened.

"You ask for what?" Jessica once again peered behind her to see what I was staring at, coming back into my line of sight. "You're talking to them right now, aren't you? Your little rebel buddies? You know they aren't real, Alice. You are here all alone. And no one will save you this time."

I shot her a glare, not trusting my mouth to open again. It kept trying, like its opinions needed to be heard. The information filled the back of my throat, ready to flood out.

"You heard her." She motioned to me. "She's asked for it. And I think we should oblige."

Cane bobbled over to my side, the tip of the needle pointed at my arm.

"I'll do it." Jessica reached for the syringe, the light glimmering off the plunger. My mind sluggishly took in something scrolled across in sparkly ink. It wasn't the measuring lines you saw on plungers, but something written out in cursive. The understanding of what it said was on the slow train up to my brain. "Grab your instruments. I think it's time Alice saw what happens when you disobey the queen."

Queen. Damn, she was full of herself, but peering at her, the title fit her perfectly.

"Blood-red queen," I muttered, the light sparking the words on the needle, distracting me again, my attention like a startled butterfly, not able to stay on one thing for long. Narrowing my lids, I tried to lock down on it.

"She's remembering." Cane gushed, his head trying to bob, but he was so chubby, it didn't really move.

"Let's help that along," Jessica replied, making Cane's smile widen with excited joy. He snatched up the pick and hammer, prancing on his toes as if he were a child on Christmas morning.

"Oh boy, oh boy. I've been wanting to use these again. It's been so long. Decades!"

"Tell us, Alice. Last chance," she threatened, the needle poised at my vein. The cursive glittered under the light, looking like it was moving, my eyes tracing over the words.

"Inject Me." I read it out loud, thinking it was a peculiar thing to have written on a needle. Seemed kind of redundant.

And very familiar.

Curious and curiouser.

Suddenly recollections of me in a gingerbread house, under a table, my head on a block, out in the forest surrounded by green monsters. *Gremlins.* What I saw had been real? A rush of *drink me, eat me*, and *use me* notes attached to cookies, drinks, and vials paraded through my mind.

All had protected me. Saved my life.

Jessica gave me a strange look, thinking I was begging her to inject me, not reading the penmanship.

"Don't say I never gave you what you asked for." She stabbed the needle into my arm, the hot rush flooding my veins, my gaze greedily drinking it up. *Please, help me now!* I begged but still felt nothing except the heaviness of Jessica's previous drug. What if it couldn't counter that?

"Now, let's see how fast her tongue will loosen when you jab that into her brain." She smirked down at me. "With or without you, I'm finding and ending him. The door will be shut and then I will place you in the corner here, where you will live out your days as my drooling ornament. Please proceed, Cane."

Cane grinned, leaning my chair back farther, hovering around my eyes. The hope I had briefly fizzled when his fat sausage fingers reached for my lid, angling for the corner of my eye where my tear ducts were. The sharp point of the pick pressed into the tiny gap between my eye and nose.

Sheer terror fluttered in my stomach, gurgling up my throat, but fell back and only a tiny whimper scoured the back of my throat. My body locked down in fright as if it were trying to protect itself. My heart hammered so loud I could feel it in my esophagus, trying to climb out and save itself.

"Nooooo!" A muffled sob parted my lips, the metal pressing farther into the corner, sliding against the cartilage of my nose. Pain registered somewhere in my body, producing bile to scorch my stomach and throat. Liquid trickled down my nostril and over my lips, the taste of metal tangy and hot on my tongue.

My blood.

The sound of metal chinking together as he tapped the hammer at the end of the ice pick, hammering it farther up into my skull.

Clink. Clink. Clink.

Saliva, tears, and snot leaked from my face; vomit hummed in the back of my throat. The idea that this was happening to me was outrageous. This didn't happen in today's world—or so I thought. Soon I would no longer be the person I was before. A stab into my frontal lobe and I would be someone my family would no longer recognize, talking slowly and softly to me when they came to visit. In time the visits would dwindle because seeing me would cause them too much pain and guilt.

Dr. Cane groaned as the pick slid up higher, like he was having an orgasm, getting off from the blood sliding down my face and the pick gliding to my brain.

Acid rose up my throat, and my heels dug into the chair, trying to back away as the rod dug into my tissue. Ferocious panic sliced at my lungs, spilling tears from my eyes, dropping pink-colored splotches on my blue scrubs. Then I felt the point collide into my lobe.

A scream bucked out of me at the onslaught of excruciating pain. Burning. Tearing. Slicing. Wails boomed in the room, echoing off the walls, the numbing drugs flushing out of my system with a whoosh. I felt every bit of the spiky tool.

Saliva and bile dribbled out of my mouth as the rest of me froze under the attack, darkness spotting my vision.

"Make sure you do it right," Jessica spoke over the horrendous noise in the room, her eyes wide and awed. "I don't want her more than a drooling prisoner in her own skin, unable to ever tell anyone anything."

"I will, my Queen. You know I want to please you."

"Yes. Yes." She rolled her eyes. "It's why you're able to keep your post as long as you have."

He twisted the rod in my brain, like a hot poker shredding straight through all my nerves at once, everything cut off. I heard guttural screams pierce the air, then they died with a horrendous gasp. No longer did I feel a part of my body. In its last attempt to shield me, my brain tucked me behind a barrier, protecting me from the unmanageable pain. Darkness took my vision, but my ears still comprehended sound.

"Think that should do it. Her brain was more difficult to dig into like others I've done." Cane's voice danced at the edge of my ears, along with the gushing sound of metal tugging out of tissue, liquid, and flesh. "Really gave it a good twist. Be lucky if she can function at all now." Metal clanged together on the tray.

"I don't really need her since she opened the door. But in case Nick tries to close it again, I still might need her." She sounded irritated. "When I finish my plan and shut it for good, I'll see how important keeping her around is. If she's so brain-dead, there's no point."

"You don't need her to answer your questions? Where Santa Clau—"

"DO. NOT. EVER. SAY. THAT. NAME," Jessica boomed.

"I'm sorry…I'm so sorry, Majesty. It won't ever happen again." Cane sniveled and pleaded with her. "Forgive me, my Queen."

"If I didn't enjoy your work so much, your head would be next. You understand me?"

"Yes," he groveled. "So, so sorry."

"Shut up," she snapped. "And no, I don't need her. Not when I got two for one tonight. My *faux* husband can lead me to *him*. I know he knows where he is too. I've been lacing his coffee with the syrup, hoping to learn anything from him, but he's as stubborn as she is.

So glad I no longer have to humor him with false smiles and concern for that phony, pathetic excuse for a child. The boy was similar to his mother in disposition. Weak and timid."

Darkness pleated its fingers in my mind, beckoning me to follow, everything sounding far away.

"We'll leave her here until she wakes. Not like she can or will be capable of going anywhere. Dear Scrooge is next. He'll talk if he thinks her life depends on it." She cackled, sounding like a hyena. "And if he obeys, his prize is a drooling dimwit. Win-win for me."

Shoes clicked over the tile, the door opening and closing. *Scrooge...* I tried to reach out for the name, but it slipped from my hand, and I fell into the darkness.

"Stay strong, Alice," a little voice of a girl called to me. "You can fight. You are filled with so much muchness..."

I dissolved into nothingness.

CHAPTER 19

My eyes opened to a dimly lit cave, my form barely covered in a torn dress shirt. Curved in a ball, I lay on the hard ground, bloody, wounded, and exhausted. I knew this place, had been here before. My gaze lifted to the figure sitting at the entrance, the moonlight shining down on his profile and sharpening his features. His blue irises glistening, ripping the air from my lungs. He was so breathtaking; he felt more otherworldly than this place did.

Scrooge. His name came to me so easily. The memory of this night draped in my head, a drunken haze of sensations, but I remembered it. We had just survived being attacked by gremlins. And I knew figures were sleeping behind me. My friends.

Tilting his head, Scrooge listened for something. Tension strained his back muscles, and I shot up with a start. "What is it?"

He snapped to me, his finger going to his lips, and turned back out. Whatever was coming, had fear pounding in my chest as I moved to him. I waited in anticipation, as if a jack-in-the-box was about to pop up.

A stunning white fox darted by and halted for a moment to peer at us before slinking over some rocks, vanishing into the darkness.

"You can take on gremlins, but a furry fox is what freaks you out?" Scrooge smiled over his shoulder, completely undoing me. Did he know every time he looked at me, he unraveled and disarmed me a bit more? It was a steady and slow descent, but this was the moment I knew I was falling for him. In a cave on Mount Crumpit, in a world I didn't belong in.

Yet, I did.

This moment was when something clicked, even though I hadn't known it at the time. This quiet beat we shared, just the two of us, in the middle of the night, when I knew I was right where I was supposed to be. With him.

My story being written.

In my gut I knew I belonged. That I was her...

Is this why my dream had taken me back here? So much was still foggy and unclear, but he was real and so were my feelings for him. My anchor. As if he were holding me to this realm I was sleeping in, he pushed me to keep going to find strength.

"This happened before," I whispered to him, his eyes going back and forth between mine, studying me. "I remember now. This place is real. You are real."

"Most likely. A place is real if you believe it to be."

"You sound like Frosty."

"Now you're just insulting me," he rumbled, moving in closer, the smirk on his face dropping away. Exactly

as I had before, I became aware of our proximity, his skin warm under my fingers, and his mouth only inches from mine.

"Ms. Liddell." His breath wisped over my lips. "Alice. This is a bad idea."

"Maybe," I replied. "But let me tell you a secret...all the best plans are."

The side of his mouth hooked up. My gut craved him; the need to kiss him was painful.

His mouth inched toward mine, but instead of feeling his lips, his words shoved into my ear.

"Time to wake up, Alice...before it's too late for us."

Then the man disappeared in front of my eyes and a piercing scream stabbed through my ear to my heart.

Scrooge!

I jolted, my lids popping open with a start, my lungs gasping for air, my gaze moving over the sterile room. What happened to me in this space rushed back to me in a sharp blow. Still strapped to the chair, the dried blood trailing down from my eye to my chin cracked as I wrinkled up my face in revulsion.

They did it; the sick fucks gave me a lobotomy...

Wait.

I paused, sending all my attention into my brain where they poked a hole, searching and prodding to assess any differences.

Nothing.

If anything, I felt stronger.

I should have been either docile or a vegetable. I was neither. Power and energy buzzed in my veins; a warmth moved around the areas the ice pick had stabbed through, as if it were being healed.

Inject me. The syringe with the scroll lettering was no longer on the tray, but I was certain it had been. It had protected or healed me. Whatever it did, it had saved my life. And I had no doubt this hadn't been the first time my "sugarplum fairies" had saved my butt.

I felt more alert, more alive and conscious than I had since coming home, like the cobwebs had been mostly cleared away.

Since coming home.

Turtle doves...

My chest pattered in quick huffs. It was all true. I wasn't crazy. All my memories weren't back, the pieces not fully connecting. But I had been in another realm where Matt was Scrooge and Jessica... I could picture her on steps, people bowing to her. Mass of grays and blacks; faces that were ordinary, but they were no longer strangers to me. Everly Green. Pepper Mint. Dr. Cane. Even the secretary at her other office. I could see each one in the crowd, their face twisted up with disgust and hate, chanting for my death. For their queen to take my head.

She called herself the *Blood-Red Queen of Winterland*.

"Holy Keebler elf." My mouth parted. "She's really a queen of a magical land. In a galaxy far, far away." I shook my head in utter disbelief, my own words ringing in my ears like ramblings of a madwoman. "Damn, I really do sound crazy."

It didn't matter; it was true. Winterland was real. I just needed to figure out how it all connected, and I sensed Matt was a huge part of putting the pieces together, my dream tugging on the back of my mind.

Erupting like a dormant volcano, a bellow echoed through the hallway, familiar and filled with agony. It was what woke me up, tearing through my dream and bringing me back to consciousness. A deep bone-chilling roar echoed and tumbled over me, freezing up my chest.

Scrooge.

They were torturing him. I could feel his pain in the air. It was palpable, coating my soul in grief and anxiety. Yanking against my binds, my instincts kicked in, needing to get to him.

Fire zapped at my skin, reverberating down into my bones as I tugged and heaved against the restraints, a cry baying from my mouth. Thrashing, I tried to wiggle free, fresh blood leaking from wounds on my wrists.

He went silent, and my ears perked up to listen for any noise. He was close, on this side of the sanatorium, but from there I didn't know.

Shoes clicked down the hallway. My frame stilled as I listened to them move closer and closer. My heart thumped in my chest as the handle of the door clicked, and panic they were coming back for me soared through my chest wanting to burst out. Lying back, I slammed my eyes shut, trying to relax my body so I appeared to still be unconscious.

The person stayed silent, but the heavy steps and the short puffs of breath from exertion led me to believe it was Cane.

His presence loomed over one side of my body. Hot sticky fingers came down on my neck. "Your pulse is high." He hmphed through his nose, his hands sliding down my neck sensually to my arm.

Trying to slow down my frantic heartbeat into a slumbering state was a lot harder than it seemed; my body reacted on its own to his foul touch.

"You really are so pretty. And this way, you will be even better. Silent and beautiful, dazzling as a star on top of a tree," he muttered. A deep inhale fluttered at my neck, making my stomach twist. "You smell like vanilla. I miss vanilla. At least I can sneak sweets when she's not looking, but everything tastes different here. Smells different. Like chemicals," he babbled, his nonsense becoming background when I felt his fingers work at the straps around my wrists. My heart leaped up to my throat, and it took everything I had to not react, to wait patiently.

He didn't even question if the lobotomy worked; he must assume I was no threat to him in any way, even if I woke up. And it would have been true if not for the serum. If I didn't believe in magic before, I certainly did now. I thought my wish went unanswered. It couldn't stop him from hurting me, but it had protected me where it could.

My teeth ground together. Cane's hands wandered down my legs, taking his time to go over my curves, air puffing out quicker in excitement.

"This will be our little secret, won't it, Alice?" He cupped my inner thigh, trailing his hand down to my ankle, undoing my ankle strap. One side was free, and the desire to kick him in the head raged in my blood, but I kept still, letting his fat fingers wander as he unlatched my other side.

"I can't help myself. You are so beautiful. Tight little body, but still so soft." His hands unharnessed my right ankle, skimming up my pants leg, a hiss coming from him. He liked me like this. A silent victim. He'd probably enjoy it even more if I was awake but no longer able to fight or even speak up for myself. A prisoner in my body who could never call out his wrongs or stop him from doing it again. "She wants me to put you in the hole, but what's the hurry, right?"

Screaming and jumping around inside, I waited for him to unclasp the last cuff. As usual, I had no plan except to escape. My lashes parted a sliver, peering over at the tray. All the instruments were still there.

"Oh, elf pudding…you feel so good." The restraint fell from my wrist, his hands sliding over, curling around the side of my breast. "You shouldn't be so temptingly sweet, Alice. I want to nibble and lick you everywhere."

"And I want to skewer you like the fucking pig you are," I growled, my elbow ramming into his throat as I scrambled in the opposite direction. Catching him off guard, he stumbled back, his hand going to his neck, choking, his eyes open wide in shock.

"Yeah, I'm not the drooling, compliant girl you thought you'd find, huh?" I leaped out of the seat, facing him, glaring, the hatred and disgust I felt looping around my spine.

"How? I felt it go into your brain." His small eyes narrowed even more. "This is not possible."

"Didn't you know?" I lowered my head, pinning him with my gaze. "I have extra *muchness*."

He inhaled, understanding I now remembered the

truth. He didn't need to know I was still uncertain of the picture and how I fit in, but I recalled Winterland.

I knew in my gut I was *her*...

I took a step, my hip hitting the tray, my peripheral drawing down, eyeing the items on it.

His eyes slid to the door and back to me, gauging if he could make a run for it or hoping to see Jessica and a herd of guards walk in. He was no match for me untethered and capable, and he knew it.

There was a pause; a beat of time when everything vibrated with electricity, vivid with life. It was just a blink, and we both moved. I whirled around, my fingers clasping onto the object, and hurled myself over the end of the chair at him as he hobbled for the exit. Leaping on him, he swung, his fist clumsily striking out as he squealed, bashing right into the eye he had just stuffed a pick into. A scream seized my throat, my figure falling onto him, the pain bursting behind my eyes, throbbing angrily, zapping the nerves trying to heal.

His head smacked against the tile, his body buffering me from the floor. The hammer in my hand skated across the room. *Shit!*

"No! Help," he screamed. "Someone help!

Dread sank into my belly. I couldn't have anyone hear him. If Jessica or a nurse found us? Game over. Scrambling off the ground, I lurched for the tray, my fingers folding around another item.

"Help! Help! Help," he screeched, scuttling for the door.

If he stepped outside, my life was over. Springing for him, my arm wrapped around his neck, constricting his airways like a boa.

His nails clawed at my arms, his hard-soled shoes kicking back into my shins in a painful blow, loosening my hold on him.

Using his weight, he yanked me forward, his hand grabbing the handle, pulling it down.

"No!" Completely on autopilot and survival instinct, I reacted, and with all my might, my arm thrust the orbitoclast into his temple.

Slurping and crunching, the sound of spearing skin, tissue, and nerves resounded in my ears, drowning out the guttural scream piercing the air. Hot red liquid ran over my hand, dripping on the floor.

I twisted the pick. His body went rigid, his scream dying in his throat. Another one of those pauses captured the room, a thump of his heartbeat, a fluttering of his lungs. Life. Then his body dropped, a lump on the floor at my feet, twitching and wiggling as it let go.

Oxygen puttered in and out of my lungs as I stared down at him in shock. The end of the instrument stuck out the side of his head, blood trailing out of his mouth, eyes, and temple onto the floor.

I had first planned to knock him out. I had never thought myself capable of killing someone outside of my imagination. My ex? Yeah, I envisioned that all the time, but not for real, never even contemplated anything past the dark fantasy.

Well…the Alice before Winterland didn't.

This Alice?

This Alice had a lot more *muchness*.

CHAPTER 20

My fingers wrapped around the end of the orbitoclast, pulling it from his temple. The sickening squelch of brain matter and tissue churned my stomach, my throat constricting.

"How's that for a lobotomy?" Using his jacket, I wiped off the rod, the blood smearing and soaking into the fabric. "Who's the vegetable now?" My lip rose in a snarl. If things had gone a different way, the *Sliding Doors* effect, my life would have taken the course they set out for me with years of torment and abuse I would have suffered at the hand of him and Jessica. Hers I could almost stomach; she was straight forward in her torture. His would have broken every last piece of my soul.

If I saved another person from this man, then I didn't regret for one second my hand in his death.

Time to move, Alice.

Stepping over him, I pressed my ear to the door, listening for movement or voices. Besides the buzzing of the lights overhead and the heater pumping in warm air, there was only silence. Taking in a breath, I cracked open the door, peering out into the dark hallway, the light from the main lobby area pooling down the corridor. The hushed chatter from the nurses was just muffled inflections. They were still in night mode, which meant I had only been asleep for a little while. Night mode had fewer people on duty and most lights were off in unused areas, but I had no doubt this place was extra jumpy after what happened, putting the nurses and guards on hyper-watch.

Creeping out, I kept my eyes locked on the entrance of the hallway. There were at least a dozen rooms on this side of the wing, and only two of them I knew he was not in: Jessica's office and the room I had been in, which were the last two on the end. All the rest of the closed doors could be possibilities. And I had no idea if he was alone now.

Scurrying like a mouse, I quietly went to the next door, listening for sounds before trying the door. I was risking everything. I understood that, but no way was I leaving without him. He came here for me, and now it was my turn to rescue him. And with my luck, there was a good chance it would go terribly wrong.

The sound of a door handle clicking down the hall made me freeze like an animal caught in headlights. I hadn't had time to open the door where I was without already being noticed. Fear gripped my muscles, strangling my lungs. I pressed myself against a door, trying to blend in the shadows, my heart jolting adrenaline into my ears.

A door two down from mine swung open, pale light trailing out of the room. Heels clacked over the linoleum floor. The grip around my lungs tightened as Jessica's profile appeared in the hallway. She peeled the surgical gown from her lean form, the fabric drenched with blood. A dagger twisted in my gut.

The *blood*-red queen fit her to a T.

A cry clogged my throat at the thought she might have done the same to him. What would I find in there? Was he past saving? A vegetable of her making?

A curvy nurse bustled out with her, bobbing about her reminding me of a nervous chicken.

"Let me take that, my liege." Nurse Green turned, facing my way, grappling for the garment.

Not a twitch of muscle nor a puff of breath left my lungs. All she had to do was look long enough in my direction to notice the lumpy shadow against the door. She was so tuned to the intimidating woman before her, her throat bobbed nervously.

"Can I say what an honor it was to be in the room with you? To watch you. You are magnificent," Nurse Green gushed, curtsying. "Truly brilliant, Majesty.

"Yes." Jessica dumped her gory gown in the nurse's open arms, barely acknowledging her praise. "I want him awake when I get back. My knave will experience every second of pain for his treason. Defying or disappointing me does not go unpunished. Do you *understand* me?"

"Ye-yes, Majesty." She dipped her body low again, fright trembling her voice. Was it sick I found pleasure in that bitch's fear? She was the person who got bullied, then turned around and terrorized someone even more to gain some power back. Something about that kind of person I hated more.

"I am still furious she was able to escape. You all failed to watch *one* silly human girl. Don't think you all won't be reprimanded for your inadequacies." She looked down at Green like a bug. "I swear, I keep thinking there couldn't be any people more stupid than you, but then you amaze me again with your incompetence. Every door is to be guarded. Let's try to not screw it up again, shall we?"

"Yes, Majesty." Green bowed, her voice trembling.

Jessica took a step around Green and stopped, along with my heart. She tilted her head toward my direction as if she sensed something.

Gulping, my fingers tightened around the pick in my hand, ready to act if I had to. *Please. Don't see me.* I was too close to him to be caught now.

Her gaze rolled down the dark hallway, my pulse pounding so loud, I was sure it would be the very thing to give me away.

"My Queen?" Green inquired.

"It's nothing." Jessica shook her head, pulling her gaze away from me. "I will be back in an hour. He'd better be awake." She turned toward the front, gliding down the hallway, her strides powerful and certain. If she wasn't such an evil, horrendous person, you almost had to admire her self-confidence. No man or outside power would ever tell her what to do or control her.

"Yes, ma'am. I assure you he will be." Green trailed after her, exiting the hallway.

A whoosh of relief flooded my body; not that danger wasn't at every turn, but for this moment, I was okay.

And I knew where he was, and he was still alive.

Tiptoeing to the entrance with a rose symbol marked on a plaque, I pulled the handle down. The door creaked open, and a harsh gasp sliced down my throat.

This room was a little different from the one they put me in but just as horrible. It had no windows, and the room was so white it was painful to the eyes. Flogging whips and torture devices I didn't even recognize were against the walls. Electric shock equipment was in the middle of the room next to a chair.

"Oh god," I whimpered, emotion blurring my eyes. Strapped to the wooden chair, bloody and broken, was Scrooge. His head dangled forward limply, the straps holding him upright. "Matt." I slipped into the room, shutting the door and running for him. My knees crashed onto the hard surface, and I dropped the pick, reaching up to lift his puffy face. One eye was completely swollen shut, cuts and bruises were shading his skin in blues and purples. On either side of his head were two burn marks discoloring his temples. Electrical shock burns.

That bitch. The urge to dart out and stab her with the pick was almost too powerful to fight.

He was no longer in his jeans and sweater but blue scrubs like mine. Burn marks peeked out from the collar of the shirt and down his arms.

"Matt?" I patted his face carefully, cringing at the abuse they inflicted on him. He didn't stir. "Matt." I tapped harder. I didn't want to hurt him more, but I needed him conscious. Now.

"Matt, I need you to wake up." I worked quickly, unfastening the cuffs on his arms and legs. "I can't carry you. Please." A noise had me holding my breath and glimpsing over my shoulder, waiting for someone to walk in. Green would come back to check on him soon.

Time ticked with my rapid heartbeat, the door to freedom closing on us.

"Matt?" I shook him.

Nothing.

Biting on my lip, I winced at what I had to do.

"Scrooge!" I hissed, my palm clapping against his cheek, his head snapping to the side. "Wake up."

A low groan rumbled from his chest, his cheek twitching in pain. "Alice." He whispered my name like he was dreaming.

"I'm here." I cupped his face again, his body flinching at my touch, pulling away. "It's me. Please, open your eyes…well…your one eye."

His lashes parted, his blue iris peeking through the good eye.

"Am I hallucinating again?" he croaked, his lid shutting again. "If I am, please leave me here."

"If I was in your imagination, wouldn't you have me dressed hotter than this?"

"Hmmm." A ghost of a smile hinted on his face until he winced in pain. "Definitely be dressed in that hot little elf costume. The one I watched you rip from your own body, wishing it was me tearing it slowly from you." He moaned, leaning into my touch. "Your hands feel so fucking good. Warm and numbing all at once. Is this how it felt?"

I jerked as a memory collided into my brain, steamrolling over my chest.

"I need these off."

"What are you doing?" Scrooge tried to grab for my hands.

"No! I need them off. They're melting to my skin. I can feel it."

"Ms. Liddell. Stop."

"I'm baking to death!"

"You merely think you are. It's the poison. You're hallucinating. Ms. Liddell. Please. Don't." He tried to grab for my hands again, but I wiggled away like a disobedient child, fumbling with the zipper. Before he could stop me, I got it down enough to rip what was left of it, shoving it off me and leaving me only in my black bra and underpants.

"Touch me," I begged. It was only him who had cooled my skin, giving me a moment of relief.

I could still feel the coolness of his touch on my boiling skin, his fingers easing the pain inside me. Was I doing the same to him? Alleviating his pain like he had mine?

"I remember," I breathed, seeing the small jail he and I were locked in together. "Your touch...it was magical." The intensity of his fingers on my skin. Clear and tangible, pulsing my thighs with the need to revisit the memory fully.

I shook my head. Right now wasn't the time to reminisce; we needed to run. "Listen to me. I can't get us out of here without your help. Please." I tilted his head to look at me. "I know you want to let the darkness surround you, protect you. Believe me, I understand, but right now I need you to dig deep and find your inner indestructible fruitcake. Need it to rise right now."

"What?"

"Durable, resilient, tough. All the things I need from you but would also say about a fruitcake."

"Now I know I can't be dreaming." His eye lifted again; his growling timbre vibrated against my hand. "I would *never* put those two together. Comparing myself to a *fruitcake*."

"Don't deny your inner fruitcake. I need it right now." I picked up my weapon, shoving it into my boot.

"You're nuts." A smirk pulled at one half of his face.

"I don't deny my nutty goodness anymore." I shrugged a shoulder, reaching for him. "I let the madness in..."

"It looks good on you." He took my hand, letting me help him rise, a groan hissing from him.

"Do I even want to imagine what she did to you?" I said more to myself than him.

"Probably no worse than what I imagined her doing to you." He breathed in my ear, hooking his arm around my shoulder, using me as a crutch. His thumb trailed down the dried blood from my eye to my chin, fury and concern flared under his skin, his iris glowing with fury.

"Not now." I shook my head, my arm wrapping around his waist. One side seemed more limp than the other, reminding me of a stroke victim. She had tortured him so brutally I hoped he would be able to recover.

"She threatened me with you...with Tim. I could hear your screams down the hall. I wanted to rip apart this world and the next to get to you."

"Same." I peered up at him, our eyes connecting with force, telling each other without a word that no realm could stop us from getting to each other. *I murdered someone to get to you.* Definitely not on the good girl list this year. "Do you remember the other world? Winterland?"

"Some." He nodded. "I know I've lived there for a long time as Scrooge, and I was her knave at one time. That I lost people. But still a lot doesn't make sense." He grunted and pulled off me, taking on his full weight, his jaw clenching in pain. "I know we need to get back there, but I can't remember why or how. I just have this nagging sensation I was looking for something."

"Me too."

"We can talk about this later." He nodded at the door. "We need to get out of here first."

"Are you going to be okay?" He didn't seem completely steady on his feet yet.

"My inner fruitcake has been summoned and risen to the occasion." He lifted his eyebrow.

"That sounds so dirty."

"You asked for it to rise. I obliged."

"Are we talking about fruitcake anymore?"

Winking at me with his one eye. "Call it whatever you want."

I grinned, clutching onto the door knob. Twisting it, I cracked it open to peek out.

And froze.

"You think escaping was going to be that easy?" a voice growled, the shadowy figure blocking the exit, eyes glaring into me. My muscles convulsed with terror, a gasp scraping up my throat as I scrambled back in defense.

Holy mincemeat pie…
We'd been caught.

Chapter 21

"Fucking lords a-leaping," I hissed, grabbing my chest, feeling it thump wildly against my palm. "Noel, you asshole."

A tiny smirk twitched on his mouth but disappeared before I could claim it really happened. The stocky man slipped into the room, shutting the door behind us.

Matt tensed, defensively stepping between us, his chin rising.

"Ease back." Noel was far shorter than him, but all muscle. "I'm on your side."

"I don't know you. I don't trust shit about you," Matt seethed through his teeth.

"I know who *you* are," Noel snarled. "And if I wasn't on your side, the guards would be in this room with me, dragging you back to the hole or strapping you back in the chair. And I certainly wouldn't be risking what I've worked for all these years for nothing, *asshole*. I'm here for her anyway."

"Excuse me?" Matt rolled his shoulders back.

"Whoa." I stepped around Matt, getting between the two. "Calm down. Both of you." I twisted to Matt.

"He's on our side."

"How do you know? He could be tricking us. Walking us into a trap. And what do you mean by all you've worked for?" Matt didn't relax, but he let me ease him back a step. Tortured, beat up, and barely standing, he didn't hesitate to challenge whomever he needed. Protect me. I couldn't deny it...it totally turned me on.

Noel set his mouth, not answering.

"You're a spy." I spun back to the nurse. "Aren't you?"

His amber eyes darted around the room. "Not here," he muttered. "Sleeping or awake, she's always watching."

"Spy...you're part of the Night Rebellion?" Matt's hand went to his forehead, rubbing it. "Wait. How do I know that name?"

"Night Rebellion?" I parroted.

"Not many of us left, but it's a group still supporting, fighting for—" Noel's sentence was cut off.

"For *him*," Matt said slowly, like it all clicked in place.

"Him?" I glanced between the guys.

"Santa Claus," Matt breathed out. "Nick."

Flashes of the grumpy naked man stomping around flowed into another one: him screaming out in grief and devastation, his face twisted in horror. Broken. Lost.

Because of her.

Jessie.

Jessica Winters.

"Holy... She's...she's frickin' Mrs. Claus, isn't she?" My mouth dropped open, my eyes widening. It was another piece fitting in place; with every new portion the picture was starting to form.

"We don't have time for this. She's heading back here soon. We need to get you out."

"How?"

Noel clicked his head to the door, peeking out, then opened it, showing us what he meant.

"A laundry cart?"

"We do mass loads down in the basement."

"Basement? Hell no." I shook my head. That was the last place I ever wanted to go again. Another dead end.

"What did I tell you?" Noel's lips rose in irritation. "Observe. Learn. Watch. If you had, you would have seen there is a loading dock on the far end they use to bring in supplies. It's the only door she doesn't have under surveillance."

An entrance into the building meant an exit for us.

"Get in." Noel nodded to the cart. "Once outside, head to the black SUV, my keys are in the glove compartment. You have one chance. Do not screw this up."

"Thank you." I grasped his hands in mine. "For everything you've done."

"I hated I couldn't do more for you earlier. I'm glad you are all right, Alice."

"You've done a lot."

"This is sweet and all, but escaping takes precedence." Matt's chest bumped into my back, his hands gripping my hips, pushing me forward away from Noel, his possessive testosterone cramming the air.

Climbing into the cart, I dug underneath the stinky sheets and soiled towels with a groan, and Matt crawled in next to me. His huge frame barely fit in the space. Curling into a ball, he pulled me tightly against his body, my back against his chest. It was so tight; not even a piece of paper could fit between us.

I could feel *everything* through the thin cotton material.

Hot toddy...did they turn on the furnace? My body heated instantly, feeling every inch of him pressing into me, his hot breath trailing down my neck, his lips skimming my earlobe.

"Comfy?" he growled in my ear, his teeth nipping at my skin, flushing scalding tingles from my cheeks to my thighs.

"Stop it," I hissed, making him chuckle. Asshole. This was not the place or the time to be thinking naughty thoughts.

Noel grunted in disgust, tucking in a sheet behind Matt.

"Night Rebellion, huh?" I said, trying to distract myself. "Have to admit I'm kind of disappointed."

"Why?" Noel's brows lowered as he clutched the end of a sheet.

"I don't know; I was expecting something like Mistletoe Mutiny, Reindeer Revolt, or even Jingle Bells Brigade. I mean, it's like you put no thought into it."

Noel blinked at me.

"She's locked us in eternal night, rotting our world and souls with her darkness."

"Oh, well...fine... If you like it, it's all that matters."

Matt rumbled into my neck, gripping me tighter.

"From now on?" Noel picked up a heap of laundry, dropping it over us. "Shut the fuck up."

🎩 🎩 🎩 🎩

My stressed heart thrummed in my throat as the cart wheeled us down the hall. Fear trampled and screeched in my stomach like a herd of elephants. I gripped Matt's fingers. Knowing he was here with me made it better. We were in this together, whatever came our way.

Filtered light glowed down as Noel pushed us into the main room, the wheels squeaking under our weight. The sound of fingernails clicking away on keyboards echoed in the quiet room. The commotion from the night had settled down, the witching hours stilling the building, settling down to reboot for a new day.

Noel twisted the cart, and I could tell he was struggling to make it turn smoothly. If only laundry was in here, it should move with ease.

"Noel?" A nurse's voice spoke, her nasal voice piercing my heart. Peppermint Patty. "What are you doing?"

"Uh." He paused, the basket coming to a jerking stop. "Laundry."

Soft-soled shoes pattered over the tile, heading toward us. My grip on Scrooge clenched down, my pulse loud in my ears.

"Now?"

"Yeah." He sounded bored. "Need to do something to stay awake. Been a long night."

Tension saturated the moment, like she didn't believe him.

"Ginger did the laundry this morning," Peppermint Stick finally spoke. Might have been my paranoia, but suspicion wrapped carefully around her words. "Seems a lot for such a short amount of time."

"Accident in Happy's room. You know what happens when he gets scared. Bea freaked him out. Every time someone wakes him up..."

"Pees himself," Nurse Mint grumbled. "Yes, I am very aware."

My eyes opened wide. What the hell? Were we laying in Happy's urine-soaked sheets?

Matt felt my slight jolt, his fingers lacing through mine, squeezing tight.

"Also found some in Star's cupboard. She's hoarding again." Noel's lies slid easily from him. At least I hoped the pee one was a lie.

"She'll have to be punished for that. She knows the rules about stealing."

"Yeah." I could hear a slight tightness to Noel's response. Was he throwing someone under the bus to save us?

"Well, go ahead." Exasperation coated Pepper's response.

Relief closed my lids, my breath sliding through my teeth. The cart jolted, Noel moving us forward, halting again soon after. I could hear him clicking the elevator button repeatedly.

The doors opened, lurching my heart with hope. We were so close.

"Noel," Peppermint cried out. "Stop!"

The hope burst like a balloon, crashing against my lungs.

"Hold up!" she bellowed, her shoes pounding the tile. *No, Noel, go!* I wanted to scream. But I heard her grab on to the elevator door, out of breath.

"Could you take this down since you're going there anyway? Toss it in the dumpster? Broke earlier." An object crashed down on us, shoving air from my mouth. Slamming my jaw, I tried to bite back the natural yelp of pain my body expressed.

"What was that?" Her voice rose with suspicion.

"What?"

"Thought I heard something."

"Like?" Noel kept his voice even.

"What else is in there?"

The utter terror of being caught, knowing if we were found our lives would be over, divided me in half. Blinding, debilitating fear froze me into a statue, while at the same time everything burst with life and awareness. Every sound: a clock two rooms away, a drop of water in a sink, the buzzing of lights.

"You found out my secret," he replied, hitching the last bit of air in my lungs. What was he doing? "Don't get mad, but it's a case of her peppermint syrup. I can't get enough..." He sounded nothing like the stoic guy I knew, but a bashful teenager.

"Noel!" Peppermint chided him, sounding suddenly exceedingly girly. "You know you're not supposed to do that. It's for the patients here."

"I know. I know. But it's *so* good."

A playful sigh came from her. "You are such a troublemaker."

"You won't tell?"

"No." She was now the one sounding like a teenager. One who was flirting. "You know I could never do that to you. Just don't get caught, okay? She's already so mad at what happened earlier."

"I won't. Thank you, Pep. You are the best. I owe you," he flirted back.

"You *so* do." Her voice curled with innuendo. "Maybe I'll come down and help you with the laundry when I'm done here. Looks like you might need a hand."

Okay, I was gonna throw up.

"Sure."

I listened as the elevator doors closed, and the box jolted down, heading to the basement.

Noel exhaled loudly, picking up whatever she dropped on us. "That was close."

"Oh, Noel." I pushed my voice up high and girly, peeling the sheets away to see him standing over us, holding a coffee maker. "Do you need a *hand* with the *laundry*?" I snorted.

He growled, glaring at me. There was the guy I knew. "I hope this coffee maker really hurt when it landed on you," he snarled, making my smile even wider.

Chapter 22

"Keep down until we're out. Eyes are always watching," Noel muttered, the elevator doors dinging, spreading open to the sinister darkness the basement embraced. I shivered. Terror, isolation, and grief clung to the walls, haunting the space from the victims who came before. I didn't know how long Jessica had used this building for her needs, but I knew this place had been used before as a sanitarium to hold the lost and broken. Misery soaked into every brick, the howls of anguish reverberating with their horrendous life here.

The moment the doors shut, Matt and I climbed out of the cart. Fear danced on my nerves. Even though we had made it through the first tier, we still weren't safe.

"The doors are on that end." Noel pointed the opposite way of the hole. "They will bring you up by the parking lot. My SUV is on the other side of the dumpster. She has cameras out there. So once you are out, don't hesitate and don't look back. Just run."

Matt nodded. "Thank you. I appreciate this."

"I'm doing it for her. Not you." Noel's lips thinned. "You have done a lot for the Night Rebellion over the years...have been on our side for a long time now, but a lot of us still can't forget, *won't* forget, what you were before." Noel's throat bobbed. "I lost family because of you."

Matt sat back on his heels, his jaw clenching.

"You may not fully remember who you are and what you did. But you will," Noel said. "And I hope those ghosts haunt you forever. Right now? You two are our best hope to find him, bring him back, and beat her. So go, now!"

With a jolt, Matt and I moved for the exit, but I swung around, hugging Noel.

"Thank you." I squeezed him.

"Yeah. Yeah." He patted my back, but his voice couldn't hide the softness in it. "Stay safe, Alice."

"You too." I stepped back. "And just curious… Were those sheets really soaked with Happy's urine?"

A slow, wicked smile spread on Noel's face.

"You're an asshole."

Which only widened his smile.

"Alice, come on." Matt beckoned me.

"Will I see you again?" I treaded backward, looking at Noel.

"If that is our story." His amber eyes locked on mine.

I dipped my head, then turned and ran, catching up with Matt. Together we got to the large rolling doors that would let us out to the car in back.

"You ready?" Matt grabbed the heavy door, ready to pull it open. "Oh, and I should let you know, I don't know how to drive those modern contraptions."

"What?" I blinked at him.

"I was born in a time when horses pulled wagons," he exclaimed. "Since then, I clearly didn't need to learn. Winterland obviously isn't in need of a DMV anytime soon."

"Good. Because I prefer to drive anyway. Let's go." I nodded at the door, rolling my hands into fists.

Opening it just enough to fit us, we bolted out, keeping close to the shadows, our shoes crunching across the gravel. My heartbeat banged in my ears, fear wiggled in my throat, sticking to the walls of my esophagus like suction cups.

"There." Matt pointed at the SUV by the dumpster, going for the passenger side and climbing in, tearing open the glove box, tossing me the keys. I jumped into the driver's seat, my heart pounding in my chest as I turned on the ignition. Pulling out, I gunned it out of the parking lot, terror gripping my lungs like a clamp, my gaze darting to the rearview mirror expecting to see nurses and guards piling out the front door. What was in front of us sank my stomach far more than that notion.

Large iron gates at the entrance leading into the property were closed; several guards stood at posts, rifles hooked over their arms. Uniformed and identical.

There was no turning back. No other way but to go forward.

"Shit...if they didn't know we were escaping, they're about to now." I gripped the steering wheel, my foot slamming down on the gas. "Put on your seatbelt and hold on."

"Oh fuck." Matt strapped himself in, his hand wrapping around the "oh shit" handle above the window, his boots pressing into the floor.

The guards jumped to face me, noticing the car not slowing down, their arms waving for me to stop.

I don't think so, toy soldiers.

For a brief second, I saw wooden toy soldiers instead of the men there, their painted mouths forming perfect circles, but I didn't have time to think about it. I pushed the pedal to the floor. The engine roared with velocity, hurling us toward the barricade.

I clenched my teeth together, watching the guards fling themselves out of the way as the front of the SUV slammed into the thick iron.

The shrill sound of scraping and crunching metal pierced my ears. The car jolted with impact, jostling us around. I held the steering wheel firm, my foot ramming down harder, the SUV bursting through the gates.

Bang! Bang!

Bullets cracked against the back window and pinged off the body of the car.

"Shitting elves!" Matt dipped lower in his seat. I only got a glimpse from my rearview mirror, figures running after us, their guns pointed at the car.

Yanking the wheel, the SUV skidded out onto the main street, smoke billowing off the back tires as they tried to grip the damp pavement. Squealing, the car jolted forward as I straightened us out, keeping us on the road before my foot crashed down on the gas again.

Crack!

The back window exploded; chunks of glass caught in my hair, slicing into my arms as more bullets plowed into it.

My focus was locked forward, feeling the wheels finally catch up with what I was demanding from the accelerator. The SUV shot forward, barreling down the dark country road. I knew it wouldn't be long before they were after us, but their time to catch up before we hit major roads was inching away from them.

Jessica wasn't the mafia. I didn't think she'd come after us, guns blazing in populated areas, giving to a car chase. Though I didn't put it past her either.

Matt glanced behind us before his gaze landed on me, his eyes burning into my profile.

"What?" I dared a quick glance at him.

He gaped at me, his one blue eye darkening with passion. "Can I say, Ms. Liddell...you...*that*...was *fucking* hot."

I looked over at him again. When he called me by my last name, something stirred deep in me.

"Seriously, beyond impressed...and can I say completely turned on?" He shook his head, shifting in his seat, brushing pieces of glass off his shirt.

Yeah, me too. The adrenaline pumped through my veins, and his heated look was giving me wicked thoughts.

"What is our plan? Jessica has to know we are gone by now." I cleared my throat, needing to keep focused on our escape and not pulling the car over and diving into the back seat with him.

Playfulness evaporated off him, his jaw rolling along with his shoulders. "Tim." He turned his head out of the window. "I need to see him."

His son was, of course, the first thing he'd want to go get. To protect him from her.

"Okay. We'll head there." I swerved the car down another road, heading for town. "It will be the first place she'll look for us. She might already be calling my parents, warning them their insane daughter is on the loose. I have a little money saved up. We can take him and run if we have to."

"No." He stared straight ahead. "No running."

"What?" I zoomed the SUV down the main street through downtown New Britain. Christmas lights and decorations were strung down the lane on the quiet street, the shops closed up for the night.

"I have to go back. This isn't my world anymore. Winterland is my home...and I know in my gut I have to get back there. People are depending on me..." He faced me, his voice gravelly. "On *us*."

He was right. I could feel it too. I just had no clue how to get there or what to do. Nibbling on my lip, I shivered, cranking the heater higher. Freezing air blew in the absent back window, streaming over my bare arms, and easily passing through the thin scrubs.

I drove the beat-up SUV down our street, parking it far enough from our houses to hopefully go unnoticed. Matt leaped out, hobbling straight for his house. The windows glowed with light, his feet coming to a halt right in front, his regard locked on the living room window.

Stopping next to him, I followed his gaze to the little boy sitting stiffly on the sofa. Beautiful, he stared at the TV, watching it, looking more like a doll than a real boy.

"What is he doing up? It's not even dawn yet."

"He never sleeps well...another sign I ignored. *My*

207

boy slept soundly. Nothing woke him up." A choked sound came from Matt, turning my head to him. Grief etched over his beaten face, his eye glistening with emotion.

"Matt, what's wrong?" I gripped his arm, the sorrow emanating off him stabbing at my heart.

"I hoped I was wrong." He choked, his lids closing briefly for a moment, anguish creeping over his features. "I knew it in my soul...but I kept pushing it away, pretending. Living in the fantasy. The hope. But I knew..."

"Knew what?"

"That he is not my son." His Adam's apple bobbed; his muscles tightened under his skin. "He's not real."

"What?" I peered over at the boy then back at Matt. "What do you mean?"

"You know how I told you he had night terrors?"

"Yes."

"Well, it wasn't him who was having them. It was me. I dreamed every night of killing my son..." He shuddered. "Why I could never sleep, afraid of myself...but most of all, afraid of the truth."

"What truth?"

"That is not my boy." He took a shaky breath. "*My son* is dead."

"What?" My stomach dropped, plummeting to my toes. I stared back at the child in front of us. "I don't understand."

"You see, Ms. Liddell." Matt twisted his head to look at me, heartache drowning his expression. "In Winterland, my son was killed..." He pressed his lips together. "*By me. I killed him.*"

My lungs whooshed like I'd been sucker punched, my feet stumbling back. "What?"

"The nightmares keeping me up at night. Watching my son's life slipping away wasn't a nightmare…it was my reality. Whomever this is. He's not my Timmy." He motioned to the boy who hadn't moved a hair, blinking in perfect repetition. "It's Jessica's concoction to torture and contain me without me even knowing. She held me with the one thing I would give my life to have back. The perfect thing to keep me prisoner without a single lock." Anguish closed his eyes, dropping his head.

I worked with enough kids at my job in Santa's Cottage to know five-year-old boys never sat still. Now, watching him, he didn't seem real to me either. Almost like a robot.

"Do you know what's it's like to have the only thing you ever loved back? Knowing I could keep pretending, living in this lie, raising my son. Be the father I never got to be to him, watch him grow."

"But it would be a lie," I spoke softly, knowing I had no clue what he must be going through.

"I lost my son once…it feels as if I'm losing him all over again."

"Then why can't we try to bring him?"

A sad smile hinted on his lips for only a moment. "Because he's not meant for that world or even this one. *My son* is gone. I will not dishonor his memory with a poor substitution because it eases my grief." He looked down at me. "I should feel the pain. Remember it every day."

He stared straight ahead, his voice low. "The moment I came for you, I made my choice."

You are the one who will end up taking Timothy away. And he will hate you for it. Either way I win. Jessica's once odd claim came to life before me. Choosing to come for me, he understood he would never be with his son again.

A figure moved into the living room, making us dart behind the apple tree. It was the same woman I saw at the therapist's office, Jessica's secretary, or she was that afternoon. They all seemed to work for the queen where she needed them. The woman sat next to the boy, taking the remote and switching the channel. Tim didn't react at all as the cartoon shifted to a reality TV show.

The ring of a phone chimed from inside, the woman picking up her cell. I couldn't hear what she was saying, but when her head turned sharply to the window, her eyes narrowed like she could see through the dark night.

With my every fiber, I knew Jessica was on the other line, warning her of us showing up.

"Shit. Come on, we need to go." I intertwined our fingers, but he didn't budge. Nervously, I glanced over at my house next door. Dark except for the Christmas lights trimming the house, and no cars in the drive.

A light came on in a neighbor's house across the street, casting us in ashen light, the early dawn starting to wake the early risers for work.

I didn't know what to do, but we needed to get off the street. My neighbors proved they were not to be trusted and would call the cops or Jessica on me in a blink if they thought the crazy girl broke out of the zoo.

"Matt." I yanked on his arm.

"Bye, little man." He swallowed, watching Tim,

soaking him in, swiping at a tear pooling in the corner of his good eye. "I'm so sorry I couldn't be the father you deserved, in any life or world. I love you." The last part he muttered so low I barely heard it. All I could hear was his heart breaking again.

Matt bit down, took a deep breath, his hand clutching mine fiercely. He turned away, slamming down on his emotions, his focus ahead. "Let's go."

The agony he must feel having to say goodbye to the life he could have had with his son…forever.

Chapter 23

The impending day hinted on the horizon, the thick clouds glowing a brighter gray. My boots crunched over the snow, chilling my exposed skin even more. The desperation to get out of sight pulled me toward my house. Finding the hidden key, my skin greedily lapped up the warmth of the house when we slipped in. Heading up the stairs, I peeked into my parent's room. "Mom? Dad?"

Their bed was empty, dresses and my dad's slacks draped all over the bed, which looked like their nicer stuff they wore to University events.

"Dinah?" I rushed for the next room; my sister's bed was also vacant. No one was home, which normally would be odd, but my sister was always with her boyfriend, especially when our parents were gone. They stayed in Hartford a lot during the holidays, with all the University parties.

It hurt knowing that's probably where they were, even though it was irrational. Life was going on for them, attending parties, laughing and joking, while I was locked in hell.

I veered toward my room, the tick of the clock downstairs batting at my nerves.

Clothes. Money. Until we figured out our next step, we needed to hide. Bloody cornflower blue scrubs stood out far too much.

"I don't want to tell you how many times I fantasized about climbing into your bedroom window at night." Matt rumbled behind me, causing my chest to flutter.

"You don't know how many times *I* imagined *you* climbing into my window." I reached for my door, shoving it open. His growl heated the back of my neck. He took two steps in and stopped.

"What the fuck?" His gaze roamed over my bedroom, landing on the wall chock full of my designs. His muscles stiffened, his expression turning cold. He strode directly to one of the sheets filled with my obsession. He tore it off the wall, his gaze rolling over it before he swung to me. "What. Is. This?" Fury lit his eyes as they burned into me.

"Evidence of my craziness?" My pulse picked up, tension swallowing the oxygen in the room.

He was in my face in a blink, his body looming over mine, the darkness encasing us. "Don't fucking joke with me right now. What is this? Where did you get this?" He pointed to one I drew of the teapot pouring into the hat.

"It's my design. When I came back…I was obsessed with it, especially the hat. I couldn't get it out of my head. It's what started to freak my family out. I couldn't stop drawing it." My finger went over the hat, trailing down the scarf.

Air heaved through his nose, his eyes watching me, then he grabbed the bottom of his shirt, ripping it over his head, displaying his ripped torso, locking up my throat. My body couldn't help but respond, sucking in roughly, desire flaming up my thighs.

But then everything stopped. My gaze landed on the ink on his chest, covering his heart and shoulder. The memory in the maze. The tattoo over his heart...the exact one I had been drawing.

It's always teatime inked over his heart with a teakettle pouring into a top hat with a red scarf.

I was right. Breathing heavy, my hand lifted, my cold fingers skating over the top of the inked lines. He sucked in, a muscle in his chest twitching under my touch, but he didn't move.

"I knew it," I muttered, my fingers tracing the art. "At the time I didn't know how I knew, but I knew I had seen it. Touched it." His breathing stumbled as my fingers continued to explore, our bodies getting closer. I leaned in, my lips grazing over the top hat. "Kissed it..."

He sucked in, his lids closing. "Alice." He rumbled my name. It felt so familiar. The need when he said my first name.

"Scrooge," I whispered without thinking. His hands clamped down on my hips, pulling me in, pressing himself firmer into me, heat blooming off his skin, forcing my teeth to saw into my lip.

"I like when you call me that." His nose nuzzled into my neck. His erection hot and heavy against me. "Feels *real.*"

A moan pattered in my lungs, needing him more than anything. This was a terrible idea and very bad timing, but as if he were a force field. I had no control over myself.

"We should be getting out of here," I said, my teeth dragging over his tattoo making both of us groan.

"We should." His hips pushed into mine, rolling and dragging the thin fabric. Friction and desire sparked up my spine. He gripped the back of my head, sending pain and pleasure through my nerves. "She's coming for us, but I can't think of anything but fucking you. I don't remember what happened in Winterland between us, but you have been torturing me enough in this realm."

"Same." My hands slunk down his body, his skin feeling like electricity under my fingertips, sliding over the band of the pants. "Like I need you more than I fear whatever is *coming* for us."

"Most likely it will be me if you keep doing that." He gritted his teeth as my hands moved down his V-line, my knuckles brushing the tip of him. "Fuck." A deep growl hummed from his chest as he grabbed my ass, tossing me back on the bed and crawling between my legs. Ripping my top and sports bra over my head, my back arched as his hand skimmed down to my breasts.

Flashes of him over me, fire burning in a hearth, a white rug tickling my skin, my back arching as I moaned in pleasure at his touch. I gasped. The images were strong, causing more raw desire to take hold of me. What was right or wrong no longer mattered.

I shoved at his pants, not caring about the danger

outside the doors. Danger only seemed to intensify my need for him.

"Alice." He grunted, tugging at my own pants and boots, yanking them quickly off my body. His lips nipped at my stomach and moved up, covering one of my breasts.

"Oh god." I bucked underneath him.

"I want to take my time." His fingers slipped under my underwear, finding me, and my hips responded to his stroke, needing more.

"Hell with that. We don't have time. I don't want to be interrupted like last time." The words stumbled out of my mouth.

We both paused. Blinking.

"We've been here before," he said slowly, staring at me.

"Yeah." Again, it was something I knew without really knowing how.

Suddenly car lights flashed across my bedroom window, stilling me. I knew it was far too early to be my parents or Dinah returning home.

"Shit." I clambered off the bed for my closet, grabbing jeans and a sweater, my body utterly furious with me for denying it yet again. Swearing at me in Yiddish and pig Latin.

He tugged his pants up, peering out the window.

"It's Jessica."

"Fuck a nutcracker." I tugged back on my shoes, adjusting the ice pick inside my boot, and ran to the window. All her guards and nurses climbed out of a SUV heading directly for my house.

"We really need to get to Winterland. That's the only place we will be somewhat safe from her."

"How?" I exclaimed peering around. "Any suggestions? Know of a magical portal we can..." I trailed off, my mouth parting. "Holy bloodsucking holly."

Portal. A memory of when Jessica had drugged me returned. A piece of the puzzle fitting in place. That's the word *she* used.

"Only one has enough magic to do that. No one, especially a human, should be capable of traveling through a portal. How were you able to fight the Land of Lost and Broken and enter the Valley of Mirrors? How did you do it, Alice? How did you pass through the mirror?"

"Mirrors," I whispered to myself. Bea's odd statement trickled in right after.

"You are the key."

"Key?"

"Look, Not-Alice...the clues are all around you. You need to open your eyes and see them. Not only what is there, but what isn't."

"Mirrors," I exclaimed again, hearing people move up the driveway.

"What?"

"The mirrors!" I jerked my head up to Matt's, realization settling into my stomach. "Somehow, I can travel through them. I am the key. I opened it...that's how we traveled here. How we get back. Why she wanted me."

"By mirrors?" he said, but then his nostrils flared, his head jerking at a noise coming from the backdoor downstairs. "Jesus, I never thought about it, but at our house, there is only one, in her private bathroom. She locks the door every day, saying she didn't want Tim getting into the medications by accident that she kept on hand."

"She wasn't worried about him. She was worried about you," I said, but my attention was already moving away from him, latching onto the large mirror hanging on my wall.

"Five milkmaids a-laying." I stared at the glass.

"I'm pretty sure that's not how it goes."

"Believe me, *no one* cares." I stepped by him, stopping in front of the mirror. "I can't believe it. It was right in front of me the whole time."

"What was?"

"Our way back." The vision of standing on that frozen lake, diamond-encrusted framed mirrors suspended over the ice. They were all identical to this one.

A loud crack of wood boomed through the silent house, like someone was busting through our garage door. Footsteps pounded across the floor.

"Shit!" We both jerked to the door in unison.

"Alice. Scrooge." Our names rang through the house, Jessica's voice full of taunting confidence. "You disappoint me. Thought you two were a lot smarter than this. The pull of Timmy or your family was too much. Love makes you weak. Predictable. How easy make this."

"Do you know what to do?" He moved over to the door, shoving my dresser in front, blocking the entrance. It wouldn't hold them back for long.

"No." I stepped onto my chair, grabbing the frame, the thing weighed a ton. I remember it took my whole family to install it after I bought it at a Christmas market which had come through town. I had instantly been drawn to it. Knew I couldn't go home without it.

Like it *wanted me.*

I grunted, trying to lift it. Scrooge darted over, grabbing the other end, both of us laying it on the floor.

Boots pounded up the stairs, skating fear over my skin and down my throat. With a bang, my door bounced off my dresser, the guards trying to push in.

"You can't run from me. I'm queen for a reason," she stated. "Now come out. Don't make this messy for your family, Alice. You know they will believe me over you. You are only going to break their hearts more."

I touched the glass feeling nothing but the hard, reflective material.

"Please tell me you know how to open it again."

"No." My voice rose, the guards ramming into the door, inching the dresser farther out. Anxiety drew drops of sweat down my back. "I have no clue. Last time…I just stepped in."

"Think, Alice." Urgency made each word a demand. He pushed back into the dresser, trying to keep them from breaking in.

"I can't! It's impossible."

"Only if you think it is."

Bam. Bam. Bam.

Matt grunted, his boots slipping over the wood floor as her soldiers barreled against the door.

"Think. Concentrate!" He growled, pushing all his weight against the dresser.

"Okay. Okay." I tried to breathe, closing my eyes, fear making it hard for me to latch on to anything.

Focus, Alice!

I knew everything was hanging on me. Our safety and lives depended on it. Pushing out the noise and terror, I drifted back into my mind to the frozen lake covered in mirrors. The tick of the clock downstairs was all I heard, the feeling of everything disappearing around me.

I could see me standing on the frozen lake like I was looking through one of the mirrors, seeing myself on the other side. Dressed in red pants and a tank, my long hair tumbled over my shoulders. I looked lost. Sad. Feeling I had no hope or ties to anything.

"Alice." A voice called out to the girl, lifting her head. Following her gaze, I saw blue eyes, his outline filling up the mirror. *Scrooge.* He stretched out his hand, beckoning her to come to him. "Let go, Alice. Let the madness in…" The other me stepped closer as if he were what she longed for most in the world. "Once you let it in, everything will be right again."

I could see it on my—her—face. She held no doubt. No fear. She believed. Nodding, she reached for the man in the mirror. Her fingers went through the glass like water, his hand wrapping around hers. A buzzing of energy rippled the mirror, hitting the one I was watching through. Even through the glass, I could feel the magic of her belief.

She stepped through and was gone.

My lids burst open, my gaze landing on Matt's, his face twisted with effort as he tried to hold the guards back, but they had already gained enough territory to stuff in an arm.

I knew what I had to do, but this time it would be me leading him.

"Scrooge." Standing up, I reached my hand out to him, letting go of every doubt and fear I had. "Do you trust me?"

"Yes," he responded, his brow wrinkling, not ready to leave his post.

"Let go." I flicked my chin behind him.

He watched me for a beat before he pushed off the dresser, moving to me, he took my hand, his eyes never leaving mine.

The dresser squealed across the floor as they pushed in, but I stayed focused on Scrooge, tossing out everything logical and practical and just believed.

"Ready for the impossible?"

"Always." He smirked.

Together we took a step...

"Nooooo!" I heard a woman scream. Jessica's cry followed us as the world dropped away, and we plummeted.

Down.

Down a dark, dark hole.

Chapter 24

My skin screamed as my form plunged into dark, icy water, my fingers losing Scrooge's as I sunk, my limbs flaying trying to fight the pull into the depths of the water. My lids popped open, the water clear, but eclipsed with darkness, swirling with my activity.

My head jerked around, trying to find Scrooge. He was nowhere around me. Where did he go? Peering down, my eyebrows wrinkled. It looked brighter down there, light shining through, reflecting, like it was the surface. I tipped my head up. I noticed the ground not far from my head, but I was sinking away from the bottom, not toward it.

What the hell?

What felt like up was down and down was up. How was it possible? Gravity tugged me the opposite way I felt I should go.

Curious and curiouser.

"Sometimes looking at something from a different perspective changes everything."

Spinning around, I faced the other way, adjusting and letting go of what my mind had set as up and down.

Like a camera flipped, alternating the scene for the viewer, everything righted itself, switching my up to down.

Darting for the surface, lungs aching for oxygen, kicking my legs faster, I reached the top. Panic bubbled in my chest when I noticed the layer of ice covering it.

No! I pounded on it, realization setting in.

It wasn't ice, but glass.

A mirror.

Panic clipped my chest, the need for air bubbling a cry from my mouth. My fists did nothing to break it.

Darkness crept around my eyes, my mind growing hazy. *Think, Alice!* I ran inventory down my body, trying to think if I had anything to help me.

Holy tinsel! I mentally screamed, my hand going to my boot, pulling the ice pick I had hidden there. The very thing that was supposed to end my life was saving it.

With all my might, I stabbed at the glass. Over and over.

Crack!

The mirror splintered, a large piece shattering, opening up.

My head popped up as I gasped desperately for air, my hands grabbing for the rim, the ice pick rolling over the glass, freeing my hands. Trembling, I dragged myself up onto the surface, hacking and gulping for oxygen, the jagged edge cutting at my clothes. I slumped on the surface with fatigue.

Spiked eggnog. I did it.

It took me a few moments, my fingers digging into

the smooth surface, trying to stabilize myself, calming my frantic heart and lungs. Taking a deep breath, I lifted my head, glancing around. Fog rolled across the frosted oval lake, the mirrors hanging around me.

I was back in the Land of Mirrors.

And what I thought was a frozen lake was actually a mirror. Identical to the one I had at home. It was as if I stepped through one side and came out the other. A portal right in front of me, waiting for me to figure it out.

Shakily, I sat up, still sucking in deeply.

"Scrooge?" my voice cracked over the air. Pushing up, I forced my wobbly legs to stand. My wet clothes clung heavily on my frame, but no coldness touched me. "Scrooge?" Only silence responded to my call.

"Scrooge!" I screamed, feeling the panic flutter in my throat. What happened to him? He was right next to me when we stepped into the mirror. Staring back at the tranquil waterhole I climbed out of, I could see nothing. Where was he? How did I lose him?

"No." I gritted my teeth. I would not *lose* him again.

Lost…

I halted, my mouth parting, my eyes leading over the hill, suddenly knowing where I would find him. Our clock had been reset. Instinct more than memory told me he would be out there, adrift in the Land of the Lost and Broken, unable to recall what had brought him here.

Santa Claus. This all led back to the man in the red suit, another soul lost amongst the misplaced.

"You will find him."

"Who?"

"The one who is lost and the one who is broken."

Leaning over, I grabbed the ice pick, my course set forward. I knew this place would *try* to take my mind...make me forget why I was here.

Gripping it tightly, the pick symbolized everything I needed to remember. The object that was supposed to strip me of my memories, my personality, leaving me a husk was the exact thing to help protect me from the place that wanted to do the same.

It had only made me stronger.

I wasn't the same Alice as when I first came through here. This Alice was not to be messed with. She killed for those she loved. Would fight anything coming her way...and she would not leave until she had a jolly fat man and her sexy tight-assed Scrooge.

Stomping toward the floating toys, I already sensed the sorrow and grief brushing at my skin, their greedy need to strip me of my hope and take away my power.

No more. I was done with being a chess piece.

I gritted my teeth, cresting the hill, watching the objects float around waiting for me.

"Game on."

The attack was immediate. The onslaught of grief and pain clawed at my mind, wanting in. As if the toys could sense my confidence, they headed for me like a magnet, wanting to strip me of the power and either take it for themselves or make me another object bobbing around shattered amongst the unwanted.

Misery loves company.

A toy moved by me, sorrow climbing over me like a

thousand bugs. My fingers jabbed into my temples as a cry splintered from my mouth. Desolation tunneled a hole through my chest.

Don't let them touch you.

My memory of this place was hazy at best, but I trusted my instincts. Another thing I used to doubt, never fully trusting myself in decisions or questioning what I really wanted. Now my instincts were all I trusted.

"Fuck off." I stabbed my pick at a purple and pink stripped stuffed cat with huge yellow eyes, pushing it off in the opposite direction and knocking it into an army of tiny green plastic men like a bowling ball.

"All of you. You get near me, and you lose another part." I snarled, holding up my weapon. Some seemed to listen, but the draw to me seemed more powerful than my threat to others.

Ducking, I zoomed past a headless doll, her woe and anger dipping my knees.

"No," I hissed, trying to steal myself against the onslaught, but I could still feel pinches of my willpower being taken. It was like when you forgot a simple word for something, the moment of blankness, your mind scrambling to track it down before it came to you again. But each time remembering became harder and harder.

Bobbing, weaving, and slipping by the ambush of toys, I pushed forward, stabbing anything that got close to me.

Perhaps it was my determination to find Scrooge caging my mind with protection. Or maybe the magic I was injected with back at the asylum still hummed within me. Something seemed to be helping me battle against the vast hole of wretchedness wanting to take my memories, my drive, my soul away from me. Either way, I knew in my gut this time they would not fully reach me.

Anger. Purpose. Stubbornness. And love...I could feel it swathing me. The extra muchness, which stomped my feet forward, helped guide me to him, wherever he was. I came for him, and I would not leave until I found him. But the vastness of the place began to chip at my determination. Stumbling endlessly through a sea of nothing was like being put in the middle of the Sahara Desert, where you walked forever, but nothing changed.

On and on, time only counted by putting one foot in front of the other, my body sagging with exhaustion, sorrow, and fear. Yet I pushed on, clinging to any snippets of Scrooge I could still remember.

Then a chill crept over my body, jolting my head up.

A line of toys hung at an invisible wall, but not one went past it. Ceaseless, dark emptiness stretched beyond, but I could tell it was anything but vacant. The air vibrated with palpable energy and despondent wails I could not hear but could feel with every nerve in my body. In my soul.

Don't go in there, Alice, a voice whispered in my head and I turned to look at a legless Transformer. *It's not for the living. Unless you want to get trapped there as well.*

"What's in there?"

Things that were torn in two and can't ever be put together again, it said. *Things beyond repair. Beyond any realm.*

I sucked in a breath, knowing exactly what he meant.

Ghosts.

Souls of those who lost everything, so broken by heartache and loss they succumbed to the despair.

I knew what I was seeking would be there.

If I went in, there was a good possibility I would become another soul trapped in this place.

Rolling my shoulders, my grip on my weapon tightened. A slow smile spread over my face, and I stepped in.

CHAPTER 25

Like stepping into a walk-in freezer, icy air drove through my damp clothes and gnawed at my exposed skin, running a chill down my spine. The hair on my arms stood on end as I felt things brush against me; the air was heavy, weighing down my shoulders.

Like with the toys, I could feel the pain of each soul that brushed against me, see bits of their memories. If I thought the toys held sorrow, they were child's play compared to the souls knocking into me as if I were a pinata.

Regret. Guilt. Torment. Anguish. Despair. The toys didn't understand regret or guilt, which was a completely human emotion, and it raked through me like razor blades.

Sobs choked up my throat as they rattled the cage that I tried to protect myself in. Their claws stretched through the bars, swiping at my soul.

"Stop!" I stumbled forward, tears running down my face, but only more seemed to come at me. And these I couldn't fight as I did the toys because I couldn't see them.

"Please," I wailed, rushing forward. "Scrooge?" I called out, hoping he was not among the sea of invisible souls floating around me. A needle in a haystack. How would I find either him or Santa?

"Scrooge! Matt?" I called out, not knowing which broken part of him was misplaced in here. "Santa?"

The names seemed to stir the souls into a tizzy, swirling the air into a blurry mass. A dim glow ignited the night, flicking and dancing around me, like hundreds of lightning bugs.

"Scrooge." I watched the light flash brighter. "Santa Claus."

Blink. Blink. Blink.

"Are they here?" The question came out as I watched the sparks glowing brighter and flickering faster.

Rudolph droppings. Were they answering me?

I bit at my bottom lip, scared my theory was in my head.

"Blink twice for yes. Once for no. Are Scrooge and Santa here?"

Blink. Blink.

"Son of a sugarplum fairy." I breathed, half not believing my eyes. "Can you show me?"

Blink. Blink.

The swirl of souls bunched together and sailed forward. Jogging to keep up, I trailed after them down a path, curving around nothing, but logic would not be found in this land.

It was so dark, only the energy the souls were creating gave the place any light. They slowed, halting me behind them, then slowly they crept forward as a group, their dim flickering light revealing a large lump on the ground.

I blinked, taking in the outline of a man. Appearing like a warped version of Sleeping Beauty. Wearing only blue scrub pants, he was draped over another object, unconscious.

A sharp gasp hurled up my throat, a boulder dropping in my stomach.

"Scrooge!" I screamed, running to him, falling to the ground with a crunch, my hands reaching for him. "Oh my god. Scrooge." My finger curled around his face turning it to me, his skin cold. Deep circles lined his eyes, cuts were on his cheeks, and the one eye was still puffy from Jessica's torture, indicating everything there had been true as well. But his wounds had healed a lot since coming back here. And though it only felt like hours to me, time was irrelevant. We could've been in here years, weeks, or seconds.

Severe torment etched his face like it had become permanent, which twisted my heart. Here, the harm was done mentally, not physically, which was worse.

"Scrooge, wake up." I shook him.

No response.

"Scrooge!" I shook him harder, my palm tapping at his cheek, trying to stir him. "Please. I didn't go through all that shit to lose you now." I slapped him hard, his body stirring, his lids fluttering.

"Scrooge!" I pounced, shaking him harder.

Both his eyes opened, glossy blue eyes staring into mine. Blank. Empty. Lifeless. Staring through me like I didn't exist.

"Scrooge?" I clutched his face, biting my lips. "Please, talk to me."

His brow furrowed, confusion, grief, pain flickering across his features, his face turning to the side, staring off at nothing.

"No." I gritted my jaw, yanking his face back to me. "Look at me, Scrooge."

"Scrooge." His voice broke over the name, no recognition reflecting in his intonation.

"That's your name," I said. "Do you know who I am?"

His eyes glossed over again, and agony twitched his face, before his eyes shut again.

"No!" My fingers wrapped around his shoulders, tugging him closer. "Stay with me."

"L-l-let..." He struggled, like speaking was something he didn't really understand anymore. "Me. Go." The agony in his eyes begging me to do just that was a blade in my heart.

"No," I growled. "There is no fuckin' way I am letting you go. *Ever.* Do you understand? You're not the only one who is selfish, stingy, and greedy. I want forever. And I'm not letting some perverse Candyland take you from me. Nor will I let *you* give up. So...get your ass up. Now!"

Sorrow so deep marked his face, and he rolled in on himself, his eyes shutting again. Broken and lost, barely holding onto his shell. I knew it wouldn't be long before he dissolved away, becoming another soul trapped in here, his body forever lost.

He was too far gone for my words to reach.

But...

"Okay." I grabbed his face, pulling it up to mine. "Not really how I planned for this to go, but you left me with no other option."

My mouth slammed down on his.

Even barely conscious, the hot-and-cold electricity between us flared to life, zapping at my skin like jumper cables, sending fevered energy into the air, creating a frenzy as the souls clamored for more, buzzing and blazing with light.

But nothing mattered outside us, my lips consuming his. In a place that took, I gave him everything I had left. Pushing every memory of us through the kiss, needing him to remember somewhere inside what we had together. What we had been through.

How I felt about him.

A deep growl vibrated against my lips, before fingers clutched the back of my head. His mouth came to life against mine, devouring me with fierce hunger, like I was a lifeline, sucking life, energy, and memories from me. The more I shoved at him, the more animated he became, latching on to the energy flaring between us.

The animal inside him roared with vitality, turning him primal and brutal. His fingers were rough as he yanked my head back, his teeth pulling at my bottom lip before he dragged them across my throat, nipping and sucking.

"Scrooge," I groaned his name, as he returned to my mouth. Deepening the kiss, his tongue curled around mine as he nipped my bottom lip. Damn, he felt so good. I wanted this, but even my inappropriate timing knew this was definitely not the time or place.

"Scrooge..." I pulled back, my palms sliding along his jaw. "Stop."

His nose flared, his blue eyes burning with hunger, his brain set on primal mode. It made sense. This place stripped you of everything, leaving you with only the barest of instincts. Food. Water. Sex.

And I woke up the last one.

"Look at me." I locked on his stare for dominance. "I really need you to dig deep. Somewhere in there you recognize me. Remember all we've been through together."

His eyes burned into mine. He seemed to want to pounce but stayed in place instead.

I wanted nothing more than for us to get out of here, but the most important thing still needed to be found.

"You came in here to find Santa Claus. Do you recall that?"

Scrooge's forehead wrinkled, and the feral animal slid away. Memories creased his face. "Santa." He rubbed at his head, anguish storming over his features again, his fingers digging harshly into his scalp, scraping, and clawing.

"Hey. Stop." I tugged at his arms. To see him so broken hollowed out my chest. He dropped his hands to the ground, his chest heaving.

"I remember," he said so softly I barely heard him. A heart-wrenching cry broke from his lips, his fists pounding the snowy ground. "My wife... my son..." He gulped. "I let them die."

"Shhh." I wrapped my arms around him, my fingers brushing through his hair, his muscles shaking with grief.

"I had another chance. I a-abandoned my boy. A-again." He gripped on to me, still stumbling over his words.

"He wasn't your son. He was not real." I tugged him in tighter. "You did the right thing. We need you here."

"D-did I? Doesn't feel that way."

His forehead nuzzled against my neck; his body heaving with a sigh, before he pulled back. Cupping my face, his gaze went back and forth between mine.

"You are why I'm remembering."

"Probably not a compliment, huh?"

His irises darkened as he leaned over, his mouth taking mine. His kiss deepened, turning fierce. Claiming. Violent. "Alice," he rumbled deeply.

I jerked back, my name ringing through me.

He stopped, staring at me with shock. "Alice." He said my name again. "I remember. You...why I came here." He blinked, his gaze darting to the side. "Holy shit."

My gaze followed his, landing on the thing he had been curled around. For the first time, I really noticed it. It was a red box tied with white ribbon, about a foot tall and wide, and a tag hanging off the bow. A present.

Curious.

I moved closer, picking up the tag, reading the name scrolled across.

Santa Claus.

My head jerked to Scrooge, my mouth parting. "Is this? Is this what I think it is?"

Scrooge's head bobbed up and down.

"Yes, it's Santa Claus's soul."

The cluster of souls guided us back to the border connecting the Land of the Lost Souls and the Land of the Lost and Broken. There seemed a big difference between the two. The souls here wanted to help us and didn't rip your memories away, but the sorrow, shame, and guilt were far deeper. It crippled and tortured you with those horrific memories instead. The ones you wish would be taken away.

Both places stripped you of your soul.

Scrooge held the box and squeezed it to his chest with one arm, keeping close to me, his jaw set tight.

"You ready?" I gazed past the imaginary boundary, toys floating like a force field was keeping them behind the line. Once we stepped out there, we would again be fighting to keep our minds, and not drown in their grief and forget what we were doing.

"No better time than the present, Ms. Liddell."

Glancing over at him, a soft smile played on my lips. My Scrooge was returning slowly, I just needed to make sure it stayed that way, and the toys wouldn't take him again.

Firming my hold on the ice pick, I nodded, both of us stepping out. The chilly air peeled off my skin like a coat, shedding it as we left the lost souls.

We took only a few steps when the toys shifted directions, coming for us as if we put off a signal they couldn't resist. Hundreds of stuffed animals, action figures, and game pieces came at us like zombies hunting for brains, sucking at our energy and filling me with gloom.

The cracked porcelain doll with one revolving eye

and yellowing gown led the pack, her dark malevolence lashing out for me. Hate and anger seeped from her, the need to strip not just my memories, but my life salivated through her emotions.

Most of the toys I encountered before had just wanted me to hear their sad tale, help them. But she was different, and she seemed to be controlling a large group of resentful toys, following her lead.

You're not leaving this time, Alice. An odd high-pitched voice slid into my head, like a little girl trying to do a very bad witch impression.

"Dangling snowballs." I jerked back, watching her advance toward us, her one eye rolling up. Was it possible they've grown stronger? Smarter? Coming together?

All because of you. She spoke again in my mind, her voice creepy as shit. *The more we take from the living, the more* alive *we become. Powerful. More clever. We don't get humans in here often...and now that we have a taste, we are not letting either of you escape.*

I glanced over at Scrooge, his head bobbing around, watching each toy, not reacting to her at all.

"Do you not hear her?"

"Hear who?" He peered down at me, shifting the box in his arms, his free hand rubbing his head, as if they were already scraping at his mind.

You are special, Alice. The moment you entered here, I could feel it. Was drawn to it. You have extra much—

"Muchness. I know." I said out loud, cutting off her sentence. "I've heard."

*I want it, s*he hissed.

"Get in line." I lifted my weapon.

A cackled laugh, like someone on helium, shivered through my mind and down my spine. *There are hundreds of us. Two of you. Who do you think has the best chance?*

"We have a slight problem," I muttered to Scrooge. "That freaky-as-shit doll has kind of formed a toy gang. She's really evil and has gotten a taste for murder and us and...well, they want to suck our brains through a straw."

"What?" Scrooge twisted his head to me, his eye twitching with confusion. "The toys aren't alive. They have no intelligences."

"They do now," I replied. "Thanks to us."

He swiveled around, taking in the horde enclosing on us like a bunch of hyenas, circling us. "Fuck."

"You know what we have to do?" I grabbed his arm, assessing the group around us.

"What?"

"Run!" I tugged on him, yanking him to the area with the least toys packed together to make a break for it, my pick raised to attack.

I only got past the first layer before the assault switched my cry from battle to pain. The toys swarmed around, stripping and tearing into my mind.

Scrooge yelled, his fist smashing into a Teletubby, his grip on Santa's soul turning his knuckles white. A torn, pink Care Bear and a bald Strawberry Shortcake slammed into me, driving me to my knees with a wail.

"Scrooge," I called his name, more for me to keep remembering it. The barricade around my mind was chipping and splintering with the onslaught. And I knew Scrooge was still weak and vulnerable, his defense no better than a newborn calf.

Do not forget who you are, Alice. What you have been through to survive.

I thought of a bunch of dollies being the ones to take me down. To take Scrooge from me. Fuck. That. Gritting my teeth, I fought against the desire to crawl into a ball and let them have me, their tales taking the place of my own.

A roar sounded near me. A pack of toys leaped down on Scrooge, too many for him to fight at once. My mouth opened to call for him again and nothing came out, his name plucked from my mind like picking an apple from a tree.

Stop, the shrill doll voice yelled, forcing my hands to cover my ears, even though it was all in my head. The toys around us halted immediately and backed off us.

They are mine. She floated to me, her eye rolling all the way back in her head.

The horde split, giving her a clear path to us.

I looked over my shoulder at the nameless man near me. I didn't recall his name, but I could feel what he meant to me. He slumped protectively over the box, but he stared around as if he had no clue why he was here.

"Hey…" I grunted, trying to dig deep for his name. He glanced up at me. "Stay with me, okay? It's you and me."

He watched me without familiarity, but he nodded his head.

"And do not let go of the box." What was in there again? It was important, right?

The doll sailed toward me, and the closer she got,

the heavier her malevolence knocked against my mind, making me wheeze for air.

You are mine, Alice. I will take until there is nothing left.

She reminded me so much of someone. Cruel and cold, wanting to take everything from me, but I couldn't recall who. She inched closer and closer to me, her greediness for me burning through my body. Her small cracked hand reached out for me, brushing my skin.

With a cry, I lurched forward, the pick slamming into her remaining eye, breaking all the way through the skull. A wild snarl derived from my throat as I pulled out the blade and smashed it into her head again, the porcelain crown rupturing, breaking and crumbling to the ground.

A piercing scream stabbed in my head, bending me over, shoving bile up my throat.

A hand reached for her, the man yanking what was left of the doll to the ground, his boot stomping on it over and over. The cries ceased, letting air through my lungs again. Taking a breath, I stood, grabbing on to him.

"Come on." My gut told me we only had so long until the other toys responded to what we did, coming after us for themselves. "Run."

He and I took off on shaky legs. Noises rang out in the air behind us. The toys that could make sounds— music, talking, beeps, or cries—wailed like sirens.

My legs picked up speed, the muscles straining as we darted and weaved around other toys floating around.

This place felt endless with its sameness. No sign telling you which way the exit was. We ran, having no idea if we were going the right way or how to even get out of here when I noticed a throng of toys grouping together in front of us.

We slowed, glancing both in front and back of us. One gang bellowed behind us, and one stood like a wall before us. A frustrated cry scraped over my tongue, my body flipping back and forth between the two groups.

Something caught my eye behind the group lining up. A strange energy wobbling the air behind them. My mouth parted with understanding.

The barricade was blocking us, acting as a defensive line. They did not advance toward us, but stayed right there, protecting what was behind them. The exit. Obstructing us from leaving.

I had a strange sense of having been in a similar situation, but the image of holly came to mind instead of toys. Holly? I had no idea where that came from, but it felt right.

The group behind us was getting closer; the warped slurring of a talking doll nipped at the back of my neck.

"Exit is behind them." I turned to the man, staring up at his blue eyes, his name dancing the crest of my mind. "Don't stop, do not look back, no matter how painful. You push beyond them and get through."

His mouth opened, his brows furrowing, trying so hard to find his words, his free hand taking mine.

"To-gether," he rumbled.

"Together." Anxiety pranced my legs as the toy troop was now just feet away, reaching out for us. "Ready?"

This was going to be excruciating.

He nodded, gripping the box, letting my hand go.

"Now!"

With a cry, we rushed forward, crashing into the barrage of toy guards. Swiping my pick and shoving at the plush toys, the agony hit me like a semi-truck. Screams tore from my throat; the rush of grief, pain, and loss blinded me, wrenching all thoughts from my head. *Fight!* Something screamed in me, turning me primal and wild. My fingers tore at the cute little playthings, ripping, stabbing, and tearing through them, their guts floating around like fluffy clouds.

A man's roars echoed in the air near me.

"No!" I bellowed. We would not lose. We would not be forgotten here.

Rage barreled me through, breaking the line, reaching the pocket of energy they were guarding. I could jump through. Be free. I whipped around, spotting his dark hair through the throng of puppets.

"You. Do. Not. Get. Him," I thundered, thrashing and slicing through to reach him, no longer feeling pain...only a feral need to get what was mine.

Reaching for him, I yanked him through. With his free hand he tried to keep them at bay, biting and clawing like a wild animal. With a deep grunt, he rammed through the last toys, colliding into me with force, sailing me back. Energy rippled over my skin as my body lurched backward through the exit. Pressure stabbed at my head, zinging through my body as I stumbled through, his body landing half on top of mine as we crashed into the snow with a crunch, the box tumbling a few feet away.

All was quiet except for our heavy breathing. The world felt alive, not like the vacuum we'd been in. The wind snapped at the trees and howled over the hill. We didn't move. Dazed and overwhelmed, our chests moved together as we gasped for air.

"Fudge nuggets." I blinked up at him, his gaze going back and forth between my eyes, heavy and full of awareness. I. Remembered. Everything.

We stepped through the door, our memories waiting for us on the other side as our reward. We had won the twisted game. Gotten out. Lived.

All my memories flooded back. My life here, on earth, what we had gone through, the torture, Hare, Dee, Dum, Pen, Rudy, and every delicious detail of Scrooge.

"You saved me again, *Ms. Liddell.*" Slowly he cupped my face, heat and knowledge blinking behind his eyes. Life fully bloomed behind his eyes. "I'm beginning to feel I'm the damsel in distress."

His body engulfed mine, his weight and erection hot and heavy on me. His skin hummed with savageness. If anything, I felt like the prey, not the savior.

Willing prey.

"If I'd known you were gonna be such a pain in my ass..." My mouth pinched on the side coyly.

"I can certainly be that...if that's how you want to be thanked." He lifted an eyebrow, his head leaning down, his breath fluttering against my neck.

"Oh really?" My fingers brushed his lips, skating down his neck to his tattoo. "I'll add it to the list of how you should express your gratitude, but I think normally the grateful damsel kisses the hero first."

A wicked grin twitched his mouth, his hands cupping my face, then lowering.

"Bah, humbug," he whispered against my lips before his mouth covered mine, kissing me so deeply, I could feel it vibrate through my bones. His mouth moved fiercely, his tongue stroking mine, and I retaliated back with the same hunger, lust consuming me in a gulp. Our hands were groping and touching each other like we needed to make sure we were there and real.

We needed to deal with so much. Jessica could be right on our heels, but when I got around him, I couldn't seem to stop.

"Shit." He hissed, breaking away with a sigh, the stronger one out of the two of us. "Our timing..."

"It fuckin' sucks." I bit down, trying to rein in my need. I knew it wasn't the time, but dammit, would it ever be? "It's as if I keep getting coal in my stocking."

"I know mine is painfully loaded right now," he muttered, sitting back, his weight and heat instantly missed, making me feel cold even though this place wasn't.

He sat for a moment, lines wrinkling his forehead, his cheek flinching, as if more memories were being dumped on him. He took a breath, rubbing his hand over the tattoo on his chest. "Fuck," he whispered under his breath, a streak of agony running over his features. It was a blink, but I felt a wall slip down around him. "Fuck." His hand continued to rub his tattoo, his lids shutting.

Tim. Belle. I could see their spirits circle him, take the joy he just held and twist it with grief and guilt.

"We have to get back." He stood, reaching out for me, his voice all business, gaze not meeting mine.

"I know." I took his hand, standing and brushing the snow off my clothes. He strode over, picked up the box, and pointed himself down the path away from this horrible place.

The images of our friends, the ones who had been haunting me on earth for so long, my conscience working hard to tell me the things I thought were crazy were the sanest: Hare, Dee, Dum, Penguin, Rudolph, and *even* naked Nick.

They waited for us.

Our last hope was in that package, ready to be delivered to the one who had the power to save us all.

Chapter 26

Scrooge led the way back to the cabin, knowing the area a lot better than I did. He didn't look back once, the barrier between us growing thicker. The change from when he kissed me to a few moments after was a wall of his making. His ghosts. His self-loathing.

My boots stepped into the prints he forged in front of me, the snow sometimes hitting our knees. Back in perpetual night, the moon lit our way through the pine trees, which grumbled and spat at us but weren't as violent as the ones on the other side of the mountain.

Sleep. Food. Sex. Alcohol. Shower. Longing for each, I no longer cared in what order.

"Did Jessica say anything?" He switched the box to the other hand, sliding the ribbon around his fingers, letting it dangle at his side. "Do you know anything she might be planning now?" Scrooge huffed, using our walk to catch up on everything that happened. His transformation felt strangely seamless. Matt Hatter to Scrooge. He was Matt on Earth, but here he was *all* Scrooge. So many things he and I had been feeling and fighting on earth made sense now. Especially our attraction to each other.

The Land of the Lost and Broken might have stolen our memories, but it didn't take away the magnetic pull to the other. The unexplainable connection that bonded us no matter if we remembered.

At least for me. Not sure he felt the same or wanted to now. And all I kept hearing was Jessica's voice repeating, *"You are the one who will end up taking Timothy away. And he will hate you for it. Either way I win."*

"I know she wanted me alive to keep the door open, planning to come in and kill Santa, then shut the door permanently, ending Winterland for good." What would that do to my world? Belief, magic, and hope lost even to children? How horrific would our world become with no good will left on earth?

"Yeah, well, her key just slipped through her fingers." Scrooge crested the top of another hill, his muscular chest moving up and down, swallowing down air. "Her game will be changing."

My fingers itched to caress his skin, to trace every inch with both my fingers and my tongue, to shatter the barrier he was trying to put between us.

"Alice?" His gravelly voice popped my head up.

"What?" Was he talking to me?

"Stop looking at me like that," his voice warned, but his gaze rolled down my body, pulsing desire through my veins.

"Then you stop that." I motioned to him like his abs were purposely taunting me.

"Jesus." He rolled his fists into balls, his hand

knotting in the ribbon. "What is it with you? You are my hell..."

"What do you mean by that?"

He gritted his teeth.

"Tell me. I'm sick of the silent treatment. Do you blame me?"

"Alice..."

"No. Tell me! Don't push me away."

Dropping the present, he swiveled on me, looming over, his shoulders rigid with tension.

"I remember *everything*." His nose flared, anger bristling under his skin. "All of it."

"So do I."

"Every hellish, horrific deed. Even the ones I even pushed down, locking away." He pushed forward, driving me backward. "You wanted to know how many women I've been with since my wife?" His teeth gritted, his face only an inch from mine. "None."

"Wh-what?"

"I died with them." He growled. "*Nothing* was left of me. My group was the only thing keeping me alive. At least technically." He lifted his wrists, showing barely visible scars sliced over them. "You think I haven't wanted to join them ever since. I've tried every way possible, but Jessica cursed me. I couldn't die by my own hand, forced to live with the pain of what I did, their screams for me. The look in my wife's eyes as the guillotine sliced down on her neck. The trust and love in my son's face when I gave him pure holly drops because I knew he wouldn't be able to fight what Jessica would do to him. He had been slowly dying since birth. Sick and in chronic pain so long, his body was giving out. He wanted to go, begged me over and over to let him sleep forever. He was in so much agony. Exhausted all the time, he couldn't play like a child or leave the house because of his immunity. But Belle and I couldn't let him go. We selfishly wanted to keep him forever, no matter how he felt about it."

Scrooge raged like lightning slashing over the sky, gasping through the agony. "I wanted it painless for him. To be unaware. To fall asleep in my arms. Finally be at peace. I thought he was too young to understand, but he *knew*—his eyes stared at me with a soul far too old for this world. He knew what I was doing. He smiled and said, 'It's okay. I want this. I love you, Papa.' Those were his last words to me."

My chest caved, ice cultivating around my ribs. He had talked about killing his son, but I had been too afraid to push him for details. This was no murder, but the most self-sacrificing act a father could have done for his son. I couldn't imagine the strength it would have taken to do that. The heartbreak, guilt, self-hatred, torment, and grief you felt from making that choice.

"Belle's belief and love in me washed away in utter heartbreak when Jessica told her what I did. The utter disbelief and abhorrence in her eyes as I watched her die. And I deserved it." He lowered his voice, self-loathing shooting out at me. "I do not deserve to feel anything but their grief, hatred, and agony..." He heaved in air, his lids closing for a moment. "And you...you..."

Pinpricks of emotion stabbed at my throat and eyes like a voodoo doll.

"I've been weak, let myself feel...believe. To want more."

"You think you don't deserve happiness?" I shook my head. "That's bullshit. You think Tim or Belle wouldn't want you to live your life? To be happy?"

"They were both so good. So pure. They would, but it doesn't mean I deserve it, Ms. Liddell."

"What happened? Why do you think you failed them? Tim didn't want to be in such pain anymore. You did the most selfless thing for him." I tried to grab for his hands, but he yanked them away. "And you didn't kill Belle. Jessica did."

"Technically." He nodded. "But I sacrificed her life to protect Tim...and I killed him anyway."

Darkness coated him like a cloak.

"The queen found our group's hiding place, our location betrayed by someone we trusted. Belle was home with Tim, who was fighting pneumonia again. I ran back to get them; Blitzen was already there. While he broke in the front, I snuck through the back, getting Tim from his bedroom." A guttural noise bumped up his throat. "I slipped out with him. Didn't fight for her. I completely tossed her to the wolves, knowing she wasn't strong enough, but all I could think was to get our sick son to safety."

"I'm sure she would have wanted you to do exactly that."

He dipped his head forward, his hands going to his hips. "Doesn't make it better. And taking Tim outside with no medicine was the kiss of death for him." Scrooge's shoulders shuddered. "We were hiding in a cave. My wife and all my friends were captured and taken to the queen. I knew our time was limited before Blitzen tracked me down. If we were found...Jessica would torture Tim and use him to seek her revenge on me as she used him on earth, keeping me as a pet to kill and destroy others like I had before." His head rotated to the side, air struggling in his lungs. "We all knew his end was coming sooner than we wanted. He couldn't even get out of bed anymore, his energy practically zilch."

"You said he was born that way?"

Scrooge nodded. "We think it's because I was from earth and Belle was from here. He was born...fragile. His DNA from both of us tore him apart, his body not fitting into either world." His voice wobbled, fighting back his emotion. "I dropped pure holly poison into his cup, and he drank. His fevered cheeks and huge blue eyes stared into mine, his little hand in mine...then with a shuddered exhale...my entire world slipped from me."

A tear slipped down my cheek; every declaration pierced my heart.

"It wasn't long before Blitzen found me and dragged me back to the castle, where I watched my friends being tortured and my wife murdered."

"Damn," I whispered, wanting so badly to comfort him but knew by his tense body he didn't want me to touch him. To hear the full story of his wife and kid broke my heart. And even more because he had to give his son up again. Real or not, that had to be so unbelievably painful. "I am so sorry."

"I don't deserve your fuckin' pity." He roughly wiped at the tear on my cheek like it disgusted him to see any grief on display for him. Twisting away from me, he snapped up Santa's soul.

"It's not pity," I exclaimed. "It's heartbreak for you. I can't imagine the choices you were faced with at the time, knowing no matter what, you would lose people. You did the best within the circumstances. No one could have done better. You can't blame yourself. You had no choice."

"There is always a choice." He stopped, glancing over his shoulder at me, rage lining his face. "Always. And I made all the bad ones. But ask me if I had the chance to do it over, would I save my son and wife or Hare, Pen, Dee, and Dum?" He rubbed at the back of his neck, not able to stay in one place. "What kind of person am I either way?"

"There is no right or wrong here. You saved Hare, Pen, and the twins. Their lives are important."

"But for what? A war is coming," he spat. "Did I save them to die painfully another way? And this time, I can too."

"What do you mean?"

"Jessica's curse broke when I went back to earth. I can feel it—I can die now—like I wanted for so long."

A puff of air stuck in my throat, another tear trickling down my face.

"And now?" He snorted derisively, his gaze moving up and down me. "The. Fucking. Irony."

"Irony?"

"I loved my wife..." He tapered off like he was going to continue but stopped.

"I know."

"No." His gaze went over me again, and for a split second longing and pain crossed his features before they were gone. Shaking his head, he uttered, "You *don't.* You don't get it at all, Ms. Liddell."

He turned around and stomped away, leaving me gutted and dejected. Even though we escaped, the Land of the Lost and Broken took him from me anyway, the thing I never truly had but had become part of my soul just the same.

Warm lights glowed on the snow from the front windows, smoke billowing from the chimney as we came over the final hill. Seeing the cabin had tears forming behind my lids. Relief and happiness rushed adrenaline into my veins.

Scrooge and I had stayed quiet the rest of the journey back, which felt more torturous than what Jessica did to me. Whatever memories from the past had settled into his head telling him vicious things about himself would not let me break through.

"We made it." I peered over at him; his eyes locked on the cottage.

Right then, the front door tore open, and Dum, Dee, and Penguin ran out giggling, Hare right behind them wearing the frilly apron, a spatula in his hand.

"I swear to Santa…I'm going to count to five." Hare shook the spatula at them. "You think you've seen me mad before…you've seen nothing yet. I'll give you something to cry about."

My hand came up to my mouth covering a snort. The warmness at seeing them filled my chest, rubbing around like a cat, happiness stabbing at my eyes.

"You are giving me gray hair, and I'm already white," Hare yelled at the three. Penguin only giggled and fell into the snow, making snow angels, while Dee and Dum ran circles around him, bumping and crashing into each other, laughing.

"There is not enough mead in the world to deal with you three."

"Think we need to save him." A small grin hinted on Scrooge's mouth, his eyes doused with love and affection for his family.

"I don't know, this is pretty entertaining."

Scrooge looked over at me, letting his wall slip for a moment. "And they call me the cruel one."

"No, they call you the greedy, *tight-ass* Mr. Scrooge."

His irises flared, but he quickly jerked his head away, starting for the cabin. Scrambling, I caught up with him, stepping out in front.

"Don't make me come over there and separate you guys," I yelled in false anger, jerking all their heads in our directions. "Just wait until your father comes home."

Right then Scrooge stepped around me, folding his arms. A pissed-off father ready to knock heads together.

"Kiss my cream-covered pretzel rods." Hare's mouth fell open, whispering, "You're alive."

There was another beat when Dee squealed.

"Scrooge! Alice!" She darted for us, leaping into Scrooge's arms first. He dropped the box as her little arms wound around his neck, holding him tight. "You're okay! You've alive! Oh my tinsel, I've missed you so much."

"Missed you too." He squeezed her tightly back, lifting her off the ground, tucking his head into her hair. "You have no idea."

"Ms. Alice! Mr. Scrooge!" Penguin waddled for me, his flippers flapping up and down frantically. I scooped him up, his beak nuzzling me. "I wrote to Santa to bring you guys back to us. He got my letter."

Dum tackle-hugged my legs, forcing me to stumble back, before he moved to Scrooge, burying his face in his pants, a little sob heaving out of his nose. Scrooge rubbed his back, still holding on to his sister.

Dee lifted her tear-streaked face, reaching for me, Scrooge and I switching Penguin for Dee.

"We were so scared. Hare wouldn't tell us where you went. Don't ever leave us again, Ms. Alice." Dee sniffed in my ear, leaning back to stare into my eyes. "Promise."

"I can't promise that." I tugged on her braid. It was so good to see her vibrant and healthy again. The idea of her not being here among our greeters tore at my gut. "But I do promise I will try, okay?"

She nodded, wiping her eyes as I set her down. Sometimes she seemed like an ancient lady trapped in a little girl's body, then other times she seemed every bit the little girl you saw.

Scrooge set Pen down next to Dee and Dum, our focus going to the porch.

Hare stood there, his stub tapping against the wood, arms folded.

"About fuckin' time." He sniffed sharply, not looking at either of us. "I've had to take care of *everything* here."

"Hare..." Scrooge took a step forward.

"Whatever, asshole." His eyes narrowed on his friend. "Hope it was worth it."

"We got what we were seeking," Scrooge replied.

"Plus some," I mumbled, thinking of all our adventures since leaving this cabin.

"Good." Hare grabbed the door handle. "Well, dinner will be ready in a few." He hopped into the cabin, slamming the door.

Scrooge scoured his forehead, picking up the package again and strolling for the house.

"Hare will come around." Dee grasped my hand in hers, her joyous face grinning up at me. "He tried not to show it because he doesn't want anyone to know he cares about you, but he's been terrified for you both. The more time went by, the worse he became. I think he was sure you both were dead." She swung our arms as we traveled to the front door, Scrooge, Pen, and Dum going in first. "I'm so happy you are back, Alice."

"Me too." I grinned down at her.

"Our family feels whole again."

Her words startled me because deep down I felt them too. They had been my strength when I was at my weakest, their words and faces were comfort even when I didn't recognize how much I needed them. When everything was crumbling around me, they were my truth.

My family.

CHAPTER 27

A welcoming fire crackled in the hearth. Scents of vanilla, lemon, chocolate, and cinnamon wafted through the cabin, causing a thundering a growl in my stomach. My tongue craved one of Hare's treats. But that's where the welcome stopped.

The small room was spewed with dirty clothes, snacks, cooking utensils, card games, drawings, towels, and blankets, reminding me of my little sister's sleepovers when she was young. Within five minutes, they exploded all over the living room with magazines, hair stuff, sleeping bags, food, and clothes.

"This is actually better than it was before." Dee let go of my hand, running for the sofa, crashing in next to her brother. "I yelled at them every day to pick up their stuff." She rolled her eyes. "Boys…right?"

"Right." I grinned, shaking my head. I never grew up with a brother, and now my sister was by far tidier and more structured than I was.

"Hey!" Hare stomped back into the living room. "I told you I am not your maid or your mommy. Pick up your own crap. And don't act like you weren't as bad."

He pointed a spoon at Dee. "You fuckin' Pucks are messy, love living in cluttered chaos."

"It's homey." Dum dug underneath himself, pulling out a pair of tongs. "Oh hey, I was looking for these earlier." He used them to scratch his back.

"Tinsel tits!" Hare bellowed at Dum. "You—you—I can't even look at you right now. I used those to cook last night's maple-butter spaghetti."

I winced. "I thought elves were supposed to be clean, neat, and organized?"

"They are at Santa's shop. Extremely disciplined, down to the last detail. The place runs meticulously." Scrooge set the package near Pen, who was humming "Santa Claus is Back in Town," swishing his flippers over the white rug in circles.

"Ohhh! A present." Pen's eyes lit up, clapping his flippers.

"Don't touch it. Not for you." Scrooge pointed at him, turning back to me. "Then they go home and are the complete opposite. Unbelievable hoarders. Disgustingly messy...and Santa wasn't much better."

Knowing Jessica, that had to drive her even more batty. Not a surprise, she was a minimalistic, clean freak.

"Alice." A low voice came from the hallway, jerking my head around. "You have returned."

Rudolph stood there, tall, fit, wearing only a pair of the red pants Nick seemed to have numerous pairs of. His wounds had healed, his antlers starting to grow back. Even though his manifestation had come to me on Earth, seeing how utterly beautiful he was in person, jolted my chest.

"Rudy," I breathed, the tie that bonded us flaring to life. Not able to stop myself, I ran for him, wrapping my arms around his torso. His arms curled around me, pulling me into him.

"It is so good to see you. I have missed you." His voice was still monotone, but strangely I felt so much depth in it. "I was so worried about you. But you came back. To us….*to me*."

"You guys never left me, even when I didn't remember you." I tilted back to stare up at huge, soft dark brown eyes.

"Great, this is absolutely touching," Scrooge grumbled behind me. "But where is Nick? He's vital in this, and we have a lot to plan and catch you guys up on."

Rudy took a deep breath. His regard narrowed on Scrooge like he could see right through him. It returned to me as he squeezed me again before he stepped back.

"He took off a couple hours ago, saying we were driving him nuts." Dee shrugged, going on her head, her legs hooking over the top of the sofa like monkey bars. Her brother instantly copied her, their legs knocking into each other. "He's been doing it a lot lately."

"Where is he going? There is nothing around here," I questioned.

Dee and Dum shrugged in unison.

"We need to find him. We have to start planning *now*." Scrooge stabbed at the table with his finger. "The queen is coming, and we need to be ready."

"Oh no…I have slaved all day on this meal." Hare slammed a stack of plates on the table. "You can take a fucking moment to sit down and enjoy it. Even if it's the last thing you do."

The urge to laugh bobbed at my throat, but I stuffed it back. Poor Hare was ready to snap. "Gathering you couldn't make more mead?"

His lids narrowed on me. "Oh, I'm sorry I didn't have time to go frolicking in the woods in search of mistletoe with all things wanting to murder me. I was too busy planning my vacation to Christmas Coast, where I would be jet-skiing and drinking cranberry piña coladas in a coconut."

"Wait." I blinked. "You guys have a beach in Winterland?"

"Not everyone celebrates Christmas in cold weather; half the world is in summer," Scrooge replied.

"Why the shit aren't we there?" I exclaimed. "Drinking cranberry coladas."

"That's…that's what you are wondering about? The beach?" Hare's voice rose in disbelief. "I-I can't. That's it! I'm done!" He ripped off his apron, hopping out the front door, banging it on its hinges.

"Uh-oh." I cringed. "I think I might have broken him."

Scrooge smirked, cracking his armor, our eyes meeting, causing my blood to flare. "Probably good for him; he seems wound a little tight."

"Seriously." Dum flipped back down off the sofa. "He's been a miserly curmudgeon since you've both been gone."

"You mean he's being a Scrooge." I tried to hide my grin, my eyes sliding over to the man in question.

"Exactly!" Dum tossed out his arms, nodding, his head still upside down.

Scrooge watched me, his head shaking with amusement. "Watch yourself, Ms. Liddell." The humor dropped away, filling with intensity. "You don't know how miserly I can get."

"Looking forward to finding out."

He took in a deep breath, a nerve in his cheek twitching as he turned away from me. "Guys, this place is disgusting. Pick up your shit before we eat. I'm gonna take a shower, and it better be *spotless*." He brushed past me, strolling around Rudy, heading down the hall.

Disappointment echoed in my chest, wishing he had given me any kind of sign he wanted me to follow, but since leaving Land of the Lost, he was keeping me at arm's length.

Dum, Dee, and Pen started picking up without question. Scrooge was definitely in charge here. Hare and I were barely able to keep it together, but with one order from Scrooge, they jumped.

Penguin started to sing "My Favorite Things," being as helpful as see-through wrapping paper, getting distracted by everything he picked up.

"Alice." Rudy walked farther into the room, his lips pressing together, his gaze directly on me. "I am so glad you have come back. The time left me with a lot of time to think. I've come to the conclusion—"

"You know what else?" Hare barged through the front door, cutting off Rudy, spinning me to him. "I haven't heard one, *'Thank you, Hare, for keeping these fuckers alive. You did an amazing job all on your own.'*

Because you know no one else pitched in. Especially that fat naked asshole."

"Thank you, Hare." I strolled over to him, going down on my knees to look him in the eyes. "You did an amazing job. I know how much the *two* of us struggled...I don't think I could have handled it all by myself. You have my utmost respect and appreciation."

He shifted on his foot. "Yeah. Well." He cleared his throat. "That's a little better."

"You know what else?"

"What?"

"I've missed the hell out of you." I pulled him into a hug, his form going rigid from the contact, but I only embraced him tighter.

"Yeah. Yeah." He patted my back stiffly. "I know. I'm impossible not to miss." He tried to wiggle away, but I didn't let him; finally, with a heavy exhale, he gave in, curling into me.

"I missed you too," he muttered.

"You did?"

He pulled back, rolling his eyes. "Don't get too flattered. I would miss anyone doing the laundry and controlling these monsters."

"Sure." I smiled, knowing he was full of shit. He and I had become such a team.

"I'm glad you didn't die." He stared off into the kitchen, his nose wiggling, like he was trying to see if anything was burning. "And I guess I'm glad you brought the asshole back with you."

"Thank you, Hare."

"You already said that."

"No, not for what you did here but what you did on Earth. For saving me in more ways than you'll ever know."

"Saving you? Earth? What the hell are you talking about?"

"It doesn't matter. But thank you for giving me strength."

"O-kay, crazy woman." He squinted with uncertainty and stepped to the side. "You know when you sound crazy in the realm of the insane, that's not a good thing. Something you should get checked out." He motioned to the kitchen, backing toward it. "I was halfway down the hill when I remembered I had zucchini-and-lemon waffles with vanilla-honey butter drizzle, sweet potato brownies, and cinnamon-sugar crepes baking—and I don't care if the world is ending—there is no excuse to let art that exquisite be ruined."

I watched him bound into the kitchen, my heart full of love for this whole group. They had all saved my life, coming to me when I needed them the most, even when I thought they were my decline, they were actually my saviors.

"Roasted Tofurky." I rubbed at my full belly, sitting back in the chair. Exhaustion tugged at my body. I wanted to curl up on the rug and sleep for days but first a freezing shower. That I did not miss. "I am stuffed. That was delicious, Hare. As usual."

"Toe fuckery?" Hare paused midbite, blinking at me.

"Tofurky." I glanced around the table at the confused expressions. "Guess you don't have it here.

263

It's a tofu turkey."

"What the hell is a toe-few turkey?" Hare's nose scrunched up. "Does it have fewer toes? Doesn't the stupid thing fall over? I mean, what is the point of that? Do you eat the feet where you come from?"

"No...it's for vegetarians who don't want to eat meat—a substitute. It's not real turkey but looks and tries to taste like it."

"Okay, let me get this straight. Those who don't eat meat will name, shape, and spice something to look and taste exactly like meat?"

"Yeah."

"And you think we're bonkers here." Hare snorted, returning to his meal.

"Earth's changed *a lot* since my time." Scrooge rubbed a napkin over his chin and pushed back from the table. He could barely sit still, worry and tension riding every nerve along his shoulders. "Where the hell is Nick? The one thing I didn't think he'd miss is a meal."

"*Here comes Santa Claus...*" Pen wiggled and danced on his chair. He had been chatting nonstop about what they'd been up to while we were away, only quiet when he gulped down a waffle. "*Right down...*"

"Penguin! Please, for the love of Santa. Shut. Up!" Hare knocked his head against the table, which just made Dee and Dum start singing with Penguin, grinning mischievously.

Hare moaned, banging his head harder.

"Guys. Enough." Scrooge paced around, running a hand through his damp hair. He had redressed in another pair of Santa's red pants and white T-shirt. "I need you to be serious."

Dee stopped, her back straightening, her expression going into her warrior mode. She elbowed her brother, coercing him to stop. Penguin and Rudolph twisted to Scrooge. All eyes were on him.

"The battle we knew was coming is here. The queen has access to Earth now. She wants to kill Santa, crush his soul, which will destroy Winterland, and close the door for good. His soul, his magic, is what keeps this world going. Without it, we're all dead." Scrooge's gaze drifted over to the box on the floor. "And we have it."

"You have what?" Rudy stiffened.

"Santa's soul." Scrooge folded his arms over his chest. "That's where I went, to the Land of the Lost and Broken to find him."

"What?" everyone exclaimed, except Hare and me.

"But Scrooge, you could have been lost too." Dee's face crumpled with fear at the idea. "Shattered and taken away from us forever."

"I almost was." His gaze flicked to mine, then returned back to the group. "Ms. Liddell is the only reason I am here." He readjusted his feet. "Two things came out of her coming after me. One, she found Santa's soul and me and got us out. And two, we discovered she is the key between worlds."

"What?" Rudy jerked to me, his long lashes batting slowly. "You can open the doors?"

"I guess." I had no idea how I did it, but it seemed I could.

"Of course." Rudy bobbed his head, his antlers slicing through the air. "That makes sense now. It is how you could follow me here. You had the ability to travel through our doors and enter Winterland when no one else could."

It did make sense how I was able to pursue him down the hole to this realm, but it didn't explain why. "But why can I? Why am I key?"

"Because you have that extra muchness, Alice." Rudy's black lips split into a tender smile, his bottomless eyes burrowing into mine with passion. "I felt it the moment I saw you. It's what connects us. You are special."

"All right," Scrooge called over, annoyance lacing his voice. "Can we get back on track here?"

"Yeah, *fawn* all over Alice later." Hare snickered, making Scrooge's eyes roll. "Oh, come on. That was funny." He peered around the table, no one laughing except Dum. "Whatever. You all are a bunch of witless snowholes."

"I thought it was funny." Dum held up his hand.

"You don't count," Hare scoffed. "You think farting in the bathtub is hilarious."

"But it is!"

Scrooge palmed his face with a groan. "Guys."

"Yep, right with you, boss. The queen blah, blah, we all die." Hare leaned back in the chair, kicking up his legs onto the table.

"Why did I come back again?" Scrooge growled, rolling back his shoulders, starring up at the ceiling.

"You love us?" Dee went on her knees, leaning on the table.

"Debatable."

"Hare bakes the best Yule log in all the land?" Pen bounced on the chair.

"Only explanation." Scrooge exhaled, rubbing his head, fatigue weighing him down. What he had gone through was causing his body to break down, and he needed rest from the traumatic events we went through.

"Do you know how to return Santa's soul?" Rudy stood up, ambling over to the box, staring at it as if the man himself would pop out like a jack-in-the-box.

"Yeah, because I do it all the time," Scrooge replied dryly, hovering on the border of irate. "No. I have no idea if he has to open it, or we have to grind it up so he can swallow that shit. I need a fuckin' drink."

"If you find one of those, let me know." Hare crossed his ankles on the table.

"I was just asking." Rudy's voice was level, but he stared Scrooge down, ready to challenge him if he had to.

Scrooge's head lifted, his chest puffing slightly, wordlessly challenging him back.

Shit. "Tomorrow." I stood up, seeing it accelerate quickly.

"What?" Scrooge peered over at me.

"It can wait until tomorrow."

"No, it can't—"

Strolling right up to him, I got in his face. "It. Can. Wait."

He blinked at me.

"Neither of us is going to do any good if we keep pushing. One night's sleep and then we can start planning." I held my chin high. "Don't fight me. I will win. Because you know I'm right. Jessica doesn't know where we are. Not yet. We need sleep. And to be honest, you're being a complete dickhead, and if you don't get some sleep, someone here, *probably me*, is going to put you down."

"Excuse me?" Scrooge's head jerked between us.

"Did I stutter?"

His shoulders rose, indignation building under the muscles like bricks, his chest pushing out until it hit me. "You want to say that again? I couldn't have possibly heard you right."

"You heard me just fine." I knocked into him, not backing down.

"You think you can take me?" He grunted, fervor flamed in his eyes, his jaw rolling, the world around us disappearing.

"It's like you're begging for it," I seethed, stepping even closer.

"Really?" He leaned over me, pressing into my body, triggering a hitch in my lungs.

"Really. Hare, is there a bottle around here?"

"In the kitchen." Hare pointed behind him. "But you promised I get to do it this time."

"That was for Nick."

"Come on, you don't get to hit all the coal bags," Hare pleaded, his hands together. "Let me. Let me. Just a teensy hit."

"You think either one of you could take me down?" Scrooge growled, stepping into me, his threatening form humming with raw energy. Wild. Savage. Sparking against me, flaring my nose with desire.

"Whoa. Whoa." Rudy tried to wiggle between us, pushing me back from Scrooge, snapping me out of the bubble we had been locked in. "Step back, friend."

"Get out of the way, *friend*." Scrooge's burning gaze still hinged on me. "This is between me and her."

"No." Rudy shoved him back a few inches, getting in his face. "This is about *us,* and you know it. It has been since the day she arrived."

"Oh hell, yes." Hare sat up in his chair, his eyes wide with eagerness. "The battle of dicks vs. horns has finally commenced."

"And I have both." Rudy's emotionless tone went against the taunt he shoved in Scrooge's face. "Do as the lady asked and go to bed, or you and I will be taking this outside. And you look nowhere near ready for that."

Scrooge huffed, his eyes blazing with aggression. "You think I will fight you for her?"

Ouch.

"Don't." Rudy's voice went lower than normal. "You aren't fooling anyone here, including yourself. You have been my friend for a long time, but yes, I will challenge you for her if it comes down to it. That is my nature. You need to stop living in the past, punishing yourself. If you want it, fight for it. Because *I will*."

Scrooge's head lifted, his shoulders widening, his jaw rolling. There were a few tense moments before he stepped back. "Do whatever the fuck you want." He snatched a blanket off the sofa and swiftly moved up the stairs to the tiny loft, disappearing behind the railing.

"But that's my room..." Hare trailed off, slumping

back into the chair. "Happy days. The angry, aloof, bitter asshole is back. Didn't he get laid once while you guys were gone?"

I cringed, imagining his time living in the house with Jessica, especially when he first arrived, believing he was supposed to be in love with his wife. Did they ever? Did she trick him into sleeping with her?

My shoulders shook, a shiver running down my spine. I really didn't want to think about it.

"Alice." Rudy turned to me, intention in his advance.

"Tomorrow." Fatigue dropped on me like cement, pushing my bones into the ground. Whatever he wanted to speak with me about, I couldn't handle it. "Not tonight." I reached my hand out for Penguin and the twins.

"Certainly." He dipped his antlers, watching me take the group down the hall to the guest bedroom.

"Wow, Ms. Alice. You are so lucky. Both Rudy and Scrooge fighting for you." Dee's eyes were glazed with dreamy excitement. The twins crawled onto the bed, while Pen made himself comfortable in the little nest of blankets he built for himself in the corner.

"No one is fighting over me," I replied, pulling the covers over them. "I'm not an award to be contested for."

"Oh, I know, but it still must feel nice. They are both so handsome and good."

"Good." I chuckled. Not the word I would use to describe Scrooge at all.

"Plum drops! When *you* challenged him..." Dum's eyes were big with awe. "He did not know what to do. He's never had someone do that."

270

"What do you mean?"

"Belle would never have done that." Dee shook her head. "I mean *never*. She agreed with whatever he said."

"Really? Even when he's being a dick?"

"Especially then." She dug deeper into the pillow, but excitement still glistened in her eyes. "Belle was nothing like you. You're amazing, Ms. Alice. Badass, a warrior princess."

"Call me Xena."

"Who?"

"Never mind." I leaned over, kissing both on the forehead. "Night."

"Night." They sang together as I moved to Pen.

"It's so good having you back, Ms. Alice." Pen's lids drooped. "I didn't mind visiting you in your realm. Though it was chilly there."

"What?" Confusion furrowed my brow. "What are you talking about, Pen?"

"You needed us." He exhaled sleepily, his eyes shutting. "Our bodies may have stayed here, but we're part of you and Mr. Scrooge. Family is there when you need each other the most. Even in our dreams…" he muttered, his voice falling away. A whistle of a snore tooted out of his beak, his body relaxing into his cocoon.

Was he aware of my hallucinations? Was it actually them coming to me? No one else seemed to remember that. Was only Pen conscious of this? Sometimes it felt like Penguin was the wisest one out of all of us. The most aware of things beyond the median, his pure innocence opening him up to see and understand more.

Leaving the room, I dragged myself down the hall, passing the shower I desired. Tomorrow.

Rudy and Hare had cleaned up and were settling down for a winter's nap.

"Please take the sofa." Rudy motioned for me to take the lumpy couch.

"No, thank you. Floor's good."

"Good choice." Hare chuckled, curling into the side chair, kicking his legs over an arm. "You don't want to know where Dum's naked ass has been on there."

"Now I'll never be sitting on it again. Thanks."

"No problem." Hare snapped his fingers with a wink, laying his head on the other arm. "Got your back, girl."

I crawled down on the rug, snagging a blanket and pillow. With Rudy's attention on me from the sofa, I curled on my side away from him. I watched the fire dance and leap, recalling another night I had slept here...another man staring at me from the couch before he joined me. Scrooge's firm physique pressing into me, hot and heavy, tingling every nerve with need.

My eyes flicked to the loft, wishing he was next to me again, craving his weight like a drug. I knew when he got all his memories back, he must have relived the pain all over again. Re-watching his wife and son die, his friends tortured. The pain, grief, agony. All things he thought he deserved.

He was building a wall between us, and I didn't know if I would be able to get through it this time.

Chapter 28

"Hairy roasted marshmallow balls!" I yelled, the drops of water feeling more like knives. Swiftly, I scrubbed at my body and hair, the cheap razor stinging my goose-pimpled flesh. "Fuck-a-nutcracker!"

An ice-cold shower may have woken me up but didn't help my grumpy mood. Once I fell asleep, it seemed only moments before Pen and Dum were bouncing on me, urging me to get up, with giggles and glee. My eyes burned wishing for sleep, my bones aching like they were just catching up on everything I put them through.

Jumping in the shower before the house fully stirred, I half regretted the decision now. No one should torture themselves like this without spiked coffee.

"Alice?" A soft knock rapped on the door as I shut off the water, Rudy's voice slinking through it. "I found you some clothes. There's not much, so I apologize."

My jeans and sweater were ripped, bloody, and still damp and now lay in a lump on the ground where I peeled them off. They had been extremely uncomfortable to sleep in, the jeans chaffing.

Wrapping myself in one of the last towels, knowing laundry would be on the to-do list, I cracked open the door and peered out.

Rudy was a work of art. Michelangelo's *David*. With a defined lean body, deep brown eyes, long nose, dark lips and lashes, and beautiful coloring, he was really pretty. Unique. The only response to him was an awed gasp.

He held out a stack of clothes.

"What the hell are those?" My eyes widened, my head automatically shaking as I lifted a tiny tank and what looked like child-sized cotton shorts.

"Elf clothes," Rudy said matter-of-factly. "It's all that's left."

"I'll wear mine, thank you."

"I saw those garments. They're disgusting." His nose wrinkled. "Did you go through a woodchipper on the way here?"

No, hands and claws of toys and shards of glass.

"Wear these until we wash and dry them at least." Rudy dropped them in my hand. "Hare is about done with breakfast. I hope to see you there." He dipped his head in a small bow, stepping back and walking down the hallway.

A small smile grew over my mouth. He was so majestic, graceful, and proper, but other times you could totally see the wild animal in him.

Placing the clothes on the sink, I stared at the mirrorless wall, recalling the moment in the facility when my brain tried to bring me back here. I thought I was losing my mind when it was only trying to show me the truth. Good thing Nick didn't have any mirrors leading right to his hiding spot, especially now that I had opened the doors allowing Jessica to go through them.

I pulled on the white tank, which hit my midriff, and probably did nothing to cover my curves underneath. Thankfully this time I had a bra. A gruff laugh came out of me as I held up the minuscule green shorts with red-and-green-striped suspenders. Yanking them on, they fit me like boy shorts, the suspender hanging high on my thighs.

"Slutty elf on a shelf," I muttered to myself, tugging at the cloth. Not that I hadn't worn less here, but trying to fit a woman's body into toddler-size clothes was ridiculous. After brushing my hair and teeth, I headed out into the main room, the aroma of delicious food hung in the air, the sound of chatter and movement greeting me. But it was *his* voice, the deep timbre, that purred over my skin.

"I need you to stay here, Hare. Help prepare food, supplies, training. It's up to you and Ms. Liddell. We need to get the word out he's back. Bring them here. We need them to be able to protect themselves against her men. The war is coming."

"And you expect to turn a bunch of sweet-eating, tree-hugging elves into violent warriors?"

"Yes. We have to."

I crept down the corridor, seeing Rudy sitting in a chair. Scrooge and Hare stood at the end of the table, while Dee, Dum, and Pen ran around the table paying them no attention, nor did anyone notice me.

"No. Fuck that! I'm not doing this again. You just got back, and you want to leave us again? How about I go instead? You stay here and babysit for once." Hare plunked down a muffin pan, steam swirling off the baked goods.

"It's better if I go, deal with him, you know...after last time." Scrooge leaned over Hare. "But if I recall, I told you to head there if I was gone longer than four days. *You didn't.* So don't cry wolf now."

"Don't play the fuckin' martyr! And these assholes wouldn't have lived a day without me. He..." Hare motioned to Rudy, who was quietly staying out of their fight. "Was useless until a couple days ago. Dee was weak. And no one else could find a pot to piss in if I left them in charge." Hare climbed on the table getting level with Scrooge, fury bristling his fur. "You might have been fine with leaving us so easily, but this group is my family. *They are all I have left...*"

Scrooge stiffened, his mouth clenching. "You think it was easy for me to leave you?"

"Seemed to be." Hare snarled, his built-up rage and fear lashing out. "You didn't give a shit what your loss would have done to *us*. You gave no thought to our feelings or how we would go on. You're so consumed with your own pain and anger you don't see *us*. That we need you. Depend on you. I'm sorry they died...but we're still here, and we are just as much your family."

Scrooge inhaled through his nose, his chest rising like he had been smacked in the face. "There was no other choice, but I-I never thought—"

"No!" Hare snapped, but his shoulders sunk down, a sorrow creeping into his demeanor, his ears sagging. "You don't think. You want to end it all so bad, you forget to see who is still here. Who loves you. What is worth living for." Hare hopped down on the chair, turning his back on Scrooge.

"Hare." Scrooge's expression twisted with pain. "I'm sor—"

"Don't. I don't want to hear it right now." Hare shook his head, grabbing another pan of cranberry muffins from the oven, his tone back to business. "So tell me while you're jaunting up the mountain, how will I get the word out to the toffee-tots, or get supplies without the queen hearing the rumblings?"

Scrooge shifted on his feet, licking his lips like he was trying to adjust back to the topic after Hare's outburst. Scrooge needed to hear it, to know he mattered, that his actions had consequences and affected those around him. Especially his best friend.

"Be careful?"

"Thanks." Hare glowered at him. "So helpful."

"Where are you going?" Rudy finally spoke, confusion wrinkling his head.

"Well..." A slow malevolent smile curled up on Scrooge's face. "In times like this, your enemy's enemy is your ally."

Rudy blinked, his jaw dropping, his eyes opening wide. "Noooo."

"Yes."

"Blood. Pudding." Hare rubbed at his nose. "You really do have a death wish. Don't you recall both him and that monster tried to eat me last time?"

"Yeah." Scrooge let out a chuckle, his head falling back. "Good times."

"You'd think that." Hare folded his arms as Pen danced around him, trying to reach a muffin.

"Come on, where's your sense of adventure?" Scrooge smirked, picking up Pen and placing him on a chair, setting a muffin in front of him.

"Muffinsmuffinsmuffins!" Dee and Dum jumped up next to him. "Make room! Make room!"

"You really think he'd help us?" Rudy leaned forward, doubt coiling in his voice.

"Hopefully." Scrooge lifted one shoulder. "Only because he wants his title of the most hateful one on the mountain back again." Scrooge glanced around the room, landing on the unopen box. "Did Nick come back?"

"He must have." Hare frowned. "All the cookies are gone and most of the milk. Bastard left crumbs everywhere but slipped out before I could catch him."

"We need to find and deal with him before I go."

"Once again, you're going to leave without saying goodbye?" I stepped into the room.

Scrooge's head jerked to me, his mouth parting as his gaze roamed over my body, taking in my outfit. Heat burned behind his eyes before he looked to the side, setting his jaw firmly with irritation.

"Uh-oh…someone's in trouble," Hare sang under his breath.

"Ms. Alice! Ms. Alice!" Pen and Dee cheered my name before returning to their breakfast.

"Wow." Dum blinked, dropping his muffin, gaping at me. "Holy candy canes! You look so *elfish*."

"Eat your breakfast." Hare smacked Dum across the head, pulling his gaze off me. "Just because Alice is actually dressed like a *tart* doesn't mean you can drool all over her like she's one."

"Nice." I glared at Hare as he winked at me.

"Got your back, girl," he teased, snapping his fingers like he did the night before.

I returned to Scrooge. "Where are you going this time? Will I have to come save your ass again?"

"Somewhere stupid," Hare spoke for him. "But really, what's new?"

Scrooge wouldn't look at me, keeping silent.

"You won't tell me?" I shook my head, folding my arms across my stomach. "Must be bad."

"So bad." Hare snorted, plopping down in the chair. "You'll hate it."

"If you think I'll stop you, then it must be even more nonsensical than your other plans have been." I leaned against the wall, crooking one eyebrow at him.

"Not really," Hare muttered, stuffing a muffin in his mouth. "They're all equally bonkers."

"Something we can agree on." I tipped my head at Hare.

"What I really need right now is for us to find Nick. All our plans fall apart if we can't get Santa back." Scrooge's gaze slid to me through his lashes. "Without him, we have no hope."

Rudy's gaze went back and forth between Scrooge and me. "Since I'm sure you have things to do before your departure, Alice and I can go searching for him."

Rudy stood up from the table, eyeing Scrooge. A twitch moved over Scrooge's cheek. "If that's all right with you, Alice?" Rudy smiled, reaching out for me. "I wanted to speak alone with you anyway."

"Of course." I strolled over to him, seeing Scrooge's

shoulders rock back, a nerve convulsing along his jawline.

"Great." Rudy's smile turned on Scrooge. "It's all settled. I'm sure you need to get organized for your mission." Rudy was so composed, it was hard to tell what he was feeling, but I could swear he was taking great pleasure in needling his friend.

"Great." Scrooge's lips tightened, not moving an inch as Rudy and I pushed past him.

Shoving my feet in my boots and stealing Dee's kid-sized cardigan, Rudy and I stepped out into the dark, shutting the door behind us, Hare's laughter following us down the stairs.

"Alice?" Rudy said my name slowly, knotting my stomach.

"Where is Frosty? Is he not here anymore?" I blurted out, wrapping the sweater around me. It wasn't cold, but I needed a barrier; his intensity squirreled me with nervousness.

"He never returned after you two left," Rudy replied, clearing his throat. "Alice, I actually did want to speak with you alone."

"Oh?" I stomped for the barn on the side. Where else would Nick go? Nothing was around here.

"Yes." He stopped me, twisting me to face him. "Though I can't say I didn't enjoy that."

"What?"

"Provoking him." Rudy smiled. "I can see how he feels about you. But he has not claimed you, and I want to be clear. I am also pursuing you. I have felt the connection between us since the beginning. You cannot deny the bond there."

"No, but…" I bit my lip. I did feel it. The attraction was there, but it wasn't the same, not what I felt for Scrooge.

"I haven't felt this way since Clarice." Rudy dipped his head. "She broke my heart when she left me for Blitzen."

"I'm sorry."

"She preferred fame and attention over the real me. They deserve each other," he stated. "But you—*you* are special."

"Right. All the extra muchness." I laughed, heading for the barn again, an awkward silence rubbing at the air. Needing to alter the course we were on, I asked, "When you were sick you kept saying *you're her*." He also said that to me when he came in my visions.

"Ah." He nodded, strolling with me. "Bit of a hazy time for me."

"What did you mean?"

"There's been a rumor, whispers of a fable, most have brushed off as made up. No substantial details, but the gossip has been around for a long time." He opened the door to the shed, letting me step in first. It was dark and barely the size of a garage, but I doubted we were out here really looking for Santa anyway.

Rudy stepped in after me, pulling on a cord, which lit up the storage barn in a shadowy light. One side had work benches cluttered with tools; otherwise it was stuffed with a broken-down sleigh and clutter.

No Santa.

"The tale has never deviated from the basic story of a girl, full of extra muchness and magic, being the savior of Winterland."

"Savior." I guffawed, nerves skipping over my body as he stepped up to me. "If anything, I've helped destroy it faster. I'm the reason Jessica got out and can obliterate this place for good."

"A hero's story is never a smooth one." Rudolph cupped my face, his skin as soft as fur. His thumb brushed over my bottom lip.

"I'm no hero." I gulped at his nearness, my heart fluttering nervously.

"We don't need a hero. We need you," he whispered, moving in closer, his mouth only inches from mine. "Tell me, Alice, are you ready to be *her*?"

CHAPTER 29

Frozen in place, my answer stuck in my throat as Rudy's mouth hovered over mine.

"Alice." He closed the gap, brushing his lips softly across mine.

"Is this what searching for Nick really means?" A deep voice vibrated from the doorway, jolting me back away from Rudy, my neck snapping to the entrance. Scrooge leaned on the frame, arms folded over the white shirt, his expression aloof, but his eyes brewed like a violent storm. Feral and raw. "Silly me, I never thought to look for him down Alice's throat."

"Of course. Perfect timing." Rudy pinched his mouth together, his hand dropping away as he stepped back, irritation huffing through his nose. "I thought you were leaving, my friend? Don't you need to get going on your journey?"

"You'd like that, huh?" Scrooge replied smoothly, but I could hear the tension, the threat under each syllable. "I can't leave until we find Nick, or have you forgotten?"

"It's more that you *won't*." Rudy twisted to face

him, but still stayed close to me. "And I think we all know it has nothing to do with finding Nick."

Scrooge's gaze leveled on him.

"You had plenty of chances." Rudy's hand took mine, Scrooge's focus dropping to our contact, a barely audible growl thundered from his chest. "But now that I am making my intent clear, now you step up?"

Rudy's statement jarred me, a rage curling in my chest. Turning, slipping out of Rudy's grip, I crossed my arms in a challenge. *Yeah, what the hell was that about?*

"You don't want her, but no one else can either? Can't have it both ways, old friend." Rudy's head went back, his horns skimming the top of my head. "She is far too remarkable to stay on a shelf. Lovers will come out of the woodwork for her. I plan to stake my claim before they do."

"Stake your claim?" I frowned. Yes, he was from another time and realm, another species, but his statement still peeved me.

Scrooge's lips twitched with a glimmer of amusement, but he hadn't moved from his position at the door.

Rudy wagged his head, disappointment and annoyance rattling through his sigh. Then in a blink, he rounded to me, his hands clutching the sides of my head, his mouth coming down on mine. Claiming. A startled wheeze escaped my throat, parting my lips, letting him deepen the kiss.

I couldn't deny the zing up my spine, his soft lips dancing over mine, my body responding to his tender kiss.

As fast as the kiss started, it ended. With a roar, Rudy's frame ripped away from mine, smashing up against the wall. Scrooge strangled his throat, fury blistering off him. The savage man inside fully broke out.

"Don't fucking touch her," Scrooge seethed, getting in his face, his grasp tightening. Rudy grappled for air, struggling against Scrooge's hold.

"Scrooge. Stop." I lurched to them, trying to pull his hand away, but he didn't seem to even notice me, his regard fully on Rudy.

"Don't *ever* touch her again."

"You ready to challenge me?" Rudy lifted his chin.

"*She is mine*. Do you understand me?" He banged him back in the wall, his fingers curling deeper around his throat.

"There he is." Rudy choked out a laugh, his eyes glistening with what looked like triumph. "I was wondering if he existed anymore. Good to see he's not completely in the grave."

"She's mine?" I sputtered, indignation grinding my teeth, shoving at Scrooge's arm with little effect. "Fuck you. I am *not* something to own. You have no say over what or *who* I do."

His eyes snapped to me, his nostrils flaring, his irises set on mine with so much force, my lungs stumbled for oxygen.

"Get. Out." Scrooge rammed Rudy again before dropping his hand away. "Now."

Coughing, Rudy clutched his throat, sucking in deeply, a strange laugh clattering up from his chest. I could feel his stare landing on me, but anger clouded out everything except Scrooge, my fingers curling up in balls, rage straining my breath.

"GET. OUT," Scrooge boomed at Rudy, his attention never leaving me, his chest puffing with ire.

I didn't even notice Rudy exit but heard the door bang closed, leaving us alone, the room suddenly feeling far too small. Scrooge's hypnotic force had always been too much for one world, blistering and tearing at the seams. Dominating the space.

Ruthlessly, his eyes drilled into me, his muscles vibrating with energy, cutting away the air in my lungs. Quiet and still, as if he were hunting his prey, he took a step forward. Fear and desire fluttered against my bones, not knowing if he wanted to end me or fuck me.

A slow smirk ensnared his lip, as if he could read every nuance. "Yeah. I would love nothing more than to take you out. Send you back to earth where you belong." He gained another step. I didn't move, not backing away from his looming figure. "Walk away."

"Then do it." I sneered, my neck crunching back as he loomed over me.

His jaw rolled.

"Do it!" I yelled, ramming my palms into his chest. "Do. Fuckin'. Something." At his silence, I shoved him again, my fury building. "Walk away from me. Go."

With one swift movement, he cuffed my wrists, shoving me back to the wall with a thud, pinning them beside my head, sparking shivers through my blood.

"I. Can't," he growled, his physique flattening against mine, his wrath hissing through his teeth. "I'm revolted. I hate myself…hate *you*." His grip strangled my wrists, only stirring my own resentment.

"Good." I spat at him. "Now get off me."

"Don't you want to know why?"

"Not especially." I tried to wiggle out of his grasp, my knee darting up.

Dodging to the side, my knee clipped his thigh; he tilted his head in warning. "Stop."

"Screw you." I shoved against him, trying to get away. "Remember, you can't tell me what to do. No one owns me but me."

"Really?" He lowered his head, his words sizzling down my neck, pulsing need through me. "How about I fuck you right here? Stake. *My*. Claim."

A thunder of hate and desire cascaded down on me like a waterfall, abducting logical thought from my head, my body betraying me, curving into his.

"That's what I thought." He scraped his teeth up my neck, rumbling in my ear. "Rudy says it and you balk. Deny it all you want, but I can feel how much it turns you on when I do."

"No." I tried to refute him, telling him he was wrong.

"Keep lying." He unclasped one arm, dragging his fingers down my chest, curving around my breast, before trailing down to the tiny shorts, his fingers dragging over me, my breath hitching. "But I can feel how wet you are."

"You only want me because Rudy showed interest." I glared at him; my free hand dropped to my side but didn't stop him. "Don't like when someone plays with your toy?"

"I have no doubt Rudy wants you, but he did that to provoke me. Wake me up," Scrooge seethed, his fingers dipping inside the shorts, finding me bare. "Fuck." He hissed, his fingers slipping deeper.

My mouth parted, my head spinning with his touch, my thighs opening for him. "Oh god."

"I've always wanted to fuck you. That's not the problem." He rubbed faster, his teeth clenching like he was angry at me for that. "I told you I loved my wife. And that was true…" He let go of my other arm, using his free hand to rip the shorts down my legs. "What I left out was what I feel for you. It's not even in the same universe as her."

Fire flamed up my legs, my back arching, moving against his fierce rhythm, my nerves sparking and tightening, my chest heaving with need.

"I abandoned her, Alice. I loved her but was still able to walk away." Animosity was thick in his voice. "Didn't even fight when she needed me the most." He snarled, feral and wild, flames burning in his pupils. "Then you come along…and I almost ripped apart the world to get to you when Jessica took you. Nothing…I mean *nothing*…would have stopped me from finding you. Even the chance at a life with my son. So yeah…" He curled his fingers inside me, blistering dots behind my lids.

"Scrooge." I say his name in a plea, my orgasm just hinting on the horizon.

He pulled his hand away, my body groaning with the need to feel him again, for him to never stop. His eyes on me, he grumbled with possessiveness, heating every fiber in my being. "I want to hate you. Hate myself. She was my wife…but the thought of anything happening to you? If Blitzen had taken you instead?" He gripped my hair into his fist, yanking my head back, his mouth inches from mine. "I would *obliterate everything*."

Seizing my hips, he tossed me on top the front of the sleigh, his hands ripping my shorts the rest of the way off, along with my boots. Spreading my legs, he stepped between them, my thighs clasping his hips as his lips crashed down on mine with a savage hunger.

Anger. Desire. Hate. Need. They all whipped together in a squall, crackling the air and tunneling our passion with frantic need. Biting. Tugging. Nipping. His mouth possessive, consuming me as much as I was him. Fiercely we demanded more as we kissed, needing to be closer.

We had created the perfect storm, thundering passion in the air like electricity, zapping the ground, burning everything in our path.

Pulling away, I ripped his shirt over his head, his torso flexing as he sucked in air before his mouth claimed mine in a bruising force.

My hands tugged at the drawstring, the red pants falling to the floor. *Oh, Christmas Tree...this man should be naked all the time.* I didn't hesitate, my fingers curling around him, moving up and down his shaft. Silky and hot, it pulsed in my grip.

"Alice." Moaning against my mouth, his teeth sank into my bottom lip, his hips jerking forward, his breath growing heavier. Leaning over, my mouth ran down his abs, licking the tip of him. "*Shit*." His knuckles raked through my hair. A groan shook the barn when my mouth wrapped around his dick. Loving the feel, the control I wielded, I took more.

Normally this wasn't my favorite thing to do at all with men, but with him, I didn't feel cheap or degraded. I felt powerful and strong with the way his body reacted, his breath strained, the moans vibrating through him.

"Alice." His fingers tugging on my hair, trailing beautiful pain down my body. "Stop." He pulled me back, his scorching blue eyes met mine, his chest puffing up. Roughly he yanked my tank over my head, unclasping my bra, both dropping to the ground. His hands glided up from my stomach to my breasts, his thumb flicking over a pert nipple. I leaned back on my elbows, my back arching as his tongue wrapped around my breast, nipping and sucking.

My body felt like it was alive with electricity, snapping and sizzling.

"Scrooge." I lifted my hips, brushing against his erection, the feel of him trembling my muscles. We had been this close before and were stopped. Nothing in the world would stop me now. Not even if Jessica walked in.

The bitch could watch.

"Scrooge." My voice was hoarse with need. "I want you deep inside me. Fucking me completely senseless," I twisted words he had once used on me as a taunt.

He leaned back, his eyes savage and brutal. "Be careful what you ask for, Ms. Liddell."

"I didn't ask." I pushed at his torso. "I demanded."

His chest stilled. For a beat the air held its breath. Growling, he pushed my spine back on the sleigh, pinning my arms to the red sled. Fiercely he rolled his hips, dragging himself through me, blistering my flesh, and flaming my nerves. My head dug into the metal, my back curving and lifting for more of him.

"Scrooge!"

He curved over me, his arms on either side of my head, crushing himself harder into me. His tongue wrapped around mine as he inhaled me, the tip of him entering me, my knees digging into his sides. Then he thrust into me, my nails clawing at the chipped paint as he filled me.

I gasped loudly. *Holy bleepin' nutcracker.*

He hissed, brutally clutching my hips as he pulled out and slammed back in, wrenching a moan from my lips. "Fuck!" he bellowed, plunging into me again, forcing a loud cry from my lungs. I didn't seem to have any control over the sounds originating from me. A current ran up my legs, exploding inside me, dotting my vision. "Holy shit. You feel so good." He grunted, pulling my leg up, sinking in deeper.

No words made it out of my mouth. I could only feel. Gasping and clawing, I bucked against him, meeting his intensity with my own, feeling him throbbing inside me, my heart pounding in my ears, losing my breath as he pushed in deeper.

Our frantic rhythm crashed against the wall, ricocheting off the metal, my skin rubbing against the sleigh, sounding even louder.

Nothing I had ever known came close to the feel of him inside me. The utter bliss plucked all lucidity from me, his size feeling like it could split me into a thousand elated pieces, and I only wanted more.

"Harder!" I matched his ferociousness, challenging the violence of his thrusts. "Fuck me."

He snarled moving deeper, picking up speed, creating another cry from me. My body was overloaded with sensations, blistering with heat. I could feel the orgasm coming, my body clenching, wanting everything from him. To reach the crest.

But I never wanted this to end.

As if he could feel it coming too, he pulled out.

"Nooo." I barely got out before he yanked me up, spinning me around, his hand on my spine, flattening me over the workbench, my breasts pressing into the woodchips, only arousing my sensitive nipples.

"I'm not done with you," he rumbled in my ear, seizing my hips. He slammed back inside me, a brash moan hitched in my throat, tears collecting at the corner of my eyes from the pure pleasure.

"Don't stop!" I cried, my fingers wrapping around hooks on the tool wall.

"Liked being fucked where children's toys have been made?" He pressed me down harder, creating more pain and friction across my breasts, my body trembling with the high to feel ever more. "Say it, Alice. You are as dark and twisted as me. Enjoy being on the naughty list, don't you?"

"Yes." I pushed back into him.

"I told you there were a lot of dirty things I wanted to do to you. And this doesn't even skim the surface." One hand moved around to my front around my neck, the other finding my core.

"Ahhh..." I croaked, my back bowing, the orgasm running along the rim, my body greedy and pulsing.

Scrooge hissed, unleashing on me. Punishing. Vicious. Ferocious.

I lost my grip, my muscles freezing as my body took a running dive over the ledge, a cry bursting from my throat.

Like a million twinkle lights busting behind my lids, a volt electrocuted every cell in my body. My body splintered, clamping him like a vise. Waves and pulses bowled through me, trampling me under the bliss. I felt as if I burst into confetti, sprinkling out over the universe.

A deafening roar came from behind me, he drove so deep, my body quaked, flooding me with more ecstasy as he pulsed inside me. Hot and claiming.

His chest sagged into my back, our skin sticky with sweat, both of us gulping for air. Neither of us moved as we came down to the ground.

"That-that was…" I swallowed, my throat dry and raw. "…cranberry sauce."

"My sentiments exactly." His mouth brushed my temple before he pushed off me, sliding out. The instant he was gone, I wanted him back, though I could still feel him, his claim on every bit of my skin.

And I didn't care.

Gripping onto the table, I turned around, my legs wobbly. "Santa's sleigh…"

"Yeah, we fucked on there too." He snorted, stepping back up to me. Clasping my face, he kissed me so deeply I lost all sense of time and space.

"Jesus, if I'd known you would feel like that." His mouth skated over mine, heating my veins again. "Actually, it might have been better if I still didn't know."

"What?" I jerked my head back.

A slow bad-boy grin slid over his mouth. "Because I'm going to be utterly useless…this might become a problem."

"Why?"

He backed me against the table, his frame pressing into mine. "The fact there is a war nipping at our heels, and all I want for Christmas is to be inside you. Incessantly."

"Oh." I stared up at him.

This would be a problem.

Because I felt the same way.

Chapter 30

My frame draped lifelessly across his naked physique on the long seat of the sleigh. His fingers tracked up and down my spine, and the smell of dust, wood, and *us* filled my nose. Fatigue and verve battled in my nerves, rattling my muscles, making me feel I had taken too many espresso shots.

After the first time, it took only five minutes before we had been at it again, this time on top of the workbench. We had been so caught up the first time, we hadn't even mention protection, which I never forgot. Ever. Not in New York. You didn't do anything without safeguarding yourself diligently there.

"Fuck, you feel so good." His hips pumped against mine. "I can't even think when I'm inside you... I may be from a different time, but I'm not unaware of modern protection." He kissed me, tugging on my bottom lip. "We don't have diseases here, but..." He hinted at pulling out.

"I'm on birth control and clean," I breathed, wrapping my legs tighter around him, wanting to feel him deeper inside me. *"Don't stop."*

Merciless, he took my demand until I had turned into liquid, melting all over the table, my cries so loud they even scared me.

Both sedated and limp, he laid us out in the sleigh where we grappled for air, our hearts thumping together. We stayed silent for a few moments, overwhelmed by what had just happened.

"How did you get here?" My hand traced his tattoo. "If you were human. How did you end up in Winterland?"

He took a deep inhale, his chest pushing against mine.

"It was so long ago; it's hard to remember exactly." He rubbed at his scruff with his knuckles. "I didn't have the best childhood, poor and always scrounging for food. My mother worked at a factory in the day and in a pub at night to make ends meet, but that rarely happened. We had multiple gentlemen live-ins in a tiny one-bedroom and struggled every day to even get stew in our bellies." His Adam's apple bobbed. "I worked hard, her constantly instilling in me if I succeeded, I could break away from this life. I threw myself into my studies. My grades and a professor who believed in me were how I got into Oxford. I turned even more ruthless, seeing all the money and power there. I wanted a piece of the pie, and I had to work ten times harder to earn it than the rich boys coming in.

"After my mother died, and I couldn't even afford to bury her, I became ruthless. Greedy for more money, for more success. Turned my back on everyone except those who could help me. Even the girl I was engaged to. Love, friendships, nothing could compete with my ambition. And I used it as an excuse. I couldn't provide for her anyway if I wasn't successful, if I couldn't give her the life she was used to. It was never enough, even when she said she didn't need anything fancy, just me." He huffed. "I would think, *how naive. She has no idea what it's like to be poor. To be hungry.* It's easy for someone who always had a full belly to think love was enough. I knew better…or so I thought."

"Don't tell me you were visited by three ghosts?"

He laughed. "No. All fables take great liberties from the truth. But unlike a lot of characters in Winterland, I'm not from here. I'm human. I was real and existed before the story. I happen to fill the role. Just like at one time St. Nick was real. Lived on earth. Every culture has their version of him. The saint, a make-believe icon, a spirit, a Christmas witch—they are all true. But he is also so much more than what people know. A man who had a wife."

"A bitter one," I replied. "Though there are moments I understand her. He treated her like a second-class citizen. *His* Jessie snapped…"

"He's also a man, who despite all the joy and magic he gives children over the world for centuries, has faults. Being a good husband was not one of those. From the day she was written for him, he treated her as such. A character at his beck and call, not a person with feelings."

"So she's from here." I suddenly understood. "It's why she can't travel through the realms unless she has one of us."

"Exactly." He nodded.

"You said Belle was from here? Was she created for you?"

"Like you, I kind of stumbled into this place. Meant to be or not, my story, my life was here. I met Belle not long after I came here. After a while, my life on earth became a blur. She was so similar to the girl I broke up with on earth, the girl I turned away because at the time her love wasn't enough. I thought I was being given a second chance to right a wrong. Have the life I let slip through my fingers. But..."

"What?" I peered up at him.

"I know the reason neither worked out." His eyes met mine. "Neither one was truly meant for me."

Emotion lodged in my throat, not sure if it was fear, joy, or shock.

"But I don't regret my choices. They led me here, all of it, even the loss of my son." He swallowed. "At least I had a brief time with him."

"Do you want kids again?" Terror danced on my tongue.

"No. At least right now it's not something I can think about. Not for a long time."

Relief escaped my lungs. That was not something I wanted for a long, long time as well.

"Plus." A grin twitched his mouth. "I have those pains in the ass inside that house. They are more than I can handle. Like having four kids."

"Three." I shook my head, grinning. "You and Hare fight too much like a married couple."

"Then this is going to be extremely awkward." He curved into me, already thick and searing against my thigh, his nose brushing into my neck.

"What?"

"Telling my wife about my mistress." His teeth

scraped the sensitive spot behind my ear, spurring heat through my body. "Though I doubt I'll have to tell him anything. Everyone on the mountain could hear you." His palms ran up my legs, stopping at my thighs, rubbing his fingers through me, slipping in. My breath hitched, my body instantly ready again. "And if they didn't, they will now."

"Scrooge…" I gasped, arching into him.

"I told you this was going to be a problem." He slipped in another finger, his mouth moving down my neck to my breast. "You have turned me into a fiend, Ms. Liddell."

"Don't you need to leave soon?" I moved against him. "Some mission?"

He rolled over on me, planting my back on the bench.

"First, I need to make sure I have a proper meal." His tongue flicked at my belly button as he inched down, his blue eyes glinting with mischievousness. "Something that will keep me warm, filled, and energized."

"Hare's cinnamon muffins?" I smirked, my breath growing heavy.

"No, Ms. Liddell." His smile widened, his hands snaking under my ass. "Yours."

He tugged me up, tossing me on the dash of the sleigh, my fingers gripping the console as he spread my legs, his mouth trailing down, kissing and nipping.

Holy tinsel and jingle my bells. My head fell back, my fingers clutching as his tongue found me, taking every bit of sense with him I might have had left.

Elf cookies—he was unbelievable.

The fable was partly wrong. Ebenezer Scrooge was not stingy, but damn he was greedy, consuming me with ravenous need. A slew of curse words hitched up my throat, and I was almost squirming away at the intensity.

"Fuck, Ms. Liddell." He licked deeply, hooking my legs over his shoulders, gripping my ass firmer to him. "Nothing tastes as good as you. You are completely destroying me."

"You?" I choked out, only able to get out one word. He was annihilating me. Setting me and everything around me on fire. Red. As if you could taste, touch, and hear the shade of scarlet. Not the darkness of blood, or the happiness of Christmas, but the color of fire. Deep, violent, consuming.

This time I cried out so loud I knew everyone on Mt. Crumpit could hear me. My fingers dug into the knobs on the dash panel as I detonated. The sleigh jerked with movement as I shattered on top of the holiday symbol. No longer part of any realm or universe.

"This is all I ever want to eat now." He growled, then lifted his head, tipping it to the side with a jolt. "Earthmoving…"

"Yes. It. Was." My bare chest heaved up and down, I was dizzy and felt like the barn was shifting.

"No." He stood. "I mean *literally*."

My head twisted, following his gaze, seeing the floor line come even with us.

Curious.

"What the—?" I bolted up as my mind took in what was happening. The ground level was passing over our heads.

"What did you do?"

"Nothing."

"Did you push something?" He reached over me, stabbing at buttons, none of them stopping the descent of the sleigh. We had been in our own world, not noticing until it was too late to jump out.

"That was *your* fault." A trapdoor in the floor slowly shut the moment we were clear. Darkness crept around us as we lowered deeper in the earth, feeling as if we went at least a full story.

"Is this just some kind of storage room for the sleigh?" The moment the question rose from my mouth, the sled hit the ground, and lights clicked on.

Curiouser.

Blinking, Scrooge and I scanned the small space. We saw nothing except cement walls and high-tech lights glowing in sleek panels over the wall. It felt more like a spaceship than a barn.

A chill skated over my skin, shaking my shoulders. I tugged my long hair over my chest to feel some kind of cover. My clothes were still above, strewn across the ground. The shorts and tank weren't much, but I wished I had them. Naked felt doubly vulnerable when you were already feeling edgy. Where the hell were we?

His hand automatically rubbed at my arms trying to warm them up, poking at the buttons on the dash again, but nothing happened.

"Reindeer balls," he murmured, peering around again. "What the hell is this place?" He stepped out of the sleigh, investigating the small space, my eyes trailing slightly ahead of him.

I shook my head, punching at all the objects on the

dash hoping I could find the switch taking us back up.

Bang!

The sound of metal unlatching echoed like a gunshot, causing me to jump. "Holy tinsel fudge!" My eyes landed on a door in front of us, swinging open, presenting only darkness beyond.

"What did you hit?" Scrooge cautiously moved to the exit.

"I have no idea." I stabbed at the same buttons, but nothing transpired.

He poked his head through the doorway. "This leads to a tunnel."

My feet hit the cool cement floor, and I headed over to him, peering into the passageway. My curiosity taking hold, I started to creep down it.

"Wait." He grabbed for me. I couldn't help but notice his form still holding onto the excitement his body didn't get to release, scuttling tingles over me like a blanket. "Do not look at me that way, Ms. Liddell."

"Like what, *Mr. Hatter*?" I cleared my throat, pointing my face to look up at him innocently.

"Dammit." He hissed and his lips slammed together. "That didn't help. At. All."

"Don't worry, even with clothes you couldn't hide that thing." I bit my lip playfully.

"*Alice*." He gritted his teeth.

I winked and moved away from the door, letting him step up.

"You gonna save me?" I folded my hands to my chest, fluttering my lids dramatically. "Ebenezer Scrooge, you are my only hope."

He glared back at me, having no clue of my silly pun. "Hell no. I'm using you as my human shield." He motioned down. "Got to protect the goods."

"Right." I snorted.

"I don't need to protect you." His eyes burned through me. "If anything, it's the other way around. You have saved my ass more than not. But…" His fingers tugged through the strands around my face, his knuckles gliding down to my stomach. "I told you. If anything happened to you?" he said hoarsely. "I won't be able to live with that. What Jessica is doing will seem tame to what I will do to the world."

Oxygen puckered in my lungs, my response evaporating on my tongue.

He turned back around, moving into the passage, his muscles locking defensively.

The space beyond, where it led, made me once again feel I was about to fall down another rabbit hole.

Chapter 31

There was no question I could take care of myself, but it was also okay to know when someone's weight and size would be a better defense if anything came for us. It didn't make me less strong or independent, it made me smart. And if we were attacked, I would be right by his side, fighting with him.

I also couldn't deny I liked using his warm body as a shield, covering my naked form. Funny how the lack of simple pieces of fabric was the difference between feeling like a newborn and a warrior.

Several steps down the path, lights on the walls similar to the other room flickered on, as if they were set to sense movement, lighting our way.

"There's another door." Scrooge motioned down, his voice low, our figures moving together toward it, my neck constantly twisting behind, making sure we were still alone.

He halted at the metal door, his fingers wrapping around the handle. We had no idea what was behind it, if anything. Could be an empty room, or a secret collection of toy soldiers ready to kill us.

Scrooge inhaled, my heart pounding in my throat as he quietly pulled the knob, the barrier cracking open with a hiss of air. With a whoosh, light and loud metal music poured through the gaps, blasting into my ears.

Scrooge glanced back at me, his brows wrinkling with confusion before he turned back, silently sneaking into the room, my feet right behind him. I flinched at the bright warm light blazing down from the ceiling, guiding us to a landing before more stairs led down.

"Holy. Christmas. Balls." My mouth dropped open, my gaze taking in what my brain had yet to fully register.

The room was huge and went down another story, giving it a large warehouse feel. One wall had a large gourmet kitchen, stocked with all the latest gadgets and appliances which would have Hare weeping at the sight of. A long dining table was placed in the same area. Another wall slightly behind us had three doors along it; two of them were open showing one was a huge bathroom and the other—*oh my frickin' garland*—was a laundry room. We couldn't see the space below us, but the one in front of us was filled with books, games, Xbox, and the largest TV I had ever seen in my life. The screen couldn't be heard over the blasting music, but it was the game *Assassin's Creed*. I knew that because my ex used to play it all the time.

Placed around the TV was a large sectional and a recliner. Dressed in only his robe, Nick sat in a recliner, clicking at his controller, snacks and drinks on the table next to him, oblivious to his guests.

"I'm gonna kill him," I seethed, my hands flexing with anger.

"Not before I do." Scrooge was already heading down the stairs, the music covering up the sound of his descent. It was fitting Nick, the asshole side of Santa, would listen to metal grunge music.

Following Scrooge, my gaze continued to roam. Underneath the stairs and on our right was a bar, pool table, and a few old-school arcade games. Everything you would need to stay entertained and happy for weeks if locked down here. This place was the counterpart of the humble, simple cabin somewhere above us.

"You asshole!" Scrooge rammed his hands into the recliner, tossing Nick forward, screaming over the shrill music. "This is where you've been hiding when you disappear?"

Nick curved, staring up at Scrooge, his nose wrinkling up. "Oh terrific. You found me." He flopped back in the chair, returning to his game.

"Are. You. Kidding. Me?" Fury flashed in Scrooge's eyes, his demeanor shifting, the crazed beast sliding under his skin.

"Whoa!" I jumped in front of Scrooge, my hands up. "Calm down."

"Yeah, listen to the tart. The very naked tart." Nick waved us off, going back to his game. "Get out or get a drink and relax."

My attention zeroed in on the bottle next to him, half full of brown liquid. "Is-is that what I think it is?" I sucked in, pointing at the container.

Nick glanced quickly over at it, shrugging. "Yeah." He returned to killing people on screen. "I have a whole wall of it."

As if I was set in slow motion, my head swiveled to the wall behind the pool table. The bar was stocked full of different liquors, but several of the shelves were filled with the unlabeled mead bottles.

Red.

This time it was the color of blood.

His.

"You-fuckin'-black-souled-ball-licker!" I darted for him, foaming with rage.

"Whoa, whoa, Ms. Liddell." This time Scrooge leaped for me, arm looping around my middle, hauling me back from attacking him.

"Let go!" I thrashed against him. "You have no idea what Hare and I went through. And here he was slipping away to this place. The grief he put us through." I clawed for the man lounging in the chair. "You selfish, greedy, egotistical jackass!"

"Hey, little gremlin," Scrooge muttered into my ear. "Breathe."

I glowered at Nick, he regarded me like I was a wild animal.

"Is that a full functioning laundry room in there?" I pointed behind me.

"Shit." Scrooge groaned as Nick swallowed nervously.

"And does the shower have hot water?"

Nick shifted in the seat, inching away from me, his throat bobbing. "Yeah."

"Oh, fuck." Scrooge sighed, pulling me firmer against him.

Blood vessels popped across my vision as a crazed scream devoured the raging music, my figure trying to wrestle out of Scrooge's grip, my hands dying to wrap around Nick's throat. Throttle him until he understood my rage.

This whole time, while Hare and I suffered upstairs trying to get through the day, scrubbing his clothes, making his dinner, listening to him endlessly bitch and whine, he had all the mead, food, and laundry facilities anyone could dream of down here. How kind it would have been to share this place.

"Ahhh! You sagging-balled cream puff!" I reached out trying to gain ground against Scrooge's hold. "You made our lives hell. Watched me scrub your clothes by hand. Never once thanked Hare for the delicious meals he made you."

"If I had let you down here, you would have eaten and drunk everything. Would have wanted to play with *my* things." Nick stood, his robe wide open, his beard—full of crumbles—dangled down his front.

"Your things." I blinked, still shocked to see "Santa Claus" be so unbelievably selfish. No matter if his soul was splintered or not. Nick was a douchebag. And I wanted to kill him. "You bastard!"

"Alice," Scrooge hissed in my ear. "Stop. Your naked ass rubbing against me is not helping at all. We're gonna have a very white Christmas soon."

His innuendo, purposefully or not, deflated the anger a bit. Falling back into him, a crazed laugh bubbled up, my hands rubbing my face.

"Can you turn that shit off?" Scrooge's hands pulled more of my hair in front of me, covering my breasts from view, his erection pushing into my back. "And stop looking at her like that."

My head darted up to see Nick's gaze run down me, then to Scrooge.

"Glad you guys finally decided to loosen up." He picked up a remote, hitting a button, silence lowering my shoulders with relief. "Free yourself of labels and restrictions." He tossed it back on the table. "Looks as if you two were having some fun finally." His gaze went over us again, his tone still gruff. "I have some mistletoe we could smoke, let things go where they may."

"Gross." I scowled, squinting back toward the laundry area. "Are there clothes back there?"

"Who the fuck knows? What do I need them for?"

"Don't move." Scrooge pointed at Nick, steering us back for the bathroom.

"You're in my place. I'm not going anywhere," Nick huffed, folding his arms.

"I can't believe this," I muttered over and over as Scrooge and I went into the bathroom, hoping to find at least a towel. "This whole time."

The huge bathroom stopped me in my tracks. Beautiful natural stone, wood, and glass made it look like it should be in one of those million-dollar log cabins you see on TV.

"Holy shit." My mouth parted seeing the stacks of fluffy towels and products: lotion, shampoo, conditioner, and soaps. None of the cheap crap in the cabin, but the really expensive shit.

Over the counter hung an oval mirror.

A door for him to travel through any time he wanted.

"Son of a bitch." Scrooge shook his head at the mirror, understanding what it meant as well. He grabbed a towel for me as he wrapped one around himself. "He even has a towel warmer in here."

Grumbling, I went farther, loving the softness of the cloth wrapped around my body, spotting a door at the far end. Opening it, I flicked a switch on the wall, a hiss of swear words sprung from my lips like Christmas lights.

A bedroom with a walk-in closet. It wasn't massive, but enough for a huge sleigh framed king size bed, nightstands, a bench at the end of the bed, and a large chair in the corner. A closed door on the wall shared with the main room, let me know this had to be where that third door had led.

Scrooge went forward, entering the walk-in closet, a bitter laugh escaping him when he flicked on the light.

"What?" I trailed after him, stepping in.

The closet was as big as the guest bedroom in the cabin upstairs, chock full of Santa Claus suits. Red with white trim, coats, pants, hats, black polished boots, belts with shiny buckles. It was here waiting for the man to return. Only a small section had more comfortable clothes. Dozens of extra-large-sized sweats with hoodies and white sneakers for Santa's "downtime."

"Perfect." Scrooge strode over, grabbing a pair of gray sweats. "Probably be huge on you, but better than nothing." He chucked a pair at me, already tugging on his.

Scrooge was taller than Nick but firm in all the places Nick wasn't. The pants hung on his hips, threatening to fall down, his V-line on full display.

I licked my lips, ambling closer, my fingers brushing his hipbone, causing a deep growl from him.

"You better stop right there," he warned. "Because I won't."

"That's not encouraging me to stop."

"Feel the same if Nick came in and joined?"

"Ugh." I dropped away with a grimace. "You might have destroyed sex for me for good."

"I hope not, Ms. Liddell." He leaned into my ear, his breath grazing my neck. "There are so many more naughty things I want to do with you."

"Tease." I tugged on the pair of sweats, yanking the drawstring until the waistband looked like ruffles, rolling it over and tightening it again.

"Tease? Funny, I think it was *you* coming on my tongue, not me."

His words were instant fire racing through my veins. Biting down on my lip, trying to ignore the desire pumping through me. I pulled on the hoodie, which almost went to my knees.

"Great. Now I look like a Stay Puft marshmallow." I flopped my arms to my side. I loved being comfy, but in Nick's stuff I felt I was drowning in fabric, actually making it harder to move.

"Adorable." Scrooge snickered, wrenching on his own hoodie. He moved to me, his hands sliding up the sweatshirt, his palms skimming my waist as he settled in closer to me, his legs widening to be more at my level. "Though I *loved* those nonexistent shorts and tight tank, this bulky, oversized monstrosity makes me want to fuck you right up against the Santa suits." He breathed against my lips, grazing them enough to send tingles over my skin.

"This really *is* going to be a problem," I uttered, yearning puffing my chest.

"Yeah." He nipped softly at my bottom lip. "It really is."

"What the fuck is taking you two so long? Don't be screwing in my bed." Nick's voice called from the bedroom door. "Yeah, I could hear you all the way down here earlier. And this place is soundproofed."

"Asshole."

"You are the one who stopped me from killing him." I stepped back, Scrooge's hands still on my waist.

"Yeah, and already regretting that choice."

CHAPTER 32

We moved back into the main area, clustering around the table, Nick scowling at us from his seat.

"So…you found my hideout." He reclined, crossing his ankle over his knee. Thankfully the table and his beard covered him.

Santa would never be the same in my eyes again.

"What is this place exactly?" I motioned around, resting back against the counter. It reminded me of those bunkers people built for the end of the world.

"I have a place to hide if Blitzen and the soldiers ever found me. Comfortable to hole up in until they moved on. Up there it would look like a vacant cabin that I had already abandoned."

"Doesn't the cabin move around?" I looked at him and Scrooge, remembering him telling me something like that.

"Yeah." His lip curled. "Used to. But it takes a lot of magic. I don't seem to have much of it lately."

"Because the magic comes from Santa." Scrooge stood near me by the table, his arms folded. "Not from a selfish asshole such as you."

"Bugger off." Nick sneered, shifting his naked butt over the seat.

"Nick." Palms on the table, Scrooge loomed over him. "It's no coincidence since we've returned, you've been hiding. You know what we brought back."

Nick moved in his seat again, not looking at Scrooge.

"It's time. We need Santa back. We need people to have something to believe in again...to fight for."

"Do it without me," Nick huffed, motioning to Scrooge. "They can believe in you. You seem to have taken on the role. Why don't you become their hero? From what I heard, she'd fully agree with me." He popped his chin in my direction.

"Because I'm not Santa Claus," Scrooge growled. "*You* are the infamous icon. The symbol people need."

"Well, it's about time they start learning to live with disappointment. And live without me. I mean, they should damn well grow up. Stop believing in a man who knows intimate things about your children, breaks into your home, eats your food, and leaves you a crappy toy in recompense."

"Shit. You really are the dark side of him." I shook my head in disbelief.

"Sweetheart, the things I've seen would turn anyone's blood cold." Nick's voice was full of condescension, wrapping rage around my spine. If Jessica had gotten any of this side, I could see why she might have flipped. "Now why don't you go back to earth and play with your Barbies. Stay out of our business here."

A roar shook through the room, bouncing off the

walls and ceiling. I jumped as Scrooge grabbed Nick's throat, knocking his chair over and slamming him back against the cabinets.

"*Don't ever* talk to her that way again, you spineless piece of shit," Scrooge snarled, his muscles rolling and tight as the beast inside tore through. Rage pinwheeled off him, sparking the air. "You are going to come upstairs with us and face yourself. Find a heart through that deplorable rubbish you call a soul. Be the man they still believe you to be."

"That's their problem, not mine." Nick's spat through Scrooge's hold. "I didn't ask for them to worship me. They did it on their own."

Wrath boomed through the room as Scrooge slammed Nick's head back against the cupboard, violent tension strung like rope, weaving around us.

"Can you stop being a greedy, self-centered, narcissistic asshole for one moment? Do something for others for a change."

"For a change!" Nick sputtered out a dry laugh. "That's all I've ever done. I give, give, give…and they just want more. I'm not the selfish, avaricious one, Earth is a *cesspool* of greed. *I'm done.*" Nick leaned into his face, spit coming through his teeth. "I *gave* enough."

"You think *you* gave enough?" Scrooge snapped back, his expression streaked with fire and rage. "Don't act as if you were the only one who lost everything they loved and held dear." He rammed Nick harder into the sideboard, grief slicing over Scrooge's brow. "So many have lost. Friends. Family. Homes. Freedom. But they are still out there ready to fight for you, in your name, what you represent. They lost everything, were tortured, and are in hiding, but still they believe. Have hope." Scrooge's face was only an inch from Nick's. "While you hide and wallow in your greasy bitterness, they are trying to rise against her." Scrooge's throat bobbed, something in his demeanor shifting, his voice going low. "Don't let the memory of those we lost be in vain."

Nick's throat bobbed, his head snapping to the side. He stayed quiet for several beats before he muttered. "I can't. I can't go through it all again. I won't."

"You will."

"You don't understand. I *don't* want to be him. To let him back in and feel all that pain again. There was a reason my soul split off. I like feeling nothing. I can live this way. And I want to be the darker version of me." Nick's conviction rolled his jaw as he stared back at Scrooge.

"Your darker side doesn't even come close to *my* good side." Detached, Scrooge's words sounded like a threat. "You want to see dark? I can show you. Believe me, you will be screaming in terror to get out."

Nick stared at Scrooge, his Adam's apple moved up and down.

"Now. We are going to go back to the cabin where you will open the box and become the man who used to believe in this place. A leader." Every word sounded between an order and talking to a toddler. "Because a war is coming. Jessica is not going to quit until you're dead. Time to get your head out of the snow and face your wife. Take back what was yours once."

Scrooge nudged him one more time into the cabinets, reinforcing what he said was not a choice, before stepping back, his regard shifting over to me. The heat and intensity of his gaze buzzed my skin like caffeine. Damn, he was so effin' hot.

"Ready?" He lifted an eyebrow at me, his eyes devouring me.

"Ye-yeah." I tugged on the hoodie, the room feeling like a sauna under his scrutiny.

Scrooge whirled around, grabbing Nick, dragging him along to the stairs. I was about to follow when my attention landed on something else. Their feet clanged on the metal steps as I walked past them, heading for my destination.

"Hold on!"

"What are you doing?" Scrooge leaned over, peering down at me.

I went to the back wall, noticing boxes of Milky Ways, Butterfingers, and Hershey Kisses stacked on the other end of the shelf. I'd be back for those later. I had priorities. My fingers wrapped around the necks of the containers, cradling them into my chest.

"Provisions." I winked up at him, prancing up the steps with four bottles of mead.

"Damn." He shook his head. "I'm so lovin' you right now."

"Show me your gratitude later." I caught up with them at the landing.

Scrooge looked over his shoulder at me, his eyes skating up my body like fingers. "Count on it."

"No, not my mead," Nick whined, stomping his foot like a petulant child.

"Be thankful I can only carry four bottles right now," I replied, wiggling my eyebrows impishly. "And I'm coming back for that box of Milky Ways later. Wait until Hare learns about this place."

Nick moaned, his head dropping forward.

"Just consider this compensation for babysitting you. I think I earned this at least." I indicated a container full of yummy sweetness.

"You knocked me out with a bottle one night," Nick cried out. "Don't think I've forgotten that."

"You what?" A laugh burst from Scrooge. "Is that what you and Hare were talking about the other night?"

"She hit me!" Nick exclaimed. "What kind of person hits Santa?"

"Anyone who knows you," Scrooge quipped.

"No one wants to hit *Santa*." Nick frowned.

"Actually, I've been dreaming about doing it for years. I'm kind of jealous."

"Get in line with Hare," I replied.

Nick huffed, wagging his finger at me. "You will never be off the naughty list, missy. Ever."

"I'll live with the shame." I bumped his shoulder and stepped into the hall, the lights flickering on.

"Welcome to the permanent naughty list," Scrooge muttered against the back of my neck. "We have a lot more fun here."

"As long as it's your lap I get to sit on, asking to fill my stocking."

An animalistic noise rumbled from behind, making me smile.

Oh yeah, we were going to be a problem.

"Switch. Switch." Dum's voice, followed by Dee's laugh, met us before we even opened the door. "Make room."

"For the love of holly trimmings," Hare boomed as we opened the door, stepping into the scene.

"You know what?" Nick grumbled, shaking his head in annoyance. "If getting my soul back means being able to tolerate this shit, I'm all in. Just put me out of my misery."

"Oh. My." I pinched my lips together, trying not to laugh.

As if I stepped back to when I first met them, Dee and Dum darted around the table, jumping in and out of chairs, giggling and knocking into each other. Penguin danced up and down on the table, kicking at anything in his path, singing "Have Yourself a Merry un-Christmas." Hare was banging his head on the table like he was hoping to knock himself out. Rudolph was nowhere in sight.

"Ms. Alice!" Penguin tossed up his flippers, chirping with excitement. "We're having an un-Christmas party."

"Isn't that pretty much every day?" Scrooge said.

"But today is a *very* merry un-Christmas," Penguin twittered. "Did you bring a present this time, Ms. Alice?"

Grinning, I moved to the table, setting the bottles down right in front of Hare. "I did."

Hare's head jerked up, his gaze traveling up the bottle.

"Please don't tell me I'm dreaming. Or don't wake me." His lids shut and opened wider. "Am I dead? Those little psycho-toe-furky dinners finally gave me a stroke." He reached out and touched the jug like it would disappear, whispering softly. "I'm in a much better place. Hello, sweet thing...."

"Just wait until I show you the gourmet kitchen he's been hiding."

"Hiding?"

I popped off the top, handing the bottle to Hare. "You're gonna need to down this before you learn the rest."

Hare didn't have to be told twice; he slugged down gulps of the mead.

"Get over there." Scrooge shoved Nick forward to the leather chair, not letting go of him. "Sit."

Nick grumbled and sneered but did what he was told.

"Oh. Looks like you found his hideout." Rudolph stepped into the room, pointing at the mead.

My spine went rigid as I stared at the deer-man.

"You. Knew?" My voice was low, my nails digging into my palms.

"Yeah." Rudy nodded, snorting through his nose. "Who do you think keeps him in supplies? You think he would?"

"This whole time, you knew where he was. What was down there?" It wasn't a question but an accusation, my voice rising. "And you didn't tell us?"

"I promised Santa I would keep it secret so no one could give away his location. Tortured or threatened, they had no true whereabouts of him."

"See?" Nick pointed at Rudy. "That's what loyalty looks like. A true friend of Santa's."

"Oh, shut up." Scrooge and I shouted at the same time.

"So that little charade earlier?" I wrapped my arms at my chest.

"I technically lead you to him." Rudy shrugged. "He was right there. Under your nose. And you found him."

Scrooge scoffed, shaking his head, and returned his attention to Nick, setting the perfectly wrapped gift on his lap. Nick leaned way back in the chair, trying to be the farthest he could away from it.

"Open it."

"Wh-what if we wait?" Nick knotted his hands on the arms of the chair. "I mean what's a little more time? I'm probably a better fighter without a soul."

The entire room burst into laughter.

"You're also lazy, selfish, and venal. You would run at the first sign of a fight to save yourself." Scrooge tapped on the bow. "Now open."

Nick's mouth scrunched up, and he glowered at the room. He acted irritated, but I saw his fingers shaking as they tugged at the bow. He was scared. None of us knew what would happen when he opened it. Would it be painful? Flooded with memories and trauma Nick was able to keep to the side? Whatever he went through was so bad, even with a split soul, his pain and torment still came out in nightmares.

Glacially slow, Nick pulled the ribbon loose, shifting in his chair and breathing heavily.

Hare hopped next to me as we all watched Nick with a silent apprehension, all hanging on the edge of a cliff.

"Oh, for fuck sake, just rip the band-aid." Hare moved to Nick quicker than I thought he could, grabbing the box lid and ripping it off.

A distressed cry came from Nick, who slammed back in the chair with panicked eyes. Santa's soul floated out of the box, and like the ones I saw in the Land of the Lost Souls, it twinkled with a warm light. It pulsated, glowing brighter than the North Star. My hand went to my eyes, shielding them from the brilliance.

"No! No! I don't want it!" Nick cried out, his head waggling back and forth, his eyes and mouth wide in fear. The soul glittered and dashed forward, darting into his open mouth, glowing as it moved down his throat, disappearing into the darkness.

Nick's eyes whizzed around the room nervously, as if he were waiting for something. Slowly his body relaxed as more seconds ticked by.

"Nothing happened. I feel like me." A smile grew on his face. "Ha, ha, asswipes! Santa's 'goodness' is lost for good. Can't compete with the dark side." His hand went to his belly, rubbing it. "Actually, I feel good. All warm and toasty insi—"

His form jerked, horror rounding his eyes as light blasted from deep under his skin, a chilling scream tearing from his gut. His hand went to his head, clawing and wailing. Like a dying fish, his body flopped and jerked, sliding off the chair, crumpling onto the floor.

"Make it stop! Make it stop!" he bellowed, writhing on the ground. His gut-wrenching pleas fired chills over my skin, my chest knotting up. "No! Please." Nick thrashed on the floor, tears spilling down his face, his expression twisted in agony. "Stop. Please, stop!"

"Santa," Dee cried out trying to get to him. Scrooge grabbed her, pulling her back into him.

A long agonizing wail tore through the room, piercing the air in my lungs. Then he froze, the cry shutting off like a faucet, his body sagged onto the wood.

Silence.

"Santa?" Dee whispered, Scrooge's arm still wrapped around her.

A heartbreaking sob came from Nick, his huge frame quivering as if his entire heart and soul were broken, as if every memory and feeling had been returned to the owner to experience all over again. Another excruciating sob whimpered from him before he went still.

Silent.

Only the sound of the fire crackling and our tense breaths hummed in the air.

"Santa?" Scrooge finally spoke, moving around Dee as he inched closer. "Hey." Scrooge nudged his arm with his boot. "You okay?"

"Do I fucking look okay, asshole?" Nick spat, his head jerking up, his nose flaring with hate.

"Nick?" Scrooge peered back at us, confusion riding his brow. "Where's Santa?"

Nick sat up, his face angry, streaked with tears and red blotches. "The gallant, bleeding heart is sniveling like a little girl in here."

"Hey," both Dee and I responded.

"What a great fucking hero you have." Nick scanned the room. "The man you put all your belief in is curled up in a ball. Can't take it. *Oh, my friends. Jessica cut off their heads. Oh, I can't handle it.*" Nick mocked in a whimpering voice. "Pussy."

Scrooge's shoulders lifted, his chest puffing out in anger.

"*Oh Jessie, how could you? How could you hurt them? Oh, my elves. My family. They're all dead,*" he parodied, raising his pitch in a woeful voice.

"Shut up," Scrooge growled.

"*No, stop, Jessie.*" Nick rolled his eyes. "Fuckin' pathetic."

Crack!

The bottle in Hare's hand whacked across Nick's temple, jolting his body to the side, his chest smacking down onto the floor again, knocking him out instantly.

"Baked biscuits, that was...*amazing!*" Hare looked over at me. "Am I right? I feel so much better."

"Dammit." Scrooge placed his hands on his hips. "I should have done that."

"Ha! Too late," Hare cheered. "I thought of it first."

"Next time, it's me." Scrooge pointed at himself.

"Not unless I do it." I winked. "I am the trailblazer."

"There is something seriously wrong with all of you." Rudy stomped by us, squatting down next to Nick. He tapped his cheek softly. "Hey, wake up."

"Want me to do that?" Hare asked, wiggling his ears.

"No." Rudy narrowed his eyes at the rabbit, patting at Nick's face again.

Nick snorted awake, his lids blinking as he came back to himself. Glancing around, his head finally lifted to us. Innocence rounded his cheeks and eyes as he looked around at each one of us, then down to himself.

"Oh my!" Nick's voice came out, but it sounded smooth around the edges and calm. He used his beard to make sure he was completely covered, his cheeks reddening. "I am not decent for mixed company."

"Santa?" Dee's voice trembled, her tiny little feet pushing away from Scrooge as if she were in a trance. "Santa, is that you?"

His glistening blue eyes went to her, blinking with emotion.

"Oh, my dear Dee Puck." He gripped his heart, then leaned forward, holding out his arms. "How I've missed you."

"Santa!" She ran into him, jumping into his arms, happy sobs muffled by his beard. He shut his eyes, sighing deeply into her hug.

Joy filled the room as two lost friends were finally reunited.

Best friends.

Chapter 33

Dum and Penguin joined in on the hug, leaping and squealing for Santa's attention. The happiness and love in the room were palpable with pure innocence.

Santa dominated the space with his magic, turning me into a little girl lost in adoration. The power he exuded was tangible, sparking joy and warmth down my spine. I couldn't fight the emotion behind my lids, a smile expanding over my face at their giddiness and the genuine affection they all felt for each other.

Eventually they eased back, letting Santa rise.

"Rudy, my dear friend." Santa reached his hand out to him, shaking it, then smoothing down his long beard. "Would you be so kind as to grab me something to wear. I feel quite exposed."

"Certainly." A smile drifted over Rudolph's face. "It is so good to have you back."

Santa blinked, nodding, a sadness lowering his shoulders.

"It is good to be back..." There was a *but* he left off, but everyone here understood. "There is so much to do."

As Rudy left the room, doing Santa's bidding, the white-haired man turned to Scrooge.

"At one time you and I never saw eye to eye." He took Scrooge's hand, his white bushy eyebrows crinkling. "What you have done for me?" A lump hitched in his throat. "There are no words for your gallant, selfless act, my dear Scrooge. You have been a true friend to me, a leader to Winterland, and a father to these beautiful souls." He nodded down at the three dancing around him. "You could even say your acts would put you on the good lis—"

"Don't say it." Scrooge shook his head. "Don't even think it."

Santa's smile curled higher, his glinting eyes sliding to me for a second.

"I promise I will keep it between us." He squeezed his hand, letting it go and turning to me.

"Alice." He stood before me.

"You know who I am?" I might as well have turned into a five-year-old, my eyes wide with awe. The aura coming off Santa Claus was ten times stronger than what Nick carried. Staring into the same face, he looked completely different to me, like the jolly-happy man the songs sang about.

I wasn't just standing in front of an icon, but a worldwide legend, fairytale, myth, and idol.

"You are *her*." He bowed his head in acknowledgment. "The Spirit of Christmas Future."

"Wha-what?" I blinked, my mouth dropping open.

"You have shown you are worthy of the lore, my dear girl. Strength, courage, loyalty, and determination. You are exactly what we need to change what is yet to come." He smiled down at me. "And when I say spirit, I mean character. You are a force, Alice. You have set all of this in motion. I thank you for waking us up."

"You-you're welcome." I stuttered under his overwhelming personality and praise.

"Hare…" Santa faced the rabbit.

"Yeeeaaahhh…let's not do this." Hare gestured between them. "Blah, blah, I'm awesome…I know."

"Of course, if that's what you wish."

"What I wish for…" He bounded back for the table. "…is another drink of mead."

For a brief moment, I saw Santa's eye twitch, his jaw setting, before it was gone, the jolly man back in place, smiling at Hare. It was so fast I wasn't sure I witnessed it.

"Santa?" Rudy came back into the room, holding out a pair of red pants and a white shirt.

"Thank you." He clutched the fabric to his chest. "I will be right back. Make myself presentable." Santa headed down the hallway, Pen, Dee, and Dum following him all the way to the bathroom door, not wanting him out of their sight.

At the table, I glanced back at Scrooge. He stood in the same place an odd expression on his face.

"What's wrong?"

He jerked at my words, his hand running through his thick hair.

"Nothing." He strolled up next to me, his hand sliding down my lower back to my ass.

"Try again."

"No, it's nothing. Just me being paranoid." The hand

on my ass slipped around, grabbing the bottle in my hand, swiping it from my grip.

"Hey!"

"Need to be careful." His eyebrow cocked up, mischief written over his lips as he took a slug. "I've heard I can be a real greedy bastard. Endless appetite."

Prickles of desire flamed up the back of my legs, traveling all the way to my cheeks.

"Ugh." Hare downed a huge gulp, falling into the chair, his lips smacking. "You guys are going to be intolerable now, aren't you?"

"Extremely." Scrooge took another drink, groaning with happiness under his breath at the taste of mead before handing it back to me. "But you get a reprieve for at least a day. Now that Santa is back, I need to head off."

"I'm going." I looked up at him.

"No, you're not." His brow wrinkled, his blue eyes lowering. "We already discussed this."

"No. *You* discussed it, and I vetoed your plan."

"You vetoed my plan?" He seemed bewildered by my claim. "That's not how it works. This isn't a democracy."

"Well, it is now, and I voted, I'm going with you."

"Ms. Liddell…"

"Ms. Liddell me all you want. *I'm. Going.*" I put my hands on my hips. "No point in trying to stop me. Think we both know how well that went for you before."

"Alice."

"You're so adorable when you think you have a say in this." I patted his cheek.

He rumbled dragging his hand over his face. "Fine. But you stay close. Listen to everything I say."

"Oh. So caveman of you."

He glared at me, only widening my smile.

"Whoa. Whoa!" Hare waved his arms, almost falling out of the seat. "If she goes, I go."

"No. No-no-no-no." Scrooge shook his head. "We talked about this. You need to stay here, and…"

"If you say watch these fiends and bake, I will knock *you* in the head with a bottle." Wobbling with drink, Hare stood on his seat. Teetering to one side. "Why don't you stay back and be the nanny this time. I'm tired of being unappreciated, ignored, and treated like a slave."

"Welcome to parenthood," Scrooge smirked.

"Do you see me with a bunch of bunnies bouncing around me?" He waved around him. "No! I wrap that shit up so I won't. I was supposed to be your partner…not your maid."

"You're right." Scrooge nudged me with his elbow. "He *is* my fucking wife. Nag, nag, nag."

"Gah!" Anger rolled Hare's chin, grunting noises coming from his throat, too furious to form words. "Gahhh!"

"Hare, you can come with us," I declared.

"What?" Both said at the same time and stared at me.

"Listen, you did leave," I said to Scrooge. "Hare and I became a team. We got through because of each other. So yeah, I have his back. If he wants to come, he's coming."

Scrooge blinked at me as a wicked smile stretched over Hare's mouth.

"Sorry, fucknutter. She and I are a *team*. Guess you'll just have to deal."

"No," Scrooge blurted out. "Who will watch them? As you've seen, Dum and Pen can't take care of themselves."

"You have the perfect babysitter now. Who better than Santa?" Hare pointed down the hall, where the group huddled around the door waiting for the man himself to reappear.

"Yeah..." Scrooge rubbed his chin, glancing down the hall, with the same odd look I had seen earlier.

"Rudy is here, and also Dee has the run entire elf workshop." Hare tossed up his arms. "They are in *better* hands."

"Dee is the only one I trust out of those." Scrooge took a deep, defeated breath.

Hare and I grinned, knowing we won.

"Shit." He scoured at his face, dropping his head forward. "My wife now has teamed up with my girlfriend."

🎩 🎩 🎩 🎩

Not everyone was thrilled with us leaving again, but as soon as Scrooge asked Dee to be in charge, to keep the place running like her workshop, her character completely shifted, turning serious, her warrior, no-nonsense attitude kicking in.

"I will not disappoint you." She got a piece of paper and started making a list, using a book as a clipboard, she started issuing everyone their duties.

"I hate you." Dum stuck his tongue out at us. "She's ruthless when she gets this way."

"Shush, Dum-puck." Even her voice commanded attention. "If you have time to complain, you have time to clean." She clicked her fingers, motioning him to the pick up the stuff in the living room.

Santa had decided to take a nap claiming a headache and exhaustion from the trauma his mind and body went through. Rudy glowered from the sofa, not happy with being left behind. Pen was asleep, his head on his thigh, while Dum pretended to clean up.

"Where was this person earlier?" I gaped at her. When I left, she was still unconscious, but she had been part of the mess when I returned, not at all the one laying down the law.

"You never asked." She shrugged, causing Hare's mouth to drop open.

"S-s-seriously?" he sputtered. "I asked you to clean up all the time."

"You ordered and screamed at us." She twisted back and forth, letting the long t-shirt she still wore of Nick's swish around her ankles. "You never asked me to take charge."

Hare's mouth opened, then shut, and opened again, his lids blinking at an unnatural rate.

"You all acted like gremlins." He spoke slowly, fury stressing each word. "Making my life hell...because I didn't *ask* you to manage the rest?"

"Elves are all or nothing." Scrooge tried to hold back a grin, winking down at Dee. "And you have to know how to ask them. It takes a certain finesse."

Dee's rosy cheeks bled into her entire face, her head lowering bashfully.

"Yeah." Hare snorted, pulling on a backpack full of snacks and kitchen knives. "I think I can see finesse comes with ripped abs."

"Let's go." Scrooge squeezed Dee's shoulder, strolling to the table holding more kitchen knives. He stuffed one in his boot and another one in his waist band. "Should only be a half-day trek to the top."

"That's where we're going? To the top?" I rechecked the ice pick I had in my boot, adding a knife to a slit I put in the pair of sweats at my hip. I had changed back into the tight tank, letting my arms move freely again. In an attack, the sweatshirt would just tangle me up and give the enemy something easy to grab onto.

"Yeah." Scrooge's gaze met Hare's, sharing something.

"What?" I responded, realizing I hadn't asked many questions about what we were doing or where we were going. "What am I missing? What are we doing?"

"Sometimes knowing just makes the knowing long for the unknowing."

"Ugh. We're gonna start that shit again?" I headed around the table.

"Start what, Ms. Liddell?" A glimmer of mischief twinkled in Scrooge's eyes. "I have no idea what you're referring too."

"Talking nonsense again."

"We never spoke nonsense or have never stopped. You just didn't understand the sense in our nonsense, or you finally understand nonsense in our sense."

Scary, it was probably all true. "You are all bonkers." I bumped by him, my hand brushing over his ass.

"As you are, Ms. Liddell," he rumbled into my ear. "Completely and utterly mad."

"The best people are." I winked at him, making my way over to the sofa, kissing Pen softly on the head. Dum leaped up for a hug, while Rudy bowed his head to me. A distance between us had developed the moment he knew Scrooge had "claimed" me, though I think we'd always have a connection.

"We'll be back hopefully by tomorrow," Scrooge said to both Dee and Rudy, heading for the door, Hare trailing behind.

Giving Dee a hug, I followed the boys.

"Alice." Rudy's unemotional tone stopped me at the door, cranking my head to him on the couch. "Be careful."

"Of course."

"No." He squinted as if I wasn't understanding. "You are exactly his taste. A sweet little tot."

"Whose taste?"

Rudy's black lips tugged slightly.

"Who indeed."

CHAPTER 34

The trek up the steep incline to the tip-top left little room for chit-chat or questions. My lungs and legs ached with fatigue, sweat dripping down my back. The warning winds did everything in their power to dissuade us, either with threatening hisses through my hair or blowing so hard our hike uphill became nearly impossible. Each step felt like victory.

"Turn around. Death is waiting if you keep going."

"Death! Demise!"

"Don't be foolish, girl." A gust whipped against my ear, tangling my hair into knots. "He's leading you to certain death. Painful. Bloody. Death!"

"For fuck sake, you guys are being extra dramatic today." Hare snarled, trying to push against the force blowing down on us.

"Look at the source it's coming from," Scrooge grunted, nodding up at the white covered tippy top of the mountain. The moonlight sliced down, shadowing us under its looming form. It curved and twisted like the back of a cobra ready to strike, threatening death as the wind claimed.

"True." Hare took a hop forward, his head bent in, escaping the brutal lashings of wind. "At least we're almost there. Can't take their constant bitching anymore. Actually making me miss the tyrants back at the cabin."

The incline gradually eased, landing us at the place the curvy top narrowed into a sharp point. Scrooge came to a halt, his shoulders inching up at his ears. Settling in next to him, I saw no indication as to why he stopped.

"Are we here?"

"Yes."

"O-kay." I peered around.

"I swear, if that thing so much as sniffs me...I'm out." Hare pointed behind him.

"You didn't have to come," Scrooge replied.

"Between being brutally murdered and babysitting, I think this was the wiser decision."

Scrooge snorted. "Come on, *hasenpfeffer*." He took a step forward, placing his hands against the mountain, his hand scouring through the snow as if he were looking for something. "Ah! There it is."

A loud boom echoed with a hollow sound. A slice of the mountain, the size of double doors, shifted, opening, causing me to leap back with a cry. "Stocking stuffers," I gasped, watching the gap leading inside the mountain open for us. I could see the beginning of a path, but darkness stole anything past a couple yards.

"Where does this lead?"

"Wrong question, Ms. Liddell." Scrooge took a deep breath, taking the first step. "It's not where it leads, but what is waiting for us down there."

"What?" I squeaked, bouncing my panic between him and Hare.

"I truly hate you." Hare jumped next to him.

"Good. Then things are right on par." Scrooge glanced back at me. "You coming? He already knows we're here. No turning back now."

"I think it's time you told me who *he* is."

"And take all the fun out of this for me?" Scrooge wiggled one eyebrow, turning back down the path.

"You are so heartless." Hare snickered, disappearing in front of him, the darkness eating him up.

Hedging for a moment, I cursed under my breath. I knew myself too well…and it seemed Scrooge did also. My curiosity would always draw me forward, always wanting to learn and explore more. Not telling me was the best way to keep me going forward. I couldn't stand not knowing.

Exhaling, I stepped onto the path. The stone, so worn and used, felt no different from pavement under my boots. I stepped inside, and instantly the door slid shut behind me. The loud boom of it closing, reverberated off the hollow mountain and pounded adrenaline through my veins.

The moment the doors shut, lights above us flicked on. The ceiling of the cave stretched far above our heads. The electricity lined the rock as if this had been an underground bunker like Santa's. Was this another hiding spot for him? Who was using it now?

The path curved, spiraling down into the mountain, reminiscent of a nautilus shell, taking us far beneath the earth. I leaned over the edge trying to spot the bottom, but it seemed to go on forever.

After ten minutes of spiraling, we came to another door. This one was thick iron, but small opening, fitting one person at a time. Another barricade for whoever was down here if they were being attacked.

"Open up." Scrooge hit the metal, staring up. Following his gaze, I spotted a camera. The light blinked, twisting to stare down at us. Then it slowly went back and forth as if it was shaking its head.

"Open. Up. Wanker!" Scrooge yelled at the camera. "You know I wouldn't be here unless it was important."

Once again the camera shook its head.

Hare muttered under his breath, then bounced next to Scrooge.

"Hey, garbage heap, let us in. The big man needs your help."

The camera didn't do anything, but neither did the doors open.

"You will be king of the mountain again if you help us." Hare taunted. "All the smarmy glory back in your court."

Nothing.

"Fine!" Hare's arms flew up. "He can lick me...once!"

Clunk.

The heavy door released, cracking open.

"Hare." Scrooge held his hands to his chest, not hiding his smirk. "If I didn't know better, I'd say you were a little too eager to give in."

"Fuck off!" He stormed past us, pushing open the door.

"I'd feel bad," Scrooge said to me. "But I think he

actually likes it."

He followed Hare inside, holding the door for me to step in. It wasn't much different from the side we just came from. I was slightly disappointed, ready to find a bunker like Santa's or something similar. Instead we were greeted with cheerless rock, reeking of unfriendly odors. I cringed at the sour smells, like I stepped into a bucket of sauerkraut. Pickled and sharp, the scents were so jarring compared to Hare's sweet treats.

"Ugh." Hare moaned, fanning his nose. "I forgot how awful it smells here."

"Get used to it; it just gets worse from here." Scrooge continued down a narrow path, the stench indeed blooming the farther we went. This went down a few more floors before entering another room at the bottom. Stepping only a few feet in, I glanced around with shock. It went up as tall as a skyscraper, bridges and paths weaving everywhere like cobwebs. It reminded me of the print, *Relativity* by the Dutch artist M.C. Escher. Upside down, sideways, reversed, upright, the paths and stairs twisting your brain where everything made sense and nothing did.

How easy someone could lose themselves here. Perfect to shred the confidence of your attacker until they were begging you to save them, stripping their strategy from them at every twist.

"And here I thought I was safe from the infamous Scrooge darkening my doorstep again." A raspy, but peculiarly familiar voice came from my right, jerking my body to the side. Not seeing anything, the smell sharpened in my nostrils, making them feel like they were burning.

"Believe me, I don't want to be here anymore than you want me."

"Doubtful." The voice came from the far left, skipping my heart, my head darting the opposite way.

"It's important."

"You creatures think everything is important." His voice came from straight above my head. His abrupt, ludicrous movements unsettled me. It fit this world perfectly; it made no sense.

"It's *time*." Scrooge didn't bother trying to follow his voice. "The queen can get between worlds now."

"And who was the fool who let it happen?"

I flinched, keeping my mouth closed.

"Not important anymore. She's looking to kill Santa and close the door forever. I know you couldn't give a shit about anything else but yourself, so let me clarify…you will cease to exist as well if this happens."

"Oh, that hurts." Fake sadness oozed from his tone. "You don't think I care?"

"Cut the crap." Scrooge spat through his teeth. "Come down here."

"So bossy."

"I swear to Santa…" Scrooge knotted his hands. "To think this is supposed to be the better version of you."

"I'm taking the lick away from him." Hare waggled his fist in the air.

"Oh, now you're being vindictive. He doesn't like it when his favorite toy plays hard to get…"

The man jeered as a deep growl came from the darkness behind us, skipping my pulse. We swung around, as a large mass stepped out of the shadows.

"Actually, what am I saying…he totally does."

"Evil vampire holly," I muttered, stepping back in fright.

A massive dog the size of a donkey, with a tan coat and long, dark chocolate brown ears would have been adorable if it wasn't for his enormous size or the snarling teeth dripping with saliva. He took slow steps toward us, ready to pounce on his prey at any moment.

"He loves you, Hare." The man spoke. "He especially loves when you run."

"I said nothing about letting him chase me. I said one lick. One!"

Now I totally understood Hare's resistance about coming here. He was a take-away dish to this dog-beast.

"You are all no fun." The voice scraped up the back of my neck, my body shivering.

"Stop the games. We came here because we had no other choice. We need your help. The war is coming. For once in your wretched life do the right thing…if only because it gets you what you want in the end. Peace and quiet on your mountain again."

Silence followed for a few beats, before an odd shape stepped up next to the dog, my lids squinting, trying to make out what it was.

"I can't deny being utterly alone, with no one to bother me, or ever speak to me again, sounds utterly delectable." He took a step closer, his yellowish eyes glowing with gluttonous need. "What do you think, Max?"

The dog and the strange man stepped forward out of

the shadows.

My mouth fell open, flabbergasted at who stood before me. "Toadstool sandwich with arsenic sauce," I muttered.

Tall, green, furry, and shaped like a butternut squash, the legendary icon of hating Christmas, stood before me.

The Grinch.

A creepy smile spread across his mouth, showing his yellow, decaying teeth, as his eyes went over me.

"Well. Well. Looks like they brought me a toy too, Max." He licked his lips, his insinuation evident.

"You won't lay a finger on her." Scrooge's chest expanded, shifting slightly in front of me. Is this what Rudy meant to be careful? That I was his type?

"Guess we'll see how much you want my help." Grinch's smile widened, patting his dog on the head. "For now, I guess Max gets to have all the fun. Go, boy. Catch the Easter bunny."

Max reared back, leaping for Hare with an excited yip.

"Fuck. Me." Hare hissed, before taking off. Max barked, tearing after Hare.

"Let the Easter egg hunt begin." Grinch leered at me, tapping his finger against his chin, wobbling slightly like he was drunk. "Think I will start with the nice eggs you have hiding under that tight see-through top."

The Grinch was really the king of sinful sots.

"You didn't think it would be so easy, did you?" Grinch tapped his foot, and my gaze was drawn to the long hair growing between his toes, his feet resembling slippers more than feet.

"As if I'd ever think you'd do something out of the kindness of your tiny heart." Scrooge folded his arms.

"What do you mean? The people claim it grew three sizes."

"And it's still only the size of a pea."

"At one time, you were no different from me." Grinch crossed his ankles, picking at his yellow teeth. "You were fun then."

"Remember, I came first. Your story is just a retelling of *mine*."

"Oooh, someone is feeling incredibly territorial today." Grinch lifted his bushy eyebrows at me. "It's not like I want to keep her for good. Just for a few hours."

"Don't even—" Scrooge took a step forward.

"Ahhhh! Get this beast off me." Hare's voice volleyed through the large cavern, my eyes catching a tuft of white zooming across one of the bridges overhead.

"Uh?" I pointed at Hare, my attention going to Scrooge and Grinch, who seemed to be in some standoff. "Shouldn't we help Hare?"

"He's fine." Scrooge gritted, his focus still on the green squash.

"Ahhhhh!" Hare's scream came from my right. "Down, you overgrown stuffed animal."

Max's bark responded, making Hare's wail a string of curse words. In the story, Max was a cute, sweet, small dog, not the size of a bear.

"If she's not my gift, what did you bring me?" Grinch leaned against a wall, feigning boredom. "You know my rule."

"Poor Grinchy…still hurt over his childhood. Didn't get gifts all those years alone in the mountain." Scrooge rolled his eyes, folding his arms. "I wonder why that was? Because you're a narcissistic, cruel bastard? Shocker you didn't get presents."

Grinch let out a deep chuckle. "It tickles me in all the right places when the very person whose words describe them, tells me I'm selfish."

"Takes one to know one," Scrooge replied.

"Get to it, pretty boy. *You* came here. You know my demands."

"Fine." Scrooge broke his contact with Grinch, looking around. "Hare get back here."

"Sorry, busy being murdered. Maybe some help here?" Hare's voice bounced around the space, but neither of the men moved. "Call off this circus pony. Down doggie! Don't even think about getting that tongue near my ass again."

"Seriously. Shouldn't we help him?" I peered around for his white figure.

"Dammit, Hare!" Scrooge yelled at his friend. "Stop playing around with Max. I need your backpack."

"Stop. Playing. With. Max?" Hare zipped over our heads again. "Playing? Seriously? Yeah, because this is so much fuckin' fun for me. Ahhhh! Don't lick me there again."

"He's just a puppy." Grinch snorted, uncrossing his ankles, standing fully up. He was even taller than Scrooge's six-three stature. "Max!"

The dog yipped and in a few seconds was at his master's side, his tongue flopping out of his mouth, his tail wagging.

"Did you have fun?" He cooed at his dog, rubbing behind his ears. Max's back foot whapped against the floor, rocks and debris jumping up around him like fleas.

"He's so big here." I couldn't get over his size, the monster dog looked sweet with his teeth tucked in his mouth.

"Oh. You aren't one of those?" Grinch rolled his eyes. "Earth-bounders? Who grew up with their version of me?"

"Yeah." I nodded.

"Ugh. They twisted my story into some moral learning crap...and Max? They thought him being cute and little would be more relatable. As if that size dog could pull a sleigh up the hill? So unrealistic."

"Sure, that's what was unrealistic about your story," I snorted under my breath.

"Fuck you." Hare, gasping for air, hopped up next to us. "And fuck you some more."

"He's *just* a puppy," Scrooge taunted him.

"You." Hare pointed at his friend then at me. "I hate you both."

Max whined, moving toward Hare.

"Back!" Hare panted, glaring at the dog. "You got in four licks...which we will *never* talk about again."

Max tilted his head, his tongue rolling back out of his mouth, making him look like he was smiling.

Scrooge grabbed for the backpack on Hare's shoulders, tugging it off him. "That had to be heavy. Why didn't you just leave it behind before you played?"

"Leave it—played—" Hare's fury stopped the words in his mouth, his whiskers quivering with rage. He shook his finger at Scrooge before stomping away, grumbling under his breath.

Scrooge opened the pack, taking out two of the bottles of mead we didn't get a chance to drink at the cottage.

"Is this what you wanted?"

Grinch's eyes widened, glowing with need and desire. Stepping forward his long furry fingers reached for the bottles, his greasy tongue sliding over his thin black lips. "I haven't been able to get any on the black market."

"Whoa." Scrooge pulled the alcohol out of his grasp, shaking his head. "Not until you agree to help us. I know you have access to weapons."

Grinch's head didn't move, but he slowly peered at us, a wicked expression tugging at his mouth. "It's gonna take more than two bottles."

"That's all we have," Scrooge seamlessly lied.

"What are you looking for? A few guns?"

"A dozen at least."

"Oh, Scrooge, you never did have the brainpower for the bigger picture." Grinch smirked. "You have no idea what I can provide." He spun, walking away, Max right on his heels.

Puzzled, I looked at Scrooge. "Should we follow?"

"That or murder him." He shrugged. "My vote is on the latter."

"Let's see if he can back up his claim. Then we can roast him over an open fire." My fingers wrapped around my knife on my hip.

"Is it scary how fuckin' hot I find that?" Scrooge's bad-boy grin lifted one side of his face. "Though I'm still not above selling you to him for a few candy cane guns."

"I might be okay with that." My voice low and purring, I turned into him, brushing my breasts into him, knowing perfectly well what I was doing. "He does have awfully long fingers. A girl might find a use for those." I winked at him and walked away. A growl followed behind me, causing me to smile in victory to myself.

"Someone is playing games with me."

"Life is a game." I winked over my shoulder, flaunting a sentiment he once said to me. "You only need to know how to play it to survive."

"Fuck, that just came back and bit me in the ass."

"I can do that too."

"Alice," he warned.

Holding my head up, grinning to myself, I hurried my steps to keep up with Grinch, not wanting to get lost in this crazy maze.

Scrooge's feet stomped behind me as he called for Hare.

Grinch took us down another two levels, before we went through still another door. Astounded at the huge space, the room was as tall and wide as several warehouses, buzzing with an abundance of voices and noise like we just walked in on a city. The sour smell dissipated, filling again with sweet aromas. The closer I walked to the railing, the more I heard singing, banging of hammers, and the sounds of machines.

I stepped in next to Grinch, peering down at the

ground below. I wasn't sure what I thought I'd find on the other side, maybe something similar to a bunker holding a few weapons. That was not even close to what I discovered.

I gaped, my eyes not feeling I could take it all in. Below, filling the entire space was….

Whoville.

"Snoof fuzzles." My mouth parted. "And tringlers trappings."

Chapter 35

"You've been hiding Whoville here?" Scrooge came up next to me, his eyes also bugging out. "After the queen took over, they had vanished in the night, leaving everything behind. No one knew where they went."

"Yeah, those asswhos came here." Grinch waved down at them with a snarl. "Whined and pleaded with me until I couldn't stand anymore of their noise, noise, noise," he grumbled, leaning his elbows on the partial wall. "Funny how for decades they wouldn't dare come here. Stuck-up bastoodles shunned me...then, ha! One day they need me. Wanted nothing more than to get into my home. So...I made them a little deal."

This time I really took in the whimsical village. The homes were actually plain beige tents painted with fun colors dulled by time. In the middle of their makeshift town stood a tree made from slabs of stone, twisted and curved, wrapped with lights and homemade ornaments.

Singing and children's laughter echoed up, but I noticed all the older Whos were gathered in the middle of the village—working.

On one side were people baking and crafting different types of candy weapons from fire and stoves. The back tier looked to be carving them into the dangerous weapons, laying them in a huge wheelbarrow when they were done. The left side seemed to be making bullets and other needed accessories. Right below me was food, supplies, bathrooms, and laundry tents. Squirrely-curly written signs above the tents let you know exactly what each was. The homes were on the outer tiers of the village.

"You are using them as slaves?" Scrooge snapped at him.

"Pppfft." Grinch's lips vibrated. "They are earning their keep. And please, like it really bothers you."

"They've been doing this since they went into hiding?"

"Took them a while to set up and get all their shit together, but yeah, for a while now."

"How many weapons have you made now?" Scrooge slowly turned to Grinch.

"Enough to confront the queen." His gnarly smile coiled up. "And far more than two bottles of mead are worth."

"I can get you more."

A smugness rolled over the green Bigfoot.

"I figured."

"What? There's more mead?" Hare wiggled between Scrooge and me.

"Oh, Hare. I think we're gonna have to sedate you when we show you the bunker."

"Bunker?"

"Not important right now." Scrooge dismissed our conversation, going back to Grinch. "A case of mead for your weapons."

"Ten cases and *her*." Grinch's dirty yellow eyes moved to me salaciously. "And you can have *all* of those pesky Whos as well." Grinch pointed down. "More soldiers for your war. She is certainly worth all those cooing Whos to fight against your queen."

My head slanted, taking a step up to him, my nose flinching at his sour smell and whiffs of what smelled like battery acid.

"You really are an appalling dump heap."

"Why, thank you." His stomach pushed into mine as he tried to inch closer. "Why don't you and I get nasty wasty skunk drunk and see where things go?"

Scrooge stepped between us, pushing Grinch from my space. A growl came from Max, a slice of teeth showing as he stepped up to protect his master.

"Try it, Scroogie." Grinch sniggered. "And Max finds his new chew toy."

I peered over at the dog, stepping slowly to him. "I think Max, like his owner, is all bark and no bite." My voice went up to the pitch I use on animals and babies. It worked as I hoped. Max's ears and tail went down. His mouth opened, panting happily as my hand slid through his soft fur, scratching behind his ear.

"Great guard dog." Scrooge let out a howl of laugher when Max melted into me, his massive size almost pushing me over, his tail thunking heavily against the ground as he wiggled closer to get more scratches.

"Max! Stop that," Grinch snapped at him. "Attack!"

Max licked my face as I scrubbed his back, his legs sliding fully to the ground, rolling over to show me his belly.

Hare and Scrooge couldn't fight back their laughter as Grinch continued to chide him, wanting him to get up. Max yipped contently, wiggling over the ground, loving his belly rubs.

"Not such a tough guy now."

"Stupid, worthless dog." Grinch huffed. "Great protector you make."

Max barked in response, adding to Grinch's glower.

"Ten cases and I get all the weapons and whoever is willing to fight for Santa." Scrooge dropped his humor like a switch, getting back to his ruthless negotiation stance.

"Santa? You going to trick them into fighting for a man whose heart is smaller than mine?" Grinch nodded in approval of his plan. "Slippery Scrooge...more cunning than I thought."

"Who says I'm tricking them?" He got into Grinch's face. Even if he was smaller than the moldy yeti, something about Scrooge seemed larger. Stronger.

"You have to be. Otherwise, you found Santa's soul..." Grinch tapered off, watching Scrooge's malevolent smile stretch his mouth. "Tha-that's not possible. There's no way you could have survived the Land of the Lost and Broken."

"I also survived the Land of Lost Souls," Scrooge replied. "Go check for yourself. He's back. All those in hiding will hear and come out."

"You lie. You couldn't have made it through both those places. Impossible."

"Let's say I had my own weapon." Scrooge's gaze slid to me, burning with heated meaning, rippling over my skin. A private smile exchanged between us. A promise of later.

"Fuck-a-strudel…filled your stocking once, and now all he can think about is coming down your chimney again." Hare sidled up next to me, knocking me with his elbow.

"You and him?" Grinch's face twisted up. "Now that's vile. Ewww! Think I'm gonna vomit. Dammit. You were hot too. We could've had fun, but I don't take slimy-sloppy-seconds from him." Grinch shoved his finger at Scrooge.

"Ohhh…noooo." My shoulders slumped, sarcasm leaking from my disappointment. "So heartbreaking. Somehow I will have to go on." I started to hum, suddenly belting out, "Near, far, wherever you are," singing the sappy song "My Heart Will Go On."

"What is she doing?" Grinch stared at me.

"I have no idea." Scrooge lifted an eyebrow.

"You know what? I think I lucked out with that one. She's nuttier than a fruitcake. Sorry man." Grinch patted Scrooge on the shoulder.

"Yeah, you might be right."

Putting a hand on my hip, I glared at Scrooge. He winked back at me, hiding his grin.

"All right. Ten cases of mead." Grinch waved his hand out to the village. "Just take them. Get them the hell off my mountain. I've been wanting peace and quiet for decades now." He swiveled around, marching up to the railing.

"Hey, losers down in Loserville," he yelled, his

voice booming off the stone walls like a speaker. All work stopped instantly, heads turning up to us. "Scrooge bought you. You pains-in-the-wazoo are now his. Get the hell out of my house," he huffed, then stomped away, disappearing into the shadows, Max trotting after him.

Instead of calling out questions or cheering, the Whos all got up and gathered around the fake Christmas tree. They gripped hands and started singing. *"Fah who foraze! Dah who doraze!"* They swayed in unison.

"What the hell are they doing?" Hare stared at them as if they lost their marbles.

"Singing," I quipped.

"Thanks. I got that much." He leaped onto the wall, shaking his head. "But why?"

"I think this is what they do when they are upset or confused." Scrooge pinched his nose. "This makes them feel safe and united."

"They sing when they're upset?" Hare burped a laugh. "Oh, good luck getting these scrambled eggs to be soldiers. In the middle of battle, they will drop their weapons and start holding hands."

Scrooge winced, taking in a deep breath, hearing the truth of Hare's words. "Hey, everyone." He held up his hand to break their kumbaya moment. They continued to sing louder.

"Stop!" Scrooge yelled out, the silence in the cave was instant. The thirty or forty of them blinked at us. "I didn't buy you as slaves. You are free to do what you want. But those who are willing to fight for Santa, who still believe, we'd like you to join us."

They stayed silent. At least thirty seconds passed before they started singing again.

"Screw this." Hare jumped off the ledge, waving his hand at them. "They are fuck-zozzled."

"Yeah." Scrooge nodded, running a hand over his head. "Let's get the weapons and go."

We were about to leave, when a little voice called from below, "Wait!"

We turned to see a small blonde Who, around the age of six. Her nose like a button, her cheeks rosy pink, she wore rags, but I could tell at one time they were pink. She was angelic, but she held her chin up with strength in the middle of all the adults.

There was no doubt who she was.

"You said Santa?" She put her hands on her hips. "You can't bamboozle us. We know he is gone."

"He's not. Santa's back," Scrooge replied, focusing on the girl. "And the queen is coming to close the doors to our realm for good. Death will find you wherever you are. You can hide here, scared, or you can fight."

"Hide!" half the Whos replied. "Mr. Grinch will protect us. He cares about us."

"They really aren't too bright, are they?" I leaned into Scrooge, whispering in his ear, the smell of him warming my blood.

"They call it 'purposefully naïve.'"

"Idiots. All of them," Hare spouted from behind us.

"I will fight." The little girl spoke above the rumblings, her stance strong. "For Santa, I will fight with all my might."

A man nodded proudly, clasping her shoulder. "I'll fight with Cindy Lou Who."

"And me!" Another joined. "I follow Cindy Lou Who too."

"And me. I follow Cindy Lou Who through too."

"And me, I follow—"

"Yeah. Yeah. We fucking get it." Hare tugged his ears.

About fifteen took a spot next to Cindy Lou, the rest gasping, appalled by their brazen announcement and actions.

"Fine." Scrooge nodded. "For those who are coming with us, load the weapons, grab what you need. We'll be leaving in twenty minutes, agreed?"

The fifteen quickly reacted, doing his bidding as I reclined back on the wall, staring over at him with a grin.

"You know you started rhyming there at the end?"

"I'd shut up before you get locked up." He inched closer, his mouth brushing my cheek.

"Take notice, you are not giving me much motive."

He growled, his mouth tipping my head back as he claimed my lips, shutting us both up.

Waning my thoughts, but not taming.

CHAPTER 36

Instead of a cautious, stealthy retreat, being aware of attackers or LSSes, the Whos paraded down the mountain with two huge carts full of weapons and their bizilbix and wums, in constant song. Scrooge's back curved with irritation until he almost hunched over. Growls and grunts came from his direction with every few beats of their quirky instruments.

Hare's ears were flattened back, trying to block some of the off-tune voices and noises. I tried to hush them over and over, but their attention span seemed to be less than a gnat. They'd nod their head, stop for a moment, take two steps, then start up again.

"These asshoozels are too stupid to live, but unfortunately we'll go down with them," Hare grumbled, hopping next to me, glancing left and right, on constant guard. "Grinch has a bigger heart than I thought. I would let nature take its course. Weed out the brainless. These walking mind-gaps are far stupider than turkeys. And I don't know about where you came from, but turkeys here will just walk off cliffs. One walked straight into the oven for me."

"You cooked him alive?"

"Easier to pluck the feathers when they're all warm and crispy on the outside."

"Sorry I asked."

Thankfully, besides one or two of those Wums *curiously* finding their way into an LSS or off a cliff, when Hare went to steer the rear of the group, the trip was uneventful.

The wind hissed and batted at us, threatening us to not go forward, which freaked out most of the Whos, but once again it was Cindy Lou who stepped up and encouraged them to keep going. She was all of six, but the girl had more force and smarts than all the rest combined.

Spotting the smoke from the cabin, I let out a breath, relaxing my shoulders as we came up on the house, the warm buttery lights beckoning us home.

That lasted for a few seconds.

Two well-known outlines stood out front. The antlers of Rudy wouldn't have drawn any concern from me, but the three-tier ice cream cone next to him did.

"Frosty," Scrooge snarled, his lips rising, his muscles locking up. He bulldozed forward with his gaze locked on the snowman. "How dare you show your face here."

"Scrooge." Rudy held up his hands, trying to dissuade his friend. "No, you don't understand."

"I understand him perfectly, the fucking traitor." Snow flew under Scrooge's boots.

Frosty skated back, his twig hands going up in defense.

"Scrooge!" Rudy barreled into his chest, holding him back. "Hear him out!"

"No!" Scrooge shoved back, his eyes flashing with abhorrence and fury. "And I can't believe you are asking me to. You know what he did. He's why I have no family anymore. Why everyone in that cabin was tortured."

As if Scrooge summoned them, the front door opened. Dee, Dum, Pen, and Santa spilled out onto the porch, their notice going briefly to the *finally* silent party behind me, then back to Scrooge.

"I didn't turn you in," Frosty exclaimed. "It wasn't me."

"No one else could have." Scrooge rammed into Rudy, trying to get past him.

"Maybe you should have looked closer to home." Frosty's claim suspended in the air, strumming silence over the air.

"What. Are. You. Implying?" Fury wiggled under Scrooge's skin, his calm, cold voice highlighting the rage simmering under the surface.

"I'm saying I wasn't your culprit." Frosty moved a little closer. "You wanted me to be so *desperately* you made it so in your head. But deep down, I think you knew the truth."

Scrooge's entire body tightened, expanding up and out.

"Come now, Scrooge, you were there. Didn't you ever wonder why your dear sweet wife was crying out, 'You promised,' over and over?"

Dread pitched into my stomach, worming it through my gut.

"She wasn't speaking to you." Frosty planted himself where Scrooge could easily grab him if he wanted, but Scrooge didn't move, letting Rudy hold him in place.

"You. Fucking. Lie," Scrooge breathed, his chest moving up and down violently. "You are trying to get me to doubt. That's what deceivers do."

"You are the only one deceiving themselves. Truth is such a funny thing. My truth is your lie, and your truth is my lie, though both our truths cannot be facts." Frosty slid a little farther away. "Tell me, did you question for a moment why Blitzen went straight to your home? Peculiar, since he had to go through the rest of the village to get to yours? He seemed to know exactly which one yours was." Frosty tapped at his coal mouth. "Was your wife screaming for help or hiding your son?"

"She was terrified. She didn't want him to think Tim was there. Probably getting him to take her instead."

"Was she?" Frosty's pipe journeyed to the other side of his mouth. "Is that what you heard her say?"

Scrooge's chin lifted, like he was trying to defy Frosty's speculation, but he didn't defend his own claim.

The sickening sensation swam in my stomach, understanding Frosty's insinuation sharply.

"You two-faced, vile piece of shit. You think I'm going to let you twist me up so easy?" Scrooge gritted through his teeth. "Belle was kind and loving. Innocent. You're trying to make her into something else because you're not strong enough to admit you're a backstabbing sellout. Knowing you, you have the entire queen's army waiting over the hill to attack us right now."

"If that was my strategy, I would have done it the first time I was here." Frosty motioned to me. "And why would I lead Alice to the Land of the Lost to help find you? I would have left you there and taken her to the queen. Or I would have let you both die at the castle."

"What?" Scrooge's head jerked with puzzlement. "What do you mean *here* before?"

Right. He had already left when Frosty showed up, and when we returned, Frosty was gone.

"He is the reason you are alive." Rudy gripped Scrooge's shoulders, forcing his eyes on him. "He's why I was able to get there and save you all."

"What? No!" Scrooge shook his head. "This is all a set up somehow. Part of his plan."

"You think I'm that bored?" Frosty replied. "This is all some elaborate plan of mine? Even if I was, the queen is not. If I was such a pet, I would have brought you straight to her long ago."

"Belle…she would never betray us. Me. And especially not our son. He was *everything* to her."

"Exactly." Frosty tipped his round head. "What she did was out of a mother's love, not betrayal. Though it can be one and the same. She knew the queen had access to medicines and doctors that might help Timmy. Her son's life meant more than *everyone* else's in that village. Even yours. She forfeited everyone's lives, giving you all up to the queen. She divulged your location under the promise the queen would help the sickly boy, which you know the queen would have never done. There was no saving him. No medication which would have saved his life." Frosty's mouth twitched. "Belle was not expecting you to slip in the back and take Tim away...to end his life. Her sacrifice was all for naught. His life, hers, all the people she sacrificed in hopes of saving him."

"Shut. Up!" Scrooge shoved past Rudy, charging for the snowman. "Fucking shut up! It's all lies!"

"Scrooge, no!" Rudy tried to grab for him.

"Let him." Frosty held out his stick arms. "You want to let your anger out? Go ahead."

Scrooge collided into him, tearing into the snowy flesh, the hat and button eyes flying into the air. Scrooge roared punching, clawing, and shredding the snowman, the beast inside let free.

Out of all the terrifying things I had seen here, he was possibly the worst. The beast under his skin was made of hate, grief, sadness, and guilt, building into a monster who had nothing to lose. Everything was already taken from him. Or so he thought. His wife's betrayal had to cut far deeper even if done with good intentions. She forfeited everyone else, even knowing they would be tortured and killed for her actions. Her desperation in saving a boy who couldn't be saved dictated everything. My heart hurt for everyone involved, but most of all it hurt for Scrooge. The fact she did that to save the son he ended up letting go of had to be crippling. Fresh torture.

My feet moved automatically; the pull to him was constant. Powerful. "Scrooge." I tried to grab his arm, but he saw nothing except tearing down Frosty. Pain grunted and cried up his throat. "Scrooge?"

"Get the hell away from me," he yelled, jerking away from me.

"No."

"Jesus, what is wrong with you?" He backed up, his face full of disgust, but I knew it wasn't really directed at me. "Everyone should get as far as they can. I'm worse than an LSS...suck you in and crush the life of everything I touch."

"No, you aren't. You are not her actions. You can't blame yourself for what she chose to do."

"I can't?" He sputtered. "We're no different. She thought she was saving his life from death, while I ended it, thinking I was saving him from a painful life."

"You were." I stood strong in front of him, no doubt in my conviction. "It was what he wanted. You did it for him, she did it for herself. He would have died painfully. Would you have sacrificed all those other lives for his?" I motioned to the porch. "Look at them!" I demanded, gesturing to the figures on the porch. His head slowly snaked around to them, then to Hare and Rudy, finally stopping on me. "Would you have let them all die and be tortured to save one?"

"Yes!" he bellowed, but his conviction crumbled instantly. "No. I don't know." Agony streaked his face, his back curving. "What kind of father am I? I would let my own son die..."

"There is no right choice here. Tim was in pain, his life not a life at all. Do you think he would have wanted them killed because of him?"

"No," Scrooge croaked, gazing around at his family. "He loved them so much."

I could hear Dee sob quietly from the porch.

"What you had to do? I can't imagine. The cruelest choice anyone would ever have to make. Your wife thought she was doing the right thing in her mind. But was it right for Tim?"

"Belle." He choked on her name. "How could she do that to us? They loved her, trusted and believed in her, and she betrayed us all. I should have seen it coming. Sensed something."

"Are you clairvoyant now too?"

"No." Scrooge's eyebrows furrowed.

"Then how would you know?" I took a step to him, taking his wrist until my fingers laced with his. "Give yourself a moment. Your entire world just flipped on you. What you thought you understood and knew. But you will someday need to forgive her…and yourself."

"I don't see how."

"Then we have no future." I touched his cheek. "I won't live with the ghosts of Christmas past haunting us. I'm too selfish. I want you all to myself."

Scrooge's lids shut, his breath still clipped, but his hand squeezed tighter around mine.

"Damn…" Hare came up to us, his gaze on the ground. "Anyone want shredded ice? Think I have some flavorings in the house."

"Let's rebuild him." Rudy stepped around us, bending down to start to reshape the snowman.

"I'm sorry if I scared you." Scrooge's forehead tipped to mine.

"You didn't. I'm only heartbroken for you."

"Really? I just slaughtered a Christmas symbol."

"Eh. He'll live." I shrugged one shoulder, a small smile hooking my lip. "Kinda jealous I didn't do it first."

"Can't have all the firsts." Scrooge stepped into me. "Thank you." He didn't say more, and he didn't need to.

I peered up into his blue eyes, my hands sliding over his scruff.

"You know I would never hurt you, right?"

"Only in the ways I like."

"Alice…" he rumbled, his hands clutching my hips.

"First, I know you won't, not because you're afraid I could kick your ass even worse, but that's not who you are." I went on my toes, our mouths only a breath apart. "Can I tell you a secret? I find the beast part of you fuckin' hot. I like that it can scare everyone else, but I know what happens when that brutal passion is alone with me."

His grip on me almost became painful, shooting electricity up my nerves as his mouth crashed down on mine, claiming and demanding. Fire exploded in my veins. Fierce need consumed me. Deepening the kiss, his hands slid back into my hair, his knuckles wrapping around my strands, tugging. A noise came from his chest, and I knew if we didn't stop, everyone would be getting a totally unadulterated version of being Scrooged.

I wouldn't be surprised if a porno was out there called Screwged. If not, then I wanted to make one soon.

Breaking apart, both of us panting for air, a slow smile crept onto his face.

"You should see the Whos right now." His lips brushed mine again. "Think they're gonna need to go to the institution I found you in."

I glanced over my shoulder, and a giggle burst from my lips.

All fifteen stood stock still...their mouths parted, eyes huge, trinkets dropped on the ground. They looked beyond frightened. They reminded me of deer, frozen in fear, but at any moment they would all freak out and take off leaping and screaming into the forest.

"The worst they probably have done is shake their fist at someone and then apologize for it later."

"And they're gonna be fighting for us." Scrooge kissed me, then leaned back, sorrow flushing over his features again. The new revelation about Belle would take a long time to process and deal with. I couldn't imagine finding out someone you loved and trusted was the one who betrayed you. "We're not fucked at all."

"We need more people. We need to get the word out that Santa's Army is recruiting."

"Another reason you'll be glad I showed up." Frosty's voice jerked our heads to the side. He still looked like a car accident, but his mouth and eyes were back in place, his three scoops on the thin side.

"I don't recall being glad you showed up for any reason." Scrooge dropped his hands from me, turning to Frosty. Dee, Pen, Dum, and Rudy were surrounding him, filling in and patching him back up.

"You should be kissing my button nose right now."

"I know what I want to do with that button."

"Hey. Hey." Frosty's one arm lifted, gesturing for him to backdown. "You're scaring the Whos."

"Get on with it." Annoyance flicked over Scrooge.

"After I left Alice, I tracked down the other spies I had working for me."

"Working for you?" Scrooge frowned.

"Yes." Smugness twisted up his coal mouth. "You should be thanking me again...*Matt Hatter.*" Frosty's smile curled higher on one side.

A name, and it felt like he crushed my lungs under each syllable.

"What did you say?" Scrooge sucked in, his chest expanding.

"Once again, I saved your life. I made sure someone was there to intervene. To help *you both* return to Winterland."

"What are you talking about?" Scrooge took a threatening step to Frosty.

Jingle bell rock...

"Noel." His name popped off my tongue, understanding where Frosty was leading us. "You are the leader of the Night Rebellion, aren't you?"

"Clever, dear girl." Frosty's grin expanded.

"What?" Scrooge jerked back, his head shaking. "No fucking way."

"Why? Because you don't want to think I've actually been the good guy the entire time?" The snowman skated a few feet away, Penguin and Dum hovering, still trying to perfect his shape. "I've been leading the Night Rebellion since the moment Jessica took hold of the kingdom, slowly invading her staff. It was slow and dangerous, but it was the only way to learn her weakness, to win the endgame. But once you two went to earth and were captured, I knew the time was up for us. The war was here. If my spies didn't leave, their lives might be forfeit." Frosty waved off the group reassembling him, gliding over the snow toward the barn. "You can come out now."

The snow crunched with movement. Lots of it. Shadows flickered over the snow as bodies moved out into the light.

"Jack Frost's nipples." Hare stood in disbelief next to me, and all I could do was blink, making sure I hadn't become bonkers again.

Dasher, Vixen, Comet, Cupid, Donner, and a mass of elves stepped out, swarming around us.

"Holy-silly-noggin-heads," Dee cried out, darting forward into the throng, crying and hugging her long-lost friends. Dum leaped in right behind her, their forms quickly absorbed by the group with excited yelps and cheers.

Rudolph was frozen in place, his mouth parted in disbelief, his eyes locked on one figure. Tracking his gaze to see who had affected the always stoic deer-man, my eyes found a stunning reindeer staring back at him in the same way. Vixen.

Curious.

Rudy and Vixen? Something was there. A history I knew nothing about but could feel like webs of cotton candy.

Curiouser.

"Rudy!" Dasher held out his arms, breaking the moment between them. Rudolph jogged to his herd, immersed in his own greetings with his friends.

Two elves parted the group, wandering up to me. The girl smiled at me. Friendly. Knowing. The guy next to her looked annoyed and bored.

"Not Alice is Alice again. Your muchness is back." The girl with long braids grinned up at me. There was something so familiar about her...about both of them. "You found what was lost."

"Dancing turtle doves...B-Bea?" I stammered, my jaw unhinging. My gaze snapped to the other one. "Happy?"

He jerked his chin but didn't respond.

"I don't understand..." I gestured to them. "You're..."

"Shorter." Happy snorted derisively. "Elves usually are. She had the place spelled, to appear normal to outsiders. Our regular size would have certainly caused notice."

Bea tugged on her braid, her voice sing-song. "Though I fit perfectly in my skin." Her eyes drifting away.

"Alice." A deep timbre came behind them. Amber eyes, dark skin, and a slight smile parting his lips.

"Noel!" I didn't even give him a chance to respond before I flew into his arms. He chuckled, wrapping his arms around me. "I've actually missed you."

"Actually, huh?" He squeezed me and then stepped back.

"Oh, and whatever he said about me peeing the bed." Happy stepped between us. "I didn't." He huffed and stomped away as Noel mouthed to me, *he so did*.

"That's one angry elf."

"He's just bitter I cut him off the peppermint stuff." Noel shrugged. "Now I'm thinking about getting him back on it after realizing Happy was only happy because he was drugged."

Bea still stood near us, playing with her hair, lost in her own world.

Noel's mouth flatlined.

"Everyone at that facility had been held captive by the queen for decades." He glanced down at Bea. "Some minds can't be healed again."

"They will never be okay?"

"What do you consider okay?" Noel responded. "She may have damaged their understanding of the world, but she never destroyed their spirit. And Bea, what she's gone through? She is a tough cookie."

"Oh cookie? Is it snack time?" Bea's eyes widen with excitement, clapping her hands.

"I'm sure we can find you something," I replied.

"The *key* unlocked all the doors." She giggled. "You let everything loose."

I sure did.

"When doors are left open." She squinted her lids in thought. "What should you fear? The monsters that can get in or the ones that get out?"

Chapter 37

"Santa!"

Excited mumblings buzzed in the air as the man himself stepped down from the porch. He had cleaned up since I'd last seen him, his snowy white beard cut closer to his chin, his hair clean, trimmed, and brushed back. He wore a pair of red pants and a white shirt which stretched over his snow globe belly, and shiny black boots.

He looked exactly how you'd picture Santa Claus. Rosy-cheeked, happiness and warmth bursting off him in gooey waves. He opened his arms, a smile lighting up his face.

"How I've missed you all."

The Whos, elves, and reindeer circled him, crying with happiness their hero was back, packing in closer and closer, hugging and crying with their idol.

"Scrooge?" Rudy's hesitant tone snapped both our heads to him. It was still level, but I could feel the caution in it. "We might want to move them back a little before…"

"Before what?"

"I haven't really had a moment to tell you—"

"Get the hell away from me," Santa suddenly bellowed, pushing away from the horde, his voice laced with annoyance. "All I need is more intruders. More eating my food. Invading my space. Why can't you all leave me the hell alone for once."

"Oh, elf tits..." Scrooge shut his eyes briefly, his lips rolling together. "I was afraid of this."

"Santa?" A handful of elves reached out for him, concern crumpling their faces.

"Jesus...you guys are all still so needy. Shouldn't the time without me have taught you to stand up on your own feet? Stop looking at me to lead you? Lead yourself for once."

"Bu-but...Santa?"

"But-But." He parroted the elf, mocking them until the elf started to cry. "Haven't I done enough? Santa, I want this. I want that. You always want more and more. Take. Take. Take! Wonder why I left you guys."

"What the hell is up his ass? A tinsel thong?" Hare thrummed his stump into the snow.

"Nick." Scrooge pinched his nose. "Shit, I had hoped I was wrong." I recalled the strange expression Scrooge had before we left. The concern to leave Santa in charge.

"Nick and Santa are having a hard time meshing together," Rudy replied. "Nick doesn't want to go quietly into the night."

I stared back at the group staring at Santa in confusion and heartbreak. Not understanding the change in the kind soul they knew.

"Seriously, go! I was happy without all you little assholes hanging on me."

"All right!" Scrooge's voice boomed, sharp and angry. "That's *enough*, Nick."

"Who are you, my mom?"

"Yeah. I'm your mom." Scrooge grabbed his shoulders, twisting him to the cabin, shoving him back onto the porch toward the door. "Think you need a timeout."

"Let me." Dee came up to them, her warrior "in charge" expression and tone stopped both the men. "I handled it before."

Scrooge looked over at Rudy. He nodded his head in agreement. "She was the only one who was able to get through last time."

Scrooge stepped back as Dee took his place. Nick rolled his eyes.

"Oh goodie, my babysitter is back."

She didn't respond to his jab, taking Nick's hands in hers and stared up at him. "It wasn't your fault. She hurt us, not you." Dee looked up at him. "Say it with me. It's not my fault."

Nick shifted on his feet, glancing to the side.

"You're my best friend. So many love and miss you. It wasn't your fault," she said earnestly. "Say it." I felt like I was imposing on a private moment between them. It reminded me of how people handled those with trauma.

Nick's lips tightened, and finally his head fell forward.

"But it was," he whispered, the agony in his voice bowed me slightly forward. "I should have stopped her.

Seen it coming. And the reason she even became that way was because of me. How I treated her."

"We can't change the past." Nothing of the child-like goofiness was in Dee as she spoke. She was the ancient elf, wise beyond her looks. "But we can still change the future before it becomes the past. We need you, Santa. We need you to be by our sides. You are the one who needs to fight her. Fight the memories. Not let them consume you."

A sob shook his shoulders, his head curling all the way over until it knocked into Dee's.

"I'm sorry." He sniffed. "I will try harder to be the man you all deserve."

"Just be the Santa we love. That's all we want." She hugged him, instantly easing the tension in the group, the delighted murmurs lighting the air. You could see how close Dee and Santa were, why she seemed to be the only one to reach him. It was pure friendship built on trust and respect.

Santa was back, Nick receding, overshadowed by love and friendship.

"Wow," Hare muttered next to me. "Anyone else find that *awk-ward*? Like the time I found out I had sex with a cousin."

"What?" I cringed down at him. "Ewww!"

"Don't judge. It was a *distant-ish* cousin… Hey, I'm a *rabbit*! I have thousands of cousins. This whole damn realm I'm probably related to in some way. As if you haven't made that mistake before?" he snorted.

"*I haven't.*"

"Aren't you Miss Perfect."

"That's a low, low bar."

"Easier to step right over." Hare smirked and bounded forward. "I'm hungry."

Food sounded excellent. And mead. It had been a long couple of days. The endless nightfall added to the feeling it was all one long-ass night.

"Well, isn't this cozy." A voice resounded over the plot, icing my heart. My lungs froze, my throat closing in on itself. "This little reunion is so sickly sweet. I feel ill."

Oh. God. No. My heart slammed in my ears, wanting to jump out of my throat. Swinging around, my eyes clarified what I already knew to be true.

Jessica.

The Blood-Red Queen had found us.

She wore black pants, heeled boots, and a long white rabbit fur coat, her red lips the pop of color in her icy appearance. Not looking much different from when we left her on earth.

A chill seemed to grow in the air. Toy soldiers stood in formation behind her. Far too many to fight when all the weapons we had were in the carts. Next to her.

Blitzen leaned on one of the carts, a malicious smirk dancing on his face as he looked upon his old comrades.

Gasps and cries rang out through our group as they crowded closer together in protection. Shrieks as most eyes in the group went to Blitzen, their tormentor, and the queen who ordered their demise.

"Mr. Scrooge! Ms. Alice!" Pen cried out, waddling frantically to us. Scrooge guided him to hide behind us as he moved in next to me, Rudy taking up my other side. Hare leaped in front of me. We stood together as a team, creating a barrier, protecting those behind us.

How did she even find us? How did we not hear them approach?

I couldn't stop myself from glancing over at Frosty, his expression held no surprise.

"You," Scrooge growled at the snowman, his body leaning toward him, ready to attack. "You led her here."

"No, I did—"

"Thought you could hide from me forever, my dear husband?" Jessica sliced off Frosty's response, her eyebrow curved up, focusing on the man standing on the deck, ignoring the rest of us. "As usual, you underestimated me."

"I may have at one time not appreciated you as I should, but I will never again underestimate the level you will go to." Santa walked to the railing; his chest puffed up. "Ever."

"Finally. That took how many centuries?" Jessica's cruel smile hung like a threat. "The stupidest animal in the world could learn decades before you did."

"What do you want?" Santa cut right to the heart.

Jessica took a few steps, her hand gliding over the rail of the large wagon filled with weapons. "Hmmm. I will be taking these. Can't let them fall into the wrong hands."

Blitzen, dressed like Rambo-deer, leaped up on the other wagon, picking up one of the candy cane guns. Stroking it, his eyes locked on his ex-reindeer friends, stopping on Vixen, his tongue sliding over his black lips. He got off on this kind of threatening dominance. Causing others fear made him feel tough and powerful.

Pen's flippers wrapped around my calf and Scrooge's, humming "Do You Hear What I Hear?" coating me in a strange calmness.

"Then I think I'll take the little girl standing next to you." Jessica's lids narrowed on Dee. "Match the other side of her face."

Blitzen sneered, his glinting eyes landing on Dee with hunger.

"You will not touch her." Santa's hand unconsciously went to Dee's shoulder, pulling her into his side.

"Ah." Jessica derided. "I see being bad with you keeps her on the good girl list, huh?"

"You are disgusting." Santa's cheek twitched. Nick was brushing against the surface. "I will not even dignify that with a response."

"Of course, you won't," she scoffed. "Another thing I am so glad I don't have to deal with anymore. You prearranged our extremely lackluster sex nights, which happened maybe three times a year. And it was far too many with you."

"I really don't want to hear about this," Hare groaned quietly. "Not an image I want to live with."

"Thank Claus I don't need a man to have really satisfying sex." The queen laughed, winking at the appalled faces staring back at her. "They make *toys* for that." Her attention landed on the man next to me, a spark of heat glowing in her ice-cold blue eyes. "Or they create playthings like him."

"Get to it, Jessica." I pushed slightly forward, physically dwarfed by the men surrounding me, but I held the power she wanted, which made me tower over the group. Plus, the last thing I wanted was to hear about her and Matt's relationship. The one she tricked him into believing they had. "You're not here to chit-chat or talk about your sex life."

"Think someone is a bit jealous." She poked at me.

"She doesn't need to be," Scrooge replied calmly, every nuance telling Jessica exactly what he meant. "Believe me."

"Can we get to the capture and torture part?" Blitzen jumped down off the cart, motioning for a few soldiers to pull it away. "That will get me more in the mood."

"Patience." The queen patted his arm. "All in good time."

"You are not hurting one person here." Santa's deep voice rocketed from the porch. "You have hurt enough people, Jessie."

Shit. I could see it instantly, her whole attitude shifting. Her backbone snapping into a rigid line, her jawline straining.

"Do. Not. Call. Me. That." I could have sworn fire puffed from her nose. "I'm not the dutiful little wife who was at your beck and call, who's greatest ambition was to dote on you, stuck in a house where you thought cooking and cleaning for you should bring me endless joy. No more a pet, a servant, a hostage. But that was what I was designed for, right?"

Grief passed over Santa's face while rage consumed Jessica's.

"I was never a person who could have their own hopes and dreams outside of yours." Wrath vibrated her body. "Now the world will know the man they idolize is a chauvinistic masochistic pig."

"Jessie—" His voice broke at the end, his head falling forward. "The pain I caused you. What I turned you into. It is all my fault. I will never be able to forgive myself."

"Good," she seethed. "You will die with your crimes and the deaths of all those who perished in your name. You'd think the weight of that would have crushed a soul that's supposed to be so pure."

"It did." Santa's chin lifted, and his eyes filled with grief.

"But here you are." She waved to him. "Still love yourself more."

"I'm only here because of the love and belief of others. Not myself. I was too weak. I did give up." He rolled his shoulders back, squeezing Dee's shoulder, knowing her love and dedication was a big reason his soul was back. "I will admit centuries of being idolized changed me. I got caught up in it. I have a lot of work to do to get back to the man I once was. I will always struggle, but every day I will try to be a better person. The person they all deserve." He indicated to the group before him.

"Anyone else want to throw up?" Jessica's eyes fluttered with annoyance.

"Actually, I agree with her on that." Hare leaned back into me, muttering.

"That was so mushy, my dear Nicky, I'm positive you stole it from Hallmark. Makes me itchy and want to do things like this." The queen took a few steps closer, raising her arm, her posture intimidating. "Attack!"

The surge of movement rushed through both groups like an ocean wave, crashing two opposing currents into each other. Adrenaline thrummed in my chest, my hand grabbing for the knife still in my waistband.

Scrooge hunched over, widening his body, knife in hand, growling as the toy soldiers marched for us. I could hear the Whos screaming as the reindeer and elves advanced forward to fight.

"Kill everyone except Santa or her." She pointed at me. "I need one of them alive," Jessica ordered her men. She only needed one of us to close the door for good.

The toy men reacted to her command, getting in formation. Blitzen was already advancing for Rudy, death blazing from his gaze.

"No!" Santa screamed, his voice getting lost in the commotion. "Stop!"

"Ready." The soldiers lifted their guns, the general ordering their movements. Fear pounded my chest, and anguish tore through me. All the people I loved. How long before we were all dead. We were weaponless against the troop. Easy prey. They were hunters plundering defenseless animals.

"Ms. Liddell," Scrooge said my name, our eyes meeting. Would this be the last moment I had with him? His blue eyes so full of life right now...would they be in a few moments? Every noise, every smell, the acid coating my tongue, every sense was heightened, but all I could see was him. The idea of losing him crushed me into shards.

"Aim."

"No!" Santa cried, his boots pounding down the steps.

"Fir—"

"STOP!" Santa leaped between the groups, his hands up.

Her general looked at Jessica with panic. I don't think he even liked the idea of gunning down Santa Claus execution style.

"Hold fire," Jessica commanded her troops, her lips turning down.

"Take me." Santa swallowed, his arms still up in surrender. "It's me you really want anyway."

"But killing them will cause you pain." Jessica traveled closer to her husband. "That gives me joy."

"Jessie—Jessica," he corrected himself, his hands lowering until they clasped together in a plea. "Please. All of this is because you want to get back at me. Then take me. Kill, torture, do what you need. Just leave them out of it."

"No!" I could hear Dee cry behind me. Dum grabbed his sister, holding her back from running to Santa.

"This is about you and me." Claus didn't flinch, keeping his attention on Jessica. "No one else."

"I adore you think this is a negotiation." Jessica placed herself a foot away from him. She was short compared to him, but in their body language, she held all the power. "I had you anyway. They..." She gestured behind him. "They are what you used to say, 'Just the whipped cream on cocoa.'"

"Please." Desperation lowered him to his knees in front of her, his head bowed before her. "I know somewhere in there is still my Jessie. The kind, loving woman I once knew. Please. I beg you. Leave them be."

Her ego lapped up his defeated position. Santa Claus on his knees before the queen.

"You killed that woman a long time ago." She started to walk around him, as she had done to Matt and me, the shark circling her prey. "She was weak and only pleased others while no one thought once about her except to mend the elves' outfits or bake treats. I could have been a robot built in your shop."

"And for that, I will always live with regret and sorrow."

"Awww. Poor Santa," she mocked. "Good thing you won't have to live with the torture much longer." She came back around, taking a deep breath. "You know what? I will let them live tonight. Because once I behead you in front of thousands of onlookers, those who still love you will lose all hope and die a horrible death when I close the door for good on this place. Shooting them here would be the generous thing to do. But stripping them of hope, belief, love, and joy will be so much more fun to watch."

She twirled her hand for her men to grab him.

"Wait. What?" Blitzen snarled, showing off his lower front teeth, which seemed to have been sharpened into points. "No."

"I'm sorry?" Jessica blinked at him. "Are you questioning me?"

"Yes!" He sneered, his bloodlust crawling over his skin, his chest heaving as he looked to Rudolph, then jumped to Vixen, licking his lips again. Rudy instinctively shifted closer to Vixen as if he wanted to put himself in front of her. "You promised me I could play with them."

Jessica walked up to him, cool and in control. "You do not *ever* question *your* queen."

"I wan—"

"Stop! Unless you want to be another decoration on my wall like your buddies. You are nothing but another man who has stepped out of his place."

Blitzen's jaw rolled, his nose twitching with rage, but he kept his mouth shut.

"Because you have been so good at your job and have pleased me until this moment, I will let you take one for your enjoyment."

Blitzen swung back to his old colleagues, a vile smugness tugged at his mouth, his eyes stopping on each one. "Eenie meenie." He passed over Comet, Donner, Cupid, and Dasher. "Miney." He wiggled his finger between Rudy and Vixen, pausing on each one for a punishing time.

"Me." Rudy stood tall. "Take me."

Blitzen smirked, his wicked gaze dropping back to Vixen. "Mo."

"No!" Rudy scrambled in front of her, shaking his head. "Don't do this. This is about us. You finally have me. Take me!"

"That's why I will take her." Blitzen wiggled his eyebrows. "To know what is happening to her because of *you*." He curled his finger at Vixen.

Her head held high, she squeezed Rudy's hand and stepped around him, dressed in tight-fitting cargo pants and a white tank. She stood tall and emanated sexual appeal and strength, her name fitting her perfectly. In half-human form she was curvy but extremely fit. Her movements were elegant and dainty, though her brown eyes burned with grit and might.

"Vix! No." Rudy grabbed her arm, trying to stop her.

A sad smile ghosted her mouth, her antlers twisting to her friend. If I thought Rudy was a work of art, she was breathtaking, almost unreal in her graceful beauty.

"If anyone can challenge Blitzen in reindeer games, it's me." Her voice was low and calm, full of power and confidence.

"Something might happen to you. If you die…"

"You're not the only one who sacrifices for love." She looked him dead in his eyes, her meaning stabbing me in the chest with utter clarity. She was in love with him. She marched forward, leaving Rudy gaping and dumbfounded.

Toy soldiers hustled around Santa, clamping tinsel cuffs around his wrists and neck, tying him and Vixen to one of the carts like cattle.

Jessica wanted to humiliate and break him down even more. I hoped Nick would take over and protect Santa, though if he did, there might not be enough of Santa left to ever return.

One jolt of the cart and Santa, leashed like a dog, jerked forward, stumbling, while Vixen held her head high, prancing behind the wagon.

"No." Scrooge stepped forward. He was ready to dive between the hundreds of soldiers and cut Santa free. Jessica whipped around, her eyes narrowing on him.

With a bellow, Scrooge grabbed his head, flinching in agony. Her magic was twisting his mind into a pretzel.

"Can you hear them? Crying out for you?" She sneered.

"It wasn't me Belle was crying out to." Saliva spit from Scrooge's mouth, his glare locked on her. "It was to you." His fingers dug into his scalp, his legs bending, a roar shaking the air.

"Stop it!" I cried, grabbing Scrooge, holding him up, but Jessica's attention didn't even flutter to me.

"So…you finally found out about your dear, sweet Belle." Jessica laughed. "How fast she gave you all up. Threw you all on the chopping block. And yes, my Knave. You too. She was so sure I would help your dying son she didn't even hesitate to surrender your life. Her husband. The supposed love of her life. Not even a blink."

"If it had just been my life, I would have been okay with that." He grunted; his back hunched over.

"So self-sacrificing. I will miss you the most when I close the doors for good. Look around. I hope you like the view because this is your tomb." She cackled, turning away, motioning for her soldiers to move forward.

Scrooge's shoulders slumped, and he inhaled deeply, with the release of her hold on him. Instantly he stood fully up, lurching for the group.

"Scrooge!" Santa looked back at him, shaking his head. "Don't."

"I can't let this happen."

"Yes, you can. You have to. You have no weapons. All their lives are depending on you now. It would be suicide." Santa's gaze burrowed into him and then me, his words slow and precise. "Take the sleigh *down* on a lovely trip *behind* the Milky Ways."

O-kay. Curious.

The cart yanked him forward, the queen yelling out orders as fog and dark hazed around them until they disappeared over the hill, leaving as soundlessly as they came, the wind encasing them in silent movement.

As panic and commotion commenced around us, Scrooge, Hare, Rudy, and I stood in the same place, our eyes still on the dark horizon.

It was then I realized the warning wind was silent. Wrapping Jessica's army in an airtight seal. Not a footstep could be heard. That's how they had approached us without anyone hearing them.

"The wind is on her side?" I uttered. "This whole time?"

"The wind is on no one's side." Scrooge cracked his jaw. "It's only connected to other things mother nature has influence over: things made from water, air, fire, or earth."

"For example, frozen water? Like three scoops of it?"

"Exactly." Scrooge's entire body snapped to the side, where Frosty had been.

The spot was empty. The snowman was absent. I had no idea when he slipped away, but he was gone now.

"Fuck." Scrooge glanced around. "The coward probably slipped out with his mistress."

"If he comes near us again. I'll turn his white snow yellow." Hare padded his foot on the ground with frustration.

"That will sure get him," I replied dryly.

"Rabbit piss is full of acidy goodness. Melt his ass for good."

"Then bring on the golden shower."

"The golden what?" Hare eyed me.

"Oh, a golden shower sounds so pretty." Pen chirped. "Like tinsel pouring down on you."

"Yeah." I cringed as Scrooge snorted. "Exactly like that."

Shaking my head, I glanced over at Rudy, who had been utterly silent.

"Hey? You okay?"

Rudy took a step forward, still hinged on where the group had disappeared, an animalistic noise coming from his chest.

"I let her go."

"You couldn't have done anything."

"Yes, I could have!" His voice rose, anger flooding his expression, which was startling to witness since he was always calm and even. "I could have fought. I could have done something. But no…once again, I let Blitzen walk away with someone I care about." He punched at his chest. "I'm nothing but a spineless coward like Clarice said I was."

"No, you are not." I grabbed his hands. "You are dedicated, loving, and will do anything for those you care about. You didn't even know me, but you risked your life to save mine." I clutched his face, pulling it up, forcing him to look at me. "It was not the moment to fight Blitzen. She knew that. I don't know her, but she seems strong and clever."

"The smartest out of all of us. And the top fighter." His idolization of her was obvious. If they were just friends or something more could be brewing between them, he respected her.

"Then she knew she was the best to go."

"He picked her because of me."

"We will get her back. Okay?" I dropped my hands away, nodding until he joined me. "We will get them both back."

"Yeah, without guns or bullets or bows," Hare grumbled. "What the hell do we do now?"

"I have no idea." Scrooge blew out, scouring his forehead.

"*Just got back from a lovely trip.*" Pen started to sing, still standing behind Scrooge, flicking at the snow. "Silly Santa. He knows the lyric is *along* the Milky Way…not *behind*. And you don't take the sleigh down…that makes no sense. He never gets song lyrics wrong. We sing them all the time together."

Usually I wouldn't think twice about Pen's musings or the curious things Santa said. But he specifically stressed that word, as if he were trying to tell us something.

Behind the Milky Ways…

Take the sleigh down.

"Sweet potato pie." My mouth opened, my head snapping to Scrooge's, my mind latching on to Santa's strange comment.

"Take the sleigh down…" Scrooge's eyes widened, the same idea connecting for him.

"Behind the Milky Ways," I finished. Plural.

Santa wasn't talking about taking the sleigh through the constellation in the sky…but down to the candy. A box of them.

Chapter 38

"He wants us to take a sleigh ride in that piece of crap?" Hare scratched behind his ear, staring at the dilapidated sled. "Wait. Are those butt cheek marks on it?"

"Wow, okay." I pinned my mouth together, stepping inside it. "We shouldn't waste time."

Scrooge tried to hold back his amusement, his gaze landing on me with heaviness, feeling like his hands were sliding over my curves.

Hare bounced inside the sleigh, pitching it to the side. "This thing is a piece of junk. It doesn't look like it can go up in the sky."

"It's not going up." Scrooge stepped in, his form rubbing up against the back of me, his hands gripping my waist in the tight space. "It's going down," he said, his fingers slipping around the band of my sweats, creating shivers to run over my skin. The memories of what we did here a little while ago were still blasting through my mind, my body craving a reenactment.

"Down?" Hare peered at us with confusion, jumping back onto the bench. He had followed us here, not wanting to be left behind this time, while Rudy and Dee tried to settle everyone and bring them up to speed on what was going on. "Why is this seat sticky?"

"Probably don't want to sit there." Scrooge lifted an eyebrow at him.

"Nut to my cracker!" Hare leaped up, leaning on the dashboard away from the seat. "Are you kidding me? You let me sit in your jingle juice."

"If you're afraid of that, probably shouldn't touch that either."

"Oh, deck my balls, I don't know if I'm really proud or I want to throw up." Hare patted at his stomach. "The sensation feels the same to me."

"Do you remember what you pushed?" Scrooge's question skidded down the back of my neck, my nipples instantly reacting to his deep voice.

"Ummm." I stabbed at buttons on the dash to no avail. "Not really. I wasn't exactly in a coherent frame of mind right then."

"Do you need me to help you recall?" Scrooge's fingers dug into my hips, twirling me around to face him before he chucked me on top of the console.

"Uh. Innocent bunny in the room."

"Please. You screwed your cousin." I rolled my eyes at Hare.

"Rabbit here." Hare motioned to himself. "I'm in some way related to *every* hare in Winterland. I have *hundreds* of siblings, so cousins become a gray area."

"Let's get back to why we're here." Scrooge shook his head.

"Yeah, okay..." Hare grumbled. "Like your time period was so black and white on cousins. At least we don't marry them."

"Yeah. Let's definitely stop this conversation now." I stared up at Scrooge, his body between my legs, settling me in the exact position he had me in before.

"I could get rid of Hare and really make you remember." Scrooge leaned over, his teeth scraping my throat, his breath curling between my breasts, his hands gripping my thighs. Lust sparked down my spine, my fingers curling with need.

Click.

"Holy shit!" Hare reacted as the sleigh jerked, the floor opening below us as we started to lower.

Scrooge stood up, a smug expression on his face, knowing exactly how to get a reaction from me.

Hare was astounded the whole trek down and through the corridor to the bunker.

"Just wait." I opened the door, the light from the room blazing down on us.

"Butter my balled biscuits..." Hare gaped as we stepped into the room, blinking in awe as we trekked down the steps to the ground. Hare hopped past me, his mouth opening as he took in Santa's hiding place. "Am I dreaming?" Like a magnet, he went straight to the gourmet kitchen, stroking the brand new, unused stove as if it were his lover.

"Santa Baby..." A whimper came from him, his cheek pressed against it, his paw gliding over the oven door. "Slip a fully stocked gourmet kitchen under the tree for me...I've been an awful good bunny."

"Just wait until he sees the other wall." Scrooge chuckled, heading over to where the bar was, going around the pool table.

"Still can't get over the laundry and hot shower." I

trailed after him, snarling at the memory of me screaming under the icy water or scrubbing the clothes until my hands were raw. "Total asshoozel."

"I will be back, sweetheart." Hare kissed the stove. "Don't worry, my love, I will not leave you. Our love is already too strong and pure." He stroked it again before tearing himself away. He whined, spotting all the gadgets and pristine cooking accessories stocked in the open kitchen. "Oh. My. Claus! He *does* have a quiche pan. That's it! Santa is off my Christmas card list."

Scrooge shook his head, stopping near the shelf full of mead bottles and candy bars, me right next to him.

I could hear Hare bounding over. A little gasp came from him, twisting my head over my shoulder.

Hare stared up at the shelf full of mead in reverence. His eyes wide, his mouth opening and shutting like he was trying to say something.

"Hare, are you okay?"

"I-I-I..." He sputtered, before he fell face-first onto the floor.

"Holy holly," I squeaked as he thumped on the ground, out cold.

"Poor guy. The kitchen and mead were just too much. We should have eased him into it." Scrooge shrugged his shoulders, turning back to the shelf.

"Nice concerned friend."

"He's fine." Scrooge grabbed at the Milky Way box, shaking it. "Probably dreaming about drinking mead as his sugar plums bake in the oven." He dumped the candy bars on the counter, flipping around the box, before chucking it across the room. "There's nothing here."

"You sure?" I fumbled through the candies, peering at the empty place on the shelf the box used to sit.

"If we need a sugar rush, sure, we're covered." Scrooge ran his hand through his hair, pacing beside me. "What did we think? Santa is a few gingerbread men short of a village right now. And we have no idea what he even wants us to find? What could possibly help us fight the queen down here?"

"Hare could bake her some poisonous Yule logs?" I countered, my hand feeling along the glass shelf, following up the rustic multi-colored feature wood wall behind, the boards rough against my fingertips. Feeling nothing unusual, I sighed, my last strings of hope being cut. Nothing was there. We either mistook him or he was talking nonsense. "Dammit." I hit my fist into the wall.

Clunk!

The sound of a metal latch releasing its hold rung in the air, and part of the wood panel wall next to the shelf cracked open. A door stood seamlessly concealed in the uneven paneling of the wood.

"Oh, my twinkle tarts," I gasped.

"What did you hit?" Scrooge peered over at me. "Damn, Ms. Liddell, it's you with the magic fingers."

No, that was most unequivocally him.

I looked back at the spot. Nothing stood out, but I had hit the spot that had been right behind the Milky Way box. "Santa sack...he wasn't crazy."

"Don't ever talk about Santa's *sack* again, please." Scrooge's eye twitched as he reached out for the partly opened door. Cautiously, he drew the door open, peering into the dark space beyond. "I can't see a thing." He took a step inside, lights flickering on the moment they sensed motion. A bluish light made the walls glow like the hallway we came down to get here, igniting the room.

"Holy..." Scrooge took another step in the room and stopped in disbelief, his lids blinking frantically, making sure he wasn't hallucinating. "Tinkering. Elf. Balls."

My chest pressed in on my lungs as they filled with shock and horror, my brain taking in what my eyes saw. The room was the size of the bedroom, but this one wasn't filled with fluffy pillows and a comfy bed.

No, this one looked like a doomsday shelter, stockpiled with *hundreds* of weapons. And not the edible kind. All earth-bound weapons: military-grade rifles, hand guns, grenades, and knives, lined the walls, shelves, or in trunks. Santa was well supplied for a war.

I licked my lips, folding my arms, a twisted smile forming on my face.

"Yippee ki-yay motherfucker...."

"I hate you!" Hare slumped back in the sleigh as we headed back up to the surface.

"You have three bottles of mead and a rifle." Scrooge stepped off once the doors below the sleigh closed. "You should be worshipping me."

"But I had to leave my love. She did not take it well."

"Somehow she will survive." Scrooge hooked the strap of the rife higher on his shoulder, waiting for us to catch up.

"She wants to be used. Get dirty. Turned on…get covered in flour and chocolate. She's begging me to heat her up. Get those flames burning."

"Oh, the kitchen's already gotten dirty. You didn't see the ass prints there too?" Scrooge grinned wickedly. I dropped my head, groaning

"Wha-wha-what-no-you-no…" He shook his head, pleading. "Y-you wouldn't. You couldn't do that to me. To her! She was so pure. So uncontaminated." Hare sputtered, dismay widening his eyes, his lips and nose quivering.

"Scrooge." I glowered at him, readjusting the two rifles I was carrying. I also had a handgun and a few knives I added to my boots. "Don't be mean. We didn't touch your kitchen, Hare."

We so did. I saw Scrooge mouth to Hare, causing the bunny to whimper.

"You're an asshole." I knocked into Scrooge's shoulder, stepping out of the sled, heading for the door.

"So you don't want me to fuck you against it?" He growled in my ear, hitching my breath, my cheeks flushing with the idea. "That's what I thought. Just preparing him for what will happen in the future." Scrooge winked at me, opening the barn door to the outside. My body collided with his as he stopped dead in his tracks.

"What the…?" I glanced around him and saw the reason for his sudden cease.

Frosty.

A rumble came from Scrooge, his physique shifting into a threatening stature.

"Now before—" Frosty held up his arms.

He didn't get more than two words out before Scrooge lunged for him. Frosty skated back, missing Scrooge's swing by inches.

"You traitor," he bellowed, jumping for him again. "You have a lot of gall to come back here."

"I never left. I just hid until she was gone." Frosty darted and moved out of his reach. "I didn't have anything to do with the queen finding you here. I swear!"

"Your word means nothing to me." Scrooge huffed, his eyes glowing with hate.

"I promise. I didn't lead her here."

"Why did you hide then?"

"Because…I have betrayed her the most. Do you think she would have walked away if she saw me? She would have me melted right there."

"You're not just a turncoat, but a coward as well?"

"Shrewd is not the same as a coward. Her finding me here will help no one."

"Except it would have been a pleasure for me to see you liquified." Scrooge snapped his teeth, swinging the rifle like a sword for Frosty's head.

"Scrooge!" Rudy's voice thundered over the night, yanking my attention to his outline on the porch. "Stop."

"Why?" Scrooge seethed, still not backing down. "We can't trust anything this two-faced popsicle says."

"I believe him." Rudy traveled to us, inserting himself between Frosty and Scrooge. "He could have let you die. All of you. But he didn't."

Frosty's coal smile widened with smugness at Rudy's defense.

"That's what traitors do. They get you on their side. Make you believe they are helping you, when all along they are setting you up."

"There's no reason to set you up anymore," Frosty spoke, still staying behind Rudy. "She has what she wants. With Santa she can close the door. Game over for all of us. I'm as dead as the rest of you. It's not like she is taking me through the door, nor would I survive in earth's realm. Too hot there now. So, what would be the reason for me tricking you?"

He had a point, but I was still with Scrooge, not wholly believing Frosty's declaration.

"Who knows why you have done anything."

"It wasn't me who betrayed you, Scrooge, though how fast you turned your back on me. Not once ever giving me the benefit of the doubt. I was your villain. You never doubted it for a moment."

"Because the one person you truly care about is yourself."

"It's important to love oneself."

Scrooge moved forward, ready to tear into the snowman again. "Leave. I say whatever debt I may have with you, in saving my life, is repaid. But go right now before I change my mind."

"Willing to burn down your own house, just to use the kindling on me?" Frosty's pipe moved to the other side. "What if I know something that might help you?"

Scrooge's muscles tightened around his ears, his pulse pounding in his neck, but he took in a deep breath. "What?"

"You think I just give knowledge away?" Frosty smiled. "If I help, I get to stay. No more threats of melting me into soup."

Scrooge's chest puffed.

"Sounds fair." Rudy shot his friend a look. "Right, Scrooge?"

Scrooge glared at the ice cream for a bit, his jaw rolling, before he muttered. "Only if his help is *actually* helpful."

Frosty's grin reached up to his eyes. "Value can be always be found, but the significance of the value sometimes needs a *key* to unlock it."

"You're already making me regret this." Scrooge pinched his nose.

"Let's say being a spy in her world, I uncovered a door in the castle."

"Hare, you want to start cooking on that new stove of yours?"

"Fuck, yeah. Corn pipe soup."

"You have the key to open a door and walk through." Frosty tipped his hat to me. "You just need another one to step into."

"That's it. You're done." Scrooge started to move forward, but my hand slapped down on his forearm, halting him in place, his eyebrows furrowing as he stared at me, but my gaze was on Frosty.

The snowman's grin doubled in size. "Ms. Alice understands me. Don't you?"

"Frighteningly, I do."

"Understand what?" Hare still gripping onto his mead, inching closer to me.

"Frosty knows where the queen has a mirror." I continued to keep my attention on him. "That could be how we can win this war. We sneak in that way. Take them by surprise."

"O-kay...but don't you need a mirror to go into to do that?" Hare asked. "Unless you're talking about going to the Land of Mirrors, which I will say a big fat *hell no* to right now. Mirrors have always been forbidden here. No one has one."

Scrooge groaned next to me, his head dropping back, understanding hitting him.

"Yeah," I smirked. "We do. Guess we're taking another sleigh ride down."

Chapter 39

"This is bonkers. You know that, right?" Scrooge leaned against the night table in the small cabin's guest room. "This plan is completely insane."

"Why it makes it so good." I took a sip from a mead bottle Hare had brought up, passing it to Scrooge. As he grabbed the bottle, his hand slithered around my waist, tugging me between his legs.

Hare sat on the bed drinking from another one, while Rudy smoked his mistletoe. Dee perched on the end, her tears dry, her face ready to battle. She was eager to get her best friend back. Pen and Dum were cuddled on Pen's bed, not really paying us much attention.

I had gathered our little family together in the back bedroom, telling them my idea. It was met with less enthusiasm than I hoped, but we all knew it was our only choice.

The handful of Whos and elves had taken over the rest of the house, plus they built a cozy camp outside. The reindeer decided to patrol the border of the property. I doubted the queen would come for us again, but it was better to be safe than sorry. It would be like her to point the Gremlins in this direction, though.

"It will take one moon rotation to get to the castle." Rudy inclined into the headboard. "Cupid can lead them. She's third in command after Vixen."

"You're the first. Why won't you?" Scrooge asked, his fingers unconsciously rubbing the space between my sweats and tank.

"Because I'm coming with you." Rudy took another hit, blowing out perfect rings.

"We need you on the front line," Scrooge countered.

"No." He stood, opening the window and flicking the end of the joint outside. "Vix is locked somewhere in the castle, and I'm not leaving until I find her. I will not let Blitzen take anything else that is mine."

Mine, huh? I lifted an eyebrow at his choice of words.

"That's not what I meant." He brushed my expression off. "She's a friend."

"Sure. If you want to believe that." Scrooge snorted.

"We've only been friends. She was just there for me with the Clarice stuff." Rudy sat back on the sill, his brow set with his sureness, but his tone of voice wobbled. Even if they had only been friends, something was brewing underneath, which was more than friendship.

"I'm coming too." Dee sat up straighter on the bed, her shoulders pushed back.

"Dee…" I started.

"No. If Rudy is going, I am going. Santa needs me."

"And you know there is no way I'm *not* going with you guys," Hare muttered from the lip of the bottle.

401

"We need you guys on the outside. Distracting them. There's so few as it is." Scrooge shook his head. "It's going to be dangerous enough with just me, Alice, and Rudy on the inside. I will not put you in that kind of danger."

"Like we're not in danger outside those walls?" Hare exclaimed. "We can be killed by toy guns as much as real ones."

"No." Scrooge stood up, inching me back from him a bit. "You guys are all I have left. Do you understand that? I will not lose you too." Scrooge's hands went on his hips, he stared at the ground. "Dee, I need you to protect Dum and Pen…"

"Hey! Why is my sister watching me? I don't need a babysitter." Dum sputtered from where he and Pen played with box soaps they turned into trains.

"Because she is the warrior in the family, and you get distracted by sparkly things."

"I do not—" He tapered off, getting sidetracked by Pen's makeshift train crashing into his. "Hey, not fair!"

Scrooge held out his hand at them. "Do I need more of a reason, Dee? We will get Santa, I promise. But your brother and Pen need you. You are a leader, and we need those. We need you."

Dee exhaled, annoyance at not going still rigid on her form, but her head bobbed, knowing what Scrooge said was true. When I stepped into the cabin, even with all the commotion, I noticed what her leadership had done. It was sparkling clean and completely in order. When she was put in charge, she got shit done.

"Hare—"

"Fuck off, asshole," Hare interjected, glowering at

Scrooge. "You need me. Rudy will be going after Vixen, you two looking for Santa. I am the perfect distraction inside. Leading the guards away while you get them out." He set down the mead on the table. "So…you can whine and bitch all you want. But I'm with you."

"Damn." I glanced up at Scrooge. "The wife has spoken."

"This is going to be bad," Scrooge grumbled, rubbing his eyes.

"We have no choice, Frodo." I patted his chest.

"Frodo?"

"Yes. And I'm your Samwise Gamgee. The real hero of the story, let's be honest. He's the only reason Frodo even got to Mordor."

Everyone in the room stared at me blankly.

"Normal people would get the reference," I grumbled. Little did they know my *entire* plan of attack was taken from *The Lord of the Rings*. A war at the gates to point the queen's eye there, while a few snuck through the back, going after the true source of power.

Santa.

"Are we ready to round our troops?" Scrooge sounded less than confident. Our "troops" consisted of untrained, fainthearted Whos, elves who wanted to hug you not kill you, Donner and Dasher who were so high they would fight if the other side were hiding their Cheetos, and Pen, Bea, and Dum who were most likely to drive our enemies more insane.

Dee, Noel, Comet, and Cupid were our only true fighters.

That was our army.

We were so screwed.

But it was do or die. We were going to perish, anyway, might as well go out fighting for what we believed in.

It was funny, at one time I didn't think this was my fight, my world. I missed my family, the thought of never seeing them again killed me. It flipped on me, and somewhere along the way this place, these people, had become my home.

And I would fight for my family.

For Winterland.

The ghost of Christmas future was ready to kick some holiday ass.

Scrooge stood on the porch above everyone, the army grouped in the yard staring up at their leader in awe and fear. Our plan laid out at their feet. Besides Cindy Lou, the Whos were freaking out about fighting.

"We are peaceful people," Cindy's father cried. "We don't battle or tattle."

"I implore you. We don't make war; we ignore," Cindy's mom followed.

"You came here knowing it was war and a whole lot more." Scrooge flinched, turning to me. "*Please* stop me from rhyming. It's making me want to cut off my tongue."

Clearing my throat, I pressed up against the railing, my voice booming. "Santa needs you and so does Winterland. Earth even needs us. If we do nothing, the queen will kill him and close the doors…your death will not be peaceful. Hate and darkness will take over and smother this land. Destroy earth. At least this way, there is a chance. I know this is scary. But we need you to be brave. Santa has given everything he can. Now it's our turn. Our turn to fight for him."

"Some of us don't even know how to shoot a gun," Happy hollered out from the crowd. "Not very fuckin' helpful."

"I can teach you," Dee declared from the bottom step of the porch, a blush forming on her cheeks when Happy's cantankerous eyes snapped to her. "I can teach all those who have never held a weapon before."

"We don't have long." Scrooge wrapped his hands around the balustrade. "At any moment, the queen can commence her plan. We can't take much time training you guys, for which I am sorry. It will take you a day to get there as it is. You will leave in a couple of hours. Noel, Cupid, Dee, and *Frosty*," he snarled, flicking his head at the snowman. Frosty was the most suitable to escort them to the castle. He knew all the secret ins and outs, where the best place to attack was. How to get there unseen. The problem was the large *if* he was on our side. We no longer had a choice. We had to take the chance. "They will be leading. Until then, you need to train with Dee and anyone else who can help. We need all hands-on deck."

Hare had slipped back down to the bunker, putting together snacks and meals for the journey, not able to stay away from his "precious." Pen and Dum had offered to help him, which meant they were running around, singing, and driving Hare crazy. Dee, Donner, Cupid, and Noel helped get others comfortable with the weapons Comet, Rudy, and Dasher had brought up from the bunker below.

Loud pops and cracks tore through the night sky, stirring up the warning wind into a frenzy as several dozen people practiced target shooting along the cliff surrounding the cottage.

"Come here." Scrooge clutched my wrist, dragging me into the quiet cabin, his legs not stopping as he slammed the door behind us, muffling the gunshots.

"What are you doing?" I glanced behind me. "Shouldn't we be outside helping?"

"Everything is being taken care of right now." He strode into the bathroom. Tugging me in, he closed and locked it. "No one will miss us for an hour or so. I need a shower. Thinking you probably do too." He shoved me into the door, his body pressing into mine, his nose skating my neck.

"And you chose the bathroom with freezing water?"

"I promise to keep you warm." His teeth nipped my sensitive skin. "The bunker is now the popular place to be. And I want no interruptions."

My chest pattered with desire, my neck tipping back. In seconds this man could set me on fire.

"I don't know what's ahead of us. If we live or die." He nipped my ear. A simple tug of his fingers and my sweats fell to the floor, leaving me in only a crop tank. "I've lived so long with regret and guilt. I don't want that with you. We have wasted too much time as it is. From the moment I met you, even when I hated you or had forgotten, I still couldn't fight the undeniable pull to you. I want to know if we're gonna die, your last thought will be of me fucking you into oblivion." With a deep growl, Scrooge grabbed my ass, picking me up. Wrapping my legs around his waist as he walked us to the shower, falling heavily against the stone, our lips consumed each other, need driving through my core like flames. My skin bubbled with heat, forgoing air as I deepened the kiss, matching his intensity with my own.

A cry broke from my lips as icy water sprayed down on us, but it felt delicious against the fire burning inside me. He pushed his hips into me, only his sweats impeding us; the friction of his movement against me made us gasp.

Clawing at his wet shirt, I tore it from his torso, my fingers running over his taut stomach muscles. I squeezed my legs tighter around him, feeling him hard and thick against me. His lips moved down my soaked tank, his mouth nibbling at my nipple through the sheer cotton.

"Scrooge." My back arched as he bit harder, pulsing need between my thighs. My hands tugged his pants down his hips, the wet fabric slapping on the floor in a heap. A rumble emerged from his chest as my hands ran back up over his tight ass. He slipped his hand under my tank and ripped it over my head, tossing it aside. The smack of fabric hit the tile.

Wet and naked, our skin glided against each other, our breaths short and heavy. My hands ran slowly up his body, his running down mine. My head fell back with desire, as the shudders of his touch sent tingles rapidly through me.

"You could leave." His hand wrapped around my throat as his lips licked mine until my breath shuddered. "This isn't your fight. You don't belong here."

"Yes, I do. I belong with you." My nails dug into his skin. He hissed, his teeth sinking into my shoulder. "It makes sense now, what Santa said. I am her, the spirit of Christmas future. I'm part of *your* story. It's why we have always had such a palpable connection. I was always supposed to be part of your world, Ebenezer Scrooge. We are written for each other. Our stories will forever be twined together."

He took a shuddering breath.

"If something happens to you…" He waggled his head. "I won't come back from it."

"Yes, you will."

"No." His grip on my throat tightened, pointing my face to look at him. "I warned you…I'm greedy and cruel…no realm will be safe from my wrath."

"Nor will it be from mine if something happens to you," I replied fiercely, every word true. Christmas future wasn't the happy, joyous spirit out of the three. I knew how I felt about him. All the bad relationships I thought were love… I never believed when people said you'll know it when it comes. I thought my mediocre feelings were the best it got.

Oh, I was so wrong.

Scrooge. Matt. Whatever name he went by, he was embedded in my soul, under my skin. He was part of my tale, and I was part of his.

"Now if I'm going to die, make sure I have a smile on my face."

Scrooge growled, raw and animalistic. His body reacted to my request, pulsing and twitching against my core.

"Please," I begged. "I need you now."

He hitched me up higher, thrusting in deep, both of us groaning loudly, the rain trickling down over our hot skin as our bodies moved together. Demanding more. Not able to get close enough. Ruthless and pounding, our energy bounced off the walls, echoing and crying out for more. Our claim for more stumbled us to the bathtub, where he slipped out of me and twisted me around.

"Like in the workshop," he said into my ear, his hands sliding down my arms, curling around my fingers, forcing them to grip onto the tub. "Hold on."

Lowering himself to the ground, his tongue glided all the way down my spine, his hands opening me up to him, hitching my breath as his tongue sliced through me.

"Oh god…Matt!" Using his other name just seemed to entice him more. He discovered every inch of me until I was threatening his life, the need consuming my body almost painfully, my cries so loud there was no way the people outside didn't hear me.

"Being on the naughty list is so much more fun." His body pressed into the back of mine; his breath hot on my neck as he came back up.

"Matthew Hatter," I growled.

"Uh-oh. I'm in trouble." His hand slid around my waist as he flipped me around.

"You will be if you don't fuck this insanity out of me."

"Think it would be more of a challenge to fuck the sanity back into you."

His hand snaked up from my stomach, wrapping around my throat, pulling me back into him as he pushed slowly inside me, stealing my breath away. "But I like you slightly crazy. Wild. Free."

I had a good retort on my tongue, but his mouth crashed down on mine as he drove in deeper. All thoughts left me, only the feel of him, of me, of us together remained. He claimed me so deep, so thoroughly, I was suspended between lunacy and sanity. Sensible in my utter madness.

He made sure if I died tomorrow, or decades from now, I would go with a smile on my face.

CHAPTER 40

"Ms. Alice." Dee's eyes floated in liquid, her nose wiggling with the need to cry.

"Don't do that." My throat clogged with emotion. "I will see you again. Believe that, okay?"

"But—"

"No." I shook my head, lowering my knees into the snow. The cluster of our army was packed in the yard and loaded with multiple weapons ready to start their journey to the castle. They carried grenades, guns, knives, and a few younger ones wore the handful of bulletproof vests we found below. Even though all dressed in dark clothes and beanies, blending in with the darkness, they still barely looked the part. Our chance of success, seeing some of these people again, twisted my gut, but all we could do was go forward. "There is no but. We will win."

"How do you know?" Dee asked.

"Because I can't imagine a world without Santa. Without Christmas. Without *you*."

"Get him back for me...for us." Dee gripped my hand, her innocent eyes staring up at me.

"We will." My palm slid over the deep scar on her face, knowing how strong so many of these people were. Most were either survivors of Blitzen's torture or lost someone because of it. They were about to face their greatest tormentor.

"Ms. Alice! Ms. Alice!" Pen waddled over, his flippers wrapping around me in hug.

Neither Pen nor Cindy Lou should be going. To me they were innocent children, but in reality, they were actually far older than me and had as much right for what they had been through.

Cupid had ordered them to stay in the back, helping with supplies, but Cindy Lou had refused. From what I heard, she was one of the best with a weapon. Similar to hobbits, just because they were small, didn't mean you should count them out.

Dum sprinted over, and I pulled all of them into a group hug, my chest heaving as it splintered in half.

"Stay safe. All of you." I squeezed them, a tear slipping down my cheek. "I love you guys so much."

"We love you too, Ms. Alice," Pen sang, the others joining in.

"Hey, girl-puck." A voice grumbled, jerking Dee's head over her shoulder. Happy stood there, his expression between bored and irritated. He was several inches taller than the average elf, making him stand out.

"Yes, *boy*-puck." She folded her arms.

Happy shifted on his feet, peering to the side. "Was wondering. Never mind…"

"Spit it out," Dee challenged him, causing his features to pinch more, his glower set on her.

"Show me that move again," he grumbled.

"Ask me nicely."

"Forget it." Happy started to walk off.

"You actually can't ask me like a normal elf?"

"I'm not a normal elf," he sneered. "I just wanted to try the roll-and-shoot move you did earlier."

"Then ask me, Happy-Puck." Dee stomped her foot, holding her head high.

His nostrils flared, his lips twitching in a snarl. "Fine. Will you show me the move again?"

"Now, was that so hard?" A smile widened on Dee's face. "I would be *happy* to show you, Happy."

"Whatever." He marched off.

Dee's gaze followed him, a rosy pink flushing up her neck and brightening her cheeks.

"You like Happy?" It wasn't really a question but a stunned statement.

"No." She looked down at the ground, her cheeks turning an even deeper red.

"Yes, you do."

"Seriously?" Dum's mouth dropped. "He's a grumpy, freakishly tall, mean elf. He's not like the other elves at all."

"I know." She kicked at the snow. That was exactly what she liked about him. He was different.

"Okay, soldiers." Cupid's voice rose through the crowd. "It's time to head out."

I gave the three another hug before standing up, Scrooge and Hare coming beside me.

"Guys…" Scrooge started.

"Don't even have to say it, Chief." Dee stared up at Scrooge. "Until. The. End. Always."

"This time it might stick." Scrooge's throat bobbed, fighting back his fear.

"No better way to go than fighting for something you love." Her warrior personality was locked in. "And yes, I believe in Santa, but speaking for myself, I fight for you, Chief. Always have. Always will."

"Same." Dum nodded his head.

"Me too!" Pen raised his flipper.

Scrooge crouched down, huddling his family into him. "Same."

They all may have been an odd grouping, but their love for each other was so bright, it would guide us through the darkest of times.

"Actually, I only tolerate you guys." Hare broke out of the hug, rolling his eyes. "My fight is to be able to come back to the kitchen downstairs. The stove needs to be used hard and often."

I snorted, shaking my head.

"Fall in!" Cupid yelled, motioning for everyone to advance, Frosty already taking lead. Dee, Pen, and Dum gave us a nod, then slipped into the throng of people, disappearing.

"Shit," Scrooge murmured. "If anything happens to them…"

"I know." I nodded, curling my arm around his, tucking myself against his strong shoulder as we watched them march over the hill, vanishing out of sight.

Rudy strolled up to us, his face serious. It was now only the four of us. The Fellowship of the *Key*.

Me.

"Now what?" Hare asked. "Enough time to get naked and play with my stove for a bit?"

"Cupid said we move when the moon hits the opposite horizon." Rudy nodded at the glowing disk crossing the mountains and nodding at the darkening sky on the other side. The moon still rotated, but as soon as the sun should have come up, the moon started to reverse, trekking through the stars again.

"Something might happen along the way: gremlins, trees, chipmunks. They might not make it on time." Scrooge stroked his cheek absently. "This plan hinges all on timing, which is not Winterland's strong suit."

"A chance we have to take. We have no other way to contact them." Rudy replied. "Until then, it wouldn't hurt if Alice worked with the mirror. There can't be any mishaps going through."

"No naked time with my new flame?" Hare blinked up at us, his eyes pleading.

"Naked time sounds good to me." Scrooge shrugged, looking at me.

"Oh no." Hare stabbed his stubbed foot in the snow. "Remember hares have exceptional hearing. If you think I didn't hear you the last two times in the cabin earlier... My last memories aren't going to be replaying that in my head on a loop. I'll put my head in the oven first."

"Okay, gloomy one." I dropped away from Scrooge, heading toward the bunker. "Mirror time it is." I swiveled, walking backward, winking at Scrooge. "Though I might need help being reminded which buttons to push on the sleigh."

"You know there are stairs next to the trap door you can—" Rudy said evenly.

"Shut up, reindeer," Scrooge snapped, jogging to catch up with me.

"Did he say there were stairs?"

"Nope." Scrooge shook his head. "I didn't hear anything like that."

Grinning, I glanced up at Scrooge. "Me neither."

"You know I've had fantasies about something like this…" Scrooge tugged on the rope. "But clothing was not a factor in it and the rope was being used a little different from this."

I leaned against the counter, wiping the sweat hinting at my brow, my boot kicking gently at the framed mirror. The glass oval had been moved from the wall to the floor of the bathroom.

"Believe me, this is not how I want to be tied up either." I shoved at the rope wrapped around my waist down to my hips, trying to pull my sweats up that buffered the coarse twine. The rope burn around my midriff stung like a bitch.

Working with the mirror meant having to step into it. Not wanting to lose me, Scrooge had the great idea of tying a rope around my waist to keep me from falling all the way through. Several times he had to yank me back.

"Did you see anything this time?" He wiped his damp hands on his pants, frowning at the sounds of Hare humming happily in the other room. The bunny really did love that stove.

"No. The rope isn't long enough." Vast emptiness lay on the other side of our refection. At least there was no water this time. Gray stone was all I could see. I hoped I was seeing the walls of the castle.

I had no idea how this worked. Frosty had given me a detailed description of the room the mirror was in, which I tried to focus on, hoping it would lead me there.

Bare feet padded into the bathroom, the shadow of antlers crossing over my figure.

"It's time." Rudy adjusted the weapon halter he was wearing over his bare chest. Guns, knives, and grenades adorned the harness, his expression tight and angry. I had never seen so much emotion in him before. If it was Vixen or he had finally had enough, Rudy was ready to fight. To kill.

He held out two more harnesses, doctored with all the same weapons. He had spent hours in the weapon room…making us all assassin harnesses.

Hare stepped in, munching on a fudge brownie, already wearing his own Rudy design.

"Brownie?" He held up a stack of freshly made treats. I learned Hare calmed his nerves by baking. A lot. "I added extra chocolate to this batch." He stuffed one in his pocket. "If I'm going to die, I want this as the last thing I taste. Death by chocolate, baby."

Grabbing one off the pile, I shoved it into my mouth as I untied the rope and pulled on the harness. Scrooge stepped up to me, tightening the straps so it fit me, his gaze heavy on me.

We had been silent most of the time, no words really feeling strong enough for what was ahead of us. Neither wanting to think that in a few hours, this might be all over.

For good.

"It's time, Scrooge," Rudy said again.

"I know." He sighed, his fingers gliding down my sides, his mouth pinched.

Licking my lips, I bobbed my head, lifting my eyes to stare into Scrooge's. "At the end of this, you better survive. Come back to me."

"I *promise*."

"But your word is crap." I tried to tease, but it fell flat.

"Guess I'm staying on the naughty list then." His mouth took mine with desperate hunger, tasting of rich, creamy chocolate and fudge, his teeth tugging at my bottom lip before he turned away, ending it as fast as it started. Taking a step around me, his boots hit the mirror, poised to jump in.

Stepping next to him, I took his hand in mine. Rudy moved in on my other side, taking my other hand as Hare went between him and Scrooge, all our hands linking us together in a circle.

"Everyone hold on. No matter what, *do not* let go." I gulped, fear batting around my heart like a cat with a toy. This really was a stupid, crazy plan. "On three we step in together."

I took a deep breath.

"One."

"When faced with life and death you think of all the things you regret," Hare babbled nervously.

"Two."

"I can only think of one thing."

"Three!" I leaped forward into the glass.

"I should have fucked more cousins." Hare's words followed us as we fell.

Down.

Down a gray brick road leading us to a wicked witch.

CHapTER 41

We plunged, twisting and rolling through the air.

My grip on Rudy slipped. "No. Don't let go," I cried, his fingers digging into my hand, trying to hold on, but the dampness between our hands slid his grip from mine with a small cry. "Rudy!" His form was swallowed up by the darkness. "Noooo."

A loud grunt came from somewhere around me, but I didn't have much time to think. Twirling and turning, we tumbled. I gripped Scrooge's hand with all my might. There was no down or up, floors and ceilings in every direction, giving me no bearing on which way to go.

I closed my eyes so my brain would stop trying to make sense of nonsense. I let go of the structured concept, accepting the crazy. I constructed Frosty's description in my head, letting it become my center. My anchor.

It was like a switch, suddenly I didn't feel my body rolling or falling through space. Everything calmed. I was floating, drifting down gently; my toes touching something solid.

"Alice." My name sounded next to me. "Open your eyes."

Slowly, my lashes lifted, and I blinked. My feet were on hard ground and I stood on the back side of an oval mirror. Like a two-way mirror, instead of seeing my reflection, I could see through to the other side. Red and black flags hung on the walls, modern crystal chandeliers, the castle waiting for us beyond the layer of glass.

"You did it." Scrooge's hand slid from mine.

I had done it. I had gotten us to the queen's fortress. "I let go. Accepted the insanity."

"I told you." Scrooge smirked. "Everything would become logical if you let in the absurd."

"Did that with you, didn't I?' I chuckled. Scrooge had been right. Though I would never tell him that.

"Oh god, Rudy!" I swung around, panic lurching my heart at the memory of his fingers gliding through mine.

A soft smile came from the figure straight behind me. My gaze ran over the reindeer making sure he was all intact.

"You made it." I sighed with relief

Hare coughed, pointing at himself. "Thanks to me. Though he yanked my arm out of the socket."

"You got us here, Alice." Rudy bowed his head to me. "I knew you were *her*."

Part of me wished I wasn't. There was so much pressure to be what the legend declared. What if I failed them?

Blowing out, I spun back around. It looked quiet and calm on the other side, but that could all change the moment we stepped in.

"You ready?" I took a breath, looking at each of my comrades.

"As ready as a Toe-few-turkey." Hare pulled out his gun.

I grinned, turning back to the mirror, and yanked out my gun, switching off the safety.

"Christmas Combat has begun," I said, and stepped through the mirror. The air wobbled and pricked chills at my skin as I slipped through, the guys right behind me.

Quiet emptiness welcomed us, but my guard was still up, scrolling every corner for a threat, my gun ready. My awareness circled the room as we came into it. There wasn't much to it. Curved stone walls and a large window, which let the moonlight stream in. Gazing down through the window, I saw an interior courtyard. Cages hung in the air, filled with prisoners, whose skeletal frames said they were either dead or near death from starvation.

I knew exactly where we were.

"That could've been me in there." Hare stared down in quiet horror.

"Nah," Scrooge replied. "You would have been fattened up and served with potatoes."

"Knowing you..." I nodded at Hare. "...you would've cooked your own dinner to be served up, criticizing her chefs the whole time that you wouldn't be garnished in anything but the best."

"Funny." Hare huffed.

"True." Scrooge snorted.

Heading for the stairs, all of us quietly followed him down the tight turret. Single file with steep and uneven stairs, Rudy had to turn sideways to get his antlers through.

Our feet echoed against the stone no matter how quiet we tried to be; the stone screamed out like an alarm. One way in and one way out. My heart pounded. This would be a perfect scenario to attack us as we came out the doorway at the bottom. We had no defense and would be gunned down before we could run back up to the mirror.

Scrooge took lead, stepping out into a room, his gun up and ready to shoot. I followed him, doing the same. We were on the second level, the elegantly designed space reminding me of Jessica's therapy office. Cold, minimal, but beautiful. It must be her private office with the same abstract art on the walls, glass desk, sleek furniture, and a blood-red rug. The tower we had come from could only be accessed through this room, which I had a feeling she kept closed to anyone else but her.

Creeping to the large door, I pressed my ear to it.

Nothing.

Heart beating, lungs contracting, I cracked open the door, slowly poking my head out into the hall.

Silence.

Unease prickled up my spine as we slunk into the dark passage. It was *too* quiet. A strange eerie heaviness lapped at my bones. No signs of a battle raging outside. Not even the sound of people moving casually around the castle.

"This doesn't feel right," I said softly to Scrooge.

"No." His eyes darted around, his body hunched and ready to defend or attack. "No, it doesn't."

That meant our party hadn't arrived, or if they had,

they were already dead. The journey here was filled with peril, they might have been killed back up on the mountain.

"We can't think about that now." Rudy inched down the hall toward the exit. "All we can do is go forward."

"You think she has Santa in the dungeons we were in?" I whispered, my head jerking around, my pulse thumping in my neck.

"No." Scrooge's lips thinned, knowledge straining his expression. "Vixen, yes, but Santa? She'd keep him close. This is personal. He'll be below. A room she once put me in."

"Right." My head dipped. "I forget you have personal experience with her. With this place."

Being her knave, willing and not, Scrooge had spent a lot of time in this castle. Knew her mind and the layout of the castle.

"Yeah. Not a time I want to remember." He jerked his head deeper into the castle.

Rudy looked back at us, comprehension sinking in.

"This is where we part ways."

"Get Vixen and whomever else you can save down there…" Scrooge verbalized to his friend. "And get the hell out. Don't even think about coming for us. You understand? Help out people on the other side."

Rudy's black lips peeled back in a snarl, wanting to fight Scrooge, but slowly his head bobbed in acceptance.

"Good luck." Scrooge clutched his arm.

"And good luck to you, my friends." Rudy nodded at each of us, stalling on me for a few beats longer. "I believe in you, Alice. You are worthy of the legend, of this story," he said before he turned away and slipped into the shadows, descending a set of stairs.

My heart lurched, and I wanted to run after him, protect him. My feet stumbled forward. There would always be a connection between Rudy and me. The thought of anything happening to him shredded my chest in grief. But it would make no difference if we didn't save Santa and stop the queen.

Rudy's belief in me to fulfill this lore didn't ease my nerves, and the doubt I could live up to the myth weighed on my shoulders.

The three of us slunk and weaved down two more levels, not running into one person, which tripled the anxiety spinning in my stomach. It felt all wrong, like walking into a trap, but what could we do? We had to try.

Scrooge was in full "knave" mode. Stealthy, meticulous, quick, and ruthless with his commands, making us follow in the exact line he wanted us in. If it kept us alive and got us what we wanted in the end, I was fine with taking his orders. He knew this place, knew where to hide, and the lesser-used paths. Hare and I stayed alert, covering all angles when we got to a crossroads.

Scrooge waved us forward, the steps taking us lower underneath the castle, darkness coating us in shadows, but also hiding dangers behind them.

Sweat dripped down my back, my ponytail tickling my exposed skin. Scrooge stopped, his head peering down the dark passages, the only light coming from tiny windows at the top near the ceiling. This level was mostly underground.

Scrooge's hand shot up, halting Hare and me instantly, the muscles down his arm straining with nerves. Scrooge tapped at his ear, then put his finger to his lips.

That's when I heard sets of footsteps come from down the hall, freezing me in place. They were precise, the clicks perfectly timed, echoing back as if they were contained in a small space.

Toy soldiers. Scrooge mouthed to us, holding up his fingers. *Two.*

The only reason they'd probably be down here would be to guard Santa. Of the many scenarios we came up with before we left, we were ready for this, though we actually had planned for more guards on Santa. Two seemed hardly sufficient.

Scrooge fanned his fingers out, ticking his pointer finger down.

One. Two. Three. Four.

Inhaling, my ears thundered in fear.

Five.

Hare darted around Scrooge, leaping into the hallway.

"Do you wood chips know where the massage room is in this place?" Hare folded his arms, his voice nonchalant. The two soldiers jerking toward him in surprise. "Gloria still does those happy endings, right? Last time she had me falling to my knees, singing, "*Oh Gloria!*"

"Foe!" one guard yelled.

"Is that a no? Guess I'll have to find it on my own." Hare snapped his fingers and dashed back around the corner to us.

"Stop! Halt!" the guards yelled as their heavy marching reverberated down the hall toward us.

POP!

A bullet from Scrooge's gun tore through the wooden head of the first one, splintering chips across the space like daggers. The muzzle of the gun so close it muffled the boom of recoil, eliminating the sound banging in the corridor.

Spinning around to the second guy, who pointed his rifle at Scrooge, I pressed the gun into his temple. "Unless you want to end up in chunks as your friend here, you will lower your weapon now."

The toy soldier hesitated, his black painted on eyes weirdly moving around his smooth face.

"Now." I pressed in harder, tilting his head to the side. Slowly he lowered his weapon, Hare taking it from his hands. "Now, you are going to unlock that door like the obedient toy you are."

"I-I-I can't. He-he has the keys," the soldier stuttered, pointing to his comrade in pieces on the floor.

Scrooge crouched down, digging through the sawdust, finding a set of keys under a leg, holding them up to me.

"See." The toy motioned to them.

"Yeah." I nodded, my finger pushing down on the trigger. "I see we don't need you anymore."

Bang!

Timber sprayed out, soldier number two spreading over the hallway.

"Damn, woman. You are *ruthless*." Hare's mouth parted, and he stared at me. "I seriously think I'm in love with you."

"More than your stove?"

"Let's not get carried away."

Scrooge brushed off the dust covering him, standing up, his body only an inch from mine, his blue eyes burning as they devoured me.

"That turn you on?" I curled an eyebrow.

"Hell, yes," he rumbled. "You're a badass, Ms. Liddell...and *that* fucking turns me on."

My lungs fluttered, my tongue sliding over my lip.

"You guys might be *worse* than rabbits." Hare shook his head, bouncing over the dead soldiers. "Come on, her stocking doesn't need filling right now."

"I beg to differ," Scrooge gravely muttered, his eyes still moving over me, making me inhale sharply.

"Scrooge!" Hare whispered hoarsely, pulling his friend's attention from me to the door. Scrooge jogged up to the closed door inserting the key. The terror that dozens of soldiers would pour down the hall, hearing the commotion, kept my gun pointed toward the hall entrance, watching their backs.

The lock clicked, the door creaking as it swung open. With a final look for enemies, we all slipped into the room. Light from the window above streaked down the wall to the floor.

"Oh god." My hand went to my mouth, taking in what my eyes were showing me.

Naked and badly beaten, Santa lay on the floor, his neck, hands, and feet chained to the wall. The stillness tapped an alarm in my stomach.

"Santa?" Scrooge called softy inching closer to the still form. "Nick?"

Neither responded.

"Shit." Scrooge moved to him, panic making each movement jerky. He scoured Santa's body for signs of life, his hand going to his neck, then bending over to his chest. "Fuck. No…no-no-no…"

Terror sprouted up my esophagus like weeds; a sob assembled in my soul like a hurricane.

"Is he…?" Hare tapered off.

Scrooge's head shook, but he wasn't answering Hare's question. It was more he was not accepting this outcome. "You are not doing this to us. *You can't.*" He growled at the lifeless form, starting to pump down on his chest, breathing into his mouth.

I couldn't seem to move, the truth ripping away all certainty and hope, and though I stood on solid ground, I was plunging down a dark hole.

Down. Down.

We were too late.

Santa Claus was dead.

CHAPTER 42

"You do not get to do this." Scrooge pushed at Santa's chest, a nerve along his jaw twitching violently. "We didn't come this far for nothing. Jessica does not get to win. You hear me? There are too many who believe in you. Need you." He bent over, giving the essence of his life into Santa, reminding me of the time I did that to him...which had saved his life. The greatest gift. The ultimate sacrifice for someone else.

Hope bristled in my throat, my eyes latching onto Santa as Scrooge gave himself over to saving this man.

Santa's chest expanded with Scrooge's air, but this time I saw it hitch.

"Cranberry sauce!" I yelped, rushing over to them, dropping to my knees, my fingers going to his pulse on his wrist and neck. It was dull, but I could feel life thrum against his skin.

"He's alive!" I cried as Santa's heartbeat grew stronger, with each breath Scrooge gave to him. Slowly, Santa's lungs started drawing in oxygen on his own. "You did it."

Scrooge sat back, fear still encrusting him.

"You saved him, Scrooge."

Scrooge's shoulders sunk, his head tipping forward, and he rubbed at his face, a long breath exploding from his lungs.

"Fuck. If I knew you wanted to make out with me so bad..." A hoarse voice muttered petulantly, lids fluttering open with a cough. "You could have asked for it for Christmas."

Scrooge's head snapped to him, his eyes narrowing. "Nick?"

"Is that a question?" He hacked, sucking in gulps of air, his voice hoarse. "And here I thought I meant something to you." Nick tried to roll over, the chain yanking him back. His face and body were covered in bruises and cuts, dried blood coating half his face and streaking back into his white hair like red highlights.

Hare snorted. "Of course *that* asshole is too stubborn to die."

"Santa's still alive, right?"

"Yeah, that feckless elf hugger is still here." Nick twisted to me, winking with his better eye. "But I think you enjoy them a little more virile and rough around the edges, don't you, sweetheart?"

"Ewww." Believing Santa was dead, I didn't contemplate much about him being naked, but now I realized it with disturbing awareness. His beard no longer covered any of his bits. And I thought I needed therapy before...

"Nick," Scrooge growled. "We don't have time for this. We need to get you out of here."

"Great." Nick held up his wrists, the chains clinking together. "Let's go."

"You know, I just realized a scenario we didn't consider." Hare tapped at his mouth.

"Fuck." Scrooge huffed, grabbing for a knife in his harness. He wedged it in where the cuffs linked together, trying to pry them apart, while I tried to do the same on his other arm.

"Yeah, twiddle-shit, that won't work. You know she has these spelled. A certain key has to open them." Nick groused, his face flinching as he curled himself forward, sitting up. "Damn, you guys really are stupid."

"You know, on second thought, I don't think St. Nick here will be missed all that much." Hare drummed his stub on the stone. "We'll actually be doing a service to people."

"Something I heartily agree with you on." Her voice snowplowed through my stomach, punching my heart up my throat.

My head jerked up to Jessica's smirking smile, her small frame dwarfed by the huge wood door, but her ego crammed every inch of space. This woman was a freakin' ninja. Silent and deadly.

Lurching up, Scrooge twisted around, his physique automatically stepping in front of us.

"Took you guys long enough." She strolled in, Blitzen and a few soldiers right behind her. Their weapons were already pointed at our heads. "I was starting to get bored."

Scrooge huffed through his nose.

"Yes, my Knave, I knew you'd come." Her eyes were locked on him, the rest of us inconsequential "I know your mind and heart, my love. You felt more like a husband to me than that soggy lump of coal ever did.

When we connected…"

"Shut up." Scrooge reached for a weapon on his holster.

"Bad boy." She waggled her finger at him. "You make another move, and Blitzen puts a hole in your girlfriend's head much faster than you can draw a weapon on me." She grinned and walked closer to him, her eyes roaming over him. "I recall brief moments you liked being my husband. Wanted it."

"Guess women aren't the only ones who can fake it."

A grimaced smile convulsed her mouth. "As horribly bad-tempered as you come across, you still have a hero's heart. I knew you'd come for Santa." She motioned to the man on the ground. "Frosty ran to you just as I hoped, the mirror too tempting for you to ignore. Though, I did think I was being a tad bit obvious…" She clicked her tongue. "Instead of the extra work of bringing you all down the mountain, you came to me willingly. Walked right in. Checkmate."

We weren't stupid, we all figured this was a trap, but she had set the game up perfectly. We had no choice but to play.

"You got us." Scrooge held out his arms. "So now what?"

"Someone's impatient."

"We have a spa treatment with Gloria." Hare tapped at his wrist.

The queen stared at him for a moment, perplexed, before going back to Scrooge.

"I've been so generous with you." She patted Scrooge's chest. "Even gave you a chance to be with

433

your son again…live a full life with him. Watch him grow up this time." Her eyes flicked to me in a sneer. "But your dick overrode your very own son."

"He wasn't my son." Fury bristled through him. "He was an empty husk you conjured."

"He could have been everything you wanted him to be. But you chose her." Jessica shook her head. "At every turn, you have chosen wrong. Such a disappointment."

"I'll learn to live with it."

"No." She chuckled. "You won't." She moved away from him, Blitzen seemingly took it as a cue, moving to him.

"I'm done with this realm. I don't need you, Nick, or Ms. Liddell anymore."

"You mean I won't get to be your drooling houseplant in the corner of the institution, you know, in case of emergencies." I clutched my chest mockingly. "I'm so disappointed."

An eerie smile peeled back her lips, her eyes rolling over me. "Not when I learned there is another I can use. You think you're the only Liddell who is special?" Her words sucked out the blood in my veins like a vampire, ice creeping into my skin.

"What?"

"Your sister might be closed off to believing right now, but she wasn't always, you know…and from my spies, your disappearance has affected her greatly. She's not quite right. You know insanity runs in families."

"Don't. You. Dare. Touch. Her." Fists clenched, I pitched forward.

"Or you'll what, Alice?" She clasped her hands together, nodding at her guards. "You'll be dead."

They moved in a blink, Blitzen eagerly leaping on Scrooge, his hatred for his old partner lighting up his eyes. Two soldiers grabbed me, and two more confiscated Hare, shoving us all to our knees on the ground, stripping us of our harnesses loaded with weapons.

"You know how I love a beheading. Makes such a fun party. But not this time." Her heels clicked around me. "Nick will once again watch his friends being murdered in front of him. By the end, he will be begging to close the doors for good and let this place die."

The soldier's wooden hand pinched painfully into the back of my neck as he shoved me down farther.

"Blitzen, you get to do the honors this time."

"How did you know what I wanted for Christmas?" he jeered, slamming Scrooge's forehead into the rough stone floor. "But I'm saving him for last. He'll first get to watch his lover lose her pretty little head." He yanked Scrooge back by his hair, growling in his ears. "Be like old times? Watch the blood spray out. Her life leaks out as she stares at you with utter heartbreak and disappointment."

A feral snarl came from Scrooge, trying to fight back, but more guards moved in, kicking and smashing him with the butts of their rifles.

"Scrooge. Stop!" I cried out, his wild eyes meeting mine. "Please." I shook my head. That's not how I wanted this to end. Emotion suffocated my throat as I looked at Hare then back to him.

"I should have made you leave." His words tore through his teeth. "This was not your world...this should not be your ending."

"You keep saying that. But it was; it is. I was always supposed to come here." A tear rolled down my cheek. "And I'm glad I did. Otherwise I would have never met you."

"You would have been better off."

"I was lost until I came here. I found friends. Family. Home. In this crazy place, I've never felt surer of anything. Of you, of my life *with* you." My words were strong, but my body shook. "I love you, Matt Hatter."

A noise curled out of his throat as Blitzen moved to me, pulling the axe from his back harness, the soldiers shoving me down, the texture of the stone the only thing I could see. This was it. Would it hurt? Would there be blackness and peace? In my mind, I told my family I loved them, wishing I had taken the chance and opened the hat shop instead of listening to everyone else.

"Jessie, please! Don't do this!" I could hear Santa was back, his voice pleading with her, his chains rattling. Hare cried out for me, but the sounds were muffled compared to Scrooge's voice. Like a blanket or a stuffed animal you curled up with when you were scared as a child, I wrapped myself up in his rough timbre, closing my eyes.

"No! Alice!" Scrooge's scream thundered through me as the soldiers tightened their grip, Blitzen's axe swinging up.

"You have the power, Alice. Don't forget." I could hear Rudy's voice in my head.

Right. I had muchness. Closing my lids, I pleaded for help, Blitzen counting down above me.

"Three."

A tinkle of glass hit my knee opening my lids. A vial sat in front of me. But it was not a cookie or something to drink.

I blinked.

An antique key slid around the inside of the container.

What the hell, Christmas fairies? How was a key supposed to help me from getting my head chopped off? Had they finally gone mad?

Terror sank in my gut so deep, bile burned my stomach, knowing this time there was no way out.

"Two," Blitzen called as I heard Scrooge roar with fury and agony.

"One—"

BOOM!

A blast tore through the castle with a jarring rattle, knocking everyone to the ground with a shriek. Covering my head, dust and chunks of stone crumbled from the building on us, falling like rain.

"Alice!" Scrooge scrambled over to me through the haze of debris. Anguish and relief covered his features as his hands gripped my face, pulling me into his body. His arms came around me. The rush of his warmth and the fact I got to feel him again shuddered my chest.

Once again, I slipped from death's fingers. Even if it was for a moment.

"What was that?" Jessica screamed as she rose back on her feet, brushing herself off, fury igniting her eyes like Christmas lights. The stiff soldiers struggled to get up, appearing like upside-down turtles.

"I don't know, Majesty." One soldier who had been holding Hare finally rose to his feet. Free, Hare darted to us, and Scrooge pulled him into our huddle, his physique ready to defend and protect.

"Then. Go. Find. Out!" she shrieked. "Your wooden brains are showing they're only good for a fire."

The guards squeaked, all rushing for the door at once, getting stuck as each tried to get out the exit, no one getting anywhere.

Boom!

Another blast went off, this one farther away, but it still shook the fortress with a hearty groan.

"Get out of my way," she yelled at the guards, rushing for the door. "And bring them. If it's that rebel alliance…they will watch their commanders die in front of them."

Jessica rushed out the door. The guards seized our limbs, forcing us to our feet.

"Move it!" Blitzen ordered, pulling Scrooge away from me, shoving him forward so hard Scrooge stumbled, ramming his head into the wall. Blitzen thrust him out of the room, sadistically enjoying Scrooge's face smashed into the hard stone, watching blood gush from his nemesis's nose. Scrooge straightened up and smiled at Blitzen with a taunting smirk.

"Let me go, you dickless dolls! That's why you're so bitter, huh? Don't even have a whittled pencil for a dick." Hare kicked and wiggled as two guards lugged him out.

The guards holding me, propelled me forward, my boots hitting an object, pitching it forward toward Santa. With a clink of glass, the metal rolled around inside, which no one seemed to notice but me.

The key.

"Let them go. Take me instead!" Santa cried after us. The guards ignored his pleas, dragging me out. "Plea…" His words were cut off as the door slammed behind me.

They marched us up and out the doors, where most of Jessica's servants already hovered. Many I recognized from the facility. Pepper Mint and Everly Green—their snarls lifting when they spotted me.

The guards stopped us on the steps overlooking the back garden. The memory of the first time here didn't feel much different from my present circumstance, except this time the forest beyond buzzed with commotion and noise.

My gaze landed on the first wave of shapes coming from the forest. People, reindeer, and elves lined up, armed and ready for battle. Torches glowed in the dark, flicking shadows across their faces, making them look spooky.

The rebel alliance *had* arrived.

CHAPTER 43

"That's it?" Jessica howled with laughter, the deep cackle skating shivers down my spine, her gaze shooting to me. "That's your army?"

"Don't ever doubt those who have something to fight for." I sneered.

"Aww. What a sweet notion." She placed her hand on her heart. "But when has fluffy hope ever *actually* won? I have thousands of men against your handful. We'll see how long your idealism lasts."

I wanted to refute her, but truthfully, she was right. The good guys barely ever won in real life.

"General?" She called over her shoulder to her head guard.

"Yes, Majesty." He stepped forward.

"Send out all your troops. Don't leave one alive."

"Yes, ma'am." He bowed, instantly turning to his troops, ordering them to attack. My optimism shriveled up, my heartache thumping against my ribs. We had weapons, but she had the numbers. Mindless toys that wouldn't stop until my friends were dead.

"What do you want?" I screamed at her. "You have all you want. Santa's in your dungeon. Scrooge and I at your feet."

"You brought this on yourself, my dear. You placed this fight on my doorstep. I'm just defending myself. My people." She motioned around to her staff, some nodding their heads in agreement and some staying quiet in the back. "Now sit back and watch the show." She gestured out to her gardens. Rows of soldiers marched across the lawn, the red glowing lights painting them in a putrid grayish color.

"On your mark!" The general called out. Like machines, the soldiers all moved as one, their weapons pointed on their targets.

I could see Cupid holding up her hand in a hold motion. What was she doing? They were all about to be shot down.

"Get set."

"Hold," Cupid ordered.

"Fire!

"Now!"

As the soldiers fired straight at the targets, our troops dropped to the ground, shooting at their legs. The real bullets shredded through the wood, dropping dozens and dozens of soldiers to the ground. At the same time, a cluster of our rebels rushed from the trees, Dee leading them, attacking from the sides.

Dee. Seeing her, fear leaped into my throat, my body instantly lurching to go to her, but the guards yanked me back, forcing me down to my knees.

The toy soldiers had been designed for old school combat. Order and rules. Straight on fighting, not guerrilla type of warfare. But there were still a hundred times more of them.

All that could be heard were bullets cracking through the air along with screams of death. Both their side and ours. A cry bolted through my lips as I watched Cindy Lou's father get stabbed through the stomach with the spear at the end of a candy rifle.

A weapon he had probably made himself.

"No!" My body thrashed against my keepers. It was the worst kind of torture to watch those you care about fighting and dying before your eyes, and you couldn't do a damn thing.

Please. Please. Help me. Help us! I begged in my head to whatever magic might hear me, but no vial or cookie appeared before me.

Bodies and wood chips decorated the lawn as more and more dropped, red blood soaking into the snowy ground.

I spotted Dee jumping on a sentinel, taking him down, not seeing his friend coming to his defense.

"Dee!" I bellowed, terror scraping my throat as I watched the comrade draw up his rifle, the javelin end of the gun narrowing in on her back.

Dum dived for his sister, trying to knock the spear away. The toy swiveled; the spike set on its new target. I couldn't hear it, but I felt it in my bones as I watched it slice through Dum, impaling him to the ground.

Oh. God…

"Nooooooo!" A wail tore from my soul, tears strangling my throat, the pain like a tsunami. I only got a glimpse of the soldier tugging out his red soaked harpoon before they were lost behind moving forms.

"Jessica. Stop," Scrooge bellowed, pain leaking through his tone, yanking my head to him. His body fought against the dozen guards who tried to hold him back.

"I thought this was what you wanted." She waved her wrist at the battle as though she were watching kids playing in a park. "Die for what you believe in. Sounds better when you foolishly believe the 'good guy' wins. But *you* should have known better. There is no good or bad guy. Just a losing side."

My head dropped, grief sucking any hope from my veins. This was how it would end. A tragic tale no one would know about.

Boom! Boom!

The earth jolted violently, explosions ripping up the ground, the force flinging us back with a painful crunch. My backbone slammed into the wall of the fortress, and I crumpled down with a thud.

Hundreds and hundreds of toy soldiers flew into the air, their forms combusting, showering the castle with dirt and bits of wood. I tucked my head in as spikes of timber sliced at my skin. After a moment, only the sound of clumps of dirt trickling down patted the ground like snow. Blinking, I looked up to see the destruction from the grenades.

It looked like a war zone, but one side had been almost wiped out. Most of Jessica's army was sprinkled over the snow, leaving a handful of bewildered soldiers to carry on with her orders.

There was another moment of shocked silence before the world surged with chaos. Screams and cries gushed into the air. Jessica's servants scurried around like rats, climbing over each other to survive, to save themselves from another bomb.

I could hear Jessica squawking through the cloud of debris, but it was all noise as my eyes searched the space for my friends.

"Scrooge! Hare?" I cried out, climbing to my feet, my bones aching, blood trailing down my head.

"Alice?" From the wreckage clinging to the sky, billowing around like cocoa powder, a silhouette emerged, the red lights outlining his huge figure.

"Scrooge!" I yelled, hobbling for him.

Our bodies crashed together, his arms wrapping around me. "Thank Claus…you're okay." He gripped me tighter, needing to feel me as much as I needed to touch him and know he was whole.

Alive.

He was covered in blood and cuts, but he was all right. That's all that mattered.

"Hare?" I leaned back.

"Right here." Hare hobbled over; his good leg wounded at his knee. "Though for a moment I thought I was going to be a rabbit kabob."

"Do what I say!" The queen's wail broke up our reunion, all of us turning to her voice.

"Are you kidding?" Blitzen roared. "She could kill us too!"

"She won't. Not when her youngster's life is on the line. She will do what I say!"

"You are a fool."

"Do not address your queen in such a manner. Release her! Now!" She demanded, her tone wobbling with panic, her strong façade crumbling around her. "Let out Jabberwocky!"

"Fuck." Scrooge's muscles tightened, his throat bobbing.

"What?" I scanned the area, seeing our army hacking down what was left of Jessica's. All her servants and friends beelining for the hills, showing how fair-weather they were to their queen.

"This is really bad." Scrooge grabbed a candy gun off the ground, swiping another one nearby and tossing it to me.

"What?" I cried again, looking to him and Hare. "What is a jabberwocky?"

"That's not what it is. That's her name." Scrooge rolled back his shoulders, his gaze forward, searching the sky. "Be concerned about *what* it is."

"What is it?" Fear sank into my stomach.

"A very pissed off mother."

Right then, a roar assaulted the sky, echoing from the far side of the castle, shivering the ground as if it knew what was coming.

"What. Was. That?" I gulped, terror beating my heart as fast as a hummingbird's wings.

"Our executioner." Hare's cheek pinched in a grimace. "Yorkshire pudding…we are fucked."

I didn't have to wait long to understand why we were screwed.

Another roar came from the side of the castle, piercing my eardrums. My heart leaped from my throat, and I jumped, seeing a creature the size of a four-story building stomp down, shaking the ground.

"Double hot toddy." I blinked, my jaw unhinging. "What the shit is that?"

"Remember the cave we stayed in after the gremlin attack? And you laughingly asking me if Abominable Snowman used to live there?" Scrooge kept his focus up.

"Yeah?"

"Well…one did. With her young." Scrooge pointed at the beast coming around the fortress. Her white fur appeared more a dirty yellow color. Dark red stained her mouth, and she had teeth the size of elephant tusks. Razor claws were on her paws and feet. "If you think mother bears are known to protect their young at all costs, you have no idea what an Abominable Snowman will do to defend theirs."

And if Jessica was using the baby to control the mom? She would have no qualms to butcher us all to get to her young.

A shrill bellow sent chills down my spine, the ground wobbling with each step it took closer.

She reminded me of the cartoon version of the Abominable Snowman, but instead of being kind of goofy and sweet once you knew it, this monster was anything but. Fury snarled her face, her arms and legs swiping everything in its path. She was like King Kong without the sweet side.

"Jabberwocky!" Jessica's voice was strong and commanding, jerking the beast's head to her. "Kill them, and you will get your baby back. The feast awaits you, *my pet*."

Jabberwocky's nose wrinkled at the queen, but she still turned in the direction of our group, letting out a thundering bellow before lunging for the tasty appetizers just out of her reach.

"Retreat!" Cupid yelled, barely leaping out of the way of the snowman's claws. Guns cracked, shots bombarding the beast. She grunted in annoyance, batting the onslaught of bullets away as if they were flies, her lids narrowing on the attackers. Growling, she swiped down at a few elves taking a last stand, their figures flying into the air like beach balls, blood spurting from the gashes her claws sliced into them.

Jabberwocky would kill what was left of our side in moments. My weapons, including a grenade, had been stripped of us below in the dungeon, and I knew if our troop had any left, they'd be using it against this thing.

The need to do something beat against my ribs, moving my feet without thinking. We had been so foolish. Untrained and scared, our tiny army tried to fight against impossible odds. But I would fight 'til the end. Stand with my friends until my last breath.

"Have you lost your mind?" Scrooge called, his feet pounding behind me.

"Most certainly."

Scrooge shook his head but didn't try to stop me, picking up weapons as we ran for the beast. Hare tried to keep up. Loaded with all the weapons we could find still intact, I cried out in battle, running toward the furry creature, spearing her leg with a javelin.

I understood she was doing what she needed to be with her family, but I wouldn't let her take mine in the process.

Jabberwocky belted out a cry, and her large claws reached for me. I leaped back, falling on my ass, barely missing the sharp daggers.

"Alice, move!" Scrooge shouted.

Glancing up, I now saw the beast's foot coming down for me, wanting to squash me like a bug. Hurtling my body, I rolled away just as its heel crashed into the snow, sending a squall up into the air, half burying me under the powder.

Scrooge and Hare shot coal bullets at its knees; her legs dipped in pain. Jabberwocky's face scrunched in rage, pounding her fists into the earth, trying to hit the guys like whack-a-mole. She staggered, falling to her knees with force; the impact flung us back. Sailing through the air, my bones crunched as I struck the ground, rolling across the turf, knocking the wind out of me. Pain exploded through each nerve, my lungs gasping for breath, my muscles locked in place like I was making snow angels.

The Abominable Snowman's claws came into view, and with a snarl, they plunged for me. *Shouldn't she be called a snowwoman instead? Or was snowman universal for both sexes?* Funny, the thoughts that came into your head moments before death.

I couldn't breathe or move as I watched the hammer drop.

"Jabberwocky! Stop!" A man's voice chimed in the air like a bell, clear and strong, stopping the beast in place, her white brows furrowing, her head jerking to the voice. "Jabber, my old friend, you will not hurt these people...or anyone else. They are not the ones keeping your baby from you."

All heads turned to the speaker, silence descending upon the fortress.

Santa Claus, wrapped in what appeared to be a curtain, stood on the highest step, slightly above everyone, Rudy and Vixen next to him, pointing their weapons at Jessica and Blitzen.

My heart thumped with joy at seeing my friends alive. For a moment Rudy's gaze found mine, his head dipping, a twinkle in his eyes, before he snapped them back to the queen.

Santa took a step, power and command radiating off him with such intensity, the draw to his power was almost painful. I had seen different forms of Nick and Santa Claus, but nothing came close to this man holding court. His magic pulsed off him, everything dark and ugly scuttling for a place to hide.

"You are not her pet or her slave. Take your baby and go back home in peace."

On cue a smaller wail bayed from the side of the fortress, twisting Jabberwocky's head toward the noise, her eyes widening, a soft wail called from her. She took a few steps toward the cry. A baby snowman, the size of a car, came running out.

A heartbreaking yowl came from Jabberwocky, who loped toward her baby. The young cried, moving toward its mom, leaping into her arms, nuzzling her face and neck. A purrlike noise escalated from both as they united.

My heart broke for her. Even if a moment ago, she was seconds away from killing me—it was hard to hate something that was just trying to protect her child. She endured the pain and agony of being kept apart and being used to fight in hopes of saving her young. No wonder she was willing to slaughter everything in sight. Any mother would.

"I am sorry for what you went through here." Santa kept his eyes glued on Jabberwocky. "You are *free*."

The beast huffed, keeping her cub close to her chest. She stood up, bowed her head at Claus, turned, and slipped into the forest behind, the vibrations of her footsteps gradually diminishing.

"How. Dare. You," Jessica hissed. "How did you even get free? I spelled those chains."

"A magical *key*." Santa winked at me as I rose to my feet. "It unlocked much more than the chains on my wrists."

The key. Holy shit. The Christmas fairies weren't totally bonkers. They had sent me exactly what I needed. The key to free Santa. And it liberated him from more than just the binds physically around him. His magic had fully returned, no longer fighting with his demons or his fears. Santa Claus was back in the driver's seat.

"Her? How did she free you? You were still chained when I took her away."

"You have always underestimated the power of love. It liberates you from the chains inside. The ones really holding you back. I was the one stopping my own magic this whole time. Not you. Me. I began to doubt myself. Doubt what I meant to the world. I had a visit from a spirit, and I was shown what our future would be if I didn't wake up. Change my ways. That I am much stronger than I thought myself capable of."

"Oh wonderful." Jessica folded her arms. "How I have *not* missed your psychological crap."

"Again, I am sorry for how I hurt you." Santa closed his eyes briefly. "But turning your hurt and rage for me onto others? Killing and destroying because you were mad at me? That I cannot forgive."

"I wasn't looking for your forgiveness," she replied, anger bristling her shoulders. "I've had enough of this. Get him," she ordered Blitzen.

Not a single muscle flexed on the Rambo-deer—a bug trapped in the glorious power that was Santa.

Lids narrowed, she glanced around, ready to order someone else to restrain him, but she found herself completely alone. Not one of her staff, even Pepper Mint or Everly Green, were left standing next to her, not one of her soldiers was still alive.

"I ordered you! You useless animal," she shouted at Blitzen again.

He was in her face in a blink; his hand wrapped around her throat.

"I'm useless, huh? For decades I've been silent, knowing what I was working for. The end game. I may have worked *with* you, but let's get this straight, I never worked *for* you. Your throat was next on my list after this was all over. You were just a means to an end for me too." She jerked in his hold, his wrath dripping off every word.

"Step back." Rudy's gun went to the back of Blitzen's head. "The game has been played out, and you lost."

"You say that now because Santa's standing behind you." Blitzen whipped around, the muzzle of the gun landing on his forehead. "But we both know you are a feckless coward. Always was and always will be. Something Clarice realized about you...and soon she will too." Blitzen nodded toward Vixen.

"I don't feel killing, torturing, and bullying makes me a real reindeer. Only those lacking..." Rudy's gaze dropped to Blitzen's pants. "...feel the need to put others down to make themselves feel good."

"If that's what you want to believe." Blitzen chuckled as Rudy grabbed him, shoving him to the entrance of the castle.

Santa stepped down, moving to his wife, his chin held high, looming over her figure.

"What are you going to do to me?" She folded her arms, her voice bored, but I could see sparks of panic flash in her eyes. "You wouldn't kill me. Santa Claus couldn't possibly do something so sinful."

"No." He shook his head. "I don't have it in me to kill."

A smug smile tugged at her mouth.

"What I have planned for you is far worse." Nick's attitude bloomed out, a glint in his eye. "You'll be wishing I had just killed you, Jessie."

"Like what?" she whispered.

"Somewhere you will be forever tortured by those you have murdered. Haunted by the lives you took."

Her eyes widened in terror, her head shaking, understanding oozing from her pores. "No, you wouldn't. Santa Claus is not capable of cruelty."

"No, *Santa's* not..." He winked. "But Nick sure is."

Chapter 44

Death was strewn across the earth, but I kept my back to it as I stepped forward, following Santa, Rudy, Vixen, and Scrooge into the castle with the prisoners. I couldn't look, my heart not ready to find the truth of who I would find among the dead.

"Hare, find who you can." Scrooge dipped his head toward the field, not looking either.

"But-but…" Hare shook his head.

"Hare. Please. I need you here." Scrooge's voice dipped low, stopping Hare in his tracks. Scrooge didn't mention Pen, Dum, and Dee, but they were written all over his face. The sorrow that awaited us, the people we lost. It was an unopened box. You knew something was in it, you just didn't know how much grief was inside until you actually peered in. The silence from the garden hinted at the worst, only a few moans and cries.

Right now we needed to deal with Jessica and Blitzen. Scrooge didn't wait for a response, moving up to the group on the veranda, guarding Jessica. Santa wouldn't hold a weapon and too much could go wrong with just Vix and Rudy guarding the two slippery snakes. Jessica still held power, and I knew she would not go quietly.

"I don't want to know," Hare said quietly, his gaze sliding behind us. I could hear a handful of people sobbing and moving through the debris.

"I know." I squeezed his shoulder, pain flinching my forehead as I headed after Scrooge. To be the one to discover who was alive...or dead...was the worst position.

I headed forward to the fortress. Vixen and Rudy kept Blitzen close, his stagger still full of confidence and ego, while Scrooge kept a gun to the back of Jessica's head. The only weapon I had left was the ice pick, which throbbed in my hand with ironic justice.

False light flickered against the dark stone walls, our footsteps echoing off the high ceilings sounding like a drum march. Not one person was left in the castle, but clothes and items were strung around showing signs of people's fast getaways.

"You disappoint me, Alice." Jessica's voice slithered to me. "Once again letting men control you, tell you your worth."

"Is that any better than letting you?" I growled, holding up my pick to her neck. "Look familiar?"

Her lips pinched with amusement.

"The same thing you used to *control* me." I skated the point to her temple. "Do you know how good it felt when I stabbed Dr. Cane with it? The irony of killing him with the very item he had in my brain just moments before, trying to turn me into a vegetable he could abuse."

"I saw your handiwork." Jessica's eyes strained to

look at me without twisting her head. "I was quite impressed. As I thought from the beginning, you would have made an excellent partner. It's not too late, my dear girl. You are far more powerful than any man here. Remember the feeling of the pick spearing into his head, the power you felt as his life slipped away. You have it in you, Alice. It calls to you...we could be magnificent together."

"Shut up." Scrooge shoved her forward, but her smile only grew, her eyes finding mine.

It scared me, the high I felt killing him. The justice of saving the world from someone like him. What if I was more similar to Jessica than I thought? What if I liked it too much? Wanted more of it? The world was better off without him. Would be better off with a lot of men who beat, raped, stole, and destroyed.

"Haven't you had enough of being kept in a box?" Her voice coiled around me. "Scrooge may talk a good game, but he and Nickolas are no different from any other men. Deep down they cannot handle your power. A woman's power. It will be gradual, putting you back in a box. All men, no matter what they say, feel too insecure at the thought a woman could rule them. Their fragile egos can't handle the fact they know we would do far better ruling the world."

A fizz of anger crackled at the back of my head, my teeth crunching together, her words sinking into places. Nooooo...

"Get. Out. Of. My. Head." I snarled.

"I wasn't in your head, my dear. Whatever you are thinking is all you." She grinned maliciously, licking her lips as a cat does with cream.

Doubt sprang like flowers, the ice pick dropping from her temple.

"You know the truth, Alice. You are scared to face it. Realize it in yourself."

"I said shut up!" Scrooge dug the gun deeper into her scalp.

"Feeling left out?" She smirked.

Scrooge grunted, his nose flaring, his jaw locking. "You can't get into my head anymore." He snarled, his voice low. "I know the truth now."

"Really?" she taunted. "Want to bet on that?"

"*Stop. It.*" A streak of pain sliced over Scrooge's face, proving she could still crawl into his brain. It was less effective than before, but continued to cause him grief. "I have a lot of guilt from that night, but Belle made her choice. You were the one she was talking to. The one who betrayed her."

"And your innocent son? Did he make his own choice?" Like an arrow, her words dug into its target. Agony curled Scrooge's shoulders, but he kept upright, his grip on her crunching down.

"Jessica!" Santa boomed, his voice an order. "Cease!" At his demand, it was as if the sun broke through the clouds, a darkness easing off my chest. Her power weaseled into your head like a worm, digging holes of doubt and hate, while Santa's lifted it away, brushing out the cobwebs she weaved into your mind. Letting you breathe again. See the truth.

Dammit. I let her get in, mess with me.

She lifted her lip in a malicious sneer, her heels clipping the stairs as we rounded up to the tower. He was taking her to the mirror.

Santa seemed to know exactly where he was going, even though he had only been held prisoner here. Something told me it was the magic of Santa. He knew more than just when you were sleeping or naughty.

Entering the small tower room, I twisted to watch Scrooge shove Jessica up the final step. Her gaze locked with mine, her mouth twitching with wickedness, a plan toiling behind her eyes.

It was a split second when understanding flooded me with alarm. Before my lips could even part, she dug her heel onto the last stair rise. *No!* My head screamed as I watched everything in slow motion and fast forward simultaneously.

At her sudden stop, Scrooge knocked into her, bouncing him backward. The small turret step not holding his huge form, he stumbled back with a shout, his eyes meeting mine. For a moment, I saw the shock and fear, the realization of what was about to happen before his physique was taken by gravity. Bones crunching, his body plummeted down the steep spiral stairs.

"Scrooge!" I screamed, instinctively lurching for him, the same time Jessica came barreling into me. Crashing into the ground, my tailbone rammed into the uneven hard floor, wind gushing from my lungs. The ice pick in my hand tumbled to the ground. Jessica clawed my face, climbing over me to reach it.

"No!" I grunted, my fingers straining to reach the weapon, the tips brushing the handle.

Pandemonium detonated in the room.

Jessica dug her nails into my scalp as she forcefully slammed my head into the floor. My skull, cracking

457

against the stone floor, caused pain to stab through my brain, my vision blurring, the ice pick rolling away from my limp fingers.

Blitzen slammed his head back into Rudy's face. Blood spurted like a fountain from Rudy's nose, a snap echoing in the chamber. Blitzen whirled around, taking advantage, grabbing the gun in Rudy's hand as his heavy boot slammed into Vixen's chest, knocking her to the ground. Her gun tumbled to the ground. Blitzen leaped for it, kicking her in the side.

Jessica swiped it up, grabbing me by the hair. She yanked me to my feet, the pick digging deep into the thin skin at my neck as she pulled me back into her, using me as a shield.

"Now, how is this for irony?" she hissed in my ear, prodding the ice pick into my neck, my pulse bouncing off the metal sticking in my throat, right at my artery. One move and I would bleed out in moments.

"Jessica." Santa stood there, his voice calm and powerful. As if nothing remarkable happened. That the situation didn't get flipped and turned upside down in seconds.

"Don't even think about using your magic, Nicholas." Jessica's breath seethed past my ear to the man across the tiny room. "I can stab this through her throat long before you can do anything to stop me."

Blitzen held both guns up, moving around to the side of her, pointing them at anyone hinting on moving. Even if they hated each other, they knew each other was the best option to get out of this. The enemy of your enemy is a temporary ally.

Boots pelted up the stairs, Scrooge appearing in the door, his eyes widening as they met mine, but he quickly hid away his emotion, his expression locking down as he stepped fully into the room.

"And you too, Knave." Jessica sneered. "Your girl dies if you try to make *one* move toward me."

"Jessica." Scrooge held his hands up as if he were trying to calm a wild animal. "Don't do this."

"Why?" the queen asked. "Give me one good reason. Since she has shown up, she has been nothing but trouble. She is the culprit. Why so many more have died."

"No." Santa shook his head. "She was the trigger who woke us up. The girl who saved Winterland."

"Saved Winterland?" Jessica burst out in a howl. "Does it look like she saved you? Look around, you idiot. The countless bodies lying on the lawn. No one is left! You lost!" She laughed again. "You are delusional. But why should I be surprised? The man who's based off fairytales, wraps himself up in his own false reality."

"It's not about winning or losing this actual place." Santa shook his head. "You've always missed the point of what Winterland is. The heart of this realm. It's not a physical place, but—"

"Ugh, no, please stop." She cut him off. "If you say it's a place that exists in my heart, I might stab my own throat." Jessica yanked me farther back, shoving in the tip deeper, trails of blood pooling at my collarbone.

"Alice saved Winterland because she roused us from our slumber. She inspired us to fight for what we believe in. For love and kindness. True freedom."

"Please. Shut up. You are giving me a migraine." Jessica groaned, inching me back again. Every step leading us closer to the mirror. Once we went through, it was game over. "Now, it's been lovely catching up, but it's time for me to depart."

"No." Scrooge lurched forward. Blitzen directed the gun straight at his head.

"Stay back." He moved with us, his weapon ready to fire. "You prepared for her to die in front of you? No matter what...we are walking out of here. If you want your girl alive for a bit longer, you stay right there."

"I mean, did you really think I was going to give in so easily?" Jessica scoffed. My skin burned as the sharp point tore into it, my head spinning and foggy. "I'm finally free of *you*, of this life. I'm not giving it up. She will close the door for good."

Santa's head drew up, his demeanor shifting in a blink, anger lifting his lip, his glower lowering on his wife.

Nick.

He chuckled dryly, stepping forward; the naughty Santa smirked with glee.

"You think you can shut the door on me?" Nick tilted his head, his bushy eyebrows lifting. "I'm the reason this realm even *exists*. I'm the reason *you* even exist. You aren't meant for Earth, Jessica. You were made up *for me*. In a make-believe world."

"Screw you. I've been living without you just fine," she snapped. "I belong on Earth. They find me very real. And capable."

"I am the one who used to be a real man before my legend made Winterland. I am the bridge between the worlds. You can't keep me out. And you can't kill me. I am more powerful than you. It took me a long time to see that I *let* you have power you shouldn't have had because of guilt."

"Let me? Don't underestimate me. You started out real and now are merely a legend, where I started out a legend and will become a real person. One who stands without you," she snarled, yanking me back. My pulse thudded in my neck; my breath was clipped with fear. My eyes constantly wandered to Scrooge, trying to find some way out of this. "I'm not the sweet little wife you once knew. And you didn't let me have anything. I. Took. It."

Could I fight her before she pierced my artery? I doubted even the Christmas fairies could save me from this. I still asked for their help, but nothing appeared. There would be a time they weren't going to be there at all. I knew I wasn't immune to death. What if they kept me alive just to get Santa free? The legend of "her" said she saved Winterland, but stupid me never asked what her fate was after.

"What do you expect to happen right now, Jessie?" Nick took another step. "You take her through? Hold her prisoner? And we would let you?"

"I love how you think you *let me* do anything. I haven't needed your permission or approval in decades," she spat at Nick before her eyes slid to Scrooge. "If you love her, you'll leave her be. You come for her…she dies."

"Like you won't kill me anyway," I growled.

"Not for a while. You are my insurance getting back to earth. But don't worry, you will be so brain dead you won't care where you are or who you are with."

"I will hunt you down. I will never let you rest." Scrooge's chest heaved with fury, his eyes burning with hate. "I will always come for her."

"Every time you try, she will get punished. Do you know how close someone can come to death without actually dying?" She scuttled us back again, a few steps from the mirror.

"You are grasping at straws. You have no one left. No soldier to order around, none of your supposed admirers fighting for you. Let it go, Jessie. It's over." Nick clenched his fists.

Tinsel my tree, I didn't know what would happen once we slipped into the glass, but in my gut I knew it wasn't good. What if they couldn't follow us easily? Or it spit us out in different places like the holly maze did? They could be lost to me for good. I looked down. Two steps and we would be ingested by the mirror, out of reach.

"I *vow* I will never be confined by you again. Being your wife for so many centuries was like being put in a box. I'd rather die. I will not be held as your prisoner again. In *any* capacity." Her heel touched the mirror, making it wobble with energy.

"If that's what you want..." A voice came from the door, jerking us to the side. Hare hopped into the room, a gun in his hand pointed at Jessica, his teeth bared.

"Hare, no!" Scrooge yelled.

Boom!

Jessica shoved me to the side as the bullet flew across the room, sinking into its target, the sound resounding off the walls.

The recoil rang in my ears, bombarding numbness down my limbs, shock opening my mouth.

Burning. Hot.

"Alice!" I could hear Scrooge yell as I stumbled to the side, grabbing for the area above my heart, hot liquid gushing through my fingers.

"No! Alice!" Hare yelled, my gaze connecting with his, his eyes wide with horror, telling me what my body didn't feel. Strange. I knew I should feel pain, but everything felt slow, as if I had been anesthetized. My mouth opened to speak, but a deep grunt broke through the room. It took me a moment to realize it wasn't mine.

A body staggered behind me, knocking into me, twisting my head slowly around.

Blitzen's eyes were wide in shock, his mouth parted, blood cascading from his lips. Crimson gushed from the middle of his chest, down his torso.

He looked down then back up, blinking, his mouth parting to say something. He dropped to the ground with a loud thud. Wet gurgled gasps rattled his lungs before his body seized with death.

I heard a cry of shock, but I couldn't decipher who it was from, my head spinning with blood loss. The bullet went straight through me, killing Blitzen, but I knew the damage it did to me, the way coldness crept into my bones, death lurking at the door, waiting for me.

My body crumpled to the floor.

"Alice." Hands grabbed me, bundling me into his lap. Scrooge's warmth felt like an electric blanket as I lost my own, my essence oozing from the bullet hole so close to my heart.

Jessica whirled around, lurching for the mirror, cutting her losses.

"Fuck, no!" Hare bellowed, his body bounding for hers, his teeth sinking into the back of her ankle.

Her scream pitched in the air, her body plunging to the ground, her hands gripping the frame of the mirror, trying to pull herself through it.

"Stop!" Nick leaped to her, yanking her back and dragging her form across the floor before he forcefully flipped her over onto her back, his hands pinning her to the ground. "You aren't going anywhere but in a box, *Mrs. Claus*."

"And without a lucky charm." Hare jumped onto her chest, his paw wrapping around her necklace, yanking his foot from her neck roughly. "Think this belongs to me, snow bitch."

A malicious smile grew on her face as he put his foot around his own neck. Rudy and Santa yanked her up to her feet. She didn't fight or fuss, a strange confidence lighting her eyes.

Nick held her, his head flicking at Rudy and Vixen. "Flip the mirror upside down and backward."

"What?" Hare asked.

"Mirrors have many paths. Entrances and exits. You have to make sure it's the right one. The Land of the Lost Souls is never straightforward."

Rudy and Vixen quickly switched the mirror. The glass turned a deep inky black, sparks of light tapping on the other side.

Souls.

They clamored at the glass, either wanting to be freed or waiting for their next meal to feed on.

Jessica swallowed, fright flickering for a moment in her expression.

"Time to say goodbye, Jessie. Get comfortable with torment for eternity."

Out of everyone in the room, her eyes found mine. "I love when men underestimate us."

"I'm sure Santa would have some emotional, meaningful moment here. But I'm not one for farewells," Nick snarled and shoved her. "Plus, I couldn't give a fuck."

Her form plunged into the darkness, the mirror wobbling with energy as she fell into it. Descending into a world of madness. Her eyes latched onto mine, as her body was slurped up into the black ink. As if she were sucking me in with her, pulling me into darkness, shadows crept around my peripheral, nausea watering the back of my throat, my head spinning.

"Alice?" My name sounded far away. "No. Hold on."

But awareness slipped from me, pulling me away from consciousness.

And I fell, again.

Down. Down. A dark, dark hole.

Chapter 45

"All I want for Christmas is my two front teeth…"

A voice slipped into my conscious, fluttering my lids. Awareness slowly towed me from the deep darkness, my head feeling like it had been stuffed with cotton balls. My skull throbbed, a sharp headache pulsing between my eyes. My vision took in the ceiling, the high-pitched roof, and dark stone walls. Turning my head, I saw I was in a room that had been an infirmary or had been turned into one…like we were on the Harry Potter set. Dozens of occupied single beds lined in rows through the large room, three huge windows were at the far side of the space, dim light flickered from the sconces on the wall.

We were still in the castle.

Jessica's castle.

The event fumbled through my mind like snippets of a movie.

Shot. A bullet had gone through my chest.

My gaze zipped down my body, expecting to feel insufferable pain. Touching the spot above my heart, it was wrapped in gauze, red stains soaking through the material. The wound was sore and tender but felt nothing like a gunshot should feel. Not that I had any experience with being shot before, but you didn't need to have it to know it should be excruciating.

Spicy mulled wine, what kind of drugs did they have me on here?

"My two front teeth..." A murmur came from the floor, and I lifted my head, peering over the side. Penguin sat on the ground, creating artwork with swabs, wiggling around as he played and sang.

"*Pen?*" My dry throat cracked, barely coming out a whisper. Emotion filled my eyes. He was okay.

His head tipped up, his eyes growing wide.

"Ms. Alice! You are awake." He leaped up, coming to the side of the bed. "I'm so glad. You've been sleeping forever. I was so worried. Oh my, my, Mr. Scrooge is going to be upset he wasn't here. But I told him I'd watch over both of you. I have *so* diligently looked after you guys. I mean there were a few moments when I got bored...and I guess the time I got hungry...and well I ran out of cotton balls a few other times..." Pen rattled on, but my focus was on the other person Pen had been "minding."

"Oh god..." I shoved the blankets away, ignoring the pain screaming through my body. I scrambled to the bed next to mine. My hands went to his face. Slow draws of air told me he was alive, but it didn't feel solid.

I gulped, tears choking me. "Dum..."

His tiny figure lay in the bed, his skin pale where it wasn't cut up and scarred. He looked to be healing, but the wounds swathed almost every inch of his skin. A bandage similar to mine was placed over a deeper injury on his hip. But it was another wound that really caught my attention. "Oh no…"

Where a pointed ear should have been on the right side of his head was a bloody stump. Taped with dressing, the cotton was stained a dark red, almost looking black.

"Santa thinks he'll be okay." Pen moved next to my leg, wrapping his flipper around my knee, making me realize I was only wearing my underwear and bra. Not that I cared. Saving my life was far more important than any modesty I might have had. Which was none. "I'm so glad you are all right, Ms. Alice. I don't know what I would have done if you weren't."

Wordlessly I rubbed his head, peering over the room at the filled cots. Every face I knew. Cindy Lou was sitting up, staring out the window into the darkness, her mom in the bed next to her, asleep. I knew her father was dead. I had watched it happen.

Bea, Happy, Cupid, Comet, Donner, and a handful of elves and Whos filled the other beds. These were the survivors.

"Is Dee okay?" I asked Pen, afraid of his response.

"I am." Her voice came from behind me, whirling me around. She stood at the doorway, her face covered in dried blood and cuts, but other than that she appeared fine. "I'm a warrior like you, Ms. Alice."

"Dee." I opened my arms, and she darted to me, her body slamming into mine, almost tipping me back into the bed.

"You should be resting, my dear." Santa came in right behind her, now dressed in a gray woman's robe, but at least it fully covered him. "Your body is still healing, absorbing the pure mistletoe extract."

That was why I was feeling so good and healing far faster than a human should. Mistletoe was magic. It had saved me from the holly attack, saved Dee from death when attacked by the Gremlins, and what cocooned me in magic from the gingerbread house and so many other instances. I wanted to kiss the mistletoe.

"Sit." My body wanted to oblige his request, but my mind was reeling with all the events and how much I could be helping instead of lying here.

Dee's pained expression went across the room to Happy's still body, then back to her brother. A split second of a fight wrestled on her features before she jumped on the bed with her twin, curling in next to him. I licked my lips, staring at the pair. It was her turn to comfort her wounded sibling like he had. What these two had been through broke my heart.

"Dum will be all right." Santa followed my gaze. "It will be difficult, but we were able to get enough medicine in his system to save him. He will never hear out of that ear again…but he is alive."

I nodded. I hated he was permanently hurt, but I couldn't deny his life was far more important than his ear. Mistletoe may heal, but it didn't grow body parts back.

"They all will." Santa motioned around the room. "At least physically. The emotional damage is a different monster."

I understood that.

"Sit. Please." Santa nodded at the bed, his eyes not landing directly on me. That's how I truly knew it was

Santa and not Nick. Nick would be outright staring at my half-naked body. I lowered myself, pulling a sheet over me as Pen scrambled up next to me, humming happily.

"I do not know how to express my gratitude for what you've done, Alice."

"I really didn't do anything except fall down a hole."

"No, my dear, you did far more than that. As I told Mrs. Claus, you woke us up, made us realize what was most important. It took an outsider to bring magic back to this land." He swallowed. "Dying for a better world is worthier than living in one because of fear. There is no freedom in living if you are *only* existing."

"Feel I've heard something similar before." A smirk tugged at my mouth, remembering Scrooge saying the exact thing when I first met him.

"You brought hope back to us, Alice." Santa gripped the metal bedframe. "The most heroic act of all."

"Heroic?" I laughed.

"Yes." Santa dipped his head, a playful smile growing on his mouth. "You think anyone else could turn the bitter, hateful heart of Ebenezer Scrooge to believe in optimism and love again? That *in itself* is a miracle."

A chuckle bounced from my chest, causing me to flinch in pain.

"Hey," Scrooge growled, sauntering into the room. "This heart is still as bitter and black as it always was." His words didn't match the twinkle in his blue eyes as his gaze roamed hungrily over me.

"Sure." Santa winked at me. "We'll let him believe that."

"How are you feeling?" Scrooge stopped next to Santa.

"Sore, but otherwise surprisingly fine."

"Mistletoe." His eyebrow curved up sensually, his gaze roaming over my nakedness. "It does wonders to the body."

"Oh, Keebler nut sack. You two aren't going to be like this *all* the time now?" Hare bounced in behind his buddy, rolling his eyes. "I *will* drown myself in scalding Christmas pudding."

"Hey, fluffy butt scrubber..." Scrooge whapped Hare behind the head. "Don't you have some groveling to do?"

"No."

Scrooge smacked him again.

"Fine. Fine." Hare sighed dramatically. "*Sorry* I shot you...though if you two keep up the whipped-cream packing in *my* kitchen...I'm not so sorry."

A burst of laughter spurted from my throat, my head shaking, as I peered around at my family. Some had a while to go, but we were all alive. Together.

"Is Jessica gone? For good?"

"Jessica will be spending eternity being tortured by the souls they murdered." Santa lowered his head, sadness creasing his brows. "Blitzen went with her."

"I thought he died?"

"He did. But that's where his soul will reside. He does not deserve to rest. Even in death, he must face his own crimes. The lives he cruelly tortured and destroyed. Believe me..." Santa's lips pursed, a flash of agony streaked over his face, then disappeared. "They will both be getting their just desserts." He cleared his throat, stepping back. "There is much to do. I have a long journey to restore Winterland to what it once was. I've been absent for too long. I need to work extra hard to be the leader they once believed in. And Christmas is only a few days away."

He gave us a last nod before drifting to each bed, checking on his people, their eyes and faces lighting up at his presence, no matter what horror they just experienced. We were all quiet for a moment, watching Santa move through the room.

I swallowed, looking up at Scrooge. "Noel?"

Scrooge's mouth pushed together with a slight shake of his head. "Dee said she saw him right before the final explosion. He was right in the middle of it...I'm sorry."

Grief expanded in my throat, emotion filling my eyes. A sob hitched in my throat, my head bowing forward. It didn't matter I hadn't known him well. The experience in the facility bonded us. Noel, my bright star in a dark place. I made it out of there because of him...and now he was gone.

"Dasher too." Dee sniffed, still curled up to her brother. "Half of the Whos and dozens of my friends..."

"I'm so sorry." A few tears slid down my face, the reality of death sinking in.

"We have each other." Pen leaned into me. Softly, he started to sing, his voice growing louder and louder until it resonated off the stone.

"Please come home for Christmas...no more sorrow, no grief and pain. And I'll be happy Christmas once again."

Liquid fell down my face, the song taking on a different meaning. My chest ached with pain so heavy it bowed me forward.

"Oh my elves...look." Dee sat up, pointing toward the window, my gaze following it.

My mouth dropped, rising from the bed, my lids blinking, making sure I was truly witnessing what I saw. My legs moved without a thought, taking me to the window. Those awake or capable followed me with the same reverence.

"Oh my Santa..." I trailed off, my palm pressing to the glass, watching what I took for granted every day on earth.

The sun glowed behind the mountains, igniting them in blues, golds, and reds as it rose. Rays speared through the window, feeling as if they were going through my chest. My heart filled with awe, like I had never seen a sunrise before. Scrooge moved in beside me, his arms going around my waist as Dee, Pen, and Hare squeezed in front of us.

Gasps and cries sounded around me, everyone taking in the spectacular sunrise. Something they had been denied for decades. Power had fully shifted. Santa Claus claimed his throne, banishing the darkness she forced on this place.

"No more sorrow...grief and pain..." Penguin's voice filled the space, the song going from heartbreaking to inspiring.

So many lives had been lost, so much heartbreak and grief. I knew this place would always bear the scars of what had happened, but I knew the strength of these people. They would rebuild.

Painted across the sky like a canvas, a new day dawned on the horizon.

And like my rebel alliance...

A new hope.

Epilogue

One year later

Warm white lights twinkled off the tree and mantle, the flicker of flames dancing in the fireplace as soft music filled the air. Crumpled Christmas paper streamed over the floor of the family room from opening our presents earlier.

"Ugh." I leaned back against the sofa, rubbing my full stomach, the turkey dinner still dancing on my taste buds. "I'm so full."

"You'll be asking for a turkey sandwich in an hour." Dinah flopped on the opposite side of the sectional, groaning. "I'm gonna have to run extra far tomorrow, feels like I'm carrying a potato baby."

"Oh please, you had a *drop* of mashed potatoes and gravy." I rolled my eyes, scooting farther up the pillows. My sister was getting ready for a marathon and taking it extremely serious. As she did everything.

Something had changed with her since I had returned home from the "facility." She was more restless, sometimes she'd space off as if she were looking at something. I couldn't deny Jessica got into my head, bringing up the fact my sister could be like me. But, whenever I'd ask her, saying I was here if she needed me, she'd shake her head and say it was nothing.

"So full..." Scott shuffled to the end of the lounge where Dinah was and fell onto her legs, stuffing another slice of chocolate-gingerbread Yule log into his mouth.

"Oh my god, you're having another one? What is that, your fourth?" Dinah moved to make room for her boyfriend. "You are going to be sick."

"I know, but they're sooooo good." He laid the last piece on his tongue, groaning with ecstasy. "Seriously, Alice, where did you get this? It's the best thing I've ever put in my mouth."

A smile twitched on my mouth. "A friend makes them."

"Well your friend needs to open a bakery, so I can eat these all year."

"I don't even think *your* metabolism could handle that." Dinah laughed, patting his stomach.

"I'd love to try." He snuggled into my sister. "If your friend makes other goodies, I am more than willing to be the tester."

"He does." I grinned. "Everything he makes is heavenly. He's opening a bakery around Easter." The property next to my shop had already been rented and was starting renovations.

"I'm moving to New York as soon as it is." Scott laid back his head, slouching more into the sofa, winking over at Dinah. "Right, babe?"

She shook her head, telling him there was no chance in hell. She liked the small town. The structure, being in control. Vanilla. She liked the same routine and what to expect. New York was the opposite of that.

"Well, thank him for us. It really was delicious." Mom came behind the sofa, peering down at her two daughters. She looked as beautiful as ever in a fluffy green sweater and long white tulle skirt, her hair pulled back in a loose bun.

"Best dessert I've ever tasted." My father strolled up behind her, putting his arm around my mom. I had come in from the city, where I was living again, to spend Christmas Eve with them.

My mom and sister had done a good job of pretending the events last year didn't happen. Though what they remember and what really happened were quite different. Jessica's peppermint syrup had faafoozooled everyone's minds. Some parts seemed to be completely wiped from their memory. Like Jessica herself. She was taken wholly out of the scenario. All they recalled was Dr. Cane and the staff, but not her. Not even as our neighbor or how my mother fawned over her. Jessica Winters never existed.

I couldn't deny it. Mrs. Claus was the epitome of evil genius. When the effects of her magical syrup wore off, they took her with it. She would get off scot-free, all her wicked deeds gone because no one could recall her. And she was more than willing to throw her staff under the bus if they had been caught.

My stint at the facility happened. Nothing could erase that from people's memories, but since everyone there had disappeared taking the money, Mom and Dinah boasted about how we were all victims of this terrible scam. They took advantage of our vulnerability. My mother thoroughly denied they never researched the place or signed over all rights to the doctors. She is sure someone scrubbed all the medical licenses she saw, along with the website, reviews, and the approval by the APA.

Both my mom and sister talk about that time where I was a little "lost," and the facility was more like a weeklong therapy session for me. My father would nod and agree, but I could see it in his eyes. He remembered more than he was putting on. I sometimes saw pain and confusion in his expression, reminding me of when I was fighting between two realities, the truth slipping in telling you not all is what it seems.

Funny what you will let yourself believe for it to make sense in your world.

"Christmas movie time." Dinah clicked the remote, the TV flaring to life. Objects moved across the screen. "Oh…maybe not this one."

My gaze shot to the movie playing on TV, scaly green creatures jumping across the monitor.

Gremlins.

"It's fine, guys." I smiled. "I won't freak out this time." I can't say *Gremlins* is my favorite movie at all anymore, but this time I recalled what happened on that hill. What terrorized me before was the images I didn't understand flashing in my head. "It's classic Christmas."

"It's okay; we can find something else." Dinah started flipping through the channels. "This is better."

I burst out laughing, the cartoon *Rudolph the Red-Nosed Reindeer* displayed on the TV.

"This movie very much took Hollywood liberties." I pushed myself off the sofa, shaking my head.

"Huh?" Everyone peered at me strangely.

"Reindeer games are to the death, not fun or cute...oh, and Blitzen is a sack of shit...and Clarice?" I pointed at the screen as I headed out. "Complete vapid bitch. He's far better off with Vixen."

I could feel my family gaping at me as I strolled out of the room, my grin spreading over my face. Opening the sliding door, I stepped out onto my back porch. The icy air instantly soaked through my red sweater and skinny jeans, the cute outfit doing nothing to hold off the freezing temperatures.

"Shit." I rubbed at my arms, my knee-high gray velvet boots giving me the only sense of warmth. Sometimes I forgot how cold it got here.

The moon glowed in the sky, daubing the backyard with a bluish white, the trees creating heavy shadows that made them feel alive. I was waiting for the day they started talking or throwing sap balls at me.

The night was crisp and clear, the stars sparkling in the sky. It was beautiful. But only one thing held my focus. I took a few moments to appreciate the fantasy standing before me.

Arms folded over his thin black sweater, pushing out his broad shoulders, his jeans cupping his taut ass perfectly, Matt was a fairytale and porno wrapped up in one.

"Hey." I strolled up to his figure, getting lost in his raw beauty. "What are you doing out here?"

Vibrant blue eyes shot to me, always filled with a deep primal hunger which made me inhale sharply every time he looked at me.

"Thinking." His gaze ran down me, gobbling me up,

as if he were still famished, before looking back out at the night.

"Do I dare ask?" My hand ran over his bicep. He instantly dropped his tucked arm and wrapped it around me, tugging me into his body with a rumble.

"Just how different last year is to this one." His large hands ran over my ass, pulling me in tighter. "The married man, who had a kid playing inside, couldn't fight the pull to come out here. How hard I tried to rationalize my attraction to you. The draw that pulled me like I didn't have a choice."

"Because you didn't." I pressed into him. "Just as I didn't."

Matt's mouth brushed up against my ear. "I miss him."

"I know." I wrapped my arms around his neck. "That will never stop."

"Remembering the other boy makes me feel as I'm betraying my real son, but then it freaks me out when my memories of the other Tim start to fade."

I leaned my forehead against his. There were no words of wisdom or anything that would speed the healing of his loss. Time might ebb it, but him missing Timothy would never go away.

Here, Scrooge went by Matt Hatter, the *single* neighbor I fell in love with. Jessica took herself out of the equation, but the few who saw or met the fragile Tim vaguely remember him. The story my neighborhood understood as truth was Matt had lived next door with his sickly son. A widowed father whose son had died of cancer this past year. We had started a relationship, falling in love—some said too quickly since he was mourning, and I was crazy, but they chalked it up to my impulsive nature. I could give a shit what people thought. The rumors of Matt coming to get me at the "fraud facility" were hilarious because none of them came close to the utter ridiculous truth.

Within the month of coming back home, he sold the house, and we moved to New York, starting a business.

My parents tried to avoid the topic of Tim or the first wife, but Matt would freely talk about them. Telling us funny stories from when Timmy was a baby, and he and Belle struggling to figure out parenthood. All they knew about Belle was she was killed in a tragic accident before he moved here. I think it was helping Scrooge heal. Not ignoring his son's death or Belle's, but to acknowledge the joy and pain openly.

His fingers went under my sweater, skating up my body, his teeth grazing my neck.

"We need to get back." My breath hitched as his mouth and hands danced over my skin, his touch still speaking like fire and ice. The connection between us only grew, weaving our tale even tighter together.

"How about we sneak around the side of the house? Fuck you in the snow."

"We were almost caught earlier." My head dropped back, his mouth nipping at the skin. A slight scar still lined my neck from the ice pick, always reminding me I survived so much. I also still had one above my heart from the bullet wound. I was thinking about putting a tattoo there. Not to cover, but to add. I loved my imperfections. Like Dee's, they were my survival scars. They told the tale of who I was today. What I went through.

My story.

"Dammit, Scrooge." I moaned as his fingers dropped down into my jeans. The man knew how to tease my body in an instant, and we had yet to find any limit of wanting each other. "We really need to get back to the city. Plus, we aren't good at being quiet. At all."

"No, you aren't." He smirked in my ear. "Had to muzzle you earlier."

A hot blush burst over my cheeks. He really did. We had snuck up to my bedroom before dinner…then the bathroom after dinner. I was sure my family knew what was going on, but everybody acted as if they didn't.

It took everything I had to step back, sucking in the frozen air, hoping to cool myself down.

"Come on." I held out my hand, feeling his fingers thread through mine, his gaze still devouring me. "Let's go home."

A naughty grin hooked the side of his mouth as he followed me back inside.

"Guys, we're taking off." I reached for my long, gray winter coat, grabbing the bags full of our gifts and a few things I took from my old room.

"I don't understand why you can't stay." Mom sighed. "Why you need to work on Christmas Day, I don't understand."

"Get used to it, Mom." I hugged her as Dad shook hands with Matt. "This is my life now. Plus, we're spending Christmas Day with Matt's family."

"Will we ever get to meet them?" Dad hugged me next, squeezing extra tight.

Matt looked at me, winking. "Someday."

We knew that day might come to pass, but right now

was not the time. I think my mom still tip-toed around me, afraid I'd fall off the secure wall and crack like an egg again.

When I felt the time was right, I would show them that I never lost my mind, though they might lose theirs. Everything I saw was true and very real.

Hugging my sister and Scott while my mom fussed over Matt, handing him more bags to carry, we finally got out of the house.

"Sis?" Dinah called out to me as I opened the car door. Matt still wasn't comfortable driving since he was born in the time of horses and wagons. He had become a fan of the metro, though.

I looked up at her, an odd sadness flickered over her features.

"I love you."

"Love you too." I slanted my head, taken back by her sudden declaration before getting into the car.

Matt climbed in next to me, tucking a bag I handed him between his feet as I pulled out of the drive. We gave my family one last wave before setting out.

"Wait. I don't think this is ours." He touched the fabric busting out the top of the shopping bag.

"No, it is." A salacious smile grew on my mouth, staring out in the dark night. "Is it most definitely *ours*."

"I don't remember opening this."

"It wasn't a present from my family." I grinned, sliding my eyes to him briefly. "It's a gift from me."

"To me?" His expression furrowed, tugging at the garment. "I know I didn't open anything with green and red stripes."

"It's something you will unwrap when we get home."

"Really?" His eyebrow curved, his finger sliding slowly over the material. "Can I peek now?"

"The naughty boys always do."

He grinned, tugging out the item, holding it up.

"Holy shit." He breathed. "Is this...?"

"My slutty elf costume?" I still had one hanging in my closet, the outfit I was wearing when we first met. "Thought tonight you might enjoy a stroll down memory lane."

"You will definitely be going on the naughty list tonight." Scrooge slid his gaze to me.

"Then you like your gift?"

"Best fucking present ever...Christmas or any other holiday. And I'm not talking about the costume either," he rumbled next to me, his eyes glowing as they trailed over me. "Now, get us the fuck home immediately, Ms. Liddell."

🎩 🎩 🎩 🎩

The snow glowed with colored twinkle lights from windows and doors, the trees wrapped up with white lights. Peopled bundled up against the chill, and the streets bustled with merriment and cheer. New York was always moving no matter the weather or time. In the quaint streets of Greenwich Village, Christmas Eve celebrations filled the local pub a few buildings down. Holiday music weaved down the street to us as we walked up to the building where we both lived and worked.

The area was one of the most expensive, and I was nowhere close to being wealthy by any means. Santa had made it possible to afford this place. A "gift" he bestowed upon me six months ago as a "un-Christmas" present on July 25th. A thank-you, though I still believed I did very little.

My feet stopped on the pavement, my gaze wandering across the crazy sign hanging over the front of the building. I still couldn't believe it, my dream alive in front of me.

Alice and the Hatter was scrolled in funky lettering pouring out of a teapot into an upturned top hat with a red scarf, appearing like it was blowing in the wind. Tucked through the scarf were subtle illustrations of a penguin, twin elves, reindeer, a white rabbit, and other depictions you'd really have to look close to see. Our family and friends up for the world to see. I couldn't describe it, but magic seemed to weave around it. Mysterious. Sexy. Playful. Alluring.

The same effect coiled inside the store over every piece I had on display. Like curled fingers beckoning you closer to hear a juicy secret, the store seemed to draw people in like moths. Since the day I opened four months ago, we had been so busy with sales and custom orders, I could barely keep up. It even got more intense when a celebrity living down the street bought one and tweeted about the store. I had to hire two employees and soon we'd be expanding the hat shop with a bakery next door. The two might not seem to pair together, but I never thought having a life on earth and in Winterland would work either.

The bonkers and rational sometimes were the perfect combination.

Matt and I were exhausted, but I ended every day with a smile, knowing I wanted to do nothing else. I looked forward to the craziness of the next day.

"I still can't believe it's real," I muttered up at *my* store, my head shaking in disbelief. The passion I had for so long but worked in jobs I hated, the sketches that landed me in an institution—it all lead me here. My crazy designs fitting perfectly in New York.

"*This* is what you can't believe?" Matt smirked, pressing into me, glancing at the closed store, the windows dark. "Reality is to accept the truth in the unbelievable."

"Ugh." I moaned, my head falling into his chest. "You sound like Frosty."

"Ohhh." Scrooge hissed, his arms wrapping around me. "You will pay for that insult later, Ms. Liddell."

"Looking forward to it." I winked up at him. Scrooge and Frosty would never be friends. It was hard to get them to be civil to each other, but they tolerated each other enough not to kill the other. No longer running the Night Rebellion had turned his focus on getting the landscape of the villages and workshop up to par. Though Frosty spent more time being the leader of town gossip than anything else.

"This time I might have to borrow Santa's whip." Scrooge's hand slid into my hair, his mouth crashing down on mine. Desire. Want. With every kiss he claimed more of me, his mouth incinerating every nerve. He devoured. Demanded. And gladly I gave, challenging him with my own need.

His fingers zinged sparks through my scalp, rushing heat between my legs, my intensity increasing, causing him to growl. We had trouble stopping. Once we touched, it usually led to wild sex in the back room or running upstairs to our apartment on a break. After closing, the display tables and cash register saw a lot of activity.

"Alice." His voice husky and dripping with lust, his chin clicking up at the sign. "You know someday I will take the 'and the' out of the logo."

Leaving…

Alice Hatter.

My chest hitched with the idea.

"But that's right, you don't believe in marriage." He nipped my ear. "Don't see the point."

"If you recall, I also said I'm not against it either. Life will let me know in time."

"I guess it will…" He grinned playfully. I'd never want to be with anyone else. Ever. Matt/Scrooge was so deep in my soul. I knew he felt the same, but neither of us was ready yet. He still had issues to work out about Belle and dealing truly with Tim's death. I was happy with our life right now, coming into my own, focusing on my career. We had time, and that someday would eventually turn into today.

His lips captured mine again, hungry and ferocious. Just the way I liked it.

"Let's get upstairs before they know we're back." I tugged on the band of his jeans, pulling him to the door.

Crash!

From inside the store came the sound of things tumbling and hitting the floor.

I didn't even flinch.

"Too late." Scrooge grinned against my mouth, his eyes flicking to the side. I glanced over my shoulder, seeing a black and white head peeking from the dark window.

"Don't worry, Ms. Alice. I got it... It's not bad... Well, not as bad as *last* time." Penguin's words to us were muffled by the window.

My hand went to my head, and I started laughing. This wasn't the first time Pen destroyed the shop. He was a bull in a china shop.

Snickering next to me, Scrooge unlocked the door and pulled me inside, quickly locking it behind us. Almost every hat and headband on the display by the window was scattered over the floor. Penguin hopped around picking up hats, but with his flippers he could only get two before they fell back to the floor.

"I got it, Pen." I bent down, kissing his head before I picked up the items, placing them back on the table. "I'll reset them before we open the day after tomorrow."

I had lied to my parents. The store wasn't the reason for our need to get back to the city. Though I had no doubt we'd be put to work soon.

"So sorry, Ms. Alice. I got bored...and then I waited for you guys...I got bored again."

"Bored?" Matt scoffed, dropping all our bags behind the counter.

"I was trying to help. I really was, Mr. Scrooge...but I got tangled in the tinsel and ribbon."

"Let me guess." I peeled off my coat. "Dee kicked you out."

Penguin let out a little muffled sob as he tipped side to side. "She *yelled* at me."

"Here." Scrooge dug something out of a bag, handing it to Penguin. The bird's eyes widened, his beak chattering with excitement. "Ooooohhh, so pretty!" He stirred up the snow inside, humming "Let It Snow."

It was a miniature snow globe my sister put in my stocking, which oddly had a gingerbread house, along with a snowman and a penguin. Little did she know how relevant those were in my life.

He trailed us into my back office, lost in his new toy. I turned on the light, igniting the tiny room swathed in sketches, fabric, and tools. It had a workspace to create my designs, which was also my desk. Several filing cabinets filled the space, along with a huge calendar. But the largest thing in the room was the mirror leaning against the wall.

We also had one upstairs, which Scrooge threatened to take out because our privacy ended up being interrupted a lot.

The mirror wobbled, rabbit ears popping through. "Fuck! It's about time you guys got back." Hare hopped into the room dressed in his frilly apron, his foot hanging around his neck. "Dee is making us all crazy. She's stepped back into her role a little too well. Tinsel my holly balls, she is on the war path to make this the *best fuckin' Christmas ever*, which is making me want to snap her like a candy cane."

After the battle the year before, Dee worked hard to get Christmas on track, stepping back in her role of running the workshop, but still so much remained to be rebuilt, and there were fewer hands to work at the shop. This year Santa's Workshop was ninety percent back up and running because of Dee's determination. Her "warrior" mode had become a little intense.

"She's telling me I'm not baking stocking treats fast enough," Hare exclaimed. "You do not tell a chef, an *artiste*, to bake faster. Oh no, girlie. I am creating art for the mouth. You *do not* rush that."

"Hare! Where are you?" Dee's voice screamed through the mirror.

"Oh fuck." Hare darted for my desk, scrambling underneath. "Don't tell her I'm here."

Dee's head came through the mirror, wearing a head mic and holding a clipboard, her face set with determination. "Har—oh good, you guys are back." She nodded at us, pointing down at her paper. "I need you guys in gift wrap. Bea will catch you up on what you need to do."

"Gift wrap?" Scrooge laughed, his head shaking. "Hell no."

Dee's lids narrowed on him until he blinked, his mouth snapping shut.

"We are at the crucial hour." She glared at him, tapping her watch, which had every time zone on it. "Santa and the reindeer are already behind schedule. We still don't have the numbers we used to, and we have three times more children to deliver to than last year."

Santa's Workshop was a lot more complex and high-tech than you'd think. They had a room that looked similar to a NASA control room, which not only kept in contact with Santa, marking his drop-offs, keeping him on the tight schedule, but they had to be on alert for weather, planes, and other complications.

The size of a warehouse, gift wrapping was like a conveyor belt of people working seamlessly together, making it look far easier than it was. The one time I tried, I quit within fifteen minutes, not able to keep up.

The actual "workshop" was a lot smaller now since not many toys were "made" anymore, except for items like stuffed animals, wooden toys, and dolls. The largest room was filled with bikes, electronics, and toys gotten from a store and held there.

"Hare, I know you are hiding under the desk," Dee called out, rolling her eyes. "We need another twenty-dozen chocolate Santas and snowmen."

"No." His voice squeaked. "You can't make me, Fräulein Miser."

"Miser?" My mouth dropped open.

"Yeah. You know the Miser brothers?" Hare replied.

"As in Heat and Snow? Those Misers?" I peered up at Scrooge. "They aren't real, are they?"

"You really want me to answer that?" He smiled at me, then shook his head. "Don't even get me started on those douchebags."

"Come on! Chop. Chop." Dee's foot tapped on the wood floor.

"Bad choice of words there." Hare scoffed from the desk.

"Time is ticking. We have a lot of work to do before we can relax for a day."

"Where is my sweet little Dee?" I teased.

"You'll get her back tomorrow." Matt nudged me. "For a day."

I knew she'd relax sometime, but her drive to get Christmas to where it used to be after so many years of darkness was obsessive. It was subtle, but even here on Earth I felt a bit more happiness, a lightness since Winterland had been restored. They destroyed Jessica's castle and built the new Workshop there. The town I had walked through to the queen's castle was rebuilt, surging with life again. Cafes, houses, and shops. Flowers sang happily in the window beds, the river bubbling with joy, and glorious sun greeted them every day. Even if it was rainy, snowy, or cloudy, you still felt the break of day, the endless night gone.

I was looking forward to spending the day with my family in Winterland after the work was done. Relaxing in the cabin, laughing, drinking, and eating, consuming so many calories from Hare's food and mead I might have to diet the rest of the year.

So worth it.

Not sure if it was Nick or Santa who decided to stay living in the cabin, using a mirror to travel to work daily. Think he liked the peace and quiet there. The two men would always live in one body, and both seemed to have come to accept the other's presence. There was far too much pain and darkness for Santa to ever be without Nick. And Santa saved Nick from drowning in the negative anger and pain.

Those we lost were still in our hearts, but a new joy was helping us through. Rudy and Vixen were expecting a baby girl in spring, which they already knew would be named after their fallen comrades. *Dasher-Prancer-Dancer.* Bit of a mouthful, but I noticed everyone already nicknaming the unborn reindeer Dash or DP.

I couldn't have been happier for him. They were so in love and happy. Rudy and I would always be close, but his world *was* Vixen and the baby.

Rudy wasn't the only one who found love in tragedy.

"Dee!" Dum's voice wailed through the mirror, his upper body coming into the room. "Oh good, you guys are back." Dum waved at us with a toothy grin.

"Dum, what is it? Why aren't you at your station?" Dee's voice pitched up.

"Uhhh...We have a *situation*..." Her second in command appeared anxious.

"What now?" She exclaimed. "I left you in charge for a minute. You couldn't even handle a minute, *Dum-Puck?*"

I snorted. Yes, I still found that funny as hell.

"You know I don't handle crises well." He tugged at his hat, pulling it more to one side, covering the healed stump on the side of his head. He still wasn't secure about being the elf without an ear, but Bea seemed to find it incredibly sexy, which helped his ego a bit. He hadn't completely bounced back emotionally from the battle. He still suffered nightmares and some down times, but every day it got better. Especially since he and Bea had become really good friends. After all his talk about "normal" elves, he oddly adored her kind of crazy. They giggled and ran around a lot like they were five.

"What. Is. It?" Dee stared at her brother.

"Happy quit again."

"Again? He can't quit. It's Christmas Eve. Tell him to get his ass back in the workshop."

"You tell him. But I think he's already at the pub, drinking."

"Ugh!" She cried at the ceiling. "That cantankerous, grouchy ass. How is he even a puck? He's everything opposite from an elf. He's an anti-elf."

"You tell me," Dum muttered. "*You're* the one dating him."

Dating sounded so funny with those two. Half the time they acted as if they hated each other; the other half you'd find them sneaking sly looks and disappearing together. The gossip on the odd pairing was ramped through the village, others trying to figure out exactly what was going on and what they saw in each other. Being Santa's lead elf, most thought Dee should be with another Christmas loving, happy elf. That wasn't her. She always liked different boys, crushing on Rudy and Scrooge.

Happy may be an elf on the outside, though he was quite a bit taller than all the other elves, but on the inside, he was a grumpy, sarcastic man. Very un-elfish and she loved that.

I was thrilled for her because I knew she was completely in love. I think I was the only one she confessed to.

"Go. Find him."

"What?" Dum cupped his bad ear.

"Dum!"

"Sorry, can't hear you." He slipped back into the mirror, pointing at his bad ear. He used this tactic a lot when he wanted to get out of something.

"Dammit, Dum. I know you can hear me. Maybe you have no brain cells left, but your left ear is working just fine." She yelled back at him. "Dum!"

He poked his head in again.

"Fine. I will deal with *him*." She adjusted her ear mic. "For now, take his spot; I need to get to the control room." She motioned for him to go. "There's a bad snowstorm in Poland. A kid won't sleep in Bruges, and as usual, dozens of kids suddenly went from naughty to nice, not wanting to lose out on presents." She rubbed at her head, sighing before she started to follow her brother back through the mirror. "Now, Hare!" she yelled at the bunny before she slipped through.

"Dammit. I was hoping she forgot about me," Hare grumbled, crawling out and moving for the mirror. He dipped his hand into his apron and pulled out a small mead bottle, guzzling it down. "Now I see why so many chefs drink or take drugs, the endless desire for our master pieces can really take a toll."

"Just wait until we open your bakery next door. You are going to be worshipped." I winked at him.

"They won't even know I'm the one baking," he scoffed. Our set up was Hare would bake in his kitchen, and we'd run the hat and bakery shop. With help of course, but because of our circumstance, it couldn't be someone off the street.

Now that Jessica was gone and the water she drugged her people with out of their systems, I met many lovely characters. Most didn't remember much from that time. As much as their faces sometimes haunted me, almost losing my head to that crowd, I had to remember they were victims too.

And many in Winterland looked like regular humans, which worked in our favor. Eve, Holly, and Joseph worked in the shop. They were giddy to travel between the realms and utterly fascinated by New York.

They loved working here and, honestly, they were the best employees. I didn't know what I'd do without them. Especially now that we would be expanding.

We had searched for the queen's harem but never found people like Pepper Mint or Everly. I had a sinking feeling they had slipped into Earth's realm, hiding in the vastness of people.

"Could you imagine? The relentlessness of fame if they found out an extremely rugged, handsome, talking hare with badass scars, wearing his own foot around his neck, was the one baking the orgasms on a plate for them? Being revered like that would be too much for him."

"So humble." Scrooge chuckled.

"Lick my nutcracker," Hare jabbed back before jumping through the mirror, leaving us with only the melody of Pen's song. He sat on the floor at my feet, entranced by the snow globe, singing to it.

"Just wait until he learns we're naming it *The White Rabbit*."

The tag line for the bakery would be, "*It's always teatime*." A nod to the tattoo inked on Scrooge's chest and our sign out front. It didn't bother me that it was Belle's phrase. I wasn't afraid of the past. Everything led us here…to each other.

Scrooge twisted me to face him, his gaze heating again. "Not too late to go upstairs for a moment."

"Think Dee will actually boil us in figgy pudding."

"Again, worth it." His hands moved down my sides.

Staring up at him I couldn't believe how lucky I was. I had known I didn't want to leave earth permanently, nor did I want to let Winterland go. Okay, I would have never let Scrooge go. But for a moment, I feared I might have to choose.

He had kissed me, the sun rising in Winterland for the first time in decades, his eyes boring into me.

"Where you go, I go, Ms. Liddell."

"You'd leave Winterland? Your family?"

"Remember, I'm a greedy, selfish asshole." He growled in my ear. "I want both. And I will take both."

Santa had been firm in his rules about traveling between the realms, but with a little persuasion, and the fact he knew I was a key and could open and close it if I wanted, he relented. There was always the chance Winterland could be discovered or a character would become reckless, but you couldn't live life in fear.

That wasn't really living.

Brought back to the present, I stared up at him. "I love you." My mouth met his, kissing him softly.

"You are really asking for me to toss you over my shoulder and take you upstairs." He moved in closer. "And fuck any trace of you off the good list."

"Think I did that when I smashed a bottle into Nick's head."

"Still jealous over that," he muttered as he kissed me.

"Santa's sack. You two are at it again," Hare barked from the mirror. "Come on, Dee's cracking the whip."

"Sounds kinky." Scrooge nuzzled my neck, nipping my jaw. "Though I'd rather do that to you upstairs."

"Go without us." I waved Hare off, my legs tightening with desire.

"Oh, okay." Hare shrugged. "Guess I'll drink the fresh batch of mead *all by myself* then."

"Coming!" Scrooge and I swung for the mirror. Scrooge followed Hare, disappearing in the mirror as I picked up Pen. Shutting off the light by the open office door, the street and twinkle lights flooding down the short hallway to me.

"Alice." Like a whisper of wind, my name slithered over my shoulder, snaking up the back of my neck, like cold icy fingers. My body came to a jolting halt. *"Alice."*

I jerked my head over my shoulder, my gaze traveling outside the huge window, fear prickling at my skin.

My gaze fell on a shadowy figure standing by a tree outside. Wearing a large hood, I couldn't make out any features, but terror stuttered the breath in my lungs. A guttural instinct pounded my heart against my ribs. I could feel eyes on me, as if it could see me way back in my office. Dread bottomed out my stomach, dampening my skin with sweat. A hiss wheezed through my throat.

Then I blinked.

Gone.

The spot was empty.

Curious.

Still staring outside, I took a deep breath, swallowing back my fright. *Nothing's there, Alice. You know she is gone. It was just in your head,* I said to myself, willing my thumping heart to calm down. *She can't ever hurt you again.*

I knew she was gone, but nightmares of her still simmered up through the cracks. I hated that even from the Land of the Lost Souls, she could still find a way to torment me.

"Ms. Alice, are you okay?" Pen tapped at my shoulder, turning my head back to him.

"Yes. Just fine." I nodded, swallowing down the lump of fear in my throat. "Let's go wrap some presents."

"And me?" Pen squealed. He loved when I decorated him like a Christmas tree.

"Absolutely." I winked. "When Dee isn't watching."

"Or she'll yell at us again."

"You better get moving." Scrooge's voice drew me to the mirror as he stepped back through. "Or are you asking to be spanked, Ms. Liddell?" His eyebrow cocked up.

"That a promise, Mr. Scrooge?" I tried to smile.

"You okay?" he asked as I moved to him, taking Pen from my arms.

"Yeah." I nodded, forcing the moment out of my head. I shook my shoulders, letting playful humor dance on my lips. "I'm more than okay. Spanking and mead?" My mouth brushed his. "What more could a girl want?"

"Fuck, Ms. Liddell." He groaned behind me as I stepped into the mirror.

This life was everything I wanted and more. I would not let her ghost destroy it. My heart full of love, I plunged into the hole.

Letting myself descend into the insanity was the only way I could rise and...

Ascend from madness.

Thank you to all my readers. Your opinion really matters to me and helps others decide if they want to purchase my book. If you enjoyed this book, please consider leaving a review on the site where you purchased it. It would mean a lot. Thank you.

Also check out my Contemporary Romance and Paranormal Romance novels listed in the front of this book.

Acknowledgements

I hope you have enjoyed Alice and Scrooge's story, along with Hare, Rudy, Santa, Dee, Dum, and Pen! Would love to continue the series with Dinah's story as I have fallen so in love with this series and these characters! I hope you guys have too. Thank you again for giving this mad tale a chance.

Kiki & Colleen at <u>Next Step P.R.</u>- Thank you for all your hard work! I love you ladies so much.

Jordan Rosenfeld at <u>Write Livelihood</u> - Every book is better because of you. I have your voice constantly in my head as I write.

<u>Hollie "the editor"</u>- Always wonderful, supportive, and a dream to work with.

<u>Jay Aheer</u>- So much beauty. I am in love with your work!

Judi Funnel at <u>Formatting4U</u>- Always fast and always spot on!

To all the readers who have supported me: My gratitude is for all you do and how much you help indie authors out of the pure love of reading.

To all the indie/hybrid authors out there who inspire, challenge, support, and push me to be better: I love you!

And to anyone who has picked up an indie book and given an unknown author a chance. THANK YOU

About the Author

 Stacey Marie Brown is a lover of hot fictional bad boys and sarcastic heroines who kick butt. She also enjoys books, travel, TV shows, hiking, writing, design, and archery. Stacey swears she is part gypsy, being lucky enough to live and travel all over the world.

She grew up in Northern California, where she ran around on her family's farm, raising animals, riding horses, playing flashlight tag, and turning hay bales into cool forts.

When she's not writing she's out hiking, spending time with friends, and traveling. She also volunteers helping animals and is eco-friendly. She feels all animals, people, and the environment should be treated kindly.

To learn more about Stacey or her books, visit her at:

Author website & Newsletter:
www.staceymariebrown.com

Facebook Author page:
www.facebook.com/SMBauthorpage

Pinterest: www.pinterest.com/s.mariebrown

Twitter: @S_MarieBrown

Instagram: www.instagram.com/staceymariebrown/

Twitter: https://twitter.com/S_MarieBrown

Amazon page: www.amazon.com/Stacey-Marie-Brown/e/B00BFWHB9U

Goodreads: www.goodreads.com/author/show/6938728.Stacey_Marie_Brown

Her Facebook group: www.facebook.com/groups/1648368945376239/

Bookbub: www.bookbub.com/authors/stacey-marie-brown

X

Made in the USA
Monee, IL
22 November 2021